Outlaw Fantasy

Outlaw Fantasy

SASKIA HOPE

BLACK
lace

Black Lace novels are sexual fantasies.
In real life, make sure you practise safe sex.

First published in 1994 by
Black Lace
332 Ladbroke Grove
London
W10 5AH

First published as *Wild* in 1992
Copyright © Saskia Hope 1992

Typeset by TW Typesetting, Plymouth, Devon
Printed and bound by
Cox & Wyman Ltd, Reading, Berks

ISBN 0 352 32920 3

Outlaw Fantasy

Chapter One

AD 2080:

*H*e first saw her as the gleam in another man's eye. He was a casual waiter employed to help the catering staff at an exclusive Zoo party. The Zoo was the nickname given to the area inhabited solely by the very rich and those who worked for them. His name was Caz and he was serving a drink to a big, plump, self-important man when he saw the man's face transform, his eyes light up, his body stiffen and his attention focus across Caz's shoulder.

Caz turned in spite of himself and then he saw her, too.

He performed his duties for the rest of the evening and when almost everyone was gone, she approached him.

Standing with her made him feel heady, peculiar. She had an aura that enveloped him when she was beside him and it separated them from the rest of the room. She was so sexy he felt embarrassed, as though he conspired with her, as though his thoughts were unclothed.

'I have lost one of my earrings,' she said. He was dazzled and hardly understood her. Her voice was accented as though her tongue was reluctant to leave her palate and lingered a shade longer than most people's. The slight halt in her voice made his loins ache.

1

'What is it like?' he asked.

'This.'

She was not as tall as he was and she tilted her head and swept back her thick reddish-brown hair to reveal one little naked pale flat-set ear. Set in the lobe was a diamond cluster.

'I'll tell my boss,' he mumbled.

She slid her arm through his and walked across with him. She wore long black elbow-length lace gloves and it was the finest short walk of his life. He smiled down at her. Her eyes were dark ovals, long-lashed and velvet with promise.

'Is this your full-time work?' she asked.

'I'm a student at the Institute. I do this nights to pay my way.'

'You work day and night,' she murmured. 'It is as well you are young.'

He was maybe half her age.

'I get tired,' he admitted.

'Come home with me and rest.'

He didn't believe his ears. He thought he had made it up because it was what he wanted her to say. He picked up on the least potentially offensive thing he thought he had heard and repeated it.

'Rest?'

It came over quite differently from what he had intended. She smiled sideways at him. 'Come home with me anyway.'

He abandoned his uniform jacket and walked out on the job. They rode the moving walkways together and he found that far from being embarrassed, he felt powerful and relaxed. She was at once confiding and deliciously mature, elevating him to her level, ignoring his eighteen years. She stripped off the long glove on his side so that the bare warm skin of her hand was in direct contact with his arm as they moved together. She stopped at her bubble house and worked the door release. As soon as they were inside, he kissed her. She came warmly into his arms and filled them, pressing herself

2

into his body, holding him to her and reaching into his mouth with her tongue.

It may have been like that. Probably it was like that. It could have started in any one of a thousand ways, but all that mattered was that it did happen, the encounter took place, and they met. Once they had met, the rest followed on. It was the game. His youth and his strength were pitted against her wisdom and her maturity, but his hands knew what to do by instinct and though she was rich and classy and he was poor and non-Zoo, he had inherited a dominant streak which narrowed the distance between them.

She was eager but slow. Every moment could be savoured. There was no grabbing, no snatching, no greediness in her. Every action orchestrated to a whole, and the whole was everything.

He stripped her, unsheathed her full ripe body so that her clothes rustled and fell about her ankles in a luxurious whisper of lust. When she was naked she released him and turned her back and walked, still in her high-heeled shoes, through the apartment to her bedroom.

He was dumb as he followed, not out of callowness or nervousness, but because of the exquisite beauty of her long female flanks, her full rounded haunches, her loins on back-view from the narrowness at her waist to the full-fleshed generosity of her firm rounded buttocks.

She had two near-dimples in the soft flesh gathered across the top of her buttocks. He came up behind her to sink his thumbs into the little cavities, to let his hands clasp her hips before they ventured into the valleys and the hills of her, but as he touched her she sighed and stopped moving, allowing herself to fall back against him. Her head was against his shoulder. Her scent was in his nostrils. Her hair brushed his face. He looked down and saw her body foreshortened, in a strange perspective, and his groin burned.

Under his chin her sloping shoulder was creamy rich and the bone within it felt like a bird's, brittle and beautiful. The flesh swung out gaining momentum until it firmed into the peaked cone of her breast.

3

Yes, her breasts were like twin volcanoes seen from above, two white conical mountains fire-tipped. Almost he could feel the heat from those foxy, fiery nipples. He would burn his mouth on them or die.

Below her breasts was shadowland, mysterious, hidden by her own ripeness. But he could see on down to her white round belly sat in the broad rift valley between the jut of her hips. Her navel, a dark empty jewel, led his eye to the whiteness below.

A fine line of down dropped with sly innocence into the silken riot of curling fleece, fox-brown and fiery as her nipples. He could not see her legs. He could not see her feet. He could not see the floor or anything except the down of her, the fox-brown down of her humped at belly-base.

His hands slid round her hips so that she filled all the space between himself and himself and she was of him as his fingers were of him, as his fingers fell inward to the star at the top of her legs.

He came back to himself feeling the warm springing hair and she moved slightly against him so that her legs were apart.

His fingers slid within her legs. He felt the cool roundness of thigh and he felt the wet heat within. He laid his head sideways on her shoulder and kissed her neck, feeling it throb under his lips, and he shut his eyes to let his fingers know her.

It was as though an animal writhed between her legs. The wet warmth moved under his fingers, he felt it move and he began to stroke its agreeable slimy body.

It humped itself and rolled under his fingers, a wriggling maze that fooled his fingers, teasing them, yet enticing them to come on in, to come further, to penetrate the mystery and find the heart of the maze. It created itself for him, so that his fingers could find it and enter. His body bent tightly over hers and he kissed the pulse in her neck and his fingers entered her and were kissed and welcomed in.

He slid to his knees and kissed the near-dimples on

4

her haunches. Then he pressed his face into the cleft of her arse and he sank his fingers deep into her body.

All around them the wet animal gripped him and quivered hotly. It flexed its muscles and rippled and was alive. It drew his fingers in and toyed with them, laughing, teasing, playing in anticipation of the real thing.

He pushed his face deep into the cleft of her arse and he breathed the smell of her, he took into his lungs the air her body had warmed and scented in its deep places. Her pussy jumped and he opened his mouth in her arse. His tongue came out and she clenched her buttocks, squeezing them on his face, masturbating his tongue in her cleft. It writhed and tasted the smell of her and found her arse and touched it.

She bent forward.

Her thighs bit his wrists but her opening expanded joyously and licked his fingers wetly. Her cheeks parted and he passionately kissed the little foxy hole and he felt it purse and kiss him back. He slid his face down and pressed his nose into it and found his mouth was wet.

His mouth was at her animal sex and the nest of it, the curling hairy warm nest of it brushed his cheeks and invited him on in, down into her lair.

He kissed her glistening flesh and sobbed. He pulled his hands free and put them blindly forward. Each palm curled round a cone hanging sharp below her, curled round its underflesh less touched, more sensitive, more nervous to the handhold of a man.

He kissed her flesh and it drew him in, kissing him back with sweet passionate kisses, murmuring endearments, calling him in, stroking him with its nest hair.

It was very wet, not surface wet but made of thick wetness, watermelon flesh, solid firm wetness that cradled and absorbed his dryness, the aridity of his life and his soul and his manness, and made them woman-wet and comfortable. He became the wetness of the first globular beings, jelly-wet to jelly-wet in the primaeval sea. He had been shaped in the sea and now he was back

in the warm wet ooze of it, firm and shapely and primaeval.

His tongue went deep into the core of her till its roots
strained and she writhed about his tongue recognising
that they were like to like and he tasted the deep thick
salty sea within her body. His hands circled her breast-
cones and milked them downwards, pulling the soft pillowy membrane of her skin that bagged the fruity ripeness of breast, pulling it and pulling it till they should
ache for the joy of him. And at each pull the strange
moth-soft skin of her nipples brushed the palms of his
hands.

She moved, straightening herself, coming out from between his hands, releasing his tongue, and turned and
faced him.

'Come into the bedroom,' she said, her voice hesitat-
ing slightly, deliciously, over the dental speech sounds.

Her bedroom was a blur like an ill-focused film. Only
she had sharp definition, only her bed.

She had a light-bed and she went and lay on it.

The room was warm and the bed had no coverings.
The translucent membrane shivered as she laid her
length down on it and the whole bed surface trembled
in a soft waviform motion that rippled the length of her
body into an exquisite slow movement, emphasising
each part of her as it rose and slowly fell to the swoop
of the rolling bed.

When it was settled, she switched it on.

It came to life in a slow glow.

The glow intensified to a muted brilliance, a white
lustre of fused starlight on which her body lay dark like
a film negative, herself dark against the white glowing
background of living light that swelled silently from
within the bed. She was suspended in light, webbed in
its filaments, and she lifted a hand to welcome him to
her.

He stripped slowly, unafraid. When he was naked he
stood there a moment letting her absorb his pale thin
body into her darkness. His body had a sort of eager

6

rawness, he was an unfinished man, his promise not yet fulfilled. His shoulders were not very broad, his muscles not very full, and he was thin and pale-white, his man's hair about his sex trusting and vulnerable like a tuft of cotton.

He was beautiful, an almost-man, and a little part of him knew it and was humbly grateful for his own sweet unripe body.

She drew him down so that he was light-webbed with her and they lay like dust upon the plane of the galaxy.

She felt him carefully all over, very happily. 'I am trying to think what you are like,' she explained, smiling at him.

'What am I like?'

'You are very hard. There is no fat on you to soften your contours. Yet you are not harsh or cold-hard like metal. I know it. You have the hardness of wood, warm and almost yielding. Your grain invites me to stroke it.'

She suited the action to the words.

'But more than this. There is a tiny surface softness, your skin, perhaps. You are very soft and then you are hard. You are like wood covered in a thin layer of velvet.'

'That sounds very nice.'

'I have it now. You are like the deer's antler. You are velvet on horn. My sweet horny lover.'

'I haven't made love to you yet.'

'No,' she agreed, 'not yet.'

She ran her hands all over his body firing his skin and then her hands fell away down to his groin and she took his manhood, his sex, and she stroked it.

'Ah,' he said softly, pleasurably. With her hand holding his cock, he reached and took one of her volcano-breasts hanging down her body by him and he caressed its baggy fullness and then he drew its fire-tip to his mouth and pursing his lips he sucked it in.

The soft skin was almost papery in his mouth and his cock leapt in her hand as he tasted her. Her nipple yielded to his tongue and he sucked on it and felt it change

7

even as his cock changed. It grew and hardened and became elastic.

His cock began to hurt.

'What is it?'

'I want you so badly,' he said and tried not to groan with the pressure in his cock in her hand.

'Come then,' she said, and he rolled on top of her and found her mouth with his whilst his body felt the long soft length of her caught under his velvet hardness. Her legs opened beneath his and he brought down a hand and slid his fingers up and down her body's opening and then he lay slightly sideways and began to slip his suffering urgent cock into the quick of her.

He gasped. Her body grasped his cock and sucked it simultaneously from all sides and through the tip and he drove hard down into her and it wasn't enough. He pulled back and her vagina was like the shingle that clings to the ebb tide when it must go. He thrust deeply into her again and for a split second knew absolute peace and calm. He drew back and threw his cock joyously deep into her and felt her rise to him.

He began to spin. He thought he might be laughing. He plunged again and again and each time seemed deeper and richer and creamier and more welcome than the last. His loins began to flame. A tornado started inside him, a whirlwind, a twister that span round faster and faster on its axis and in ever-decreasing circles. When it reached the centre of him it caught fire and exploded outwards the length of his shaft and he was coming. He shot hard into her until he was done and then hung almost sobbing with pleasure over her light-framed body.

Her sex was in spasm around his cock. He felt it vibrate and suck the last juice from him, then her body eased and she allowed her arched back to soften and drop, taking him down with her to rest on her. He eased his weight to one side and kissed her neck. His cock fell out of her and trailed across the roundness of her thigh, and from her opening came a little flow, lustrous and opaque, a thickened stream of light, glistening testament to the woman's parallel bliss. His cock had been held in the dark of her whilst the two of them rolled cocooned in light.

He kissed her a little and then he sat up and began meticulously to explore her splendid body. He had made a poor awkward sort of love to a couple of girls at the Institute before this, students like himself, but they were all bones and lank limbs and they took the fruits of his body with a kind of sulky greed.

This woman held up her breasts to him, offering the nipples and the pillowing generous flesh. This woman rubbed his face gently between her breast-hillocks and put her nipples in his ears. This woman put his quiescent prick into her navel and belly-danced it back to half-life. This woman lay on her back and lifted her legs, bending them at the knee and holding her knees wide apart so that he could explore her pussy-country with eyes and fingers and palms and prick and belly and tongue.

And tongue.

He put his mouth to her little sensitive cone and played with it. He tasted it and let his tongue slide on between the little ramparts of her sex, the little soft wandering walls and he tongued-walked their lengths until he found the way into her maze. His tongue was drawn down by her whorls and vortices into her grateful hollow, sticky salty full of her own exuberance of lust. He sucked her and felt her pussy live and twist under his lips and kiss him back. He kissed it with urgent passion and it kissed him urgently back. He kissed it frantically, sinking in his tongue, darting into it again and again and it trembled and opened like a dark flower welcoming him in. Her hands were about his body. He felt pressure on his cock and knew that it was hard again and eager. Her hands came around his balls in a cradling benison that warmed them and his hips were nuzzling up to find her hips and match his hard thrust of cock to her full pulpy hollow.

9

This time his cock felt every moment as it entered her, slowly savouring the pulpy squeeze that gloved his cock in a warm poultice of pleasure, her walls leech-tight to his cock and drawing through it his goodness but passing back their own savour and ripeness and ecstasy.

He took a billion years to ride her, great long slow surges in and out of her body, while every bad thing, every frustration, every confusion that was in him calmed and focused into the cock-story, the story of his cock within her, and its definition of himself and his pain and her offer of balm and release. He evolved through pain into the light and now he rode her triumphantly, in a blaze of pleasure knowing that his cock was taming her sex-need and, by Christ, he could satisfy a woman!

Her body rolled under his and she made small inarticulate cries as he held her with his cock, her head tossing from side to side with all her chestnut-brown hair a thousand shades of red on the glowing white light of the bed. Her vulva stopped being clever and began to shiver its need through his cock, begging his cock for release, mewing to be satisfied, pleading for fulfilment. He felt her orgasm begin, felt her come hot and suddenly quite different around his cock, a thick splintered heat that fused into a blaze and she spasmed on him. Then he was kind and he dropped his barricade and all his pent-up desire shot through from him, cleansing him in a series of hot bursts that left her gasping and laughing with delight at his cleverness and mastery of her.

He fell back on the bed glowing as much as it. Happiness flooded him. He slept briefly and when he awoke his cock was in her mouth.

He opened his arms and laid them out straight either side of his body. He lay flat on his back cruciform with the woman hanging over his body sucking him. He felt the softness of her hair on his thighs and hips. He felt the brush of her cheek and forehead now and again as she bent seriously to her task. Her chin grazed his balls

10

and his cock expanded in the domain of her mouth to brush against her teeth and feel the whip of her tongue and the deep strength of her sucking cheeks. His sapling cock grew like a tree, an oak tree, with a stout strong stem and a great flowering of branch and leaf as she sucked him into bloom. It was spring in her mouth, early summer, and he was in full leaf, a wet floppy new-leafing as the sap rose in his stem.

He thought his cock would explode. His hips began to jerk. His foreskin was drawn back over his tender flesh and this expanded and expanded until it must burst. Her mouth grasped him hard and sucked deep as her hair tickled his hips and belly and thighs. He jerked violently, slapping her in the face with belly and balls, shooting into her mouth. He felt her swallow with his cock actually jerking in her mouth, filling her mouth, and he jerked himself to peace.

He fell back grasping, huge-eyed, and tried to see her face. The light blazed up from the bed and whitened the edges of her features and she smiled and bent to kiss him.

He opened his mouth and they kissed, lips clinging to lips and tongues writhing in a welter of juice that they both gulped at and swallowed.

He broke free. 'Tell me your name,' he gasped, laughing. 'I don't even know your name.'

'My name? It's . . .'

Up in the right-hand field of his vision a red square bleeped with quiet insistence. The insubstantial edge of the room wavered and faded. Every part of him screamed but the light-bed dulled. Her warm pressure against his body faded feathery-soft and dissipated. He screamed and gave a great sob as the room smoked into a grey wisp and vanished. He lifted his head and dropped it back against the headrest and felt the tears run down his cheeks. The booth was dark and the screen blank save for the red flashing square high up on the right.

He had checked into the public booth with his VR disc and fed it into the machine after paying for the hire.

There was no woman. It had been a virtual reality disc like none he had ever known. He was bereaved by the shock, orphaned.

They all played with VR discs, he had played himself on several occasions, but you always knew, however compelling the action and of whatever nature the action was, that you were in a false and eminently enjoyable fantasy world. There was no confusing it with life even as you underwent the experience. That was part of the fun, almost. It was life with no responsibility, because it wasn't real and you knew it, yet you felt all the appropriate sensations of the type of disc you were using. They covered all human activity except the very darkest. You could find sweet romance, compelling adventure, titillating horror and perfectly wonderful sex. But you always knew it wasn't for real.

Caz had been utterly and completely fooled. He ejected the disc and trembled. His body was in shock at the rupture between the two worlds, false and real. The experience was the stuff of fantasy, right enough, the sort of thing that would warm the blood of any eighteen-year-old, the voluptuous welcoming older woman rich in experience, but though improbable, it was not impossible. It had fooled him completely. His sense of loss was intolerable, yet since he held the disc in his hand, presumably he could access the experience again and again.

He pulled himself to his feet and wrapped his coat round him and shambled out of the booth into the wet cold of the windy night. He didn't even know her name, he grieved. Then he remembered, she had no name, she was the figment of a programmer's imagination, a false-woven woman-world to pleasure him.

Looking back, there were clues to it being a VR world. The edges of each situation, whether he had been at the party as a waiter or on the walkways or in her apartment, had been vague. The experience had the unnatural smoothness of VR fantasy where everything goes on a linear path with no byways and obstructions. He couldn't remember his boss telling him off or firing him from the catering firm, for example. He had decided to go with the woman and he had gone. He couldn't remember passing other people on the way to her apartment. A VR world was a monorail experience with all the clutter of the real world trimmed away. No, it was a question of intensity, of quality of feeling. The disc was frighteningly real. And it was a preferable reality to that which faced him now.

He plodded through the sodden streets wind-whipped and cold, his head tucked down between his shoulders. He passed through the commercial and retail areas and too poor to take a taxi, he walked on grimly through the residential blocks with their gay rectangles of opaqued light and on and up the long tree-lined hill to the Institute.

It was funny. He had never been in the Zoo. The rich lived there and Screen programmes depicted it but he had never been in it. You couldn't unless a Zoo-dweller took you in or you worked there. It was a thinly spread series of bubble houses planted in the deep jungle, linked by enclosed moving walkways that led through large public areas also under plastiglass. No one could access the jungle which rioted free from man's influence and was full of wild animal and plant life, but it was said that the bubble houses had glass walls and Zoo-folk made love whilst tigers padded by and the black panther wove with sinuous grace through trees chattering with monkeys and shrieking with brilliant birds.

So they said. There was a lot of romance attached to the Zoo for those who lived on the outside. Caz wondered how accurate his disc's representation of it had been.

He climbed the long hill, very tired and hungry. He would heat food when he got to his room. If nothing else, there was Sludge. Food wasn't free, but mundane food almost was because it was so cheap, and the

13

cheapest of all was Sludge. It was a sort of mushed compressed biomass impregnated with nutrients that would keep you in blooming health and alive if you ate nothing else for the rest of your excruciatingly boring life. Sludge came in blocks and you could gnaw it if you could afford nothing else. Pounds of it cost pence. There was no need ever to be hungry. It was perfectly balanced boredom. The phrase Sludge-high was oxymoronic – except that some of the chemistry students at the institute had succeeded in doping Sludge bars with hallucinogens – but high intelligence coupled with poverty has always produced criminals, and always will.

Finally Caz was in his eight-foot-by-six cubicle with desk and bed that was his only home, and he took off his coat and sat down to look at the disc.

The wrapping had faded with age or excessive handling and he could decipher only a few disconnected letters. This was peculiar because there had been no screen credits either, though it was normal that there should be. He had bought the thing at a second-hand shop that afternoon and because it was a pig in a poke the shopkeeper had thrown it in for next to nothing. Caz had been buying slightly out-of-date editions of standard text-cassettes for his science course at the Institute. The rogue VR disc had been amongst them and the shopkeeper had not even known it was there. Caz had asked him about it idly and been told he could take it.

Caz didn't know what to do about what had happened to him. He realised he was emotionally, even psychologically, disturbed and that he should do something. The experience had been too powerful for him. Not in its nature or its content – no way. If the experience had happened for real he would be whooping with delight and well able to adjust to it. Deliciously able. But that it had happened only in his mind as a computer experience was all wrong. Indeed, it was indecent. He had tried sex discs before and had terrific fun with them. But this experience was so strong and so personal, and attacked such deep layers of his pysche,

14

that he felt insulted and turned inside out. The programmer had become a voyeur. The whole damn thing was too successful and Caz's innate sense of privacy had been violated.

So what should he do? He was in training to become a scientist so he should approach the problem rationally, and the first approach that suggested itself was to find out who had made the damn thing and were there any more about and how come computer virtual reality had taken such a quantum leap forward and he didn't know anything about it?

He debated consulting someone on the computer course, or better still someone who taught the computer course, but felt reluctant. In order to explain his inquiry, he would have to emphasise how compellingly real the experience had been and since it was a sex disc, that was faintly embarrassing. It made him sound like a gullible fool, as though he didn't know what real sex was like, which he did, and so couldn't tell the difference between fantasy and reality.

He went to empty his coat pocket and found something strange there. He drew it out. It was black, cloth-like, soft to the touch like something gauzy. He opened it up and it was a glove.

It was a long elbow-length woman's black lace glove.

Caz held the glove and began mechanically to stroke it through his hand, drawing it through one lightly clasped hand with the other. This warming of its texture released a faint perfume and suddenly in full force the entire emotional intensity of the experience returned and Caz writhed on his bed with his cock hard erect and longed for the woman with no name. After a while he dealt with his immediate need and tried to think about things.

The glove. It was undoubtedly her glove. He must have tucked it in the pocket of his coat – hold on, there. Backaways, insanity. He wasn't going to be caught so easily. There was no woman. There was a VR disc. So there was no glove. As a process of thought this was fine, only with obstinacy the glove remained.

Caz knew when a problem had him beat and he went to bed.

He slept astonishingly well in the circumstances, tired out by so much nocturnal . . . no, there had been no nocturnal activity. The damn woman didn't exist. Mind you, Caz could have stood to have his balls tested because if ever anyone felt as though they had had a damn good fucking session, it was him. His balls felt light and drained. His cock felt strong and limbered up by exercise. And he had solved the problem of the glove.

It was obvious that he had found the glove at some time between when he last emptied his pocket and the previous night. He had forgotten finding it, which was odd, but the memory existed in his brain and the VR disc had taken it and used it, weaving it into the fantasy-world it offered its clients. It was an interactive disc and had fed direct from his brain in some way, stealing thought patterns and reproducing them.

So that was that. There was no irrational agency involved. The disc was terrifyingly real and he would try it again when he felt strong enough. No doubt he would feel the illusion, the delusion a second time because he would be mentally prepared for the classiness of the experience. It wouldn't fool him twice.

Felmar Arnqvist was a cleaner at the Institute and she knew all about right and wrong, especially wrong. Felmar knew it was wrong for her husband to drink alcohol, wrong for him to bet on the horses, wrong for him to use the legally available opiates for mind-pleasure and above all, wrong for him to enjoy sex with his wife. Felmar made damn sure about this last one and very righteous was the feeling it gave her.

Felmar worked at the Institute though they taught heathen nonsense 'cos anyone knew the world was made four thousand years ago, but a woman was born to suffer in a pagan world and she would have her reward in the shining mansions of the next. There would be no sex there, either. No, sir! Meantime she had to earn credits to live.

16

Felmar knew all about the dirty loose-living students. She made it her business to know all about them, even to the extent of checking their sheets for suspicious stains and the like. She was in Caz's cubicle when he was at lectures, poking about the sinful clutter on his desk, when she came across the VR disc. It had a little green triangle up in one corner of the wrapping and she knew what that meant. It was a sex disc. She tried to read the writing to see if it was one of those perversions that she had taken time to find out about so that she could abhor them in knowledge rather than in ignorance, but the wrapper was blurred and the print missing or too ill-defined to read. Felmar communed briefly with her conscience and then lifted the disc and slipped it into the pocket of her overall. She would force herself to suffer and partake in the disc so that she could learn better the ways of the devil and be properly on her guard, more able to recognise sin and wickedness as she came across it in the world.

After work she hired a booth in the pleasure area of the Institute and settled smugly into it, shutting out the noise and roar of Satan going about in the guise of young people drinking and indulging in licentious behaviour. She felt pleasantly titillated. She was going to get a real dose of sin first hand to set her teeth into, cross-sex sin, too, unless it was a homosexual disc. There were those who claimed cross-sexing could be fun, filthy beasts, and valuable fun at that because it helped you to explore the byways of your human nature more fully and it helped you to understand the opposite sex better. Felmar understood everything about the opposite sex already but was prepared to suffer for righteousness' sake, even to the exent of simulated sex with a woman and she went first to table 34 and stood with her notepad to take the order. She noticed that the man was fat and his skin pockmarked which was unusual. The creases on his face were shiny and below where his overshirt stopped she could see his thighs bulging out tightly within the straining material of his trousers. She found all these features exciting because she liked big powerfully built men and he had that aura of confidence and money and the expectation of getting his own way that Felmar found the most potent aphrodisiac in the whole damn world.

'Whaddaya recommend, baby?' he asked.

Felmar smiled and stuck out her chest. She was wearing a corset, all black and crimson satin on a tight whalebone structure that plumped out her breasts into hard bulging globes of flesh that looked as if at any moment they might pop right out of the retaining garment. She waggled her upper works near the man's face noticing his appreciative grin and then she moved her pelvis so that he noticed it too with its tight shiny short skirt showing the big bump of her sex. She ran her rounded tongue along her full reddened lips.

'The swordfish steaks are really great today, honey.'

'I don' see no swordfish.' His hand touched her naked leg and her skin shivered. His palm was sweaty and she felt his excitement communicate itself to her.

She bent over him and his eyes bulged like her cleavage. 'Xifias,' she said, pointing to the entry on the menu. His hand slid up towards her thigh.

'Ya reckon it's good?'

'It's very succulent,' said Felmar and she licked her lips again and straddled her legs slightly. Her chin came up and she gave the man a good saucy grin so he knew she dared him to go on.

'Hey,' said the fat pocked man to his companion who was a lissom blonde looking very bored. 'She says it's succulent.'

'Yeah,' said the blonde. She looked at Felmar who looked slyly back. The man's hand was sliding up her leg, on up to her strong bold thighs and now she felt him brush her intimate hair. The sensation was exquisite. She didn't know him, she had never seen him before, but she knew all she wanted to know about him. As his hand touched her belly hair desire knifed through her and she longed for him to go on, to probe further, to excite her within and without. His companion, the skinny blonde, could see his wrist disappearing up under Felmar's skirt and knowing that she could see it excited Felmar still further.

'An' if we don' fancy the ziffus?'

'The locust with pomegranate salad is popular.' His hand was now finding its way within the interstices of her flesh, touching and feeling her wet parts, frotting her labia. Felmar had very exceptional labia, very long and thinly made so that the foliate flesh drooped well below the rest of her vulva. She felt the man feel her special hanging lips and pull them slightly and even wrap them about his stumpy fingers.

'Ya fancy locusts?' the fat man asked the blonde.

'I had locusts yesterday. Do you have any pepper-clams?'

The fat man's thumb penetrated her. Felmar kept her face straight in an agony of pleasure. 'I'm sorry,' she said. 'The chef said they weren't fresh enough today.'

'What's this, then?' asked the blonde. The fat man released Felmar's sex and she moved round the table to come between the two of them. She bent over the menu held by the blonde to see what she was indicating. As she did so, the fat man slid his other hand straight up and between her lips, putting his thumb back within her. The blonde grinned and slid her cool palm up Felmar and she found the fat man's hand in Felmar and tickled it, and Felmar, round her vulva.

The fat man and the blonde paddled hands up Felmar's skirt and she waited to take their order. She grinned proudly across the room to the other customers to let them see she could take two there and give them a good time. Officially she worked in a feelie bar for the pay. A girl had to live. But Felmar admitted to herself that she loved the work. She was paid to wait on the customers and permit them to finger her private parts whilst they made up their minds to order. They usually took a while. Indeed, the longer they took to order, the prouder Felmar felt because it meant she was doing her job well. She was aware that the boss of the feelie bar,

Mr Jackmann, knew she put her heart and soul into the work. It had only one drawback and that was that it left her as randy as hell.

When her session was over she went through to the washrooms and removed her skirt and hung it in her locker. For a while she drifted round, her tight corset ending at her hips, enjoying the nudity of her lower half. Then what she half hoped would happen finally happened.

Mr Jackmann put his head round the door and saw she was alone.

'Can I come in, Felmar?' he asked.

'Sure thing, boss. Did I do good tonight?'

He came slowly over to her, a big man like she liked them, and good looking too with his square-cut chin with the dinky cleft in it. He had thick brown hair which he swept back from his broad forehead. Felmar looked like she suddenly remembered she was half-naked and she looked down shyly.

'Should I put something on, Mr Jackmann?'

'Hell no, child. We're all grown-ups here.'

Now she let her eyes rise, slow and sure, till they met his. He then let his drop just ever so slowly, going down hot and strong over her bulging breasts, down via her narrow constricted waist to the full womanly flare of her hips. Her pale belly swam above the thick fleece of her private hair and her strong thighs gave promise of strong sex with a real woman. Felmar stood there and let his eyes rake her front and slowly she slid her fingers down the silky stuff of her garment till they reached the flat plane of her lower belly and she went on down with her fingers into her strong hairy mound. She pulled at her labia till they projected down between her legs and then she came down with her second hand and she held the folds delicately apart with her two hands as far as they would go as if to let something big get up in there without any obstruction. And Mr Jackmann watched.

A drop of her juice, signal of her intense state of arousal, fell from her open orifice to land on the floor of the washroom.

'Anything I can do for you, Mr Jackmann?' she said. 'You know I like working here. You are a real good boss to work for. A girl appreciates that.'

'Felmar child, why don't you come on up to my office and we can talk about arrangements? Yeah?'

'I'd like that, Mr Jackmann. I had better just slip my skirt back on, unless you would prefer me in my own clothes, rather than my working ones?'

'I don't think your clothes matter a damn, Felmar. Know what I mean?'

'I do. I'll be right up.'

Before she left the washroom Felmar used the sprays to cleanse herself thoroughly underneath. She wanted Mr Jackmann to appreciate what he was about to get because she was an ambitious girl and she wanted to get on. She felt intuitively that pleasing Mr Jackmann would be good for her career, though what that career was was ill defined just at present.

In Mr Jackmann's office she felt unaccountably nervous. She had had the hots for him for some time and she didn't want to let herself down with clumsy overenthusiasm now that the moment of fulfilment had come.

'Now then, Felmar,' he said pleasantly enough. 'Why don't you come over here and sit on my lap?'

She went over and quite shyly sat on his lap. She smelt his man-smell and when his hand came on her thigh she thought she would faint with pleasure. His hand slid up her legs and she wriggled her skirt up a bit so that she could get her knees apart and then she put her arms round his neck and slowly drew his head forward onto her bosom. One of his hands snaked up and he released the topmost fastening, then the next, with his breath hot on her cool skin, and suddenly one of her big strong pear-shaped breasts fell free, the nipple dark and excited, glad to be out of its prison. Felmar raised a hand under it and lifted the heavy flesh and fed her own nipple into Mr Jackmann's mouth. He sucked it and his fingers wriggled between her legs. Below her she felt a growing bump in his lap.

21

He was all man.

She let go of his neck and began to undo each of the fastenings of her corset in turn until her whole splendid bosom hung free before him. He kissed and nuzzled it as fingers slipped within the tight trapped flesh of her pussy. Felmar felt her inner flesh literally throb with excitement. She wondered if he could feel her sexual pulsing.

'I gotta get this skirt off,' she cried in a real agony of desire for him. They had far too many clothes on between them and she longed to find his big naked chest so she could rub her own soft flesh against it. He must have agreed with her because he stood up, holding her, and she was able rapidly to strip off her clinging little skirt and let the now open corset hang quite free so that Mr Jackmann could get at any part of her body that he pleased.

He pleased. She opened her legs and he ran his fingers deep within her heat. She bit and kissed his neck, moaning with pleasure, and began to undo his shirt at the neck so she could slip it off over his head.

He undid his trousers whilst she laid her head against his chest and rubbed it in an ecstasy, feeling through her cheek his hard muscled body with its wiry hair thick down the centre of his chest. She kissed and lipped at his little man's nipples whilst her hands fumbled into his groin and it was with triumph that she drew back with his treasure in her hands.

He had a beautiful cock, big and thick like the man himself, hard and full of masculine brute promise. Felmar fell to her knees and almost worshipping she put the great torpedo of flesh into her mouth and closed her hot lips about it. As she began to take him with her mouth, part of her tried to keep cool in the sexual frenzy that gripped her, so that she would keep her skill and pleasure the man before her to the full extent of her expertise.

She sucked him deeply and heard him grunt with approval. Her hand cradled his balls behind and below his soldier cock and she thrilled within herself at their big swinging promise. They were fat with the proof of pleasure yet to come. One of her hands was on the front of his thigh. As she sucked at his cock and tasted its delicious strong nature, she felt his thigh start to tremble and she knew he would shortly come. She redoubled her efforts and received her reward. He began to jerk and tremble violently. His balls leapt in her hand and his cock leapt in her mouth and he was shooting into her, onto her face, and her head was back as she laughed and let the spunk flow freely all over her face and in her mouth. She gloried in it.

When he was done he gave her a towel and she wiped her face, eager to see if she could stay and what more he might want of her. She felt too humble to demand his cock within her, but she craved it, she ached for it, she lusted to feel his arrogant shaft hot within her, pounding her until she was saturated with his power and force.

He was lovely naked, a real big man with bull-like shoulders massed with muscle and half covered with hair. His waist narrowed a little, not too much for he was muscled all over his body, but neat hard hips supported the barrel torso with a flat belly, and even more exciting, he had a hard tight shapely arse. God, he had an arse to him, a beauty, that could tempt a woman to invade and insert what she could between the clenched buttocks. It was an arse to challenge and it brought lewd thoughts to her mind that made her smile with anticipation.

Meanwhile, he was the boss.

'Come through here,' he said, leading her into an inner room. She caught her breath with hot excitement. She was still wearing her high-heeled black working shoes but otherwise she was stark naked and now she tittupped from the office to the inner room and nearly fell over at what she saw.

It was a pleasure room, all laid out with artefacts to aid and abet the act of love in its most interesting and diverse variations.

'Come here,' he ordered and she caught the note of excitement in him now, his breathing running quicker and little ragged.

He took her to a rack. 'Lie on this,' he said, his eyes glittery hard and she was pleased to obey. She laid herself down and he took each wrist and each ankle and he spread her, star shaped, on her back and he buckled her wrists and ankles so that she could not move.

She didn't want to.

He began to stroke her splayed body, running his hands around and between her breasts drooping one to each side of her body in their heavy pull of flesh. He felt all her belly and pressed his face into it, moving down till he was kissing and sucking at her mound. Then he slid his fingers back into her fanny and began to masturbate her there so she strained against her bonds with pleasure. He held her flesh open and looked deep into her, deep into her secret sex as though he would know her, as though his eyes blazed with secret knowledge and power. She thrilled to his mastery of her.

His cock bounced big and hard in front of his heavy naked body. He picked up a big shaped object and brought it up between her legs. He began to penetrate her with it, she felt its cool thick invasion, and he slowly drove the massive dildo further and further into her elastic straining sex.

She lifted her hips to receive it and cried out as it touched within her sensitive buttons that triggered her full sexual response. He had switched it on and now he stood watching the woman spread starfish-fashion on the apparatus, squirming as the living juddering piece of machinery frotted and fretted her to orgasmic peaks of pleasure. Her breasts swayed heavily about as she writhed, her belly jerking upwards, and after several minutes he climbed up onto the apparatus with her and straddled her body. He began to masturbate his cock.

Felmar opened her mouth in a plea to be penetrated afresh. She could not bear that he should come outside of her. She felt she owned his desire, she was responsible for it, and she had a right to demand it.

24

He obliged, kneeling forward and dropping his shaft into her gobbling mouth. Her lower abdomen jerked and twitched convulsively as she danced to the dildo's tune. Meanwhile she sucked him and she did it well. She sucked him once more to climax. He pulled back at the last moment and shot all his pearly tribute over her shaking breasts.

He climbed off her and released her from the dildo. He peered inside the open shaking dark flesh of her and she could see he was pleased at her wetness. She smiled. She knew she was a real woman, meaty and strong, able to take a man and his desires and not quibble and snivel about what he liked to do.

He poured himself a beer and stood watching her. She had veiled her eyes under the bright lights and was watching him. She watched him liking the split open legs of her with their little juicy run down her thighs, her fleece wet and springy with her own musky juices. She watched him liking her flat pale belly that had bounced so hard as she writhed with the dildo in her. She watched him liking her full, almost gross breasts. She knew that often a woman's breasts could make a man feel very good when he was down. When perhaps he didn't have the time or the energy for penetrative sex, or sex games, a man losing his hands or his face in the full generous bosom of a compliant woman could smooth ill temper and give great comfort. Many men liked to work themselves between breasts as well and Felmar liked that to happen to hers.

She wanted him to like her face. She knew it was a good face, strong and canny. She looked like a woman who would be loyal to her man, who could keep close about his affairs, who wouldn't blab, wouldn't make a fool of him, and wouldn't always be too tired for fun. She looked like that sort of a woman because that was the sort of a woman she was.

She looked a hard woman to tire. There was no petulance in her. She was grinning at him now, daring him to think of something more.

He accepted the tacit invitation, leaning forward and releasing her ankles and her wrists but she didn't move straight away, continuing to lie there exposing her body frankly to his eyes. He fetched a scourge and gave it to her. Without speaking, he went to a large old-fashioned beer barrel chocked to lie on its side, and he carefully lowered his heavy body over it, face down.

He heard her move slowly off the rack and he heard the sharp click of her heels.

'I'm glad you kept your shoes on, Felmar honey,' he said hoarsely, not looking at her. 'I get a good feeling seeing that bushy cloud of hair under your white belly, and then your long strong legs all tight set on your high-heeled shoes.'

She stroked his back with her fingernails, raking his flesh gently, like a cat just baring its claws in the lazy promise of more to come. His words pleased and excited her and she thought he was poetic. His skin shivered involuntarily. Then she stroked the same skin with the thongs of the scourge, tickling what she would mortify. He was silent now.

He jerked and gave a great groan. She had flicked hard and the pain knifed through his back till it focused into light in his prick.

She struck him hard again with a vicious snap to the thongs. His body shivered and once more all the thrills of pain came together and quivered in a blaze along the length of his prick.

She struck again and his prick burned. She struck again and again and suddenly he had release. He sobbed as the great glow in his body rushed through him channelling itself through his burning member, shooting outwards in spray of pain and glory. The finest essence of himself had been driven into his prick and exorcised joyfully and now his whole body shivered into peace. He climbed off the barrel and moved his stiff haunches, the pain from the scourge a pleasurable reminder of the burning release of spunk.

He was vaguely surprised she was still there, droplets

of his juice still dripping from her swinging breasts. He was satiated now. She reversed the scourge and deliberately inserted the leather-wrapped handle into herself. She squatted slowly in front of him and she began to masturbate herself with the weapon of abuse. His mind groped for her name.

'Do you want me to go now, Mr Jackmann?' she said softly. All the while the leather of the handle darkened as it got wetter and wetter. He moved slowly over to a chair and sat down awkwardly on it. He watched her as she approached her climax and it seemed to him she would do this in public, for money, to his profit.

She sighed and stopped. After a moment she stood up, still keeping the whip-handle within her body. As she moved across the room towards him the thongs swung between her legs. It was a very interesting effect. She came over to him and stroked the hair back from his forehead, noting the perspiration there. Her big breasts moved close to his face and for a moment he rested his hot face on their coolness.

'Felmar,' he said.

'I'll leave you now, Mr Jackmann,' she whispered. 'I guess you wanna be alone for a little while. But anytime you want a little horsing around, a little fun like we had tonight, or maybe something else you think you might like, you let me know, honey, yes?'

'Yes,' said Mr Jackmann. 'Arrangements. I think you deserve certain arrangements, Felmar dear. You are wasted down in the bar, honey. I guess you know that.'

'Whatever you say, Mr Jackmann,' purred Felmar. 'I'm all yours.'

'So I suggest . . .'

The red light bleeped insistently in the top right corner of Felmar's vision. The room, the naked man, the heated air all vanished. In psychic shock Felmar Arnqvist realised it was all the VR disc and none of it real life.

She sat in the darkened booth before the blank screen trembling. Between her legs was a deep gorgeous glow and as she breathed she could feel the slow rise and fall of her rich bosom. She remembered the sliding cool spunk daubing her breasts. She remembered the great dildo thrusting inside her and touching off fireworks of lust within. She remembered the aggressive feel of a man's invading fingers working within her, then wriggling there and piercing her with pleasure. She could still feel the pressure of the bonds on her ankles and wrists and she could feel the whip's handle as the thongs struck, she could still see in her mind's eye the set of red weals drawn across the big pale back of the heavy man – Felmar shook herself. 'The devil,' she whispered feebly, trying to remind herself of the old verbal cabbalas with which she shaped her world and her experience. They slipped, meaningless, and she trembled and began to cry. The man had gloated over her with his eyes, her body thrust naked at him in lustful abandon, and she had gloried in her exposure. Her belly flexed, trying to recall the leathery feel of the whip handle rubbing with hard sensuality, rubbing her till she orgasmed crouching on the floor in front of the man she had scourged.

She forgot the disc, leaving it in its slot as she stumbled from the booth and home to her husband, that he might help her in her strange and fearful trouble.

Caz found the disc gone and for a few minutes was beside himself in a blaze of anger. As his outrage abated, he sat trembling on his bed, automatically feeling the glove which never left his person.

He had intended to use the disc again but had not done so. Each time he decided to access the experience, something held him back, some delicacy of feeling, some sense of embarrassment that was completely irrational. The woman did not really exist. She was a figment of a programmer's imagination. He could not catch her unawares, he could not intrude doltishly upon her life, he could not exhibit inexperience and immaturity in his handling of the relationship because there was no relationship. There was only the disc. He could not behave crassly because he was programmed as surely as she was to play the perfect lover.

Perhaps that was what the problem was. Not having the ability to be less than perfect in the discworld, he could not take satisfaction in his mastery of her and of his body. Somehow, this had not been a problem with other sex discs. You accessed the disc, went through the screen and revelled in the antics it contained. Caz had had two women simultaneously in a discworld but it had been a three-dimensional elaborate full-sense fantasy, no more.

Not so with the disc he had lost. It had been a real world to him, another existence. Indeed, he knew that it was a respectable position for the quantum physicist to take, the many worlds explanation of particle behaviour. He was at home with the idea as a mental construct. Not as an accessible physical reality though – that was just science fiction and pleasing nonsense for the Screen.

Caz walked up and down his tiny cubicle like a caged beast. It was one thing that he had not chosen to use the disc again. Yet. It was quite another that someone had stolen his property and predetermined his options in the matter. He had come by the disc quite honestly even if his reason rejected its casual appearance amongst old text-cassettes. There was no way something of such quality would have been left lying about like a used glove – Caz caught himself up. It was really strange about that glove. With a wrench he abandoned that train of thought for the time being. The point was that the disc had an owner, he was sure, someone who knew all about it, and that owner had lost it and Caz had come upon it by chance.

How would the owner set about getting it back? How could Caz set about getting it back? His mind shrank from making a fuss to the Institute authorities that something had been stolen from his room.

Caz lay on his bed and in his mind's eye he saw her again, saw her brown velvet personality reaching out to

29

caress him and enjoy him, her utter femininity and her happy abandonment of self in the act of sex. They had ceased to exist as two separate individuals. They had woven themselves into one glorious humping animal, an organic machine that once connected, once plugged together with his sex in hers, allowed the power to surge freely between them and create something new.

Caz decided he would get the disc back. He had a fair idea where he should start looking.

Lexie's eyes were shut. Their lips met and Lexie faintly tasted lip gloss and mouth perfume. The girl parted her lips and pressed harder, opening Lexie's mouth under hers, and the whole sweet aroma of her soft mouth came into Lexie's and flooded it. The girl's heavy fair fell in a solid swath of black silk to brush Lexie's face and forehead and cheek and shoulder, a silken flood of hair to match the silken mouth.

Lexie groaned faintly and stirred. The girl laid a hand on Lexie's breast and caressed it through the fine latex sheath that fitted Lexie's body like a second skin, clinging, revealing, suggesting and offering Lexie's full generous curving body to any girl who might appreciate it.

This girl was bone thin, finely made, as delicate as a bird, and as her brittle fingers caressed the fullness of breast gripped by the fine rubber material, her mouth worked insinuatingly within Lexie's, tongue to tongue.

Lexie felt her breast heat and swell under the soft stroking and finger-ripples it was subjected to. The girl was dressed in silver scales that tinkled sweetly as she walked and now Lexie ran her hand over the scales and as the girl swayed gently with pleasure, it was echoed in a faint tintinnabulation.

The girl drew back and Lexie opened her eyes. They smiled at each other. Lexie was voluptuously made, clad in ghost-grey fine latex that shaped her nipples and her navel, shaped the deep cleft between her breasts and the valley between her buttocks that revealed the mound at the apex to her legs, and hinted at the mysteries within.

30

Her blonde hair was strained tightly back to frame her skull.

The girl was a wraith in silver fish scales that trembled and rang bell-clear. Her black hair was a long solid sheet about her face, hanging to caress her shoulders. Now she bent to kiss Lexie through the rubber skin and where she kissed her mouth left dark wet rings. Lexie found the fastening to the silver fish dress and as she released it, the girl stood up and the dress fell to the floor in a carillon of thin music. She had tiny pointed breasts and thin jutting hips but between the hips was a luscious dark riot of black silken foliage, pussy-hair of such gleaming silken thickness that Lexie gasped in admiration. Her breasts heaved. She grasped part of the latex that gloved her body and ripped it away. It was in sections and now her bosom swung free, hanging down over her ribs still confined by the elastic sheathing.

The girl reached over and touched one long pale pink nipple with reverence. Then she dropped to her knees and kissed and sucked at the hot rubber over Lexie's sex, between her legs so that it was all dark and wet there, shining greasily. As she licked and sucked she reach up and began to milk Lexie's breasts, drawing the long nipples between her fingers again and again.

Lexie began to pant. She stood heavily with her legs apart, her large rounded thighs shaking slightly in her excitement. The covering rubber was black where the girl had sucked her and Lexie's long plump full breasts hung down her body pulled by the girl's milking fingers until they almost brushed her belly. They were very pink and quite shiny, for Lexie had greased all her body before inserting it into the rubber suit.

The girl released the breasts and pushed her head between Lexie's legs and kissed upwards. The heat was tremendous. The whippy thin body wriggling between her legs, bone hard and black-helmeted with hair, made Lexie come terribly close to climax. Her breast-balls bounced fatly, released from their downward pull, and beside herself with pleasure Lexie began to squat slightly, bending her knees, to let the girl get at more and more of her rubber-clad underparts. With the sound of tearing silk the rubber began to split under the strain. A thin wavering line appeared pinkly in the dark wetness of it, and from the inside flesh, began to thrust and pout strongly through. The flesh bulged the rubber lips back, flowing over them as its confinement eased, and Lexie felt first cool air at her naked vulva and then hot breath. The girl reached up and with her teeth she gripped and then ripped the fine material until the full length of Lexie's sex pushed out just above her face.

Lexie moaned. She felt as if she liquefied and flowed in a river of longing out through the sundered latex into the face of the black-haired girl. The first poking tongue-touch was electric, a harsh shiver of burning lust stabbing up. Lexie screamed and began to jerk up and down on the tongue-phallus. She came quite quickly with coloured lights flashing in front of her eyes, so intense was the orgasm.

The red square light flashed incessantly and Lexie felt the whole scene quiver as if they were in a heat-haze. The black-haired girl stood up suddenly, commandingly, and wiped Lexie's field of vision free of flashing lights. She laughed delightedly and took little bulbs and attached them to various parts of Lexie's body and began to pump.

The double-skinned latex suit was in sections covering all of Lexie save for her head and her hanging breast-balls, great globular pink shining masses pinkly tipped and bouncing on her front. As the girl pumped, each section filled with air and became bloated. Lexie's body lost shape and definition within the bulging air-pads and they pressed on her till she felt faint and uplifted. She fell slowly backwards and bounced slightly, spread-eagled on her back, a mammoth shapeless woman whose breasts now poked oddly upwards trapped between pumped airbags of latex. The black-haired girl stopped pumping and felt between Lexie's legs. Lexie was quite helpless, her arms and legs sticking out like those of a balloon toy, but the pad about her vagina was flat and unpumped because of the ruptured skin. Now the girl slid her hand between the massive thighs and felt upwards and inwards till her fingertips found the little naked slit in the suit, in Lexie's body, and she wriggled her fingers up and into Lexie. She held Lexie open as best she was able and with her other hand she slid a tube up and into Lexie's womb. Having inserted the tube, she slid a cluster of thin rods up through it. Gently she worked the tube down off the rods, leaving them penetrating the bloated woman. Now she inserted the other end of the rod cluster into a plasma cube. Setting this on a table she went round to Lexie's head and squatted across her mouth. Lexie felt the great silky hairy fleece fall across her face and she smelt the musk of the girl's sex. The red square light had begun flashing again and making a grunt of irritation, the girl stood up and wiped it out of vision once more. She settled herself back over Lexie's face and with her fingers drew her thick glossy pussy hair carefully apart so that Lexie could taste and tongue her sex.

As Lexie aroused the girl, her own loins shivered in sexual response. That shivering and its attendant variety of bodily changes were transmitted via the rods to the plasma cube. Now, above it, colours began to quiver in the air. Pink and fuschia glowed and interwove in a liquid flow suspended in nothingness above the cube as Lexie sucked the girl's sweetness and made herself ooze sexual juices. Now a brilliant sapphire blue shot through the pinks and trembled in them. Purple slowly bloomed and with osmotic slowness penetrated the other colours. The whole display flexed and quivered as it hung in the air, a visual manifestation of sexual arousal between women, a hologrammatic colour-coded suckfest that was spoiled only by the incessant bleeping of the red square of light.

The black-haired girl began to swear horribly in a monotonous vicious mumble but even as she swore she faded. The pressure on Lexie's flesh eased and gentled and disappeared. The hologram evaporated.

As the scene dissolved Lexie heard faintly the distant, piercingly sweet tintinnabulation of sound from the black-haired girl's fish-scale dress.

Chapter Two

*T*hey met like strangers, the big man with the mane of dark curling hair and the woman with the porcelain skin and long slanting ice-green eyes. On one of her cheeks was a filigree-fine scar so beautiful and strange that it made his balls ache. They entered the ascenseur together without a word spoken, ignoring each other, and the woman let the man key the topmost floor, the Canopy Bar, where they were both going. She turned her back on the man as the cubicle that enclosed them was sucked hard up the shaft to the top of the building.

The man grabbed the woman suddenly, doubling her forward and raking up her skirt. He tore the flimsy material of her panties and with one smooth fierce movement he injected his rampant cock into the gape in her flesh. She gave a muted cry and his strength had her locked, doubled over, whilst he shafted her from the rear. His hips pumped ferociously, his belly crashing into her buttocks, and he came with the hot ejaculate surging along the length of his thieving member, even as the lift spewed them up the shaft to their destination like a champagne cork.

He grunted and pulled out of her so suddenly she almost fell. He fixed his trousers and pulled her upright. He laughed and lifted a hand to push her tumbled hair

back from her face. She snarled and bit his hand playfully.

They arrived. She jerked her skirt down, ignoring the
little drift of fine material that lay crumpled in the corner
of the cubicle. The man took her arm and together they
walked into the public area of the Canopy Terrace and
Bar.

'You bastard,' smirked Fee Cambridge.

'It pays to be quick sometimes,' said the man with
lazy arrogance. His hazel eyes slid over to her needle-
sharp ones. He loved the look of her when he had shafted her, especially when it was a rude stolen fuck like
the one he had just enjoyed. Her skin took on a peculiar
resonance after sex. It was like bone china, almost translucent and blue white, and she glowed with it now despite her mild chagrin.

He felt the big open-plan room stir as they crossed it.
They were in the latest bar-restaurant meeting place to
open in the Zoo, the flashiest lushest venue for the
richest society on Earth. The circular room and terracing
swayed atop a vast tower that pierced the sky above the
jungle canopy and below them almost as far as the eye
could see were rolling hills clad in the rich green velvet
of the rainforest. Yet even the occupants of this room
could not fail to stir when Fee Cambridge went by because not only was she beautiful, but her least movement, even the quality of her repose, was intensely
sexual.

'It could have been better, of course,' he admitted.

'What!'

'I like best to steal a screw when we meet after that
smooth-arse husband of yours has had his way with
you. It always shows on you, Fee. I can always tell when
you've had sex and you scream with it now. It makes
you so beautiful.'

She slitted her eyes, unable to stop the provocative
wiggle of her backside and not really wanting to. 'I'm
going to stop meeting with you, Will,' she said. 'I can't
take too much of this, you know.'

'Sure,' he said amiably. They were shown to a table and the silence grew between them. Fee lifted one elegant eyebrow but Will merely smiled.

'OK,' she capitulated. 'I admit, I like it. From you. But I wouldn't tolerate anyone else.'

'Good. Not that I believe you for a moment. One husband and one thief – that's not enough for you and you know it.'

They ordered and when the table waiter was gone, Fee leant forward. She was not young, nearing forty, and she was the most compelling woman Will had ever seen.

'We've got a big problem,' she said.

'Oh yeah?'

She met his eyes frankly. 'The VR disc has gone missing.'

She saw his pupils dilate with shock. He rocked emotionally for a moment, absorbing what she had said, and then an imp of mischief danced in his eyes.

'Damn,' he said softly. 'That's going to cause some trouble.'

'I daren't think,' confessed Fee. 'It wouldn't surprise me if admissions to mental-impairment homes shoot up. That disc is dynamite and you know it.'

'How did it go?'

'It was in my office. I had it out from the safe because I was taking it home for Rollo to try. I went out for lunch because I was meeting a friend and when I got back it was gone. We employ a cleaning firm and I think it must be one of them. I find I don't want to mistrust the office staff if I can avoid it.'

'How long has it been gone, Fee?'

'A couple of weeks.'

'That long?'

'I've made some investigations. It's hard to pursue it without admitting what it is. The last thing we want is publicity.' She dropped her eyes and fiddled with her napkin. 'After Rollo had used it I was going to destroy it,' she said.

'Hey, lady, it's mine too. We made it together, remember.'

'You've used it. I've used it. I wanted Rollo to use it. Frankly I thought that was enough.'

'You're being very unilateral about this. Maybe you've destroyed it and you are spinning me a line right now.' Will began to look angry.

'No, Will. Look, you won't tell me what it did for you and I won't tell anyone ever what it did for me. If people like us can't talk about it, and we know what it is and how it works after all, how can I leave it to be used by any member of the public?'

'I hadn't reckoned on so much social concern.' He was openly sneering now. 'I mean, you are in the business of making money, Fee Cambridge. You kind of like to control all the options and maximise profit, don't you? It would suit you fine to tell me it was gone and then quietly patent it and make your fortune.'

'It would be banned,' said Fee reasonably. 'There is no fortune to be made. It is simply too successful. The effect can't be moderated because it is in the fabric of how it works. It is an on-off situation. You know all this, Will.'

He was silent for a while, his face dark. 'Have you thought what to do?' he asked eventually.

'I'd welcome your opinion. The only thing I can come up with is very weak. We have to distance ourselves from it in case of future trouble. But we need to try mighty hard to get it back. I think we have to take someone into our confidence and employ them full time to trace it and either get it back or destroy it, preferably before it causes too much mayhem. I have to say I have discussed the situation with Rollo.'

'So what does your husband say?'

'He fails to see the urgency because of course he hasn't tried it. He still can't realise how qualitatively different it is from ordinary virtual reality discs. He keeps asking what sex I programmed into it and I keep explaining I didn't.'

'I could trace it,' said Will.

For the first time Fee's face softened and genuine affection showed through. 'No, you could not,' she said softly and with amusement. 'You'd scare the hell out of any poor soul you questioned and if you roughhoused you'd be up before the police and then we would be in big trouble. Yes?'

Their joint history was a secret between them, to warm them in bed, not that they needed any such extra warming. Will had been a pirate, an auto thief, earning his living in the past by hacking the computer control nets of the fabulous Connet cars, kidnapping the owners and ransoming them. That he was not in jail for life was down to Fee who had helped him when he was on the run and made it possible for him to create a new identity. Why had she helped a lawbreaker, especially when she herself was the owner of a Connet car and therefore a potential victim of the pirate hackers? She had helped him for the perfectly wicked reason that he gave her a very spicy time in bed and her loins ached to have him shaft her at intervals. Fee might love her husband, indeed she did in her tigerish way, but she liked to vary her sexual menu and Will was very very hot in bed. She had helped Will to make himself a new identity so that he could enter and take part in normal society, but if he got into trouble again it would not take too much investigation for the police to discover who he truly was. And though he maddened her and offended her and insulted her, he gave Fee some of the best sex she had ever had and she adored his unpredictability in her bland world, his wildness amongst her tame domesticated acquaintance. He moved like a great lone rangy wolf unrecognised in the baaing flock of sheep that was respectable society.

'Who, then?' he asked. 'Who could we trust?'

'Rollo has a name. He might not see the urgency but he accepts my judgement of the situation. I think it's a good idea. She is someone who used to work for me some years ago and we became very fond of her and helped her to get some education and a better start in life when she left our employ.'

'She?'

'She is just over twenty but very bright and very, how should I put it, very emotionally perceptive. I think that will prove to be a necessary quality if the disc is to be retrieved.'

'What if the current owner doesn't want to give it back?'

Fee smiled wickedly, her scar vivid. 'She can report to me and you can steal it for us,' she said sweetly. She could smell Will's scent on her body and her naked mound still reverberated from the rogering it had had as they came up the building.

'Can I meet her?'

Fee's grin widened. 'I reckon so,' she drawled. 'Of course, I haven't put any of this to her yet, but I feel I can be completely honest with her.'

'About us?'

'About the disc.'

'What if she finds it and uses it and then won't hand it over?'

'It could find a worse home.'

'You mean you think this young girly could handle it?'

Fee looked down at her plate. For a moment she seemed to be wondering how to say what was in her mind.

'Give,' said Will softly. He knew her of old, knew she was devious.

Fee looked up slantwise at him with a rueful grin on her face. 'I guess I've been just a little foxy,' she said.

Will said nothing, waiting.

'She's a sexual therapist, honey. She's hot as hell, too.'

Fee vidicommed Janine as soon as she got home and was pleased to have her call immediately answered in person. Janine had been her maid, her lover, her husband's lover and was now her good friend. Most people who came to know Fee at all well had their lives somewhat skewed by the experience and most of them in the end didn't regret it. Janine was no exception. Fee had assisted Rollo in deflowering the girl and she remembered it with intense and gleeful satisfaction. She had continued to feel a proprietary interest in her. That Janine was a sexual therapist with a developing practice right now pleased and secretly titillated her. She and Rollo had created Janine's first sexual experiences and here the girl was, a professional in the field. It was all a kind of compliment, really, when you came right down to it.

'Fee,' cried Janine with genuine pleasure. 'How are you? And how is Rollo? Still working as hard?'

'You bet. How's tricks, baby?'

'Great. Things are going very well. I'm slowly getting busier.'

'I've called for a purpose. I'm in a jam.'

'Is there anything I can do to help?'

'I think so. If you want to. It won't be easy.'

'I'm intrigued.'

'Let's meet and I'll explain properly. It's a sensitive situation, to say the least.'

'Right. Name a time and I'll check my diary.'

They met in the evening in an intimate bar in the Zoo. Janine didn't live in the Zoo as Fee did but by being invited she had access. The ordinary public were kept out of the Zoo unless they were working for or were guests of the Zoo-folk. It was a tight-knit society of the rich and successful, who lived entirely within the closed artificial environment of the domes and arcades of buildings that lay scattered thinly in the deep lush ever-rolling sea of trees. For years more and more land had been given over to the forest, and its denizens had been protected by being entirely enclosed in wire, fenced around and above the canopy. Now they let the jungle spread naturally and the canopy was unwired so that the birds and animals roamed freely. It was the humans who were enclosed and restrained.

Fee laid it on the line for Janine. 'I made a disc,' she said. This was a reasonable start because Fee was head

41

of a little computer company she had created called Intimate Software, making customised discs for business and industry. 'We were thinking of getting into the entertainment scene,' she continued. She was lying but she did not want to explain what she and Will had really been up to. 'We wanted to do something new in virtual reality.'

'Surely that's all tied up with patents, isn't it?'

'There are two hundred and seventy-four valid applicable patents in the field right now. That didn't stop us. Any innovator can work on patented processes though they can only make a commercial product if they add some significant twist to the process, something that in itself is patentable. We did that, all right, although we won't go into production. The trouble is, we made a Frankenstein, honey, and it's got away from us.'

'I don't get you,' said Janine. 'You made something monstrous and you've lost it? This is a virtual reality disc?'

'It's monstrous, certainly, but it's a gorgeous monster. It's a sexy monster. And now it's gone missing.'

Janine goggled at her former employer.

Fee dropped her eyes. 'I tried it,' she said. 'I wouldn't admit to a damn soul what happened when I tried it. It struck too deep in my psyche for me ever to admit to anyone what took place.' She lifted her eyes and faced the girl across the table. 'The trouble is that you believe it. There is no distinguishing it from reality. It isn't like any VR disc on the market. It is utterly comprehensive, ultimately compelling, totally believable and as real as real can be.' She leaned forward urgently. 'It's so wonderful! You could die when it stops and you are jerked back to the real world.'

Janine could not understand. 'So what did you put on it, Fee? What would the user believe is real life?' Janine knew that Fee had rich sexual tastes. If she had loaded the disc with her own personal style of lovemaking the disc would be very hot to handle, but Janine still couldn't see quite what the panic was about.

42

'First, you have to understand it looks just like an ordinary VR disc except that the wrapper has no markings and there are no credits when it ends. Now, I've tried it and my partner and co-worker has tried it. He's a male but it isn't gender specific. I was going to get Rollo to try it and sit down and seriously discuss destroying it. But it was stolen from my office. I never got it home to Rollo. The point is that the user supplies all the activity that he or she experiences out of their own mind. The disc supplies the feelings, that's all. It doesn't actually use the screen at all except to signify that it's ending. We found a way to tap the pleasure centre of the brain directly and the disc triggers the pleasure reaction. The, um, sexual pleasure centre, because we rather naughtily specified it.' Fee grinned, looking anything but repentant. 'The user feels pleasure and then fits a fantasy to account for the feelings. Only he or she doesn't realise that he or she is making it all up because it feels exactly the same as real life. The brain can't differentiate. The damn thing is dangerous, Janine. The shock when it ends is terrific, really mind-shattering. We have to get it back.'

Janine nodded, slowly beginning to comprehend the reason for Fee's uncharacteristic anxiety. 'You said you wanted to ask me a favour. You wanted me to help. I understand the problem and I can see how serious it is. But where do I come into all this?'

'I want you to play detective, Janine. I want to employ you to find the disc.'

'Me? Why not the police? You haven't broken any law.'

'No. But they won't get it back, they aren't clever enough, and I don't want the publicity. My partner is particularly shy. I think it will need your special skills, Janine. If it has been used it will leave signs, signs that you are uniquely qualified to recognise. You need to find someone who has had access at the relevant time to my office who is in sexual shell shock. And you are an expert, honey, aren't you?'

Janine and Will met before she agreed to take on the job, though she made plain she doubted her competence to retrieve the disc. Janine was shocked by Will and felt instant hostility to him. She thought him very ugly with his wide swarthy face with its Mongolian slant, and she felt the brutality and wolfishness of the man, his latent capacity for violence. The very aspects of him that aroused Fee, his unpredictability and unconventionality, appalled Janine, who saw him simply as a man lacking in self-control.

Will's reaction to Janine was more complicated. She was a slim, sweet, peach-coloured girl whose long wheat-fair hair was bound into complicated plaits about her head, giving her a look of unnatural serenity for one so young. She had innate dignity and an air of self-restraint. Will saw in it complacency and self-satisfaction. It was strange to see her on such good terms with the alley cat Fee Cambridge who would rut in a dustbin if he suggested it.

There were some wild factors in the situation, too, that pleased and intrigued him. Among these was her reaction to him which he read accurately. Janine did not like Will one bit.

There was another wild factor that Will didn't say anything about, keeping it on hold, as it were. It frightened him a little and he was a hard man to frighten. He would just have to see how things developed.

Meanwhile, Janine agreed to try and find the disc.

Whippet lived in a pipe. It was a big pipe and they all shared it. Blankets hung at either end to give a semblance of privacy and weatherproofing, but it remained a pipe for all that.

Whippet and the boys had got hold of some synthetic alcohol and they were all happy as Jack and whooping it up with some girls. The girls were happy too and very very obliging and for some time now none of them had had any clothes on, but Whippet remained disappointed.

It wasn't all bad. One of the girls had given Dinko a suck-off and whilst she was doing it, Whippet had got his hand-friend into her business end and given himself a real treat. Even now, when he was done for the time being, it was worth keeping his eyes open. Just down the pipe one of the girls was dancing with another. They clutched each other amorously, holding each other up as they stumbled round to the music and whilst they did so, little Fruity, who had more sexual stamina than the rest of the gang put together, felt their naked bodies each circuit. They kept giggling and pushing his hands away but Fruity was remorseless and every time he succeeded in getting a digit into an orifice he cheered and sucked it before renewing his attack. After a while the girls gave up and began to kiss each other, still revolving to the gut-rock, still being fumbled by the expert and tireless Fruity. The Zootman was asleep, looking cherubic as always.

But Whippet was disappointed. What maddened him was that the orgy, as he liked to think of it, was a rare and precious event for the gang and it had been (and still was) highly successful. The combination of booze and sex was perfect, just perfect. He should have been out of his skull with satisfaction. He had pleasured himself with a woman. He had had some sucky fun early on before the booze made them all too inert, when they had with some ingenuity formed a chain in the pipe, each sucking and licking at someone's end whilst at their other end the next one along sucked and licked them. Zowee, it was the greatest life had to offer.

But Whippet was disappointed. Whippet was a sometime messenger boy who had worked briefly for a special delivery service. In a plush office in a business mall in the Zoo one day, Whippet had stolen a VR disc. He didn't know what the disc was but he was in the Autolycan tradition and he reckoned the disc was a trifle to the stinky-rich Zoo-bitch he was delivering to. He had seen her, some old dame with black hair and green eyes. You knew straight away she was the boss, she had that air about her, and it was funny because although she was old enough to be his Ma, and some, Whippet knew he would die to get inside her heat-duct and give it to her with his personal pump. He got hot just thinking about her lower parts gloving his hand-friend and making sticky-tricks with his man's juice. Some hopes, though. The bitch never even knew he was there.

The disc had blown his mind. He still trembled over the experience. He hadn't realised how classy discs had become and his total absorption into the discworld had fooled him at first and almost broken his mind when he was catapulted back into the grim reality of his normal existence.

Using the disc for a second time was even more staggering than the first. Not only did it fool him again into believing for real what was happening, it was a different happening. He had examined the thing very very carefully afterwards but he couldn't see how the separate programs could be accessed intentionally. You just shoved it in like a normal VR disc and the experience started with no join. A different experience from the last time.

When he came out of the second session, he was almost as upset as the first time, but he could remember the first time and marvel at the two wonderful happenings.

Whippet tried it again. Once more whilst undergoing its action he was totally fooled, but the action was different again. When he emerged the third time, he did some serious thinking.

He had no idea how many worlds the disc contained, or how he got into them. He knew his mind-frame couldn't go on standing the psychic shock indefinitely of being dragged from the one world back to the other. The one world was so paradisiac and the other was so godawful. It was even more godawful now, because of what he had experienced with the disc. He had a real living vivid knowledge of what things might be like, but weren't. Even this orgy, which should have been fantastic, was pale in comparison to the discworld. Discworlds. So he was in a situation where he could experience the best thing in the world for very limited periods of time, but at the cost of enjoying anything else the rest of the time, because it was so dumb in comparison.

Whippet knew it was impossible to find in real life the set-ups he had found in the discworld (that programmer's mind! Jeeze, it was as freaky as his own), not because they were inherently impossible but because he, Whippet, was a born loser and had been practising ever since. It would be easier to imagine earning enough credits to get a bubble hose in the Zoo than it was to imagine having for real what had happened on disc.

Being a realist, Whippet accepted that but then his snaky mind set to work to find the angle. The angle was to hire out the disc. If he let others access it, charging them for the privilege with the gang helping him to ensure that the disc's ownership did not come under dispute, they would get as hooked as he was and come back for more. Life might be grey and grim out of the disc, but with the help of his friends he could use the disc to make reality a little more colourful.

Then the bottom had dropped out of Whippet's meagre world. He had woken in the pipe and found sand. That was curious. The ocean was leagues away, somewhere beyond the vast desolation that used to be the city. All the cities of the advanced world were being ploughed under now, gradually, year by year, including the one nearest Whippet, and turned into savannah or prairie or grassland or bare plain where the damned animals could roam freely. There weren't nearly so many people as there used to be and they were giving the planet back, they said. Dumb fools. The city must've been fun, once upon a time. Whippet hated grass.

The sand was silvery white and it smelt of salt and spice and coconut. Whippet sniffed it and was agonisingly reminded of the coral island where his discworld had transported him to revel as the only man in the all-female tribe of warrior maidens who had found him

47

and nurtured him and worshipped him and practised their incredible libidinous erotic mysteries with his body as focal point. The whole thing had been deliciously multi-layered because the warrior maidens had been eager starlets and he was a film star and not only did they act the various erotic activities all out in full in front of the cameras, but the girls pursued him as the romantic lead afterwards and re-enacted certain parts with him for his private and continuing pleasure. Because he was the all-powerful and all-important star, any little extra kinky wrinkle he thought up was added to the script and rehearsed and enacted and the whole thing went dizzyingly on and on in an increasing spiral of sexual convolution. It was as though he had his personal harem and just to spice things up, they acted like warrior maidens. Whippet couldn't have imagined anything better himself.

As Whippet examined the sand which had not been there before, he could swear, he had felt in his pocket for the disc, because even the feel of it reassured him like an amulet now. It was his luck, his talisman, his success, his future prosperity.

The disc was gone. Whippet had become instantly demented. His frenzy had disturbed the whole gang and they had all, in the end, gone out to search for the missing disc. He must have dropped it on his way back the previous night, after hiring a public booth to use it.

They searched till their eyes burned but the disc was gone.

The orgy had been undertaken on their combined resources because Whippet had been totally convinced they would be earning limitlessly once they started hiring the disc out. They had bought the alcohol and arranged the girls before Whippet realised he had lost the disc. Only Whippet felt the utter desolation of life without the disc because only Whippet had used it, though he had promised it to the rest of the gang. That was the point of this orgy which the gang would not have permitted him to cancel. He wanted them to know the best the gang could ever have, then he would let them access the discworld and see what things could really be like. Actually, it was weird, but he found himself reluctant when it came to the point to let anyone else access his treasure, his toy, and share his fabulous and highly personal experience, but as with a pander's girlfriend, sharing was the name of the game if he was to have a source of income. He had now used the disc five times and he had a strange attenuated feeling at times, as though he was becoming as insubstantial as the discworld itself. He felt grey.

One of the two girls dancing together fell over and the other tumbled squealing on top of her. They began to writhe together. As they kissed and then turned top to tail with Whippet glumly watching, Fruity inserted his body into whatever bit of the girls remained free.

I've got to get the disc back, thought Whippet. One of the girls got astride the other's face and was sucked by her friend. Fruity managed to get his cock into the girl on her back and whilst he pumped her, he kissed the bouncy boobies bobbing in front of him. It was a really nice sight and Whippet's hand-friend began to rise again in interest; but even as his lust faintly stirred, the thought crystallised in his mind.

He liked seeing naked girls. He liked playing with their dark wet holes and he liked it when they put their eager mouths over his friend and played sucky games. He liked bouncy boobies, he liked putting his cock in a girl's cleft whether it was her bum-cleft or her boobie-cleft and he liked jerking off there. The only way he was going to get available girls to play all these luscious games with was if he had credit and the only way he could get credit was if he had his precious disc back and apart from all the preceding, he could not bear life without the disc now that he had sampled its delights. It was his! Some bastard had stolen it from him. He and the gang must get it back. They must find out who was hanging around the booths the previous night and they must pursue the disc and retrieve it.

The person who currently had the disc might not want to relinquish it, of course, but that thought only made Whippet smile. He reached into his boot (all he was wearing was his boots) and slid his ankle knife out and flicked the silvery blade into life. People could be persuaded to give back what didn't belong to them, and Whippet and the gang were good at persuasion. Whippet giggled. He would find the disc and get it back, whatever the opposition. He could handle it.

'I hate people who take something good and dirty and turn it into a crusade,' said Will.

'What are you talking about?'

'Your little friend, She's so holier than thou. So butter wouldn't melt in her mouth. She goes at sex like she's a missionary burning to convert the world.'

'How do you know?' Fee licked the flat hard disc of his nipple.

'I can see it in her great big innocent eyes, like sky-blue pansies.'

'She's not so innocent.'

'Yes, she is. She doesn't know what sex is all about.'

A corner of Fee's mouth started to lift. 'You pompous bastard,' she said. 'Janine has studied the subject. You and me, we're just amateurs.'

'It isn't what you know that makes a professional,' said Will softly. 'It's how you use the knowledge you've got.'

Fee slitted her ice-green eyes. 'Have you bedded the wench, that you talk so know-all?'

'I don't bed girlies,' said Will. 'I like my women grown up, full strength.'

Fee grinned and moved her head slowly down his big powerful body till she could softly bite his thighs. The thick curling hair made her think of Pan with his goat legs. Will would have made a good pagan god from the old days, a wild man, powerful, sensual, untamed. He was how she liked a man to be, beyond her control. She pulled his thighs apart and licked his fur with her

50

pointed tongue, purring in her pleasure as she did so. Gradually she worked closer and closer to the apex of his legs, taking her time, teasing out the enjoyment as long as possible. Even before she touched it his prick was hard erect, jutting from his groin like a weapon. She was delighted, almost adoring. The phallus was her endless joy, a column of pure carnal bliss. She moaned slightly as she kissed its slick silkiness. Will had already made love to her twice in the last hour and she felt a sadistic thrill putting his powers of endurance to the test. A man's body was a palace of delights for her, every room a new and increasingly exotic experience. Her sexual appetite knew few bounds. She would screw till she keeled over with the need to sleep if the screwing was good. With Will, it was up there with the best.

She began to lick the length of his shaft, her eyes dreamily closed as she let her tongue sense fully the silky texture of his skin, the ridges of his veining, the crumpled foreskin where it had retracted over the swollen head of his shaft. She could faintly taste the residue of their last coupling and it made her light-headed, high on the dark pleasure to come. She was subduing this strong potent man by the caress of her tongue. The warmth of his groin beat up into her face. She ran her tongue hard around his prick and then let the fat head of it fall into the hot cavern of her mouth. Very very slowly she closed her mouth about him, till she held him safe within her. She pressed her head down and forward till he butted the back of her throat. She tightened the grip of her lips and drew her head back with infinite slowness, pressing on the shaft all the while, as if her mouth was a vulva that he withdrew from, instead of her withdrawing from him. As she pulled back she sucked, her cheeks hollowing at the effort she put into it.

His cock seemed to grow in her mouth. As she sucked and pulled on it, it lengthened and it was an age before she tasted the strange flesh of his warhead. She tightened still further the grip of her lips and sucked his knob cruelly hard.

His gland jumped suddenly and she almost lost it. She pushed back down on him, taking him back into her mouth, covering his member with flickering tongue darts that stabbed every part of his weapon of sex. Then she began that long slow dragging sucking withdrawal that she so loved. He was fat and salty, luscious, savoury and satisfying in her mouth. She adored sucking a man and she adored sucking Will most of all. At least, that was what she thought as she sucked him, when she could remember who he was. Sucking a man did something to her, burnt her blood, and somehow when she was sucking, the cock in her mouth became the best cock of all.

Will looked down the length of his own body at Fee's black head bent dreamily over his groin and smiled to himself. Damn, but she was good! She turned his dick inside out with pleasure and if he caught her eyes, she wouldn't recognise him. He knew her of old. She was hyped out, beside herself, dazed with sex, unfocused on anything but the gratification of her eternal itch. He had ceased to be Will her pirate lover and was simply a man. The prick-hungry woman was never satisfied for long. That was what he liked so much about her, that and her complete lack of shame. Her talent for sex and her gluttony were nicely matched.

She had his wellhead tight in her mouth now and was sucking at it like she knew the black gold was there, if only she could increase the pressure enough. His belly jerked as he felt the urge to climax come upon him. He could feel the cool silken skin of her full breast run against his thigh and in his mind's eye he saw the great pale globe for a moment, heavy as a melon ripe with sweet flesh. Now his cock jerked and he reached a hand down the bed and grabbed Fee's black curling hair where it fell about his belly. He was damned if she was going to have it all her own way. He pulled himself out of her hot mouth and thrust into her hair. He gripped himself through her hair and felt the pleasant abrasion of the coarse fibres as he frotted himself urgently, close to coming. She rolled frantically, unable to free his grip on her hair, and he saw her big breasts flop over. She had gorgeous breasts, unnaturally large on her slim narrow-waisted body. He came up on his knees in a swift movement, let go of her hair and caught her two breasts. He leant over her face, trapping it between his powerful thighs so that his balls fell across her nose and open mouth. He pushed his almost-exploding cock into the tight cleft of her breasts. He pulled back and felt her teeth close deliciously over his balls. He thrust forward and came, his juice in great gouts that spurted over her breasts and deluged them, and beyond them, her belly. He thrust more weakly till he was done, feeling the pleasurable tug on his balls trapped by her teeth as he moved over her face. He was spent, empty, happy. Her mouth went slack and she let him move from over her face. He sat by her and looked at her long firm rich body smeared with his juice.

Slowly Fee opened her eyes, the dazed look passing and a certain softness succeeding. She was totally slack, totally relaxed, totally fulfilled. She smiled, catlike in her smug satisfaction. Idly she lifted her head and peered down her spunk-slidy body. She let her head drop back on the bed. She had the quality of looking immensely beautiful when another, lesser woman would look merely crude or vulgar. As always after sex she looked bone blue and translucent, deceitfully fragile, the effect her own orgasm had on her.

Her eyes met Will's in a conspiracy of illicit congress. Adultery meant little to her. Will watched her with amusement, wondering what she would say. She was so damn dirty. When she spoke, it was an order. 'Lick me clean, you bastard,' she said, her eyes wicked slits. He laughed and bent to obey.

The following day Fee Cambridge attended the Institute of Science in some state. She was to give the annual lecture to the computer faculty. They always had a notable, a non-academic big in the field, and the lecture was a public event that attracted many outsiders and many non-faculty members. It was to be televised for transmission at a later date on the Screen. Fee was something of a coup for the faculty, for she was not only a big noise in the computer world, she was a personality, a socialite and she had glamour. Married to the leading financier Rollo Cambridge, her articulacy and her beauty were well known. Fee Cambridge was news and the lecture was eagerly anticipated.

Caz did not belong to the computer faculty but there were few students at the Institute who were not taking advantage of their priority seats in the lecture theatre, and he was not among them. He was well back in the tiered rows, behind the solid block of the computer faculty and the Institute nobs who had turned out en masse, but he could see and hear well enough. Fee's charisma was legendary. Caz was interested to see if she could exert it to include half a thousand people at one go. And he was interested in what she had to say.

Fee was good, very good. She had the facilities set up around her and her lecture was illustrated by beautiful computer art, chaos, matter-state graphics and math-illustration, all the latest technical artistry that her software firm produced. She wound up with a computerised stroll through the solar system, a program that combined the best virtual reality simulation with all the latest data sent back to Earth from the various probes and satellites and scanners that cluttered interplanetary space.

Then it was question time. This was hogged, not unnaturally, by the computer faculty students. It was their annual lecture, after all. But Caz was patient and eventually he got his chance.

Far below him above the massed heads of his fellow inmates, the slim pale woman with the black hair looked up as he was given the go-ahead to ask his question.

'What level of user interaction have you achieved in virtual reality discs?' he asked. He knew it was a long shot.

The lecture theatre hissed slightly with disapproval at the dumb question, so simplistic that a child of five might ask it in the home. It was a waste of floor time here in the Institute.

Fee was caught right off balance and she stared up into the dimness straining her eyes, trying to read what lay behind the childish words. The silence grew. She could feel a buzz of discontent and knew they would think her too embarrassed at the apparent inanity of the question to answer. She licked her lips.

'There's a short answer that isn't worth giving and a long one that is, if you are really interested,' she said in her husky voice. 'Why don't you come down here afterwards and I'll see what I can do?'

'Thank you,' croaked Caz and sat down. Faces about him looked puzzled and slightly resentful. Then the next question was put and Caz was forgotten.

It was difficult to get to Fee afterwards. She was surrounded by unctuous men and abrasive women congratulating her and trying to lead her away to the little reception they had planned for her now that her duty was over. Yet she caught Caz's eye through the crowd and motioned him forward.

She eyed him narrowly as he came close. He was not very tall, a slim honey-coloured youth with dark hungry eyes. She smiled at him and he staggered as the force of her personality caught him face on.

She didn't have much time. 'What is your name?' she asked politely.

'Caz Luckett. Look, about my question . . .'

'I found your question very interesting, Caz. I don't think the others here understood.' She was aware of listening ears around her.

'It's just that . . .'

'Interactive,' she interposed swiftly. 'You mean, almost as if you had created the VR world yourself, as you went along. As if it was a fantasy out of your own mind.'

He was taken aback. She had put it so crisply. 'Yes,'

he said uncertainly. 'Yes.' He had more confidence now. 'Just like that.'

She leant right forward and took his arm. He felt splintered by her extraordinary ice-green eyes, cold as charity, deadly cold, and flatly contradicting the sensual slant of her cheekbones, the sexual lift to the line of her lips and the full voluptuous promise of her ripe body, narrow of waist but flaring at hip and breast. Her personality engulfed him and emotionally he reeled, dazzled, almost burnt by her heat.

'How many times have you used it?' she murmured.

The lecture theatre, the dull important men and women, the whole world fell away from Caz and he entered Fee's world and stood alone with her.

'Once,' he said.

Her eyes danced, mocking him. 'Very commendable,' she murmured. As live sexual experiences went, it was one of the more intense Caz had had.

'I lost it,' he said ruefully.

'Shit,' she said. He blinked. Her coarseness surprised him. So much moneyed elegance. So little ladylike behaviour. He started to grin.

People were pulling at her almost in their eagerness to get away, 'We have to meet,' she said urgently. 'Give me your memo pad.'

Caz gave her his little pocket-sized electronic notepad. She accessed it and typed in her vidicom number. 'Call me tonight,' she said, checking her watch. 'I'll be home about seven. You won't forget?'

Caz grinned and shook his head. Endearingly, she had entered her name, Fee Cambridge, after her vidicom number as though someone of her eminence could possibly be forgotten. He backed off and she was swept away in the crowd, laughing, talking, charming, a glittering prize making the academics who surrounded her seem like a flock of pigeons round a golden eagle.

When Fee had time to think, she found herself irritated at the student's carelessness with the disc. You'd think he'd hang on to it, see it for the treasure it was, she thought, not leave it lying about. Pity it was such dangerous treasure, though young Caz appeared to be mind-whole. He'd only used it once, he said. Fee wondered what his fantasy had been. He looked about eighteen or so. What would a child-man like that really want? Lots, Fee supposed with a grin. The boundless vitality of the young was rarely satiated for long. No doubt Caz had imagined an endless line of luscious young lovelies.

At four minutes past seven he vidicommed her as arranged. Fee wasn't surprised. Men didn't often break the engagements she made with them.

'Thank you for calling,' she said, as though the issue might have been in doubt. 'Could you possibly come over, meet me here somewhere in a bar? I could buy you a drink and you could tell me about my disc.'

'Your disc?'

'I lost it. Seems like you found it.'

'I bought it, if we are talking about the same thing.'

'I guess we are, but we can hardly talk about it over the vidi. Are you free tonight?'

'Yes. You mean meet you in the Zoo?'

'I certainly do. I'll send a taxi for you. Will that simplify things? They'll let you in.'

'Thank you, Mrs Cambridge.'

'Oh, please, call me Fee.'

On balance, she decided she wouldn't contact Will or Janine. She would play this little game by herself for the moment. Rollo was away for a couple of days and their apartment seemed empty without him. She was looking forward to the meeting with Caz.

For Caz the trip into the Zoo was like entering a dream-world. He had seen a representation of it on the Screen. He had entered it in cyberspace via the mysterious disc. Now he was in it for real, and he was in it at the behest of one of the most beautiful women of his time. She was the Cleopatra of his society, matchless, ageless, legendary, fabulous. Fee Cambridge had invited him, and he was just one student among thousands at the Institute, to meet with her personally in a social situation, on her home ground. Caz shook his head. He could hardly believe this was happening to him.

True, she was head of a successful computer firm and a rich and successful woman in her own right. True, she was married to Rollo Cambridge, financier and water baron, one of the men who had control over this increasingly scarce and increasingly valuable resource. But it was more than that. However rich, however intelligent, however commercially successful she was, the first thing that hit you with Fee Cambridge and the last thing you remembered was her beauty. Her beauty and her sensuality. She was carnal knowledge made manifest and there could be no red-blooded male on the planet who would fail to respond to her sexual ambience.

Caz did not want to appear gauche and schooled himself to behave as an equal rather than as a moonstruck boy. Yet when the taxi dropped him off, telling him which walkway to use to reach the bar Fee had told him of, he found his heart was thundering unpleasantly in his chest and he felt sweaty and red. His ears seemed to have doubled in size as did his feet. His hands would not have disgraced an old-time washerwoman.

She was there before him and he joined her in the dim booth, sliding along the seat to sit opposite her. A waiter appeared and he ordered his drink. Then they were alone together. He could smell her perfume, very faint, very subtle, little more than a colour in the air between them. She leaned forward and a green light from somewhere touched her hair, turning its blackness into the iridescence of a starling's breast. Quite suddenly Caz relaxed and the tightness left his chest. She was only a human being, after all, like himself. Maybe she had been a poor student once. Maybe he would be wealthy and successful himself when he was her age. She had a powerful personality but they had common ground. He was her equal.

'Thank you for coming.' Her husky voice caressed him indecently. 'You must wonder what all this is about.' She smiled at him.

'Is the disc yours?'

'I made it. A co-worker and myself made it. It was stolen and we need to get it back.'

Caz leaned right back so she shouldn't see his skin flush. 'It had amazing quality,' he said carefully. They were talking about a sex disc. She knew what he had experienced. That made him uncomfortable. Perhaps she was laughing at him behind that pleasant mask. Damn her, he thought, beginning to sweat again.

'You used it once?'

'That's right.'

'What happened to it then?'

'Someone stole it from my room.'

'Do you know who?'

'I have a fair idea. Look, I bought it, you know.'

'Tell me about that.'

'I was in a second-hand discassette shop looking for cheap stuff for my course. It was lying in amongst some junk there. The shopkeeper didn't seem to know what it was. He let me have it cheap. The markings were all worn.'

'We made it that way to disguise it.'

He was puzzled. 'What's special about it?' He caught himself. 'That sounds stupid. I know it's special. Unique, in my experience. But you are very concerned to get it back, aren't you?'

She took her time answering. 'It is unique, Caz. It is the only one of its kind and its kind is very different from all the other kinds there have been.' She fell silent, nursing her drink.

'I wasn't aware of the interface,' said Caz. 'It started like a real-time experience and when it stopped . . .'

'I know. That's why we have to get it back. It hurts, doesn't it?'

'You've used it?' He couldn't help the slightly lascivious overtone of the question. It was a strange thought and it made a hot lick in his groin, the thought that she had been with the brown-haired woman.

Her eyes flicked up at him, intelligent, reading his

thoughts. 'It isn't gender specific, Caz. I don't actually know what experience you had in it. Mine would have been totally different. If you had used it again it would have been different for you.'

He was baffled. 'I realised it had an interactive element,' he began haltingly.

'How did you realise that?'

'Because of the glove.'

'The glove?'

He went red. 'The experience I had involved a glove,' he said stiffly. 'Afterwards I found the glove in my pocket. I don't actually remember picking the glove up, as it happens, but when I did it must have stuck in my mind, in my subconscious somewhere. Then it appeared in the discworld. It really threw me for a while.' He laughed self-consciously.

Fee's eyes were like green diamonds in the darkness of the booth, hard and bright, staring at him. 'Let me get this right,' she said. 'You found on your person after using the disc an artefact, a glove, that you had no previous memory of, and it was involved in what happened to you on the disc. Is that right?'

'That's what I said,' mumbled Caz. He didn't believe she didn't know what had happened to him. He was sitting opposite a beautiful creature old enough to be his mother who knew he had licked and sucked a woman's sexual places and had the woman do it to him. He felt both humiliated and excited and he writhed under the brilliance of her glittering stare.

Fee absorbed what he said, turned it over in her mind, and finding herself unable to comprehend it she filed it for future consideration.

'It's a sex disc,' she said abruptly. 'You don't have to be embarrassed. I don't know what your fantasy was, just as you don't know about mine.'

'My fantasy? It wasn't my fantasy. You made the disc.'

'I didn't program a cybersynch onto it,' she said softly.

Her coarseness shocked him. 'Yes, you did,' he said hoarsely.

'I programmed your pleasure. You did the rest, Caz. You filled in the detail.'

He fell quiet, thinking over his brown woman, thinking of her as his personal property now, if what Fee Cambridge said was true. Then his scientist's mind woke up.

'How did you program pleasure?' he asked. 'You mean, like an injection of a chemical, like a drug?'

'That's what I mean,' she said and laughed. She buzzed the waiter and ordered refills. When they had been placed on the table she leaned towards Caz and he felt the warmth of her body lap him about.

'Let me explain it. You know how agonists work?'

'Not properly. I haven't done much molecular biochemistry yet.'

'Well, for example, the opioid receptor in the brain has a definite shape. If something the right shape binds to it, we experience pleasure. You mentioned pleasure-inducing drugs. Heroin and methadone have almost the same molecular shape and that's why methadone can be used to block heroin addiction and prevent craving. The methadone locks into the receptor and satisfies, yet doesn't damage the organism like heroin. Now, not only is there a physical locking between the molecules of the opioid and the opioid receptor, but this creates an electrical pattern of activity in the brain which is characteristic. What we sought to do, my partner and I, was to create a VR disc that instead of presenting an agreeable fantasy the user could lock into for a spell, the disc would generate an interference in the brain that would mimic the characteristic electrical pattern and kid the brain that chemical activity, that is pleasure, was occurring. We didn't program the discworld at all. We programmed it to cause a temporary repatterning in the brain. Pleasure is the same for all humans in terms of chemical and electrical activity. Er, sexual pleasure in this case because I admit we specified the disc.'

'You mean if someone uses the disc, it just gives them general feelings of sexual pleasure?' Caz was struggling to understand. He found that being given advanced scientific information by Fee was a little like learning the periodic table whilst masturbating. It was distracting.

'It is a little more complicated than that. The disc tells your brain you are receiving fabulous sexual pleasure. Your brain trawls through its knowledge and experience and hopes and fantasies and supplies a real-life scenario to give an apparent justification for the feelings you experience.'

'I made her up?'

'You made her up, honey. Was she gorgeous?'

'Yes.'

'And kind?'

'Yes.'

'She made you happy?'

'Yes.'

'You must miss her.'

'Yes.' Caz said this last so bleakly that even Fee's hard heart was moved a little. She reached over and took Caz's hand, holding it in her own. He stared at her, his eyes large and dark and hungry.

'We've got to get it back,' she said. 'It upsets people.'

Caz looked down. Her hand was having an extraordinary effect on him.

'You look tired,' said Fee softly. 'Why don't you come back with me? I can give you something to eat whilst we discuss where the disc might be now.'

She didn't live far from the bar, the moving walkway taking them to her bubble house in ten to fifteen minutes. Caz was dumb, quite dumb. He didn't know whether he was dreaming, whether he was back in the discworld or even if it was really happening. The dark jungle beyond the plastiglass walls pressed claustrophobically close and the green images made a mosaic in his numb mind. All he knew was that she was not the woman in the disc. She was not the woman of the glove. He must remember that at all costs. She was Fee Cambridge and she could crush him if he was stupid, if his behaviour was inappropriate.

She released her door lock and then they were inside. She flowed into his arms in one smooth natural movement and he gave a great groan as all the longing locked up in him ever since he had been ejected so cruelly from the disc burst its dam. His mouth came down over hers and he felt as if he drank from her, felt he drank great heady draughts of liberating lust that cracked the shell he had erected around himself and allowed him to be at peace with his own nature and follow its lead.

He held her tight, against him, feeling her softness against his narrow hard chest, and he kissed her with dizzying passion. She responded totally, swept up into his greed and fierce need, giving herself to him. He put his hands on her neck and ran his stiff fingers up into her hair, forcibly twisting her head sideways so that he could kiss her throat. Then their mouths were back together and they were biting at each other, sucking and kissing each other, in each other's mouths, till he thought he would drown.

He pulled her face back off his and held it between his two hands, searching her face. Her lips were slightly parted and her body curved sweetly into his own. Her eyes were dazed and heavy-lidded. He kissed her eyelids and then fumbled with her clothing. She helped him and suddenly her garment fell away from her body and she took a step back away from him and let him look at her.

He was not wholly given over to lust, although he almost was. A small part of him that was not his aching cock could appreciate even at this moment the sheer aesthetic beauty of the woman, the proud head set on the long pale column of neck, the downslope of her shoulders, the inward sloping line of her body as it came to her narrow waist and then the outward swoop of her high wide hips. She was long-legged, not much shorter than himself, but his eyes were ravished by the flat plain of her belly with its dusting of black hair at its base. Her legs did not join in a point but left a wide space between them that the hair masked. His cock throbbed as he realised the implications of that hidden treasure with its broad easy entrance.

It wasn't just her mound that stole his eyes and dazzled him. She had big firm outward-hanging breasts dark-tipped and nakedly inviting him into their hinterland, to explore and know her body's intimacies. He knew he should not have dared to do what he had done, kiss her, control that kissing as he had done, undress her without cautious preliminary moves to make sure he was welcome, to make sure he was safe to do this with a woman of her power, of her beauty. She should have been unattainable to a boy like him, a sexual novice, yet he had swept at her with his lust taking for granted her full free response. She was so completely unafraid, so completely generous, that he felt marvellous and powerful and competent, her equal. As she began to back away from him he knew she was leading him to her bedroom. He followed her.

She made him sit on the bed and she bent over him solicitously, undoing his clothes and taking them off him. Her green eyes had softened and seemed kind as she began to kiss his face and to bring her breasts up to his face so that he might put it into them and feel them with his lips and cheeks and nose and mouth and tongue. He had never known such breasts, mature, shapely, heavily full and offered to him for his sexual delight. Their texture was wonderful. They were springily soft, and faint under the skin was a tracery of blue lines, delicate veining, giving them the patina of warm old marble. As the delight of her hands busy about his body faded, he gave himself up to the voluptuous pillowy assault on his face and as he succumbed he fell slowly backwards onto the bed. She came down over him, a tender lover, adoring his youth and the sweetness of his sapling flesh.

She kissed his silky chest, bare and thin and hard, and he felt her craving for him rise in her and as her need grew, so he brought his own under control. She knelt on the bed with her hair brushing his skin and kissed down his body as he lay there on his back. As she reached his belly he shut his eyes. He could feel his manhood tremble and bounce. Her hair brushed it. Then her cheek. She was kissing the extreme base of his belly, nosing at the column of his prick, butting it gently and then suddenly he felt her fingers steal around his balls and catch them up and he was knifed by desire so sharply that he almost came upwards into her face. She swung her body round in one smooth expert motion and was astride him. She lifted her haunches. He opened his eyes wide in the shock of the moment and saw her impassioned face. She was beside herself. She was doing him no favours that she was not doing herself. He grasped her hips and his cock was so full and hard it stood quiveringly upright even as she met it and began to absorb it into herself.

He shut his eyes again to feel to the full his cock encased in her hot satin-smooth clench of inner flesh. The hard dark thick wetness gripped him tightly. She began to lift and he moaned as he slid out of her but she reversed and began to come back down on him, so deep and hard that he felt the movement of her muscles at the very base of his prick, holding him and flexing themselves against his elastic column.

He began to move synchronously with her, pulling down into the softness of the bed as she went up and then flowing up to meet her downthrust of wet heat. She missed a stroke suddenly and he felt her insides shiver the length of his cock. He was on fire. He swore sharply and the flame burnt up the length of him and he was pushing raggedly into her, gasping and panting, sweat springing from his forehead as he came in powerful plunging movements.

He came to himself again lying on his side face to face with her, her hair tickling his brow, her breath warm on his face, her breast against his chest, her belly against his wet tender cock and her knees crooked through his. He put his arms round her and felt how vulnerable she was, how soft for all her womanly strength, and he pulled her to him and rubbed his body against hers like a cat. She moaned softly and opened her mouth. He kissed her, tasting her tongue, and rolled round on top of her. He leant on his elbows and looked down into her face. She opened drowsy eyes and looked up at him.

'I want to look at you,' he said. 'I want to look at your back.' He raised his eyebrows in polite query, as though his request was unreasonable.

She laughed and as he moved his weight she rolled over.

Her back was fabulous. He lifted her hair and kissed the nape of her neck and then massaged her there until she wriggled with the return of lust. She had lovely smooth shoulders from behind and her back had the most delicious inward curve to her waist before it swooped back out to the upswell of her buttocks. He kissed the slight padding of flesh at the top of her buttocks, across the back of her hips, and then he began to kiss her bottom, the two lobes of firm rounded flesh with their dark secret cleft down between them. He put his nose into the cleft and ran it around, feeling her lift slightly to increase the pressure. His hand came round on the back of her thighs and he parted her legs, bringing his face down onto the round. He had never done this with a woman, never done it in real life. Only on the disc.

As he bent over her, she lifted still further, coming up on to her knees and spreading them at the same time. He pulled himself down and round and took a look at what she offered him.

Even as his cock hardened again, a great peace came over him. He reached in a gentle finger and touched where her little tight hole would be, buried between the cheeks. He felt it, felt it flex slightly and she gave a tiny sensuous wriggle that made him laugh and made his penis leap. He trailed his finger down and suddenly he was in a mangrove swamp, wetly mysterious, still and

66

full of roots, a foreign country to explore full of danger and promise. His finger ran over ridges and fell into hollows. Warmth beat up at his hand. He skirted the sides of her crevasse and found he had reached her tiny volcano. She thrust back hard into his hand as he aroused her and suddenly he grasped both her buttocks hard and pushed his face into her wet offered sex, kissing and sucking and mumbling at her flesh, biting it and sucking it and nuzzling as deep in as he could get.

She quivered and bounced in his grasp, trying to push still harder onto his face, masturbating herself on him. He sucked her incredible juices, sticking his tongue hard in, licking at her and drinking down her wine. He was young enough and new enough to the game to be aware of himself as he did it, gloating over the incredible thing that was happening to him even as it happened. Then, harshly, he pulled himself free of her and arranged himself kneeling between her legs. His cock was fully erect again. He began to come forward, prising her buttocks apart, his eyes feasting over her pulpy flesh swollen with her own orgasm and his recent penetration.

The head of his cock butted softly against her. He got it to the mouth of her sex and then with his mouth held wide open as though he was about to yell, he began steadily to drive forward, to sink himself within her, to allow his shaft to be swallowed up inside her hot body. He began to ride into her with long steady deep plunges. His balls swung forward and brushed her thighs at every stroke. His cock squeezed deliciously within her. His belly began to flutter. He saw the cheeks of her arse flush and darken. He could see her little arse-hole and it kept opening and shutting as he went in and out of her. His chest was heaving. Now when he went into her he felt himself bloom, expand, flower open in her dark place. He drove harder into her feeling her buck backwards into him. Her clitoris grated on his stem with each thrust. He felt her squeeze so tight it almost hurt him. She went hot and pasty around him. His cock slithered and he realised again that she had orgasmed before him and he gave a whoop of joy and released his desire in a thick hot stream. He thrust again and again with savage strength, emptying his cock, his balls, his soul into her.

He stopped. After a moment he pulled slowly out of her, admiring his member as it emerged dripping from her depths. He sat down on his heels and looked at her. Her intimate flesh had flushed a deep rosy colour, now covered with her own juices; a pearly lacework over her pinkness. He reached out a hand and pressed at her so that she rolled on her back and lay wide open in an ecstasy of wanton abandon on the bed. He heaved himself up alongside her and looked at her heavy breasts. They had been thick and creamy in texture but now the nipples were extended and dark as her sex, plum-coloured and long. Her skin had a blue-white sheen almost as if it was transparent and he saw as if with X-ray vision the delicacy of her bones within her ghostly cloak of flesh.

He put his arms around her and buried his face in her breast. She held him to her. No red square of light broke his peace now the first blaze of his passion was over. He fell asleep knowing she was flesh and blood, real, no product of his heated longing mind, and he knew that she would be there when he woke.

Chapter Three

*I*t did not take Janine long to find out that there had been a special delivery the day the disc went missing and that the messenger could have accessed Fee's office. The cleaning staff were all experienced and had held their jobs for a long time. It didn't seem likely they would risk so much for one disc. No one would know that it was special until he or she had stolen and used it. Hire of VR discs was not expensive and it was absurd to think of a cleaner stealing it.

The messenger was a different proposition. With some patient legwork Janine soon found out he was a temporary and had walked off the job two days after the disc went missing. The manager hadn't liked the thin sulky youth with the slidy eyes but he had had no reason to complain about him, save for him abandoning his job.

Janine followed up on the messenger's address but found only his mother who denied all knowledge of the youth's whereabouts with a limp lack of interest that felt real. Moreover, the mother hadn't had a compelling sexual experience in twenty years or more, if ever – Janine would stake her professional future on it. So she hadn't used the disc. Janine hung around the lacklustre neighbourhood and tried to find out where Sigmund Wheredale, the missing messenger, might be, and soon discovered that no one knew who she was talking about. Eventually she discovered he was universally known as Whippet.

A tall youth who eyed her with unpleasant interest finally gave her the clue to Whippet's whereabouts. He affected leathers, the gear best associated with the pirates, the old-style car hackers who had been busted by the HeliPolice several years before. Now all they were was a romantic memory, the stuff of Screen drama, and a fashion for down-market kids.

Janine began to feel very uncomfortable. She hadn't reckoned on going alone into the sewers of society and she found it unpleasant and a little frightening. She kept telling herself she was safe, but it didn't feel that way. She reported back to Fee without letting her feelings show about where she had to go to pursue the Whippet character and Fee didn't find any objections about her going alone. They discussed the amount of compensation Janine might have to offer to get the disc back. Fee was actually very busy because the following day she had a lecture to deliver at the Institute of Science, very much a state occasion, and she was a little distracted.

Whippet lived, if that was the appropriate word, on the edges of the old city that skirted the town. It was flatland being returned to grass and wilderness. On one side it was bounded by rising land thickly planted, forming the edge of the jungle that contained the Zoo. Far away beyond the city on its other side was the ocean. It was still filled with junk and rubble and decomposing buildings, but gradually all that would go.

Whippet, it appeared, lived in this shadowy rubble-world, so that was where Janine would go to find him and retrieve the disc.

Janine caught a bus to Townsend. The town was orderly, dull, neither ugly nor attractive. People had finally learnt to control their breeding and not live too close together. The town was full of plazas, open spaces, green rides and there were trees, trees everywere. Once a human had his territory again, his defensible space, the urge to kill his neighbour had subsided. The detection rate of crime in the town (there was no known crime in the Zoo) was almost one hundred per cent. Psychology had progressed out of nappies and criminals were 'helped'. People weren't hungry and they didn't have to rub shoulders with each other all the time and with all the synthetic pleasures around there were plenty of escape routes from a bland reality. Janine had never knowingly met a criminal and had come to believe that they almost didn't exist.

There were rumours about the city, that it gave another and more stimulating environment to those who require genuine excitement and danger in their lives. Janine couldn't believe this, didn't understand it. She knew the city was gone. Almost all the cities were gone, swept away on a tide of change. All that was left was a little rubble waiting to be cleared. A few very peculiar types who couldn't fit in might choose to live in the rubble; Janine could hardly imagine why, but she had been told it was so so she supposed it was so.

She had never been to Townsend before and it was something of a shock, as had been the neighbourhood that Whippet apparently grew up in. But she could not believe in danger to herself. In times past there had been danger, like when the pirates throve and took prisoners from the cars they hacked. There were rumours about what the pirates did to the ones they took prisoner, the female ones that is, but Janine thought this was likely just the agreeable fantasy of bored matrons who would benefit from a little sexual therapy to enliven their own experience for real, instead of feeding pointlessly off their imaginations.

Behind Janine the dull grey cubes of the Town spread over the low hills, softened somewhat by the broad vistas of trees and flowering plants, the whole topped like icing on a cake by the glittering white sprawl of the distant Institute of Science. Before her stretched a desert, a wild and windswept plain broken by the tortured shapes of crumbling towers and massive chemoconcrete

71

blocks where once people had lived and worked. The whole scene was like a decomposing skull, eyeless sockets blindly gazing, stumps of rotting teeth grinning from the gaping mouth of hell, and long tatters of flesh flapping in the eternal whine of the wind. Only the highways scything the sky above the cityscape had grace and beauty and cleanliness of line. Occasionally they winked at Janine as a Connet car flashed along their soaring lengths caught in a web of sunsparkle. Janine grinned weakly. She had never been in a Connet, a plaything of the very rich. She now found even the distant sight of them reassuring but the city frightened her and shocked her and it made her angry. She had been led to believe that it was almost gone, almost completely flattened, yet here it was gaping curiously and furtively at her, rustling its dreadful skirts to welcome her into its noisome embrace.

For a moment it occurred to Janine that it would be nice to have a big friendly male alongside her. Even as the thought coalesced in her mind, she rejected it, affronted by its innate assumption that a man's strength went for anything these days. She thought suddenly of Will Maffick, Fee's horrible friend and co-author of the disc. The man was a natural primitive. An interesting type, I suppose, thought Janine primly. She began walking. If the city was dangerous she would know about it. The police had a civic duty to prevent citizens going unwittingly into danger. So there was no danger, only strangeness. Janine put one foot in front of the other and forced herself on. She went past sad dusty weedy lots with little sheds and shacks crumbling on them until she left the Town completely and found herself walking along a broken paved road, full of potholes and little meaningless heaps of rubbish, whilst all about her a curious shantytown developed. And there were people in it, people who peered and giggled and watched her as she passed. Janine got a grip of herself and stopped by a girl lounging against a plank wall.

'Hi,' she said uncertainly. 'I'm looking for someone

called Whippet. I was told he lived down her some-where. That isn't his real name,' she added hastily, talking over her own nervousness. 'It's his nickname, I think.'

She fell silent. The girl watched her and she watched the girl. When the girl spoke her voice was very deep, almost as if she had something wrong with her throat, very deep and quiet.

'Whippet,' she croaked.

'Yes.'

'Here, in Half-Way.'

'Half-Way?'

'Here.' The girl was impatient.

'Yes,' said Janine. She was curious now, her fear al-layed. Why Half-Way?

'Try the pipes.'

'Where are the pipes?'

'That way.' The girl folded in on herself and vanished round a corner. Janine stood a moment, then set off in the direction indicated. It took her further from the Town, deeper into this strange new territory, closer to the city.

She found Whippet in his pipe. Only Fruity was with him. Fruity crouched close to her all the time she spoke with Whippet and her flesh crawled. Her forehead prickled with sweat and her nose was revolted by the earthy sour organic smells that she was experiencing for the first time in her sanitised life.

Fruity's arms seemed to be longer than his legs.

Whippet was thin with flat hungry eyes that constant-ly slid sideways, not always both eyes in the same di-rection at the same time. He had briefly raked Janine upon her arrival and she still felt dirty as a result. She was wearing a clinging black bodysuit in fine wool, little high-heeled ankle boots with knee-high thonging, and a black hat pulled low over her brow. Her hair was loose and hanging in a solid sheet straight down her back. Perfectly ordinary clothes, and yet no one down here in Half-Way was anything like her.

'They call you Whippet?' she asked, upon her arrival.
'So what?'

'If I could find the one they call Whippet, I might have some good news.' She smiled winningly and it was an effort.

'Such as?'

'I would have to know you are Whippet.'

'I am.'

'What is your given name?'

'Whippet.'

'Your birth name.'

He licked his lips. 'Sigmund Wheredale,' he muttered.

'It's about a VR disc,' said Janine.

The two in the pipe went so still that they might have been turned to stone. Little noises crept in on Janine as her nerves stretched. The silence in the pipe was deafening. She saw then Whippet's eyes properly for the first time and knew he had the disc. Her heart misgave her and for a moment she felt pity for him and wonder at the power of the disc.

'Disc?' said Whippet. His voice cracked on the word. He tried to make his mind function.

'You know what I mean,' said Janine softly, kindly. 'We need it back now.'

'Who says you need it?' demanded Fruity. Janine felt a faint sense of shock that he was developed enough to speak, that he was that close to being a member of the human species.

'I represent the owners. It shouldn't be out here on the loose. We know that. We are prepared to offer compensation.'

'I need time to think,' said Whippet. It was one of his rare honest moments. Should he admit or deny the disc's existence? He couldn't work out which was the best option.

Janine tried to meet his slidy eyes squarely. 'You stole it. We will overlook that. It has harmed you. Now give it back.'

'Compensation?' said Fruity.

74

'Because you will find it hard to give up, even though you have no right to it. We know that. We know what it is.' Damn Fee, she thought. This is a police job.

Whippet made a great effort. 'Come back tomorrow. Same time,' he said.

'Why not now?' Janine knew she did not want to come back here.

'I don't have it here.'

'Tomorrow,' said Janine coolly. 'Give it to me and you'll be generously compensated. Otherwise I'll get the police.'

Whippet sniggered. The sound stayed with Janine as she began to make her way back to Townsend, looking forward to when she could shake the dust of Half-Way from her feet.

Then Whippet had his great idea.

Once the fancy Town-sister in the sharp black get-up had gone away, he cudgelled his brain to think of a solution to their problem. She didn't have the disc. He didn't have the disc. But he couldn't afford to lose touch with her because she knew where the disc had come from and she was currently his only viable link with it, his only hope that he might ever get it back.

He could admit to her that it was gone and follow her for the rest of her life until she found it again and take it from her. It was strange she had been sent to get it back. It must be mighty expensive or the owners would simply cut their losses and make another one. Unless there was some way in which it was special. It was special. He knew that, he had used it. But was it unique? Why were the owners going to all this trouble? Why didn't they simply make another one?

Another disc. If one had been made, there must be more. The thought of a production line of the discs made Whippet drool, quite literally drool. But if they existed, they existed in the Zoo, made by that company he had stolen the master disc from. That was it! He must have taken the master, perhaps before they got it copied. In that case they would move heaven and earth to get it

75

back, using all their resources and paying no heed to the expense.

Whippet broke into a sweat. The phrase he had actually thought that was equivalent in meaning to 'paying no heed to the expense' rang in his head like a bell. For a moment it blotted out the incessant shrill clamour in his blood to get the disc back and access it again. And again. And again. He was dizzy. Limitless money or limitless sexual experience stood like two giant goals, with him darting like a nervous rabbit between them. He must pull himself together. He must get the girl back. She was coming the following day but what could he say to her that he hadn't said today, except to tell her tamely that he no longer had the disc.

Yeah! The girl. There was something very strange about the girl with her Zoo-smell coming down here to Half-Way. Why had she come in person? Why hadn't she got the troopers to do the dirty work for her? After all, he had helped himself to the disc and she would be within her rights to shout about it.

Now Whippet's mind really began to get moving. There was something illegal about the disc. That was it. They were tracking it and trying to get it back because whoever had it shouldn't have it, for whatever reason. Whippet grinned broadly. He could bet they had stolen it themselves, maybe from a competitor, and now they had the nerve to put the heat on him. No wonder they were offering compensation, the cheapskates. They were trying to buy him off.

Well, he, Whippet, was too clever for them. He had the measure of them now and he knew the police were no threat, just empty bluff. That cleared the ground a little. Moreover, the disc was valuable, very valuable. It was blackmail material in its own right, besides its value as an object for him to use.

The problem was that for all this very very clever thinking he was doing, none of it told him what he should do when the sister returned the following afternoon to collect the disc he didn't have. He would know

76

what to do if he had the disc. He could pretend to sell it very dear to get an estimate of its true worth and then blackmail the people who claimed ownership whilst he kept it. Then he would have money and the disc. But he didn't have it. He'd lost it. Moreover, despite its importance to him, he simply couldn't remember what the firm was, who it was he had stolen it from. He had had a certain amount of problem with his memory lately.

At this point Whippet had his bright idea. Janine had been gone only about fifteen minutes and she would be going by road, the long way, back to Townsend. He and Fruity could short-cut through the back-alleys of Half-Way and make up that time easily. Whippet nudged Fruity into action and they both set off, Whippet explaining his idea along the way.

Fee was able to tell Will from information she received from Caz that the probable thief of the disc from him was one Felmar Arnqvist, cleaner at the Institute. Caz had explained that he was by no means sure and indeed, he had not challenged Felmar himself though he knew her to be a nosey interfering half-crazed kind of a woman who saw sex in every corner and appeared to hate it all. She was a religious nut.

'Perhaps the girly should go and see her,' said Will over the vidi. 'This woman doesn't sound my type.'

Fee chuckled. 'I know. But I haven't heard from Janine for a day or so and she doesn't seem to be in her office when I call, either. I meant to tell her not to bother chasing up the messenger who stole it in the first place. This student I met had it so the messenger boy must have lost it. But I couldn't get in touch with her.'

'Strange how it keeps getting lost,' said Will. 'That messenger lost it and the student you met lost it. I wonder if the cleaner lady still has it.'

'Just plain damn carelessness,' said Fee tartly.

'And you, honey?'

'I beg your pardon?'

'You lost it too.'

77

Fee was silent for a moment. Will had some truth in his observation that the disc got lost a lot. Then there was that peculiar business Caz had told her about, that glove he had found. She had seen it and smelled its faint perfume. For a moment Fee thought of telling Will about it but then rejected the idea. He would think her crazy.

'You'd better get on over,' she said. 'Before it goes missing again. Take it gently, big man. We don't want the law down on us.'

So Will went to see Felmar. He wanted to see her alone because of the sensitive nature of what he had to say, and so when he had her address he watched her house till he saw that her husband was out but she was home. He intended to accuse the woman of theft and he could do that easier without a furious spouse. He wondered if she had used it and what effect it might have had on her. He could hardly discuss its nature with her husband present.

He pressed her door buzzer and after a minute she came to open it.

She was a surprise to him. Somehow he had got it into his head that she was small and old and shrewish, a pursed-up sort of woman, and when he saw the big raw-boned coarsely made woman on the doorstep, not old, glaring at him, he shifted his ideas rapidly. There was a heat in her. He could detect it quite easily. She had used the disc, then.

Will had considerable charm at his disposal though he rarely used it. Hurriedly he switched it on now.

'Mrs Arnqvist?'

'Yes?'

'I have something I want to discuss with you. Nothing you need worry about. Could I come in for a few minutes?'

'What sort of thing?'

'My company has lost something we want back very badly. It's possible you might have come across it. It's quite sensitive,' Will added. 'Please let me come in.'

Felmar liked big men and she liked the one in front of

78

her now. His shirt was open a way down his chest and she could see the tanned skin matted with wiry hair. He looked muscular and fit. His face was craggy and wildish but for all that he had a nice smile. His eyes were dark, sort of mixed-up in colour, and they looked as if he was a man who knew a thing or two. A nice smile and knowing eyes made an exciting combination. Felmar opened her door a little wider and let the stranger-man in.

They sat either side of her kitchen table. 'My company made a software disc some time ago, Mrs Arnqvist,' explained Will carefully. He couldn't make out the woman sitting opposite him. 'It was an experimental disc and it was a one-off. We decided for various reasons that it was not suitable for mass production and so we would not go in for commercial manufacture. But the disc, which looks very ordinary, has gone missing.'

That got a reaction. He saw her eyes flicker and felt her tense.

He leaned forward earnestly. 'We feel very guilty about letting the disc slip out of our hands. I have to tell you we are frightened someone might use it and sue us.'

'Why d'ya come to me?'

'You work at the Institute of Science?'

'So?'

'We know someone had it at the Institute. We wondered if you might have seen it, might be able to tell us where it is.'

If she rejected the soft approach, he would go for the hard, he decided. Accuse her of stealing. Threaten to call in the troopers. Get her sacked from her job.

'How would I know what this disc was?' she said woodenly. She was watching him like a cat watches a mousehole. Will was not used to being treated as a mouse and he found the situation amusing.

'I think you are a very intelligent woman,' he said deliberately. He smiled at her.

Felmar eased herself in her chair. Suddenly Will was aware of her as a female of the species, though a tough one admittedly. He saw her big breasts, her hard strong body, and he felt a slight stir in his loins.

'If Mr Arnqvist was here, he'd throw you right out of the house,' said Felmar. A hot thought ran through her mind and she smiled slyly back at Will.

'I guess I'm kinda glad he isn't here,' drawled Will. Good god, the woman wanted him. It would be a rough mating.

'If I had any information to give you, what might it be worth?' she asked, purring at him now.

Will got up and walked round the table. He sat on the edge of it, close to Felmar and put a finger under her chin, tilting her head up.

'The disc,' he said softly, 'is different for everyone who uses it. That's its special talent, Felmar. So what did it do for you, honey?'

'Hell, I can't tell a stranger, and a man at that, what happened to me.'

Will bent over her and brushed his lips on hers. 'I understand your reticence,' he whispered. 'So why don't you show me instead?'

He kissed her whilst she made up her mind. He could almost feel the tendrils of lust weaving her capitulation. She was strong, all right, and hot for sex. She wasn't anything like Fee's student had said. It just shows how ignorant the young are, thought Will.

'You're kinda like the guy on the disc,' said Felmar hoarsely.

'I am? I'm flattered.'

'You should be. He was a helluva man. You know what I mean?'

'Perhaps I am as well,' said Will. His flecked hazel eyes were like hot stone, granular and hard.

She giggled. Her eyes had a slightly loopy look and she was very excited. 'Come into my bedroom,' she invited.

'I thought you weren't going to ask.' Will caressed the shape of her breast through her clothes and she leered up at him. Then she got to her feet and led the way through the big apartment to her bedroom.

'First of all, we gotta pray,' she said.

'What?' Will didn't think he had heard right.

'Down on your knees, buster.'

Will dropped obediently to his knees. Felmar came over to him and put her hands on his head. Will looked up at her and she pushed her body forward so that he felt her pelvis thrust at him. Her slightly bulging eyes took on a glazed look and as she continued to thrust her groin into his face, she cast up her eyes and chanted. 'Great All-Maker of everything,' she intoned rapidly, 'you who know a poor soul's thoughts, talk with me now through the holy act of bodies coupling, like you showed me how. Amen.'

'Amen,' said Will dazed. This was the oddest sort of a prayer he had ever come across. What had she been like before the disc? Surely it hadn't done all this to her, made sex into something that it sure as hell wasn't.

Felmar let Will go and moved back till she could sit on her bed. A red light shone out of her eyes and Will braced himself for what was to come.

'I worked in this bar,' she said. Will had the sense to keep quiet. Her eyes were unfocused as she recalled the disc. 'I wore these tight tight skirts, real short.' She stood up dreamily and began to hold her hips, sliding her skirt up and moving sensuously. Will held his breath. 'Men came into the bar and put their hands up my skirt.'

She hesitated. Will recognised his cue and came forward, laying a hand on her leg.

'They moved their hands right up till they touched my private parts.' Her eyes came down and looked at him. Will was still kneeling. He slid his hand up and found she wore no underwear.

'My boss was a Mr Jackmann. He saw I enjoyed my work. He wanted to see me privately. He was big, like you.'

Will kept his body still, frightened to break the spell. His hand brushed her sex.

'I came into his office and I sat on his lap.' Felmar moved away from Will and indicated the bed. Will got up and sat on it. Felmar arranged herself on his lap. She stroked Will's neck and hair and wriggled on him. Then she began to unfasten her top.

'I was wearing this corset thing, real pretty. I began to bust out of it and Mr Jackmann, he acted like he liked what he found.'

Will put his hand into her clothes and hooked one big firm breast out. He bent his head and kissed it, caressing it, and then Felmar took it from him and held it up so that the nipple pointed at his mouth.

'He sucked me real pretty,' she said hoarsely. Will took the big nipple into his mouth and sucked it strongly. Her back arched and she whimpered in her throat.

'I took my clothes off then,' she shouted and she got up off his lap and began to strip. She was panting, her breasts heaving, but her coarse hot lust was affecting Will and his own eyes were bright and hard now.

'He put his fingers inside me,' Felmar whispered rapidly and she sidled close to Will who brought up his hand and sank his fingers inside her body. She was very wet and pasty, already close to climax. He moved his fingers inside her and felt her vibrate in response. 'Then I found his treasure and I took it out. Oh, the beauty of the thing,' she moaned and she felt in Will's clothing and delicately brought out his heavy erect cock. She cradled it, crooning slightly, and dropped to her knees, letting Will's fingers slip from within her. 'I worshipped it,' she said, laying her cheek on Will's shaft. It jumped as desire went through him. 'Oh, I loved it,' she whimpered, rubbing it against her face. 'I adored it. Oh, Mr Jackmann, I'm gonna kiss your cock and kiss and kiss it to death.' She dropped her head and took Will into her mouth. Pleasure blazed through his belly as she started to suck. She continued to croon wordlessly with his shaft in her mouth, sucking and kissing and licking and crooning whilst her fingers curled in his hair and stroked and caressed his balls. Will felt the hot fierce pleasure mount and knew he would come soon. He hoped Mr Jackmann had come because otherwise Felmar was in for a shock. She sucked him extra hard, her hand flat on his thigh, and he felt his thigh muscles start to tremble as he lost control. He climaxed hard into her mouth. She let her mouth hang open as she threw her head back and his tribute went all over her face. Will shook with the release from tension and stroked her hair back from her face. She brought her head up, stared at him and swallowed.

'I wiped my face,' she said, reaching for a towel and doing it, 'and then I laid me down on this rack thing.' She spread-eagled herself on her bed. Will stared at her splayed naked body. 'You tied my wrists and my ankles and then you got this great dildo, it's over there, and you put it up me and watched me as I writhed, I writhed, shuddering to the machine-thing up inside my body. Hallelujah!' she roared. Her hips were lifting and twisting off the bed, her mound thrusting itself up again and again before his eyes.

'Jesus,' muttered Will. He searched rapidly beside the bed and found the dildo.

'You put it in me,' croaked Felmar. Her eyes glittered as she watched Will. He put the big swollen head of the plastic organ at her entrance. She moaned, her head going from side to side and her breasts heaving. Will began to push. As he did so, he brushed against her labia. He felt them inquisitively, pulling them out of the way of the dildo, stretching them, fascinated by them. Felmar's lips drew back into a snarl. Will pushed the dildo harder and felt the end of the thing slip through into her. 'More, more, more,' she pleaded, rolling on the bed but keeping her hands and feet always in the same place as if they were, in truth, bound. Will pushed the great thing in with a sudden burst of savagery and he switched it on. As it juddered into life he thought she would scream in instant orgasm. But she rolled and moaned and lifted her hips in such violent animal enjoyment that he felt his cock begin to swell again in a contagion of raw explosive lust.

'You had your clothes off by now, Mr Jackmann. You got on top of me . . .'

Will hurriedly stripped and climbed on the bed.

'No. The dildo was still up in me. You got astride me and began to work your beautiful member. Oh, glory, just like that, you worked it up and down and I felt so damn greedy I wanted it back in my mouth and you did that for me.'

Will, astride the demented woman, masturbated feverishly and then allowed his rod to drop into her open mouth. She lifted her head so that her neck-thews strained and shut her eyes as she sucked at him again. Under him her belly jumped and twisted as the dildo continued to take her. His balls bounced and he felt himself come to climax. He pulled back to stop himself being bitten in the extremity of her emotion and came all over her breasts. She shouted and he knew that her frenzy came not from him but from her own epicentre. She was in orgasm under him. He slid off her and as she trembled and shook herself into some semblance of quietude he switched off the artificial monster from within her and slid it out.

He sat on the edge of the bed watching her. She lay in a daze and a kind of creeping fear ran though him at the power of the disc. She turned her head and looked at him and a slow deep smile of satisfaction came over her ace. 'You untied me, Mr Jackmann, but I guess I liked being starfish-naked under your eyes and I just laid here a little letting you know all about me with your eyes. I could feel my womanly juices slide real easy out of my little girl's place and you had a look down there. See, Mr Jackmann. See my great big lips just aching to cock-kiss you.'

Will looked between her splayed legs. He saw her labia, took in their length and broadness. He touched her. She was hot and slick-wet. He gently pulled the flaps of skin and they elongated and pulled free of the damp curling tendrils of her intimate hair, down between her legs. She sighed deeply and pleasurably when he did this. 'Mr Jackmann,' she murmured, and Will felt his skin crawl. Her cyberghost had done this, had he?

'Then I whipped you,' said Felmar. She sat up, pearly juices still on her big pear-shaped breasts, and her hot crazy eyes peered slyly at him in challenge.

Will had felt real pain in his life and was not sexually aroused by it. But he knew she was deep in her fantasy and he needed to carry on. He needed to know what the disc had done and how it was still operating on her as she relived her fantasy. He had made it. Only he and Fee knew the truth of what they had made. In a crazy way they were parents, the disc their child. It had developed some strange tricks since it had left their care.

Felmar directed him to bend over with his naked back to her and she then took a little multi-thonged scourge and began to belabour him. Will made appropriate noises whilst his back and buttocks stung and wondered how long Mr Jackmann had required this particular behaviour from Felmar.

She stopped, her chest heaving and her eyes bright and excited again.

'You sat on the chair now,' she said. 'I guess you were pretty done in. I wanted the show to end good so whilst you sat there I did something to myself.'

Will clambered stiffly to his feet and went over to the bed and sat on it. She was a hell of a woman, there was no doubt about it. He spared a moment's thought for her husband and felt a certain admiration for the man. What had he made of the transformation of his wife? Had he any idea about the disc?

Felmar faced him and gave him a broad cool smile. She squatted and because she still had her high heels on, she could sit comfortably in balance on her toes with her knees bent. She reversed the little whip and began to slide the leather-bound handle up inside herself, working the labia free so that they made a gateway for the intruder. Then she began to masturbate herself before Will's astonished eyes. He saw the handle go in and out, the leather soaking up her sexual juices and becoming wet and dark as her excitement increased. Her tongue came out from between her lips, gripped by her teeth, and her eyes grew dazed as her frenzy mounted. Noises came from her throat, small inarticulate groans and whimpers, mews of sex.

She came, swaying, almost falling, but she was able to haul herself to her feet instead. The whip was still inserted within her and the thongs dangled between her legs. She was triumphant, tired but childishly pleased with herself and looking for his approbation.

'You are a very special woman, Felmar,' said Will. He meant it.

'Was I good?'

'You were beautiful, honey. A real dynamo.'

'I like big men,' she whispered. She dropped on her knees and began to stroke Will's chest adoringly. 'You will want me again, Mr Jackmann, won't you?'

'Of course I will. Where did you put the disc, Felmar?'

'I left it in the machine. It wasn't there when I went back.' Her face puckered and she started to cry.

If Fee had cried Will would have laughed at her. He didn't feel sympathy easily for his fellow creatures. Life hadn't been good to him for much of the time and he reckoned you made your own fate. Sympathy was another name for contempt. It was something you reserved for the weak. But this big rough crazy woman with her power-house drive, she was like an over-engined car. She had a kind of demented quality about her. Her desire to please and be pleased was genuine, she just didn't know how to handle it. He pulled her into his arms and stroked her.

'You're the best, Felmar,' he lied. 'I guess Mr Jackmann is a lucky man and he knows it.'

'You think so?' She brightened instantly.

He gave her a hug. 'I know so.'

She began to preen. 'Good. Well, hell, baby, this has been all right. Maybe we'll do this again sometime?'

'Sure thing.' Will began to dress rapidly.

'Do you want the whip back, honey?'

'The whip?' He felt stupid. He didn't understand.

'I guess it's yours since it came from the disc. That's where I got it from.'

'You keep it,' he said when he could find his voice.

He was no further forward in the search for the disc, but he had as sure as hell added to his experience.

Fee had tried to reach Will several times whilst he had been out and he got back to her when he had tracked her down to her office.

'What's the excitement?' he asked.

'Where've you been?'

'Out.' Will was annoyed and showed it. Fee didn't own him, no one did, and he didn't put up with being spoken to like that.

Momentarily Fee was distracted. 'Not with that cleaner lady?'

'If I was?'

'Did you get it?'

Will grinned to himself. He had certainly had it. 'No,' he answered. 'She left it in the machine after she tried it and it was gone when she got back.'

'Damn,' shouted Fee incredulously. 'The thing practically has legs and walks away from people.'

'What's all the fuss, lady, all of a sudden? You're blocking my vidi you call so much.'

'It's Janine,' said Fee, instantly sober. 'She's gone missing, Will.'

'Like the disc?'

'Hell, it's no joke. She went off after that messenger boy we think stole it from my office and no one has seen her since. She has missed sessions at work, she isn't at home, her secretary is frantic and I'm getting seriously worried, Will.'

'Why did you let her bother pursuing the boy? We aren't going to institute proceedings for theft against him, are we? You knew the student had it so the messenger must have lost it.'

'I didn't tell Janine that day I gave my lecture and met the student. At first I was too busy, then I, uh, forgot. I told you this before, Will. I tried the following day but I couldn't get through, or the day after. I did keep trying

87

though it was hardly urgent, but she must have gone off by then. I think she went the day I gave the lecture. And she doesn't seem to have come back.'

'Did she give you the address where she was going?'

'He didn't have a proper address, Will. He lives in the city.'

'What!'

Even though they were only electronically linked, Fee knew a real fear at Will's response. His face went greasy pale and ugly. His bones stood out and his eyes were flinty-hard.

'Just the edge of the city,' she added nervously. 'Not right in. Hell, Will, things have changed since the old days. I couldn't see any harm in it.'

Will's face still looked tight and mean. 'That wee girly,' he said deliberately, 'knows less than a baa-lamb about how bad people can be. She's prissy and know-all and ignorant as a skunk. You let her go into the city, Fee. How come? Has Rollo still got the hots for her and you wanted her off the scene? Is that it? You're frightened you'll lose your pretty-boy husband or something? Or does another of your lovers want her and you don't fancy the competition?'

Fee broke the connection. She was in shock. She didn't know the meaning of sexual jealousy. She was so man-rich she didn't have the time or the insecurity to fear a threat from other women. Her own wild beauty enabled her to satisfy her hungry lust where and when she chose to feed. Few men had ever held out against her and Will was a case in point. They had first met in the city when he had held a knife at her throat. In seconds, he had found a better use for his hands, roving her hot places, revealing her secrets, sampling her expertise and fulfilling the ripe promise of her generous full-blooded body. Fee had walked on the wild side of sex, her tiger-nature voracious and insatiable. Caz was the latest in a long line and Rollo, her husband, would have satisfied a normal woman two or three times over because he was good, very good, flesh to flesh. But Fee was not normal.

She had seduced Janine when the girl was barely sixteen, a virgin, a new-fledged woman who had not learned how to fly. She had tempted Rollo with the girl and he had been the first man to penetrate Janine's tight little unused hole. Fee had gloried both in the girl's naive body and Rollo's revitalised dynamism. Sometimes she had gloried in their two bodies at one and the same time, in one and the same bed.

Now Will accused her of this infamy, of being David sending Uriah the Hittite into danger because Janine and Fee fancied the same Bathsheba. Damn Will. Damn him for thinking so little of her, that she could be jealous of one such as Janine, and that she could be so spiteful that she would have Janine harmed.

Fee clenched her fists and tried to think what to do. She realised she had been expecting Will to take action. Now he had put himself out of the frame. Should she go down after Janine herself, or should she contact the police and explain it to them?

Reluctantly Fee decided it would have to be the police. First she would talk to Rollo and she would be seeing him in an hour or so. Things would have to wait until then.

Will forestalled her by waiting outside her office and joining her on the moving walkways as she travelled home to her bubble house. He had an office in the Zoo and could get in and out as he liked, although he didn't live in it, saying he preferred the outside and a little freedom.

'I don't want to speak to you,' hissed Fee, her face very white and her scar a livid line over her cheek.

Will laid a heavy arm across her shoulders and let his fingers bite into the soft flesh of her upper arm. She was trembling. He had never seen her so angry, so revealed as she was now. He thought absently that she was even more beautiful than he had realised. Her beauty always caught him short. She was sly, sensual, hard and with a razor-sharp mind. They had met as equals. Now he was deliberately trying to dominate her.

'I'll go after her. Tell me what you know.'

'I'm going to speak to Rollo. I want to get the police in.'

Will gripped her shoulders and forced her to face him. 'I've forgotten more about the city than the police will ever know. If she is in trouble, if she is still alive, I'll bring her out.'

'The city isn't like what it used to be,' insisted Fee.

'Don't. Be. Stupid.' Will shook her at each of the three spaced words. His eyes locked cold and hard on hers.

She capitulated. 'His given name is Sigmund Wheredale. He is known as Whippet. He finished his messenger job two days after he was in my office. His mother lives in Valley Suburb and she told Janine he hung out on the city fringes with his pals. Janine was going to take a bus to Townsend and walk. Will, I'm fond of her.'

'I know.' His face softened slightly. 'It's the ones you are fond of who need protecting.'

Her mind flew to Caz, sweet Caz. 'Don't say that.'

'But I do,' he mocked. 'No police, Fiona Cambridge, you hear me?'

'I hear you.'

'Good.'

The Zootman said: 'I'll get her to talk. Just leave us alone together.' He had a very nice smile that filled all his pretty face and left no room for the rot to show through.

'Shuddup,' said Whippet hoarsely. The gang was in trouble and they were blaming him and however unfair that was, he had to get them out of this mess.

He felt out of his depth. They had moved from Half-Way and were in the city proper and he felt exposed and vulnerable and afraid. He had just planned a little teaser but suddenly he was into major crime and the Zootman going on only made it worse. Whatever sort of a mess they were in, the Zootman's idea would make it a whole lot worse. Whippet knew what the Zoot planned to do once he was allowed at the Town-sister. He would quite like to do it himself. But things hadn't come to that yet and if they did, he would have to accept living in the city for the rest of his life and Whippet wasn't sure that he was ready and able to make such a big move.

Damn her, he thought fiercely. Why was she so stupid? All he wanted to know was who had sent her, who her principals were, and where the disc had come from. Who they had stolen it from. He knew they were the owners of the company in the Zoo he had delivered to that day, and from whom he had stolen the disc, but he couldn't remember who they were to look them up. Somehow, since he had used the disc so much, his memory had begun to play him false and it was very hard at times for him to concentrate properly. His mind would fade like the discworld and it would be a while before he could focus his thoughts again. None of that would matter if the Town-sister spilled what she knew and he could put the bite on them, for the girl, for the disc, it hardly mattered. He could sell the girl for credits. Maybe he could sell her for the disc. That would make them find it, all right. Or get another. But if the Zoot had his will with her, they could never send her back and since they could hardly keep her indefinitely, that meant they would have to erase her, and Whippet didn't kind of feel up to that yet. It wasn't the action that he deplored. It was the consequences of the action. If they rubbed out a Town-sister, the retribution would be immense. That would bring the police down into the city searching for them and the city-folk would be angry at having their squalid peace disturbed and would hand him and the gang over. Whippet had no doubts about that. He had never heard of a Town or Zoo-sister being rubbed out, not for years. Part of him might long to break the mould but he didn't think he could handle what would come after. There were no more heroes now, not since the pirates were exterminated. The city lived by wolf-law, the rule of the pack. If he broke the rule, the pack would tear him to pieces.

If she had squealed right away, he would have made contact with her principals by now and things would be well in train. By the time he gave her back he would have the disc, or a great many credits, and she would be all right. Whippet knew her principals were on the wrong side of the law anyway, else they would have used the law to retrieve the disc, and as long as he didn't harm the girl, no doubt they would be glad enough to keep their mouths shut.

Whippet didn't believe, though, that they were so far wrong with the law they would swallow rape or murder. There would be no turning back if he let the gang use the girl. So he had to protect her and he was getting tired.

Fruity came in with food and a girl. The girl was giggling, clearly aroused, and for a moment Whippet was angry, angry enough to cuff Fruity and risk a fight. Then he restrained himself and was glad that he had done so. Dinko and the Zootman stopped looking bored and resentful and brightened up.

During what followed Whippet was surprised to find that he remained content to be a bystander rather than a participant. The strain of command was telling on him, he reckoned. It was good to see the boys well and happy but he was on a different level.

Maybe. Maybe it was just that since he had used the disc so much somehow the real thing was a bit pale, took a lot of work, was always disappointing. The disc was more real than real life, better, richer – everything. Whippet groaned mentally at losing it for the hundredth time. He no longer even cared much about using the disc to earn money from other people. All he wanted was to use it himself, to lose himself in it, to be the Whippet in the cyberworld, Whippet the king.

The girl was giggling in the middle of the three boys, letting them open up her clothing. Fruity kept stroking her, he loved to feel female skin, and this made her laugh even harder. The Zootman stood up and carefully removed his clothes, folding them neatly as he did so. The Zoot was always tidy even though it made the others laugh at him. The Zoot didn't care.

Fruity pulled down his waistband and hauled out his hand-friend like he was going to take a pee. Fruity had no technique at all. The Zoot and Fruity were now pushing between the girl's open legs, seeing who could get inside her heat-duct first. She was ignoring them and fumbling in Dinko's clothes. Dinko was crowing like a cockerel and hopping up and down in excitement, making things harder for the girl.

Fruity hooked one of her legs over his shoulder to increase the access route and suddenly she got interested in them as she realised that they were trying to get in her at the same time. She found this a novel idea and got her hands down to hold herself wide open where it mattered, craning her neck to see if she could see. The two men had their cocks side by side, rubbing against each other as they tried to slot in to her simultaneously. Suddenly Fruity came. It never took much to make him spout. His hand, the girl's hand, his cock and the Zootman's cock were covered in his spunk, and quick as a flash Zoot used the borrowed lubrication and whipped inside her. Instantly he began furiously to pump his hips.

Fruity was unperturbed. He moved up her body and wrestled briefly to free her boobies. Then he settled happily with his hand-friend nestled between them. The girl had finally freed off Dinko's member and was now frotting it crudely.

The Zoot stopped and sighed happily. He pulled out and wiped his satisfied organ fastidiously. He was always easily satisfied and his real happiness shone from his angelic face. He put his clothes back on and settled to watch.

Dinko was trying to get in the girl's mouth and she didn't want him. All the time the argument heated up, Fruity continued placidly to work her breasts. Finally and with a lot of grumbling Dinko came down around Fruity and shoved himself into her hot wet place.

Fruity came again and suddenly the girl had had enough. She got up, which meant that Dinko fell out of her and was left with his member bristling uselessly, and began to walk around the room. Whippet had dropped into his private fantasy world trying to recreate the discland and he wasn't really paying attention.

The girl opened a door and went through into the next room.

Janine lay on a blanket with her hands tied behind her back. Her hair was loose and tangled round her face which was dirty and she looked and smelled stale. Her face was bleached and her big blue eyes were hollowed and darkened underneath them.

She stared at the girl. The girl was now naked apart from some thonging that still remained up one leg after the boys had stripped her. She was around Janine's age, maybe a year or two younger, with a thin body and a thin face. Her breasts were little and pointed and she had dyed her nipples black. One of them was pierced with a small gold ring that caught the light and winked at Janine. Her head was shaven and painted with an elaborate green and red pattern that left her face a white mask. Her eyes were ringed with kohl and belladonna bright. She reeked of cheap synthetic food and sex.

Semen adhered in droplets to her little breasts. Her ribs showed harshly under her skin which was dull and papery. She had shaved her intimate hair so that it formed a zigzagging line at her belly-base, a lightning strike. Her upper thighs gleamed wet between them.

It had never occurred to Janine that she might risk real danger in her life and she was having trouble adjusting to the idea. She didn't know why the gang had left her alone and the one she feared the most was the pretty one who looked at her with a kind of hungry cheer, as if she were a titbit for him to consume. He was like fruit with an unseen worm at its heart, rotten within, pretty without. She knew that Whippet was nominally in charge of them and that her safety rested on his ineffectual grasp of leadership. He seemed to be the only one who had a thought of the consequences of their actions and so far that was holding him back. Janine didn't know how long his self-restraint and good sense might last.

The girl tottered over to where she lay and poked her with her foot.

'Who are you, sister? You make the boys angry, huh?'

'I belong to the Town,' said Janine in a husky voice. She was very thirsty and no one had thought to offer her a drink in a long time. Her throat felt swollen and half-closed. Pain and discomfort were almost as alien to her way of life as was the idea of living in danger. She was having to make too many adjustments in her ideas all on top of each other.

'The boys are crazy,' she whispered. 'Let me go. I'll bring trouble down on you all.'

'How?'

'They'll come after me. The police, I mean.'

'Why are you here?' The girl squatted by Janine, unbothered by her used sexual parts on full show. Her hot rank smell made Janine feel physically sick.

'I want something they've got. They won't give it to me.' Janine closed her eyes and tried not to cry. She didn't know why she was here. None of it made sense to her, but she sure as hell wasn't going to send these crazy boys to Fee and let them threaten her.

'Come out of here now,' said a gentle voice. The girl turned where she squatted and fell over, starting to laugh as her legs flew up. Whippet stood in the doorway looking at them a little sadly. One eye slid towards Janine and the other took in the girl's nakedness. At last he wanted her. He shut the door carefully behind him, and dropped his trousers. The girl stopped laughing and eyed him cheerfully. She knew he was the boss and was a little annoyed by his restraint earlier on in the other room.

Whippet knelt down between her legs and very carefully inserted his cock within her skinny body. She felt good, warm and snug and wetly welcoming. She got her shoulders onto the floor and used her hands underneath herself to lift her hips. She was balanced on her shoulders and elbows and on the soles of her dirty feet so Whippet had a good thrust and was able to take her nice

95

and slow. Meanwhile he watched Janine. He didn't think she would be shocked by what she saw. Anyone could watch live sex on the special channels on the Screen any time they wanted, though it wasn't the same as live sex in the flesh. No, Whippet expected her to be afraid because that was what he was really saying to her. As he shafted the little city-sister, he was saying in words that were loud and clear, this will happen to you, Town-sister, if you don't wise up.

Janine got the message. It wasn't that she thought her body a temple or any of that crap, but she used it like she used her income, the way it pleased her to use it and no one else had any say over it. That these smelly corrupt little nobodies might make free with her was a thought beyond thinking, a sick fear drawn out of nightmare country with no place in her real life.

Janine knew that even if she got out of this mess in one piece she would not be the same ever again. Her stable secure world had been knocked sideways. She was going to live forever with the fear of this particular moment.

Whippet finished his business and did up his trousers, helping the city-sister to her feet. She went out of the room with him without a backwards glance at Janine. Whippet looked over his shoulder though, and it was a very meaningful look.

Rollo Cambridge lay in his big bed and listened to his wife breathe. It was very late yet she had not given up trying to sleep naturally and had recourse to a pill. No, she just lay there, awake, worrying.

'Fee,' he said quietly.

She sighed and stirred slightly. 'I'm sorry, Rollo,' she said, her voice low and sad. 'I didn't mean to disturb you, sweetheart.'

'Are you going to tell me what's wrong?'

Despite her tigerish ways, theirs was a good marriage. Fee lay in the dark and looked for the words.

'Is it business?'

'No.'

'What, then?'

'That disc, Rollo.'

'Have you got it back yet?'

'No. It has a life of its own. Everyone who has it loses it. We keep finding it and then losing track again. We are always too late.'

'You'll get it in the end, honey, surely.'

'I guess so. Rollo, Janine went off after it and she has disappeared.'

There was a long thoughtful silence. 'I don't see how,' said Rollo reasonably.

'She went down into the old city, well, almost the city, looking for it. We think the messenger stole it from my office and apparently he lives down there.'

'When was this?'

'Three days ago.'

'She hasn't come back?'

'Not to her home or her office or to anyone who might know her that I can chase up. She has missed important appointments.'

'You've told the police?'

'I was going to. I was going to talk to you tonight and ask what you thought. I didn't realise for the first couple of days anything was wrong. I just kept thinking I was missing her and she would be in touch. Then her secretary, Adéle, told me that she wasn't turning up for work, that she was leaving clients flat. Then I got worried, Rollo.'

'What stopped you going to the police or talking to me?'

'I told Will Maffick. He said he would go down into the city and not to worry the police. He would bring her back.'

Rollo considered this. He was a far from stupid man. 'Does Will know about the city, then? Has he some special knowledge that he thinks he can do better than the police?'

'He used to be a criminal, Rollo,' said Fee tiredly. She

was beyond dissimulation, too worried about Janine and her own responsibility for the girl's situation.

'You knew this when he came to work for you?'

'Sure. I didn't care. I was getting the services of a molecular biochemist cheap.'

Rollo nodded in the dark. He understood this. He was used to seeing situations from a financial rather than a moral viewpoint.

'He knew the city well at one time, then?'

'Uh huh.'

'He maybe has the rights of it. The police would be clumsy if Janine is in real danger.'

Fee felt a great wash of love and gratitude run over her. All the questions Rollo didn't ask! 'I knew she was going,' she said guiltily. 'I couldn't see that there was any danger. I still don't understand it. She was going after a two-bit disc thief prepared to offer him money for what he had stolen. Why should he harm her? Unless she fell foul of someone else down there. I thought almost everyone was gone. Oh, Rollo.'

He began to stroke her face, letting his finger glide over the thin cicatrice on her cheek. He had learned long ago not to ask Fee too many questions and he wouldn't risk losing her now by changing his ways. She was equally incurious and trusting with him. He let his hand run on down from her face, over her neck until it reached one of her full heavy breasts. He stroked her for a while until she quivered slightly and he knew his method of comforting her was beginning to work.

He let his lips start to follow where his hand had been. He kissed the delicate line of her cheek, her throat, and then the rounded cool firm flesh of her breast. His hand trailed on down until it lay lightly over her belly. The base of his palm, where it met his wrist, could feel the silken touch of her hair springing black and sweet over her sex. He remembered the time that she had had her mound depilated, leaving it a satin smooth gleaming roundel of hard flesh that invited the hand to slip over its smoothness and fall below and between the lobes

98

beneath it. Her belly had drawn the hand in even as fruit invites the bite, with the same promise of juice squeezing from riven flesh.

Now she had her hair again. Rollo teased at it and pulled it gently, feeling the lift of her hips in response. He slid a finger between her thighs, crooking it till it invaded up into the wet fleshiness of her sex. She sighed and settled her legs further apart.

For a little while he felt around the clustered protuberances of her parts. He paid gentle attention to her clitoris, an organ he had fiercely bitten and sucked at other times. Now he looked to soothe her and was gentle.

Her breathing quickened and became noisier now that her lips were parted. Her breast rose and fell as he pushed her thighs further apart and then worked his body down the bed. She lifted her knees and let them fall almost flat to the bed. Rollo kissed down the inside of each thigh allowing his head to caress her as he did so. Then at last he brought his mouth forward and delicately extended his tongue.

He ran its tip around the tip of her erect clitoris, tasting the pungency of her arousal. She gave a small deep sexual moan and he pressed harder with his tongue. She was unable to resist pushing down on him to increase the pressure and he grinned in the dark. One of the very nicest things about Fee was her sheer inability to exercise restraint. He opened his mouth wide and moved closer to her and huffed outwards a hot damp breath that bathed her entire mound. Then he too could no longer resist her naked enticement and he closed his mouth fully over her vulva.

God, but the musk of her was divine. He sucked deeply and felt her shudder in his mouth. He couldn't get enough of the taste of her and brought up his tongue to lick the length of her sex and to penetrate her body. He pushed it in as far as it would go and wriggled it about. He could feel her muscular spasms gripping his tongue. He sucked around it and drew her juices into his mouth, swallowing them down as fast as he got them.

His upper lip could feel her erect clitoris and for a moment he abandoned her inner velvet and pursed his lips tightly over her quivering cone of flesh. He sucked hard and then bit it, toothing it, and then drawing his teeth, scraping them almost, along the valleys and the ridges of her vulva. He put out his tongue with his mouth open wide and, starting with her arse, he licked hard the full length of her again. She began to push into his face and he closed his mouth once more over her cleft and stuck his rigid tongue inside.

A few sharp probes and she came, a wet flood of nectar that had his hands gripping her knees in his intensity to suck it all down that he might taste her forever.

At last he drew back and sat up on his heels between her legs, looking down at her.

The darkness was almost but not quite absolute and he could just see the glitter of her needle eyes.

'Fee,' he said.

'Yes, darling?'

Rollo grinned again to himself in the dark. The only time he ever heard that submissive tone from Fee was straight after sex. 'Let's get a light-bed.'

'A light-bed?'

'Yeah. You know.'

She considered. 'A nice idea,' she ventured.

'Any problems?'

'Gimmicky. We might get tired of it. We'll have to store this one in case we want it back.'

'I'll see to it tomorrow,' he promised. He sighed and stretched himself luxuriously beside her. Fee turned her head and kissed him mouth to open mouth, seeking to taste her own sex in him and finding it.

'You mind if we sleep top to tail?' she asked.

'Not at all. I just thought you might like to be in my arms.'

'I love to be in your arms, Rollo. But right now I want to sleep with your cock in my mouth.'

He laughed. 'A comforter, Fee? A dummy?'

She twisted in the bed and he felt the velvet mouth of

her caress his member. 'No dummy, Rollo Cambridge,' she said. 'It's the real thing.'

At last she was able to sleep.

Chapter Four

*J*anine had worked herself up onto her knees and had backed into the corner of the room as far as she could go. The whites of her eyes were showing and she was terrified.

All four members of the gang were in the room. Whippet was explaining her near future to her.

'We're gonna have you,' he said simply.

'Me first,' said the Zootman. Janine shuddered.

'I wanna go first,' cried Dinko who felt hard done by. He was the only one who had not made it with the city-girl who had been with them for a while. He reckoned he deserved something for that.

'I could go first and last,' said Fruity with simple pride. It was no more than the truth. He swung his long arms apishly and sniggered.

'Everyone is gonna have you as often as they like,' said Whippet, speaking directly to Janine. 'Or we will let you go. It's your choice, sister.'

'Maybe she likes the idea,' said the Zootman.

'Maybe,' said Fruity hungrily, 'she doesn't believe us.' He began to pluck his waistband.

'She believes us,' said Whippet. He waited with what patience he could muster. He was taking a chance getting the gang all excited like this, and he was relying on their recent activity with the city-girl to stop them from getting out of control. If the Town-sister still refused to play, he would have to make the decision he was putting off. Either he would really let her go and risk his loss of credibility with the gang, or he would commit himself to a life forever in the city.

'I can't send you to my friends,' croaked Janine.

'They sent you to us,' reasoned Whippet cleverly.

'I don't understand. If you won't hand over the disc, why won't you let me go? Why did you bring me here?'

Whippet decided there was nothing any longer to lose about admitting they didn't have the disc. 'You tell us who they are,' he said. 'That's all we ask. We've lost the disc. We want another one. We'll give you back if they give us another disc.'

Janine stared at him her mind moving sluggishly. 'There is only one disc,' she said.

'Oh, tough luck,' said the Zootman and giggled in anticipation.

'I don't believe you,' said Whippet. 'If there was one, there's another. It stands to reason. Unless your buddies stole the disc off someone else. You'll have to tell us, though.'

'No,' whispered Janine.

'I'll give you an hour,' said Whippet in a lordly voice. 'Then if you don't tell us, we all get to play games.'

Fruity crouched down and put his knuckles on the floor. Dinko copied him and they both began to leap and gibber round the room. The Zootman clapped, his face shiny and pleased at the entertainment, and Whippet watched them indulgently. They were good boys. Then he looked at Janine and felt a lurch of satisfaction. It was going to work. There was no mistaking the look of naked terror on her face. Her lips had drawn back, her mouth was wide open, her eyes were huge and staring and she was jammed back against the corner.

Something in her rigid pose, her focused terror, made him turn his head. His jaw dropped. A man was standing in the doorway to the room, legs straddled, his weight evenly disposed, and his arms folded across his broad chest. He was big and menacing. He was masked and a red bandanna round his forehead tied his hair back. His chest was naked but for a broad leather strap across it, and his shoulders gleamed with living colour. He had liquid crystal patterns injected under his skin and the pictures writhed and lived as his body heat altered their projected colours.

He wore leather trousers and looked every inch a pirate.

The gang fell silent and clustered together. They knew some ferocious types lived in the city, but they hardly knew what those types were. Though they were four and he was one, they instinctively felt their disadvantage.

'I'll take her now,' said the man.

The contempt in his voice stung Whippet. 'She's ours,' he said. 'Get out of here.'

The man crossed the room and hit Whippet savagely. Janine screamed. He frightened her more than all the boys put together. There was a pure ugly rawness in him that she could sense clear across the room, clear through her fear and fatigue. If she gave way to the gang she might get back to the life she knew. If this man took her she felt that there was an end to her. She would go further into the city and be lost forever.

The Zootman pulled his knife and leapt at the man. He was tossed aside and Dinko was back-handed at the same time. Blood dripped from a cut on the man's arm. His arms and hands seemed to go everywhere and when his blur of activity stopped, all four gang members were broken dolls, lolling against the walls of the rotten room. The violence stank louder than sex, louder than fear itself. He slid a knife out of his own belt and reached over and grabbed Janine. He slit her bonds and held her.

'They take your body, sister?' he asked coldly.

'No,' said Whippet urgently. It hurt him to talk and his lips felt swollen but he knew he had to clear himself and quickly before the trouble got a whole lot worse.

The man shook Janine slightly. Fear made her loose-limbed, like a puppet. 'That right?'

'Yes,' she croaked. 'They were going to.'

The man grinned unpleasantly. 'Not now, they ain't.'

'I belong to the Town,' she pleaded. 'Let me go, before the police come.'

'The police don't come here,' said the man. 'They got too much sense.' He began to walk out of the room hauling Janine with him. She dragged back and yelled helplessly to Whippet. The man picked her up and slung her effortlessly over his shoulder. He turned and grinned coldly at Whippet, daring him to attack.

Whippet let his eyes fall. He knew when he was beat. The man was quality, he was what Whippet wanted to be. The gang couldn't touch him.

Outside it was dark and raining slightly, a thin mizzle that clouded sight and hearing. Janine let the damp touch her fevered skin and fought to control her fear. She had met up with an intelligence of a sort, she knew. Maybe she could reason with him.

He put her down. 'Can you walk?' he asked.

'Let me go.'

'It's Will Maffick, Janine. Sorry it took so long.' He pulled the mask off. 'I only found out today you were gone. Now, can you walk? We need to make time. Nights are bad down the city.'

'Will Maffick? Fee's friend?'

'The same. We met once.'

'But you, but you're an animal. What you did to those boys!' She was genuinely outraged, beyond rational thought. It was disgusting that a man from her own world should behave like this, like she had seen. Violence was the hallmark of the primitive, the underevolved, the mentally backward. The deranged. Maffick was a mature and educated man yet he had savaged the silly boys from Half-Way like he was a shark with raw meat. She wanted to vomit.

'Steady on, sister. Those boys have been holding you captive. Don't get on at me.'

'Why didn't you bring the police? They would have been sent to prison then. You didn't have to hit them around.' You liked it, she implied.

'Can we argue later?' Will was barely polite. 'We have to make a move. It isn't safe here.'

'You're as bad as them,' said Janine, stumbling along beside him. 'Worse, because you know better.'

He didn't reply but instead set a nightmare pace that in her weakened condition she could hardly keep up. He was a brute. This was showing off, dressing up in those silly clothes and coming down here to get her back like some old-style hero. She could have been rescued decently and in order by the police and even now be in a helibuzz being taken to hospital. Instead she had to half run like this through the dark and the rain with this violent animal by her side.

She stumbled and cried out, then sat down to nurse her ankle. He was crouched beside her in an instant.

'Can you still walk?' he said urgently.

'What are you frightened of?' she demanded hysterically. 'You think the gang will come after you?'

'I'll carry you,' he said.

'No!' She didn't want his hands on her.

She felt him go stiff. His crouch became rigid and he had his head up like a dog's scenting the air. Very very slowly he began to ease himself to his feet. 'Stay down,' he muttered.

As he stood up Janine was suddenly aware of the magnificence of the man, of his masculinity, his size and his strength. Somehow he emphasised every difference there was between the genders, emphasised and exaggerated them. She wasn't used to men in the raw. The men in her life veiled their physical strength, muted their maleness under a gloss of smooth manners.

She saw they weren't alone.

They were in a patch of open ground. Will towered over her, tense and stiff, his hand hovering by his belt. Spaced around him were figures obscured by the dank mist. There seemed to be very many of them.

Will straightened himself completely. 'I demand the right to pass,' he said coldly, his voice powerful and full of menace.

'No demands,' was the gentle cool amused reply. Her voice by contrast was pitched both quiet and confident. She moved forward slightly and faced Will across the rubble-strewn ground.

'I will pass and not return. I have urgent business,' said Will.

'Not so urgent that you must needs cross our territory,' she corrected.

'It was in ignorance.'

'Ignorance is dangerous sometimes,' she said. 'Your name?'

'Wolf.'

'Yes. A good name. It is a pity you trespass, Wolf.'

'I will go back,' Will said matter-of-factly. 'Or fight, as you wish.'

'We are many.'

'Yes, I see that. But I will fight and many of you will suffer.'

'You cannot win.'

'No. But your winning will be bloody.' Will drew his knife.

'You can't fight women,' said Janine indignantly from the ground. This was worse and worse.

Will kicked her.

'Let the sister speak,' said Will's interlocutor and now there was no lazy amusement in her voice.

Janine started to rise and felt Will grip her shoulder, his fingers digging painfully into her flesh. 'I was kidnapped from the Town,' she said clearly. 'This man . . .' Will knocked her down and she fell with a startled gasp. Immediately the women attacked him. He danced clear of Janine with his knife held forward but there were twenty or more of them, all yelling and making a curious high ululating wail as they closed to take him.

For a few terrible moments Janine thought they would kill him. Their savagery was instant, intent, disciplined.

107

It occurred to her for the first time that perhaps Will understood the city better than she did. Then she saw him staggering but upright in their midst. There was a rattle of chains and they had him at their mercy.

Their leader, the one who had challenged his right to be there, approached Janine. As she came close Janine was startled by her bizarre appearance and she saw it was in some sort of uniform and they were all dressed alike.

The woman's head was shaven and her face was elaborately made up with thick dark colours that emphasised her eyes and her cheekbones and her mouth. She wore a little cloak tied so that it went across one shoulder only and hung to elbow-length, the other shoulder being left bare. Under the cloak she wore something tight and black but one breast was exposed, not on the cloak side, and in the poor light its skin was pale, black patterns swirling from the nipple.

'Go,' said the woman coldly.

'I . . .'

'Go, and you will not be harmed. We have no argument with women.'

'What will happen to him?'

'That is none of your business now. Go.'

She turned away from Janine who stood on one foot uncertainly, her ankle throbbing. She did not know what to do. Will himself was silent. The women crowded round him and together they vanished rapidly into the murk. Janine heard the rattle of his chains and the whisper of their little cloaks. Then she was alone in the darkness.

Will loped along steadily with his captors cursing silently and fluently. He had only just stopped Janine from telling the women he was not from the city but from the Town. That would really have signed his death warrant, though he wasn't any too sure it wasn't signed already. He knew who these women were by repute though not from first-hand experience. They were the Amazenes, a female pack that lived down here and kept all men away

108

from themselves and their territory unless they wanted a plaything for a while. It was against their code to let a man go after they had used him. He didn't know whether he was on the punishment list or the plaything list. He rather hoped it was the former, though their reputation for ferocity and bloodthirstiness was matched only by their reputation for beauty.

He was not a man overendowed with a sense of chivalry and yet when it had come to hand-to-hand fighting, he had not been able to let himself go as he would have done with a man, or with a pack of men. He knew he could not have beaten them. They were too many for him and they were acknowledged as skilled and courageous fighters. But he could have harmed them much more than he had done and he cursed himself for his weakness in this. They would have no mercy on him. He was a fool to show compunction for their sex.

After some time they came to a building. They went into it and through it and then Will found that he was in a courtyard and the building bounded them about on every side. It appeared intact for several storeys and then the telltale rot showed, glassless windows, crumbling corners, broken and stained cladding. Most of these buildings still had power connected because power was so cheap it wasn't worth disconnecting. A few lower windows were lit but none of the upper ones. Girders stuck up like twisted broken limbs from the upper levels of the building.

They put new chains on Will. The two wrist manacles were joined by a long metal bar which went across his shoulders. Once he was secured, his arms stuck out on either side of him. The bar lay cold on his naked skin across the back of his neck. Then they put him against a wall and left him whilst they lounged at their ease around a fire in the centre of the courtyard.

They ate. Some came and some went. Evidently they posted guards around their territory. The night wore on and Will stood, his arms stretched out, and bore with it as best he could.

Eventually the one who had had command over the pack that had taken him prisoner came up to him. She was flanked by two lieutenants. She stood for a while in front of Will, considering him, and then she said: 'Let him be cleansed and brought before me. We shall see what we have caught in our net, how fine a beast he might be, how well adapted to our needs.'

'I am no beast for your delectation,' snarled Will.

'The meat speaks!' She laughed and turned away from him, disappearing into the building.

Then Will's humiliation began.

He was led into the building and along a corridor and into a bathroom. They removed his chains but now some of the women were dressed in white flowing robes. They had long pretty hair and they giggled a lot. The black-clad shaven women stood guard around the room, knives and kukris held at the ready in case Will should have foolish thoughts of escape.

The robed women stripped Will and he saw a bath was prepared for him. Their hands were gentle, fluttering over him, playing with him as they laughed and teased, and in other circumstances he might have enjoyed the attentions of so pretty and feminine a collection. The guards made an ominous background that he was unable to forget.

He stepped into the warm scented water and lay back with his eyes closed. Hands came in with sponges and gently worked all around his big hard muscled body. There were worse ways to go, he reflected, relaxing, and unable to prevent a certain telltale response to their ministrations. This made them laugh the harder and he found he could not prevent himself from becoming erect within the soapy warmth. They were playfully fighting to be the one who washed him there, but it was more a caress than an ablution.

Eventually they told him to stand up and they wrapped towels around him though even their thick swathing failed to hide the effect the girls had had on him. Now he was led to another room, sumptuously fur-

110

nished with warm bright silks and velvets thickly scattered with cushions. The air was scented and distantly slow music played with an insinuating rhythm. Will was dried and powdered, scented balsam was rubbed into his skin, his hair was dried and then he was left. He appeared to be alone in the room. He stood up and prowled round. He could find no window behind the wall hangings and when he tried the door, it was locked. He was quite sure it was guarded on the outside.

He considered his life briefly since he was sure his freedom to live it on his own terms had just become a matter of strong doubt. It had been a curious affair. He had had a conventional enough start and early career. Then had come the abrupt break and his years as a pirate, a computer hacker living in the city. Then, with Fee Cambridge's help, he had taken on a new persona and become respectable again, working quite successfully in the Town and the Zoo.

He had never admitted to Fee that he found life dull, a little empty. Apart from Fee herself he found the women in his life bland, uninventive, repetitive. If he showed his nature too abruptly they were frightened of him. He had run on a curb rein for five years and he was restless and sick of restraint. There was no passion in the world he had moved into, no excitement. Janine's response to him was typical.

Perhaps then to end this way was fitting, the plaything of warrior women, a final submission to the humiliations life seemed to have always in store for him. He was sure that the female leader of the pack would be as vital and uninhibited in her lovemaking as he was himself. They might waste him afterwards if he refused or failed to cooperate, but his life was all one slow dull waste now, eating at him like a canker. He would go in a blaze of glory.

It was a pity about Janine. She would probably survive and get back to the Town, a little roughed up by her adventures but not harmed in any way he would reckon as meaningful. She looked good. Those big candid blue eyes of hers had a certain subtlety behind them even if she didn't exploit it. He knew for a fact, because he had actually witnessed it himself, she was capable of something very fancy in bed. When he had been on the run all those years ago, Fee had hidden him in her apartment and he had spied on the tricks they had got up to. Fee was the very devil for sex and Will had looked secretly on Janine and Fee at erotic play together. It still had an effect on him, the memory of the two women twisting together and using hand and tongue and lips to arouse and bring each other to climax. Moreover, Will was halfway to being certain Janine had had the hots for Rollo and the two of them had gotten together also.

Will felt ambivalent about Rollo Cambridge. It was beneath him to feel jealous and he was not visited by requisite feelings of possession when he enjoyed a woman that made him edgy about her enjoying another man. Women weren't like one's personal computer. A man didn't own one. But Will knew that whatever Fee said and did, Rollo was the man for her and if she was forced to it, she would satisfy herself on his lean bronzed body alone, leaving Will and her other playthings cold. Probably Janine still wanted the guy, too. So when she was prissy and cold to Will Maffick, it was because he wasn't like Rollo Cambridge. Damned little disapproving judgmental ignorant bitch. She was far too young for him, too. Yet Will felt an itch. He itched to get between her long peachy thighs, to open them and to enter and possess her so that she finally knew for once and for all what the act of sex could be, how hot, how satisfying, how gratifying, how you could lose yourself and blind yourself in the act, leaving yourself drained and exposed yet satisfied, uplifted, complete.

Will laughed at himself. He was getting poetic in his old age. He looked down at his ravaged body. He was scarred. His skin was naturally dark and roughened because of his erratic career and because he did not tend it like the Rollo Cambridges of this world tended their skin. Because of its sheer size his body was powerful and aggressive even when he didn't mean it to be. Even his muscles bulged far too much to wear the fashionable clothes of the Town and the Zoo and look smart. No wonder the Janines in his life were scared of him. He wouldn't compromise. He never had. He had something to offer and it wasn't his fault that the little girlies round about him weren't feminine enough to recognise him for what he was, for what he had for them, what he could do.

The door opened and he was not alone any more.

She no longer wore her cloak but otherwise was little changed. She had on long close-fitting black leather boots. Her ebony thighs were bound by thonging – she wore no full garment there at all – and Will saw that though the individual thongs became broader, they were all she wore about her hips also. Indeed, he could see the jutting shaven mound of her sex painted electric blue under the black shiny strapping and his own sex stirred at the sight of her.

On her upper half was the clinging silky tee shirt he had seen before, cut so that it went over one shoulder only and one full ripe breast was completely exposed. The nipple was painted blue also, and very dark blue patterns in intricate whorls came from the nipple over the swelling of her dark flesh. She wore fine black leather gloves that came up to her elbows and she showed no intention of removing them.

'You know what I require?' she demanded.

Will lay at his ease amongst the cushions. 'I know what you require,' he mocked gently.

'The bathing attendants tell me you are a real man.'

'Thank them from me,' said Will politely.

'You say you are called Wolf.' She looked at him with a faint frown in her eyes. 'It seems to me I should have heard of you before.'

'I have been in another city for some years. That is why I did not know your rules. I was helping the little Town-sister else I might have been more careful.'

'She did not enjoy your help, it seemed to us.'

113

'Town-sisters are stupid,' said Will coldly. 'Yet it was better she should go back to where she belongs. Trouble will come if she is harmed. It will be slow but it will be sure.'

'How do you know so much about her?'

'That is my business.'

The woman knelt slowly with a creak of leather before him. 'Your business is my business now.'

'No.' Will was positive.

'It will not go well with you to cross me, Wolf.'

'I think it will not go well with me anyway,' he said and smiled.

She crowed slightly and clapped her hands gently together. 'I like you, Wolf. You should have been a woman, the way you laugh when I threaten death.'

Will leaned into her, then, and slid his hands around her neck. Her eyes were painted in an exaggerated Egyptian style. He looked into them and tightened his hands. 'How will you meet death, sister?' he asked.

She laughed delightedly and ran her hands down his body, across his ribs, feeling his wiry growth of hair. She pushed in against his hands until she could touch her mouth to his.

At first it was just a brush, a question, then as she felt his lips part she opened her mouth and pressed it against his.

Will found her good to kiss, strong, fierce, knowing, and his body leapt in response. The sense of danger woke his sex-need, made him tingle. He felt her power, her confidence in herself, the touch of cruelty in her nature. She was himself made female. It was narcissistic, his desire for her. Excitement rippled through him. Here would be no holding back, no pretence, no forced softening of his lust and deference to one weaker in nature than himself. His breath was ragged as she wove her body in against his, caressing his naked flesh, running her hands up and down his back and clawing him gently there.

He curved himself over her, pressing her down, domi-

114

nating her with his strength. His mouth was cruel and demanding, his fingers digging into her shoulders and forcing her in hard against him. He felt her naked breast crush between them. He drew back suddenly and caught it and sucked the dark painted nipple. It moved in his mouth and he sucked hard, drawing the decorated flesh of the breast into his mouth and biting at her. Her breast was tattooed, he discovered.

She gasped. His hand slid down and he felt within the interstices of her curious lower garment. His fingers slid within the lattice and he found her bare mound with its soft wrinkled folds of sexual skin below. His fingers went in, urgently, and he touched her clitoris and felt it fire her as she jolted in his grasp. He slid his fingers on further and felt them go into her. He made them thrust hard and deep. The hot wet velvet embrace of his questing fingers seemed to complement his mouth eager at her breast and nipple. He sucked and probed and felt her throb under his assault.

He drew back, his breath harshly rasping, and looked into her face. 'Take this damned thing off,' he said.

'No.' Her eyes were dilated with passion and with open lust but the negative was firm. 'We take a vow. We never remove the *caffada* when once we have put it on.' She touched the thonged garment woven about her lower quarters. 'It is dishonourable to our sect to do so.'

He did not know the word she used but the meaning was plain. He pushed her roughly back so that he could see how he would cope with taking her whilst she still wore the thing. He had no compunction at enjoying the body of the woman who might order his death if he refused to play this way again. There was a sense in which it pleased him. It was fitting that this supreme act should go with life's last laugh on mankind.

He saw then that as she lay back sprawled on the cushions, her legs apart, so the gaps between the straps became wider and her dark lusciously gleaming divide was revealed to him. He used his fingers to open her, to look within her, and she responded without coyness or artifice but with the blatant enjoyment that he so enjoyed from a woman. She arched her back and purred as he fingered her crudely. He saw then she was painted down below also, or perhaps the skin was dyed. It was berry-purple, the colour of crushed plums, until he had forced her open so wide that he could see deep within her body. There she was a natural ripe rich dark pink.

Gently he worked her clitoris free. It was unstained, a deep gleaming pink, and Will laughed and bowed his great head with its wild black mane of hair and sucked her on her clitoris till she writhed under his hands.

At last he came forward between her legs, his cock erect and trembling with the need for satiation. She drew her legs up and back and he began to push at her. He was beyond caring about life and death. He was beyond caring about a little prim girly who gave him an itch, who galled him when he saw her. He was beyond his anger at Janine's stupidity in thinking he could have received the answers to the questions he had asked searching for her if he had brought the police with him into the city. He was beyond everything but the thick hot part of a woman where he could sink his need and find release. There was a flame between her legs and though the flame was cupped by his humiliation or even his death, yet he must bend to it, bend and burn and damn the consequences.

His cock pushed and was inside. She closed around him with voluptuous tightness, a firm squeezing that put an equal pressure on every part of his manhood as he drove steadily into her. She would not often get a man in her web, he guessed, and she was tight. His cock opened her body before it and then allowed it to close darkly and hotly and cling. Will shook slightly, drew back, and plunged deep into her again.

He rode her like it was his last ride. He rode every woman he had ever had as he drove into her dark wet hole. He held nothing back. He drove ferociously again and again because he was going to satisfy his own need and be damned with them all. They could do what they liked afterwards. Everything in his life had been a disappointment save for this, and he would have this gasping truth now, this thing of bodies meeting, and he would make no concessions to this partner.

Only one woman had ever let him be like this, fulfil his nature so completely and give back as good and better as he gave her, and she preferred her damned husband. Will laughed at the madness of it all and screwed the leader of the Amazenes as a valediction upon screwing and upon his life. He felt her lift and take him, he felt her come back at him, and suddenly the world blazed and he was in the throes of a powerful orgasm.

He came to, bent over her, his cock at peace within her still and her vagina making little after-ripples from her own orgasm. His belly was warm and clear. He felt a kind of peaceful exhaustion that the struggle was over, not the struggle with her but the struggle to make a life worth living.

To his surprise she pulled him down to lie beside her, sinking her hands into his hair and nuzzling up into his neck. She could feel him retreating into himself as he accepted their inequality, her total power over him and his future where only his thoughts would be free.

By her face his shoulder glowed. The liquid crystals inserted under his skin to make intricate patterns changed colour and shone through his skin as they were affected by heat. He had had them implanted to mask his pirate tattoos when he became respectable. Now she kissed them and rubbed her face against him. She came round right on top of him, feeling the power latent in the body under her.

'It is not often I feel regret for the harshness of our ways,' she said. 'They have their purpose and it is a good one.'

'Don't give me that pap, sister,' he said lazily, insultingly, far away from her though their bodies pressed hot and close.

She waited a moment. Then she said: 'I must put the mark on you now.'

117

'What mark?' He sounded bored.

'Normally we permit a painkiller,' she said.

His dark eyes opened and he looked at her without interest. She saw the little hard gold chips in the hazel irises gleam like splinters. This close she could see that there was something very faintly odd about one of his eyes, as though it had taken damage at some time or another.

'We give the mark this way,' she said and drew back her lips into a snarl that bared her teeth.

As he watched, he saw her upper canines extend and double in length, the thin extension coming from within the normal tooth. She could not close her mouth properly now and the long teeth hung over her lip and pressed against her skin.

'They contain the mark,' she said with some difficulty. 'I must inject it under your skin now to show that you belong to us and no one else may touch you.'

'The hell you will.'

'I will, Wolf-man. It is our way.'

'Over my dead body.'

'Before you are dead, my fine friend, which I hope will be a long time. Your body is a fruiting tree that I would wish often to feed at. And I do not think you will be unwilling, judging by tonight's performance. You have value for a woman, Wolf. You can lead a useful life with us and in return we will make it agreeable and comfortable for you. Now, do you wish the painkiller? We do not do this to hurt you. Not this.'

He looked at her for a long moment and then let his head drop back. He closed his eyes again. 'Do what you wish,' he said in an empty voice. 'Yet I think the results will displease you.'

She sat up astride him, her leather bondclothes rubbing his naked skin. He felt the leather of her boots cool against his sides. She took up his hand and held it for a moment.

When eventually she bit him he jumped with the pain of it. She sank her fangs into the fleshy mound of softer

118

skin at the base of his thumb. She sank them in deeply and held them there as his body tensed steel-hard below hers whilst he absorbed and contained the pain of it. Then gradually, slowly, she withdrew her awful teeth and they retracted.

Will opened his eyes though he knew they would show that he was dazed with the pain. She was looking down at him with a peculiar expression on her face, no little part of which was admiration. She still held his tortured hand and now she lifted it towards him so that he might see what she had done.

Sapphire blue, the whorls of colour flooded slowly through his thumb pad. They were overlaid by the developing purple of bruising and the blood sat where her fangs had punctured him like crimson beads. Will looked at it bitterly and then lifted his eyes to hers.

'If you cannot find it in yourself to enjoy your stay with us,' she said in a silken voice, 'and let us take pleasure in your enjoyment of our company, then you will be disposed of as a useless dog. As men indeed are. But I tell you this, Wolf, I would be very happy to have you for my pleasure. Truly, you are more than I have met with in many a long year. Almost you might have the spirit of a woman though you are dressed in a man's body.'

'And when the pleasuring is done?'

She shrugged. 'Everything has its ending. The law is universal.'

Abruptly she stood up and went over to the wall and pressed a button. After a moment the door opened and a group of guards came in. Will didn't bother to attempt to cover his nakedness. There seemed to be little point. He stayed where he was among the cushions. His hand throbbed and he wondered how clean her damned teeth were.

The guards knelt beside him impassively and fitted a collar to his neck, a cold metal collar, though they were careful to pull his hair free of it at the back. Then they told him to stand up and when he eyed them lazily they

119

jerked on his neck. The collar was attached to a chain which they held. The inside of the collar was rough and spiked, so that when they jerked on it it bit into his skin. It was clear that if he dragged against it for any length of time, it would abrade his skin until he bled.

He stood up and was rewarded by the return of his trousers which he slid into. The Amazene he had possessed stood back, leaning against the wall with her arms crossed, smiling faintly.

'Would it be so very bad, staying with us to serve us?' she asked.

'How would you find it, supposing our positions were reversed?' countered Will.

She threw back her head and laughed. 'That would transgress the very laws of nature,' she said. 'It is known that men need to couple more often than women and have less self-control. It follows therefore that if we keep you in comfort and satisfy your needs, you should be happy. There are many of us to please, Wolf-from-another-city, and I guarantee you would not be idle. Come now, admit the idea pleases you.'

'You might have some poor broken-spirited men somewhere but do not think you will get me to join them,' said Will and he snarled as he said it.

'You will do as we wish. We are your owners now and as we are noble, so you should be proud to serve such as us.' The Amazene's voice had the lash of the whip in it.

'If you break my spirit, sister, the only use you will find for my body is six feet under.'

'You are a fool. Yet I will have my way with you. Take him away.'

Thus Will was led from the room.

Janine blessed her all-over black suit and cursed her long fair hair. She had tucked it into her collar to hide it as best she could, and she had blackened her face with mud from the ground. Now she stood with beating heart pressed tight against the building in which, somewhere, she believed they held Will Maffick. Her common sense told her she should leave him, fade away through the night and ask of those she passed her way to Half-Way. But she could not. She despised him. He frightened her. But she could not go and leave him here, captive, when he had come to help her get free.

She was sure she despised him. She had disliked him on sight when she had met him in Fee's company. He had appalled her when he had appeared just now and been so savage amongst the pathetic silly boys who had taken her prisoner. But he had been right about the city being dangerous, more dangerous than she had realised. She was uneasy, feeling stupid, even blind in this strange new environment.

She had steered clear of the courtyard entrance with its constant inflow and outflow of guards and sentries, edging her way round to the back. Surprisingly, there were few of the women here. They guarded a wider perimeter, it seemed, not taking proper account of someone well within their territory already.

Janine was patient and finally found what she was looking for, a way to climb up the outside of the building.

The longer she was away from the ghastly youths who had held her captive, the more strength of mind flowed back into her. Her helplessness was gone, for the time being at any rate. Gone with it was the numbing of her intelligence. At last she was beginning to adjust, to believe in the reality of the city, to come to terms with it and turn what she could of it to her own advantage.

She began to climb up into the night, using broken sills, balconies, projecting masonry – anything that came to hand. When she was some three storeys up and sweating with fear at her height above the ground, she allowed herself to slip in at a broken window and enter the building.

Very quietly and carefully she went through the dark room and out into the corridor. On velvet feet, wary for loose rubble and always conscious of her nagging ankle, she began to explore where she had penetrated.

It took her three hours to find Will and by the time she had done so daylight was coming up and she crept away to hide. She had found one or two other thought-provoking things also.

He was chained in a small room that had two women guards outside it. They were feeding him. More than that Janine did not know. She had seen food being taken in, she had heard the rattle of his chains. She had not seen him.

Janine slept for part of the day and used part of it to steal food and water. She delicately explored the upper levels of the building and was astonished and delighted to find the armoury, quite unattended. Plainly the Amazenes had no fear of intruders in this, their headquarters.

Janine helped herself to a couple of small machetes. There were guns there but no ammunition that she could find so she left them. She knew she would have to break Will's chains and so she took also a heavy-duty set of cutters though they were awkward to carry. It was while searching in a far corner with one eye kept on the entrance in case she was disturbed, that she came upon the real treasure.

She found Amazene uniforms.

When darkness fell she was ready. Even her hair was covered by a skull-helmet with patterns already painted on it. It left her face bare but she had made an attempt at the Amazene make-up and felt she would pass muster at a distance. The laser cutters were strapped up under her little cloak. The machetes hung with one on show at her waist. She had a knife tucked in at her waistband also. Her naked breast was cold, unused to the air, but its discomfort was a small thing and she set herself to ignore it. She was beyond embarrassment. Yet she kept the lower half of her original bodysuit upon her, finding no leather thonging to tie about herself and unclear as to the details of the lower garment that the Amazenes wore.

She saw them take Will from his cell and lead him by

122

the neck. She followed as best she dared but hung well back when he was taken into a room. The guards came out with his trousers and the neck-collar. Janine's lips tightened still further when she saw the pack leader enter the room. There was some coarse jesting outside and then everyone settled down.

It was an hour before the pack leader called the guards in. Ten minutes later Will was led out and Janine faded quietly back as he was led to his cell. She nerved herself, giving herself strength from her anger at Will's activities, and she attacked as they pushed him into the room. She would not be able to break the lock and must get to him before the door was shut. She ran forward, her boots noisy on the bare floor, and the guards turned, surprised but unalarmed to see what they took to be one of their number running towards them. She drew the machete when she was almost at them. They fanned back still more in surprise than alarm, their own hands going hesitantly for their belts. Janine thrust a machete at Will. The guards had dropped his chain when Janine had drawn her weapon and now he came out beside her.

He bared his teeth. 'In,' he hissed at the two women. They hesitated, still unable to take in the betrayal by what they took to be one of their own, and Will slashed quickly and expertly forward. Janine gasped and one of the women back-pedalled rapidly into the cell. The thonging that bound her stomach and hips and thighs began to unwind and she cried out and grasped it. The other came forward at Will but Janine gritted her teeth and lifted her weapon. Will went for the *caffada* of the second woman and she gave up at the threat to her religion though the threat to her life had left her unmoved. She joined her companion.

Will followed them into the cell. 'Don't kill them,' pleaded Janine. But Will took their weapons and gave them to Janine. Then he grasped the leather *caffada* that was cut and pulled it. The woman spun round and fell and lay there, moaning at the heresy. Janine saw the

123

deep welts in her flesh made by the holy garment, her sex now bound in welted flesh rather than black leather, but Will ignored her and tied both women firmly by the hands and the ankles, then binding their mouths. He came out of the cell and Janine shut the door, hearing it click as the lock engaged.

'Which way?' he snapped at Janine. She gestured and they set off along the corridor.

Two levels up she told him she had the laser cutters. He knelt before her, she had time to find this strange, and she put them to the collar where it locked. She directed the cutters away from his neck but it took her two goes to get him free and she could smell burnt skin by the end of it.

Briefly Will put his arms round Janine, still kneeling. 'You done well, baby,' he said, his voice muffled in her stomach. He drew his head back. His eyes danced. 'I guess we're quits now.'

It was perhaps the first time in their short acquaintance he had spoken to her as an equal, without patronising her or letting contempt edge his voice. Janine had her hands in his hair and was astonished at the warm animal silk of it, clean and sweet-smelling. She crouched down in the dark and touched her cheek to his. 'Thank God you are safe,' she murmured. 'I thought they would kill you.'

'They would have,' he said calmly. 'They had some uses for me first but I was already threatening not to go on playing.'

'That's disgusting!' Janine's voice was low and choked with emotion. 'I don't know how you could. I saw a place that looked like a seraglio. I couldn't believe it. Did they drug you?'

'It was very nice, actually. I don't need drugs to get it up, sweetheart. Ever. It was just that I was refusing to become a permanent fixture.' She could hear him laughing at her. She stood up abruptly.

'We've still got to get out of here,' she said.

'I guess we'd better go now before they find what we've done,' he said.

They went via the armoury and took rope. This meant they dropped down the side of the building very quickly. In less than ten minutes from when Janine had confronted the guards, they were both outside and on the ground.

They began to run in a half crouch that kept them as low to the ground as they could get, taking advantage of whatever cover there was available. Janine found that the leather boots gave her ankle support and though it twinged, she did not limp and could make good time. At last she understood the need for urgency, for speed. They had to get out of this awful place as fast as they could and get home.

Several times they saw groups of Amazenes at a distance but always before they were too close Janine and Will were able to duck and weave and find somewhere to hide themselves till the danger was past. More time passed and they covered much ground and saw no Amazenes. Then they saw some strolling couples at a distance and at last Will relaxed, much to Janine's relief. She was exhausted.

Will began to walk slowly with his arm around Janine as if they, too, were a couple. Their clothing was bizzarre enough even by city standards to warrant them keeping to the shadows. Janine felt the return of all her old dislike reinforced by his open admission of enjoyment of sex with his captors, but she remained glad of the strength of his arm about her. There were some lights but she was dazed with fatigue now. She heard noises, strange music, and then it fell quiet again and got very dark.

She lifted dull eyes and saw a ribbon cut the sky. Meteors ran along it and it was some moments before she realised she was seeing one of the starways, the highways up in the sky that were the sole preserve of the Connet cars. She had a longing to be in one, safe, lapped about with luxury, far above the filth and fears of the city.

The man with her was guiding her but her feet were stumbling.

'How much further?' she pleaded. 'When will we be home?'

'Home? I don't know.'

She shook herself awake. 'What do you mean, you don't know?'

'What I say. We'll rest up and I'll get us something to eat. Tomorrow I'll find out where we are and see what direction we ought to head in.'

She stopped. 'You mean we've come all this way and it might be the wrong way?'

'Sure. In fact, I'm certain it is.'

'Are you doing this deliberately?' she demanded hysterically. 'Take me home, I say!'

Will went cold on her. 'I came to get you away from those little boys,' he snarled. 'I reckoned I could do a faster better job than the HeliPolice, with less risk to you, and I was damn well right. You and your foolishness nearly got us killed back there when you were whining at me so's I didn't see we had walked into a trap. OK, you got me out and I admit you've surprised me there. Now we have to get out of the city and if you don't understand that that is no easy thing yet, then you never will. Damn it, I don't know my way around any more. Things have changed so much. I'm aiming to avoid the sort of nasty mistake we have already made. So shuddup, sister, and let me do the thinking.'

'You've been here before,' said Janine in a curious voice.

'Fee found me here,' said Will and laughed.

'Perhaps you want to stay,' said Janine thickly. 'It seems you belong.'

'Perhaps I do,' said Will rudely. 'But I promised Fee I'd bring you out and bring you out I will.'

She had nothing to say and she could not understand why what he had said hurt her so much. He forced her into a black building and found an empty room in it set away from the main corridors, where they would have to be unlucky for anyone to come across them accidentally. Will left Janine there and spent some time roaming

126

the dark corridors and rooms till he was sure that it was unoccupied, like an early man must have searched caves to ensure he wasn't accidentally sharing his home with a bear.

Then Will went out, telling Janine he would be back with food in a while. He didn't tell her he intended to mug a local using his machete and get money. The city used cash of course though it was long gone from the respectable Town and Zoo, and Will needed to buy them both much-needed food. Especially Janine. He hoped that much of her ill temper would go once she had eaten and slept. He feared they had a long walk ahead of them before they were out of this place, maybe more than they could make in one night. They could not travel by day, that was certain.

He hoped Fee would not call the police. He hoped she would trust him. He didn't intend to tell her what a fool he had been, how near he had come to blowing everything with his carelessness.

Janine was asleep when he got back to her. He shook her gently and as she woke, he felt her hysterical start of fear as she began to remember where she was, and that she was not safe. He sat down beside her, hunkered down in the dark, and told her that she had to be on the move again.

'No,' she groaned. It seemed to her that he did this deliberately, to torment her and that he was a naturally cruel man.

'I've found us somewhere to stay,' he said quietly. 'You'll get a bed and you will be able to get some real rest before we make it back to the Town. I don't think that that will be too easy. We made some waves tonight, baby. They'll be out on the prowl, looking for revenge. They won't wave you goodbye a second time, after what you did for me.'

Janine sat stiffly beside him, trying to make her fogged exhausted mind take in what he said. After a moment or two, he hauled her by main force to her feet and pushed her into shambling movement. Together they

127

left the building and went back out into what was left of the night.

Fee was worried and the worry made her restless. Her restlessness stopped her working and stopping working left her bored. With too much time on her hands, she worried.

Will and Janine were down in the city, possibly at great risk. She couldn't know. She had it in her to regret making the beautiful disc and certainly if it fell into her hands again she would destroy it, but she could not regret the experience she had had with it. She used her intelligence in so many ways. She was brilliant in her chosen field, that of creating customised computer software. But in the other great area of interest in her life, she operated almost entirely on instinct.

Fee adored men. They gave her power. Sex with men drove some internal dynamo that enabled her to live fully and richly. Without sex she could barely function. She lived and breathed it and knew that Rollo, once the most possessive of men in the physical sense, now accepted her infidelities and was possessive of her mind, of his own mastery of her, of his primacy in her emotions. He let her use her body as she willed.

Fee did not think she could live without Rollo who was her life's blood. Other men came and went but always Rollo was there, knowing her as no other man knew her save perhaps Will Kid. No, he called himself Will Maffick now. Fee grinned at the thought. He was a wild man. She was surprised he had accepted society's confining bonds for so long. She knew that she was withdrawing herself from him, preparing herself for his departure from her life. She could sense a change in him. She had that kind of intuition where men were concerned.

As Fee grew older, her mind grew stronger and her intuitions grew sharper. Yet she was mellowing emotionally and she knew it. She was soft where once she would have been hard. She had sympathy where once she would have felt only contempt. Now, at this time, she was more in control of herself than ever she had been, the slight easing of her sex drive enabling her to channel it more cleverly, more knowingly.

She wanted the boy, Caz, the boy with the light-brown eyes. She wanted his honey-coloured slimness pressed ardently to her voluptuous body. She didn't care about his naivety, his touching ignorance, his excessive tenderness with her. They charmed her, though once she would have considered all three major faults in a male lover, weaknesses to despise. She had knowledge enough for two but she was too wise for her own good. Caz's freshness and lack of guile, his lack of sexual trickery touched her flinty heart somewhere and brought a new fragrance into the act of love for her. He was spontaneous, adoring, young. For the first time Fee considered the effect she might have on a lover and whether it was entirely to his benefit.

Always she had considered the act of sex fair exchange. But now the thought nagged that with Caz perhaps that was not so. She was not a vain woman but she was realistic and she knew her looks had an almost mystic effect on men. Even Rollo after all these years caught his breath at her sometimes. The thin scar over one white cheek seemed to add to rather than detract from her looks. She had a sharp hard face, very white when black faces were more fashionable, with long narrow ice-green eyes set on a distinct slant above prominent cheekbones. Her mouth was wide and delicately modelled, the line of her lip beautiful. She adored to suck men and she thought perhaps that years of eagerly pursuing this deviant hobby had somehow invested her mouth with a sensual lift that men intuitively recognised. Maybe, maybe not. Fee was not given to inward communings and self-analysis where men were concerned. The thing was, she could have whom she wanted and she wanted quite often and the pleasure never palled. Perhaps they liked her long black tumble of starling-coloured hair, iridescent with green and blue lights. How could she know?'

Caz. He was so young, perhaps only half her age. She would swamp him, she thought desolately. She would make other women pale and uninteresting for him and he would not realise that she did it until it was too late and he was abandoned. She was not only beautiful, she was somebody, she was a society leader, a celeb, famous in her way, and rich beyond any possible dreams of avarice that Caz might have. Her transport was worth a million credits by itself, and that was only something to get her from A to B. For Fee had a Connet, a monster-machine, a powertube that flew over the ground at a speed once reached only by aeroplanes.

He would be dazzled and Fee didn't want to dazzle. She wanted to go to bed with him. Moreover, she did not want to be boasted of, and the young could be so crass in the matter of sexual achievement.

Fee wanted Caz. When she had finally decided that she could not have him, she sent a message to the Institute asking him to vidi her.

When he did, she knew only heartfelt gratitude.

'Could we meet again?' she asked baldly when he got through. Her heart was thumping like a teenager's.

'Mrs Cambridge,' he said and his voice was strangled. His lower lip trembled slightly and she saw with amazement how moved he was. He looked pale and a little whipped, she thought. Perhaps he worked too hard.

Artifice left her. 'I enjoyed meeting you so much last time,' she said earnestly. She could hardly be more explicit. She was laying it on the line.

He was in a public booth, standing up. He wiped his brow with his sleeve and she saw his hand was clenched into a fist. 'I want to go to bed with you again,' he said.

She was slightly shocked. She had thought that she was being plain. She knew perfectly well he didn't mean to be crude. He was telling her he wanted her so much that the only terms on which he could bear to be in her company were sexual terms. It was a compliment. It was a direct indication that he felt as strongly about her as she did about him. It was honesty.

'Good,' she said with a calmness she didn't feel. 'Then that's what we'll do.'

She fixed to send a taxi for the following day. Rollo was attending the annual meeting of the water cartel to set the price for the coming year. The OWAC meeting, the Organisation of Water Carriers, was always held in the flesh instead of being a computerised conference because it was the only way to keep the proceedings secret. Rollo headed a company that was one of the world's largest carriers of fresh water. Their price decision would affect financial markets and they reduced jitteriness by keeping speculation as much under control as possible. Rollo might hate to leave her, but he could hardly have a more important commitment on his annual calendar. He would be gone at least a couple of days, longer if they could not reach an agreement.

She had meant to be civilised when Caz came, to look after the boy and set him at his ease. In the event, when she released her door lock and let him into her apartment, she went straight into his arms as if drawn by a magnet. His mouth was on hers, stronger than she remembered it, more possessive, but still fresh and lively and of a sweet savour. He kissed her mouth, her throat, her shoulder, her hair and then her mouth again, with an intensity that she adored.

'I want to make love to you,' he mumbled into her skin, tasting it, kissing it, holding her soft curves hard against his thin urgent frame.

She began to pull his clothes apart, desperate to feel his skin against hers. She dropped to her knees because they felt strangely weak, kissing down his chest, wrenching greedily at his trousers, intent on kissing every part of his body that she could reach. He fell back against the door, only just inside her home but unable to get any further.

She hadn't meant to do this but Fee was beyond herself. She had got his clothes open at last and she had freed his wand, his delicate member, his sweet slender strong beautiful shaft coming out from its little cloud of

131

hair. She groaned and put her lips to it. Caz shut his eyes and clenched his fists, pressing his shoulders hard into the door and feeling his thighs tremble. Fee's mouth closed about his prick. As she drew back and the hot velvet of her mouth left him, a groan leaked out of him. She came in again, sucking him, her chin grazing his balls, her hair tickling his naked belly, her hands coming up now to help. He felt a hand cup his balls, hold them and roll them and press delicate knowledgeable fingers deep into the baggy sac of flesh that held them so that they leapt and firmed and filled with juice.

His glans burned and swelled in its cavern. At the touch of her teeth it jumped and he felt a little spunk ooze from it. Now he could feel her tongue, wrapping round and round in quick snaky movements as though his cock were within a coiled spring that was being stretched and tightened, squeezing him, milking him.

Beads of perspiration ran down from his brow. His erection palpitated in her mouth. As she sucked him light flickered on the edge of his vision. He felt his belly swell as if it would burst. His legs trembled uncontrollably. His cock was a huge dark bloom in her mouth. Her fingers held his balls as if they were two bombs.

He cried out and began to come. It was ecstatic. Hot fluid jetted the length of his shaft. His backside slapped against the door as he vibrated into the mouth that held him. Fee was crazy, swallowing him down, still sucking, and then he was done.

He held still for a moment trying to get his body back under control. He looked down at the woman kneeling with her face at his loins. Her head was thrown back so that her hair fell away below her and her eyes were shut as though she was having a religious experience. Caz let his penis slip from between her slack lips and he crouched down with her, holding her. She brought her head up slowly and opened her dazzled eyes, looking at him.

'I didn't mean to do that,' she confessed, her voice cracking slightly. He saw then that moisture glittered at the side of her face and he kissed the corners of her wicked slanting eyes and tenderly he kissed her brow and gently he kissed her bruised and salty mouth. He thought he kissed a lovely lady. Fee knew he kissed a cobra, a black widow spider, only he couldn't see it. He didn't know it.

'Come with me to the bedroom,' she said in her soft low husky voice. He was pliant like a sapling and he came with her. Before she reached the doorway he came up behind her and pressed against her, his hands busy with her clothes. He stood away from her and what she wore fell about her ankles. He laughed and stood back. He looked at the tall pale woman, turning this way and that to see her from other angles, touching her narrow waist, touching where her hip swelled smooth, touching her heavy swinging pendulous breasts with their nipples smoke-dark and pouting at him in naked invitation.

Fee stood patiently, feeling her own body new and intensely sexual under his scrutiny. He came close up behind her again and kissed her shoulder. He laid his head sideways on her shoulder and kissed her neck. Then he looked down the front of her, seeing her in strange perspective, seeing her volcanic pointed breasts, seeing below them the rounded softness of her pale belly, seeing the black fuzz of hair swim dimly at its base and unable to see more for the sweetness of her body and the coarse strength of his lust for her.

He had thought of her poetically. He had wished for the gift of words to frame his feelings on paper during the time that had passed between their last meeting and this, when he had assumed he would never see her again. But now, with her, he didn't give a damn if the talent of Shakespeare coursed in his veins. Quite crudely, and with every passing moment more strongly, he wanted to shaft her. She had just knelt and sucked him to glory. He wanted that again. He wanted his cock within her, pounding her. He wanted her to feel disabled by the strength of his lust for her as he had just been by her lust for him. He wanted to dominate her. He might be young compared to her, but he was a man and he would master her body or die in the attempt.

They went into her bedroom and he cried out in fear. 'What is it?'

He swallowed. 'You have a light-bed.'

Fee was puzzled. So? 'What is it?' she said again, forcing patience into her voice. The tiger in her was growing and it was becoming harder to contain herself, to keep herself in check with this baby-man, this sex-cub. She mustn't frighten him off.

He looked at her strangely, his face darkly glowing as if lit by internal fires. A slow smile crept over his face, curving his lips, and for a second it was Fee who felt the moth-touch of fear. Something otherworldly had just entered the room.

'Lie on the bed and switch it on,' said Caz. His voice was low and assured, the warm lick of confidence in it like the breath of hell. She went to obey, allowing her weight to set the bed in motion so that its surface swayed beneath her like an oily ocean swell, lifting her body in a long slow ripple, elevating each part of it as if she was offering herself in stages to his hot eyes.

He stripped the clothes she had torn open, casting them aside with his innocence. She saw in his slimness a whippy strength and a resilience now, no weakness. He was pared down, refined, the essence of man in his hard slim body, but it was all there, all that was necessary.

The bed glowed round her body making of it a dark negative in the living light-web, the white brilliant lustre cradling her darkness. She was an invitation to him to enter the darkness with her and taste its thick delights. He sat on the edge of the bed and laid a hand on her belly. Light shone up into his face stealing its texture till all there was was a satin gleam that shone like polished bone. His eyes were yellow ochre and deep within them a pinprick of light flamed. Fee could almost see the little horns curving up from amidst his disordered curls. Her

134

eyes fell and she saw how the dark shadow of his leg was blurred by the thick fuzz of goat hair on his long fine flanks. No doubt he had hooves where he should have had feet.

She felt his hand on her belly like a branding iron and she let her legs come apart, inviting his hand to go down and in her. He twisted it so that his fingers pointed downwards and then he bent his body over her in a graceful curve. As he lowered his head he let his hand slide where she invited. His lips touched her breast as his fingers touched her clitoris.

He bit her breast-skin gently, a series of little nips that made her nipples inflame and lengthen though he did not touch them. As he bit her skin, his fingers pinched her clitoris so that fiery tingles burned through her upper stomach. She wanted to beg him to penetrate her.

He released her. 'Turn over,' he said.

She obeyed dumbly.

'On your knees,' he said.

She raised her bottom in the air.

She felt him come fully onto the bed. 'I am going to do things here,' he said, laying his finger on her. Her flesh jumped at the intimate invasive touch. 'Then I am going to do things here.' He touched another part of her, projecting lewdly back towards him as she knelt submissively. 'Then I am going to do them both together.'

'You can't,' she said, trembling, her bottom quivering and faintly flushing in her excitement. But she had forgotten the potency of youth, so long was it since she had played with the young.

His mouth over her anus was a shock but a welcome one. He licked her wet and knelt, holding her haunches, and then he guided his erect prick within her.

Fee buried her face in the light-bed and fought not to come. His shaft in her rear was a spiky violation that pierced the armour of patronage and reduced her to his equal, to his mate, to submit to him. She revelled in the submission and was secretly amazed at his perverted lust so early in their relationship. She pushed her bottom

135

up and back, biting his prick with her tightness and shuddering at the force of him in her illicit delicious place.

She felt him gather himself and explode into her. She shut her eyes and gritted her teeth as her backside clenched around his shaft. He juddered into her, emptying himself, and then he pulled out.

It was too soon and she felt the rupture as an emotional loss. She groaned and flexed the muscles of her buttocks, savouring the memory of his fatness in her whilst she enjoyed the illicit pleasure of what had just occurred. Briefly he left the bed and she heard water run in her bathroom. Then he was back and she was shocked when she felt his erect member enter her from the front.

He had definitely climaxed yet here he was, barely minutes after, penetrating her afresh. He pumped steadily into her and she felt him grow larger and press more firmly against the inner walls of her sex. Admiration for his prowess grew in her guts. She clenched her muscles feeling the tingle of her violated anus and squeezed his clever lively indomitable cock.

Now his hands stroked the cheeks of her bottom, cupping their points as they projected back at him. He fondled them harder, pulled them open, and Fee knew he must be able to see her most intimate anatomy. She felt the walls of her passage tremble and flutter. Then she cried out and jerked, making him break stroke. He had plunged his thumb into her arse and was moving it about in the warm wet stretched tunnel he had recently invaded. His cock was swollen to full size now within her and with his thumb inside her complementary passage, she was stuffed with sex. It was becoming alarmingly difficult to contain her approaching orgasm. She could feel her breasts burn. Her muscles were beginning to go out of control, pinching down on him, on his cock, on his thumb, and now, by God, he had his other hand down and round somehow and he was pinching her clitoris as he ploughed into her.

He must have a hand between his thighs, she thought

136

dazedly. The tiny pinches made her nipples ache. His hips swung in and out, his thumb stirred and pressed within, his finger stirred and pressed without. Fee glowed in every part of her, the length of her vulva and beyond, and within, glowing hot with fierce caresses. She shouted and began to come. Her pussy convulsed and almost expressed him in the power of its muscular contraction but he only laughed and pushed harder into her screaming flesh. He got his hands free and held her buttocks. Savagely he plunged into her, riding out her orgasm, matching his plunges to her contractions until he released himself again.

This time he held himself in her, allowing her orgasm to come to quietness whilst it hugged the stranger within it. His own cock began to shrink and his belly was warm with satisfaction. When he thought she was finally done, he pulled out of her and let her roll over. Luxuriously he stretched his full length on her dark soft body, revelling in her curves, feeling her soft points press gently into his firm youthfulness. After a few minutes she moved, causing him to fall to one side of her. Now he was all dark, framed in light, and she was all gleaming planes as the light radiated up into her face.

He saw her face was secret and closed. His own body felt unstrung and lay limp on the warm bright surface of the bed. She bent her head over him and began to kiss him.

She took her time and he shut his eyes and gave himself over to the feel of her lips pressing on his skin, accepting it as his due as though she made him an act of homage in gratitude for the wonder of his performance. She kissed him everywhere and he stopped her in nothing. After she had kissed all his chest and his thighs and his throat, she kissed his groin and his slack wet member, licking his hair there as though she were a cat cleaning him after a meal. He felt her velvet tongue wrap his cock round and she licked it with strong rough licks, pulling the tender silky skin. She licked his balls and between his thighs and then she gathered his cock into her mouth.

He felt her hair spill over him and he reached down a hand and idly gripped her. He pulled slightly but she kept his cock in her mouth so that by pulling her hair, he masturbated himself in her mouth. It was very nice. She let her head drop onto his belly and began to suck him in earnest. He gave her no help, not using his mind to encourage his cock to grow. He let her do everything and so his cock grew slowly but completely in the warm cave of her mouth.

Caz let his thoughts drift as the wonderful thing went on in his groin. He felt liberated, raised, free. His body was full of warmth, its focus his cock rhythmically sucked by the woman who wanted him so much that he could do anything to please himself with her and she would deny him nothing. It might have been his soul that she sucked, so that his soul grew and swelled in triumph. Still the lovely pulling, the wet grip, the slight abrasion of teeth went on and on. Her tongue wove round his tip till he was dizzy and he let the fine detail of the instrument at his cock go whilst the orchestration of what she did to him built into a swelling chorus of sound that dazzled his senses and threatened to overload them with the volume and intensity of the crescendo.

His balls began to ache. He felt his muscle bulge. His eyelids burned. His hips twitched and his lower body rolled slightly in the extremity of his pleasure. She sucked with the fierceness of demons and suddenly he was crying out and jerking into her face.

She took him and made his climax stupendous, as though never before had he so totally spent himself. When he was done and mindlessly slumped, she crooned over his cock and pressed her cheek to his belly. Then she brought herself up to lay beside him, drawing his head onto her breast and stroking him. He wrapped himself tightly around her and pushing his fingers into the wet hole between her legs he fell asleep.

Chapter Five

*H*e was a big, plump, self-important man and though he was rich and lived in the Zoo, he liked a little rough now and again. When the urge came over him he would leave the Zoo and go down through the Town, perhaps taking a taxi because there was only one sort of exercise that he was fond of, until he came to Half-Way, the shantytown beyond Townsend. Here he would go on foot through the crazy cabins of those who couldn't or wouldn't fit into mainstream society until he came to a feelie bar.

His name was Jace and he liked feelie bars. It wasn't that they were illegal in the Town. Little to do with sex between consenting adults was illegal, little or nothing. But it seemed there was no call for them in the prissier society there and so when Jace felt like going to a feelie bar, he had to come down here to Half-Way. He didn't mind, either. He liked the women down here better than the Zoo women or the Town women. They struck him as a little too wholesome, a little too equal. Jace was a man who liked to feel on top.

The feelie bar he chose had the added attraction of serving meat. Jace was not much of a man for vegetables, for synthetic proteins, for insect cuisine. Jace liked meat and he liked it hot and greasy and clinging to a bone. Altogether he was a hot greasy kind of a man and he didn't see one damn thing wrong with that. There were quite a lot of women who agreed with him, women who liked their men strong and rough and who thought flesh sat well on the bones of a rich man. Jace was generous. In Half-Way he was popular. He liked women to carry a bit of flesh too, thinking skinny women weren't meal enough for a man with his hot temperament. He had been born in the wrong age, really. Jace liked a lick of sin about his sex and there wasn't much sin left and Jace missed it like he would miss chilli if it was left out of Mexican food.

He came swaggering into the bar and commanded instant attention. The maître d' scuttled up to him wiping his hands on his white apron and asking him which waitress he would like to serve him. Jace ordered beer and a big blonde.

She came over to him and he saw she wasn't young. On the contrary, she looked knowing and wise in the ways of men, with little lines of usage radiating out from her eyes which crinkled as she smiled a deep slow suggestive smile at him, preparing to offer him the menu and getting out her notepad.

Her face showed she was a woman who knew a thing or two and was happy to share what she knew with a man. She wore plenty of make-up, like he liked. Jace hated the baby-bare sweet look of clean healthy skin. Much like the way he found a clothed body more sexually exciting than a bare one. Society was too damned explicit now for a man to enjoy himself properly.

'What's your name, sugar?' he said.

'Theo, short for Theodora,' she said in a low rich winy voice that caught him in the gut.

'I like what you're wearing, Theo,' he said. 'You can call me Jace.'

She had on a short ghost-grey rubber skirt stretched so tight over her front that he could see the tiny dip of her navel and better by far, the big rounded hump of her sex. She had on old-fashioned stockings and Jace knew

140

by the little bumps in her skirt that she wore suspenders. He found that very exciting. On her top was a many-buttoned satin garment that strained tight over her magnificent bosom and left its upper curves exposed. Their half-revealed, half-confined state excited Jace still further. He loved any suggestion of boundaries or limits, because then he could cross over seeking the thrill of the illicit that he so desired.

'So, Jace honey, what can I get you to eat?' She stood provocatively close to him. Jace could feel her warmth. He laid a hand on her leg and let it savour the feel of her stocking. He moved his palm slightly and it faintly rasped. Every nerve in him was quiveringly erect.

'I'm not sure,' he said. He slid his hand up her leg and felt the top of her stockings. He lingered there, feeling her nylons and her flesh side by side, running his finger over and within her stocking top, feeling its warmth and her leg's cooler flesh. It was an interface that pleased.

'I'll show you the menu,' she said and bent over him, holding the card, her breasts bulging from the top of her tight blouse.

He put his hand further up. Now her womanly heat came down to him. He felt her intimate hair and the confusion of flesh within it. She closed her thighs on his hand and briefly squeezed it, letting it go to show she didn't mean to stop him going on up.

'I want beef,' he said. He pushed his hand up. 'And I want it well done.' He could feel her wet places now with the side of his hand. He rotated it and began to wriggle his fingers up. She squirmed deliciously.

His fingers were now inside her. Her hair brushed his hand but his fingers were actually within her flesh and he could feel it close and hot. He pressed and pushed. It gave under his pressure but sprang back as he released it. He rammed three fingers in together and tried to hold them apart, to widen them within her and so hold her open. His thumb went between her labia and nuzzled her clitoris.

She gasped and slightly staggered.

'Bring the meat raw,' he murmured. 'I'll cook it up here.'

She giggled. 'You reckon I'm hot enough, Jace?'

'Hallelujah, I certainly do. Why, I could fry an egg there right now. Squeeze me some more, honey.'

She obliged. Then Jace began to work her as she stood talking over the food he wanted. All the time he grinned slyly up at her as he masturbated her, watching her get hotter and hotter.

'I'm going to come before your food at this rate,' she said in the end, gripping his shoulder for balance.

'Nuts. You're just pretending.'

'Not with you, honey. Not with you.'

Jace rooted in his jacket pocket with his free hand. She certainly felt genuinely horny, much wetter than when he had first invaded her.

'You're the greatest, sugar,' he murmured, unable to remember her name for the moment. He passed what he had taken from his jacket pocket up her skirt and hooked it with his busy hand. Then he began to feed it into her opening.

'What are you doing, Jace?' she said, sounding almost alarmed.

'Giving you a present, Theo. You are one good girl.'

'A present? I like that. Are you putting it . . . up there?'

'Surely.' Reluctantly he withdrew his hand and wiped it on his scented napkin. Theo stood for a moment, her attention inturned, sampling with her inner muscles what he had done to her.

'You've put something hard up me,' she said.

'There's something else hard I'd like to put up there.'

'You sweetheart. Can I take it out?'

'You walk real careful so's you don't drop it. Since I can't put my meat in you, you just damn well get that cook hopping and get some meat to put in me. Yeah?'

'Yeah,' she said softly in her wine-thick sweet low voice. 'Coming right up.'

It was a ruby.

* * *

Jace felt good on his way back up through Half-Way. His belly was satisfied with solid fare and his hand still tingled from its massage. His face was red and his heart thumped like the powerful organ it was in his solid strong body. It was a beautiful day of bright warm sunshine with a dazzling glint in the air that would mean rain before nightfall. The proximity of the Zoo with its massed square miles of lush jungle created a micro-climate that suited it to perfection, with warm and frequently wet semitropical weather. That they were well in the northern hemisphere always came as a surprise when the season changed and autumn blustered about them. But even then it was rarely cold. The trees blanketed the planet's surface and held in the warmth.

He decided to walk through the Town. Away to his left up on its hill the Institute sparkled quartz-white. The Town was pretty, the utilitarian cubes of building thinly scattered and half-hidden amongst parks and groves and water-gardens. Jace came to the retail areas with the gaudy shops.

There were people about now and several of them, catching his eye, thought he was a benign grandfatherly sort of man, a kind man. Jace was wondering when he would next visit a brothel, the thought making him smile with anticipated pleasure. He was unmarried and satisfied his itch this way. He preferred the brothel women whom he paid to girlfriends. A girlfriend was an equal and too much like hard work. Jace was a man who would have been at home with a harem.

His foot caught. He looked down, irritated. Clean streets were something they all took for granted. He saw a VR disc lying on its side and he bent to pick it up.

It was dirty, its wrapper faded and blurred as one would expect from something that had evidently been out in the rain. He couldn't read any writing on it. It was probably spoiled by damp, he thought, unless its internal seals were still intact. It depended on how much rough treatment it had received since it had become garbage.

He was about to throw it indifferently into a bin when he noticed the little green triangle in one corner. So it was a sex disc. That made it more interesting.

It was warm in his hand and friendly. Without thinking very much about it he slid it into his pocket. It was just right, slim, neat, not spoiling the line of his clothes. Jace felt unaccountably jaunty. Damn, life was good! And because he was by nature a gambler, he interpreted his feelings as meaning his luck was in and he should take advantage of the fact.

He could see the jungle like a smear all along the horizon now, rippling upwards towards the hazing blue sky in a series of treeclad tiers, each layer a shade smokier in tone than the previous one. He would need a taxi soon to take him across the no man's land between the Town and the Zoo. It would be good to be home. He would take a bath, lay a few bets and maybe access the disc. Yes, that's what he would do. He would access the disc.

Jace was a deeply superstitious man, though he would never have admitted it. He would have described himself as subtle and perceptive if anyone cared to ask. Jace felt he saw through the thin outer fabric of things into their depths. Now his mind ran idly, pleasantly, as he wondered what to lay a bet on. There were no big horse races at that particular moment. He thought through the various animals whose antics provoked gambling and rejected them all, one by one, and then he noticed that a puffy white cloud had rolled down over the folded hills and was finely drenching the jungle.

He thought about the water gardens where he had found the disc. He had already forgotten he had found it on the streets. It was the water garden he remembered. He thought about his plan to bathe when he got home. He thought about the rain. Was life nudging him, trying to tell him something? The secret of the successful gambler was how finely he could tune his ear to these virtually subliminal promptings from fate. Any sequence of ideas, however mundane taken individually, when added together into a pack of three (garden – bath – rain) made a significance. Water was especially potent as a symbol at this particular moment because any day now the new water price was to be announced. Jace faintly knew Rollo Cambridge, the Zoo was a small society, and he knew the world's water barons were in conclave right now.

Jace owned a lot of water stock. All at once the gamble came to him and he grinned and busted out in a sweat at the audacity of his thought. He would mortgage his Connet and buy. He would buy massively and when the new price was announced and the stock began to rise, he would sell and pocket the difference, keeping his Connet.

It was a simple gamble but one that required substantial resources to make enough profit. The profit was assured. The price had to rise, prices always did, and it was known from the previous quarter's published figures that TransFlow, Cambridge's water company, was skating on thin ice. Their stock had dropped slightly as one or two nervous investors had moved out of the market.

The company was tackling a lot of major problems though none of them was out of the way for a project of this nature and Jace had no worries about the long-term viability of the enterprise. But just now they would want to reassure investors by upping the selling price of water per carried litre. Rollo Cambridge was a persuasive sort of a bastard and Jace was sure that what was good for TransFlow, his company, would be reflected in the deal struck by the cartel.

The thought that it might be a big price hike made Jace rub his plump palms together. Sure, he was gambling on Rollo Cambridge getting his own way, but Rollo Cambridge was a man who had the authentic stink of success. Jace remembered Rollo's wife. His temperature soared. Jeez, a hot baby, with those witchy eyes and big plump bosom where a man could grab when he needed. She could be snooty at times and look cold down that long thin nose of hers, but Jace had a way with women like that. He imagined them with their hands tied behind their backs wearing something pink and lacy just too small for them so that they were bursting out all over. Jace could see himself with a whip and all the pretty snooty ladies cowering, breasts bulging, thighs straining, pleading with him to release them.

Jace chortled. Disc nonsense, but fun for all that. He remembered the disc he had picked up. Yeah, he would access it when he got home. He was in the mood for a disc and he hoped it was a hot one.

Fee Cambridge did what she should have done long since, what might have prevented Janine from taking off and then Will from disappearing in her wake. It was no help to them but it was no help not to do it, so she went ahead.

She bought a box number and started placing ads in Screen magazines. Most of what went out on Screen was magazine material, endless features, gossip, games, chat, newsy items, and these were the padding material between drama and romance and genuine news. Fee took two slots, one in the morning and one in the afternoon, for a week. It was very expensive. Her advertisement read: *You've used it and you know it's different. VR with no boundaries. It hurts to come home. We've lost it and will pay.*

Now she had to wait for a response. Whippet took it from her office. He lost it. Caz found it in a shop. He lost it. The cleaner at the Institute found it, took it, and she lost it. Where did it go after the cleaner lady? Who had it now? Had anyone managed to hang onto it? Why was the disc so slippery?

Lexie sometimes saw the girl from the disc at the corners of her vision but if she turned her head too sharply, the girl was gone. She was like starlight. The harder you stared, the more she trembled into nothingness. She was more an atmospheric flicker than she was a boiling nuclear furnace, however distant, and on the whole Lexie felt the nearer and more insubstantial air-waver was preferable to something hard and real and impossibly far away.

These days Lexie watched the Screen all the time, there not being much else to do, and she watched it so much that sometimes she didn't have to put it on as soon as she came in because she had forgotten to put it off before she went out. Lexie saw the advertisement Fee had placed and Lexie understood it.

Lexie didn't want money as much as she wanted the disc. She wanted the girl in the fish-scale dress again. That girl had made her feel like something really special, that girl had brought her alive in a way she hadn't believed possible since Joe died.

Joe had been a policeman and he had died five years before in the great raids on the pirate nests down in the old city, when the police had finally tired of their criminal impudence hacking Zoo-folks' cars and then selling the Zoo-folk back to their own kind like they were slaves, like they were meat, not people. Lexie wished a malediction on all pirates for the killing of her Joe and it hardly mattered that there weren't any pirates any more. Connet-hacking was a thing of the past. The police had bested the pirates once and for all but it had taken Joe's death to do it and Lexie still mourned her Joe. She was not a poor woman. Joe had earned well as a policeman when alive and his widow took home a fat pension now he was dead, but what use was that to a woman who loved cooking and had no one to cook for?

Their apartment (she still thought of it as hers and Joe's) was large and airy and bright and from the balcony you could just see the jungle that hid the Zoo. Lexie always said she lived within spitting distance of the Zoo, but if she was honest it was a mighty big spit. Now she wondered if her feelings for the fish-scale girl weren't some sort of explanation for why she had never taken another man after Joe. She was a warm woman. She was a sociable woman. She liked having someone to look after. But she had never felt the itch that Joe had aroused in her since his death, never from another man and there were plenty of men who had indicated at one time or another that they would like a large cuddly warm friendly woman who enjoyed cooking and pleasing her man. That is, Lexie had never felt the itch till she synched with the girl on the disc and now Lexie was hot, hot for sex, but she was all alone and the disc was gone and she didn't quite know what she was going to do, only she felt so lonely, fat and lonely. Then she saw the advertisement and it did not take her too long to decide to answer it. She didn't have the disc any more, but it couldn't do any harm.

Maybe that girl would see the ad and come out of hiding. Lexie was sure the girl had enjoyed what went on between them as much as she had herself. So she replied to the box number with her vidicom number and sat back and waited to be contacted.

Jace had this very sneaky idea. He knew he wasn't a handsome man in the classic sense, but he knew he had a powerful coarse attraction for a certain sort of woman. Modern men, particularly Zoo men, were soft and unmanly, even effeminate these days, thought Jace. They depilated their body hair, not just their chins but many of them depilated their chests and their legs and their armpits too. It wouldn't be too long before they shaved their pubic hair, thought Jace. Now he was proud of his body hair and it seemed to him that a woman who really appreciated a man would be proud also of this symbol of his virility.

The question was, what sort of a woman was Fee Cambridge? She had a reputation for being hot. But her reputation was based on her looks and the way she walked and the sort of clothes she wore. Jace had never heard of her linked with another man's name save for that of her husband. Her husband was a very smooth man. Admittedly he was big and he looked as if he used the gym. But smooth was the word for Rollo Cambridge with his bronzed good looks and streaky blond hair thrust oh so carelessly back, his wide mouth and his blazing blue eyes.

Perhaps he roamed. Any girl would be proud to be shafted by the great financier. It would be surprising if he didn't play the field a little. How would the beautiful Fee Cambridge take that?

Jace thought the man so good-looking he must be narcissistic. Again, how would the beautiful and no doubt vain Ms Cambridge take that? Would she want the sun of her good looks shadowed by the sun of his? The more Jace thought about it, the more he thought that perhaps Fee Cambridge might find him attractive. He was a real man. A woman would be quite clear about that when he had sweetened her up a little. Maybe Fee would overlook his lack of physical beauty long enough to get to feel his aura. Jace reckoned he had an aura worth feeling.

He vidicommed her and when he could see her sharp slanting beauty on his screen, he introduced himself.

'My name is Jace Harvon, Mrs Cambridge, and I live right here in the Zoo.'

She frowned. 'I think I recognise you. Just.' Her voice was cool and unwelcoming.

'We have mutual friends, I think. Monroe and Diva Jackson.'

'Yes.' Fee nodded. There was no softening in her response to him.

'The thing is, I'd like to meet with you, Mrs Cambridge. Take you out for a meal someplace. There are some things I want to talk to you about that won't go well over the airwaves.'

'What sort of things, Mr Harvon? I'm a busy woman and I'll need to know more before I make an appointment.'

Make an appointment! That was how she described being invited out by him. He would punish her for that insult before too long.

'Water,' he said.

There was a long silence. Fee watched him calmly.

Then she said: 'I'll get back to you,' and she cut the connection.

Jace fumed. The damned woman. But Fee was as good as her word and she got back to him within five minutes.

'Where and when, Mr Harvon?'

He suggested the Company Bar that evening. There was nothing to be gained from hanging around. He turned up on time and was surprised to find that she did also. He didn't mind a little unpunctuality in a woman, he thought it kinda sweet as long as it didn't go too far, but he soon forgot all about the smaller niceties as for the first time he found himself in Fee Cambridge's company.

He might think he had an aura but it was nothing against hers. Her personality swept him round about and he felt the glittering force of the woman, her dazzling furious personality channelled and controlled into one powerfully icy stream as she concentrated on him. In the flesh her beauty was marvellous, slitted ice-green cold eyes, the white sharply-accented face with the famous trickle of scar like diamond dust across one cheek, the perfect flaw. He felt the force of her strong slim tall body with its overlarge pendant breasts like great heavy jewels on the front of her body. She wore very high heels and a very short skirt and all her black tumble of hair was restrained under a low black broad-brimmed hat. There was no give in her expression, no weakness.

Jace smiled. He had tamed fiercer things.

'I checked you out, Mr Harvon. You own a biochemical company that specialises in fluid analysis. You tell me water over the vidi. So what is this all about?'

He leaned forward earnestly with insincere goodwill on his face. 'The thing is, Mrs Cambridge, we have found a new bug. We found it some time ago and we can't do damn all with it. It has a toxicity rating of 8.7 plus or minus ten per cent and it is growing. It grows slow but it grows sure. We are pretty certain it has penetrated the public supply.'

Fee maintained her calm. 'If this relates as I suppose

it must to my husband's company, then I must tell you that TransFlow is fitted with very sensitive monitoring devices. I am a director myself, Mr Harvon. We have heard nothing of this.'

'It has a threshold. It simply hasn't reached it yet as it has in our laboratory. When its parts per million go over 0.2 you'll detect it, all right. It isn't in sufficient quantity to be toxic before that.'

Again she took her time to answer. 'I find the method by which you have chosen to impart this information very curious,' she said finally. 'I presume you have notifed the authorities?'

'Not yet.'

'Other water carriers?'

'Not yet.'

'The media?'

'Not yet.'

'Your professional colleagues?'

'Not yet.'

'Why me, Mr Harvon? Why TransFlow?'

'They don't have your looks.' He saw he had been too precipitate. 'They don't have mutual friends as we do. They don't live in the Zoo. I guess I think Zoo-folk should stick together.'

'It doesn't respond to normal antibacterial agents?'

'It's not a bacteria. That is, the host is, but the host is not the problem.'

For the first time a faint flush bloomed on her cheeks and he saw she was disturbed. 'A virus?' she said.

'A virus.'

'Of all the dichotomies,' she said, 'I've often thought the most potent was not light and dark, nor heaven and hell, nor earth and fire, nor male and female, not even life and death. It seems to me that it is all of us, everything, all that is alive, against viruses. Us and them. And one day they will win.'

'Maybe that day has arrived.'

She became brisk. 'So what's the deal? Why have you told me about our little hydrophilic friend?'

'I will give you what we have which is a great deal and includes a rundown of their protein coats, so that you can get ahead of your competitors in the research to defeat the beast. Or you might decide you are licked. It can mutate around five percent of its DNA every thirty minutes. You could quietly sell up whilst your stock holds out.' Jace grinned.

'I don't think we could sell without causing a little flutter,' murmured Fee.

'Nonsense. Don't insult me. You put the stock into a wholly-owned holding company for tax reasons and then quietly sell the company when everyone has stopped watching.'

'And what will we do back for you, Mr Harvon? What is your price?'

'Call me Jace, Fee. And come back to my apartment.'

Jace lay on his couch and watched her. 'My boys will undress you,' he said. The smoulder in her eyes delighted him. His two houseboys came forward and knelt by the magnificent woman and began to strip her. They took their time. All the time she never took her eyes from Jace, lolling before her, watching. Her skirt was released and lowered down her legs in a whisper of sound in the room that was silent but for her heavy breathing. Her chest lifted and fell. She wore a brief clinging red top that did nothing to hide her full contours. Her panties were clinging also, an elastic stretchy material that held her fleece tight against the base of her stomach but let him see through its lacy texture. Suspenders made a crimson slash on her white thighs and he liked the dark silk stockings she wore. He would make sure they stayed on.

His boys had removed her hat and let her hair tumble about her shoulders. Now they lifted her shirt and drew it up over her head. She wore nothing underneath it. Her nipples were as crimson as her suspenders and he saw with a quick intake of excitement that she painted them.

Her face was flushed in her mortification. She remained upright in her high heels with her dark stockings, but otherwise, barring her panties, she was regally naked.

'The panties,' said Jace. His boys hooked their fingers in at her waistband and ever so slowly began to ease down the last vestige of privacy that she wore. Jace was about ready to purr.

She kept up her malevolent glare unflinchingly until the very last moment. As what she kept between her legs was bared to his hungry eyes, her eyes closed. The boys made her lift each leg in turn and then they drew back, leaving her alone in the middle of the floor.

'Come here,' said Jace softly.

'Yes, master,' she said, and her fine proud head drooped.

'Undress me.'

She obeyed, keeping her eyes humbly downturned, and yet it seemed to Jace she was not averse to him as his strong broad body was revealed.

'Stroke me,' he whispered. She had long white hands and it amazed him they were warm, so cold was her manner, her appearance. 'Stroke my cock,' he said more harshly as excitement began to fire him up. 'Kiss me.'

'I hear you,' she groaned and he felt the cool press of her lips. Her hands ran over his chest as her head was busy over his groin. He became firm and rose up under her caresses and she let her cheek rub against him and kissed his wet tip.

He lay back on the couch. 'Get astride, sister,' he said. 'Fill yourself with me.'

She cried out as she lowered herself over him. 'You're so big. I can't handle it. Help me, help me.'

He helped her and slowly her woman's place absorbed him, took him in, and he felt how tight he was in her and he knew that she would not forget going with Jace Harvon, oh no. He was more than a match for her.

She began to move up and down and it was very fine, .very good, and knowing that he had bought it with information made it all the better. As they warmed together and sweat sprang from his chest she began to moan and plead and pray for him to do this to her forever, he was so good, it was so good. She began to whisper things about other men, how poor they were beside him, how meanly made, how weak beside his rampant virility. Then he was coming and the familiar everchanging blaze of glory caught her by surprise so that she screamed how he was her lover, her joy and at last he had what he wanted.

She begged him to do it to her again, to give it to her like that, so she could know what a real man was.

'The deal is honoured,' he said a little thickly. 'I'll give you what I promised.'

'Promise me more of this,' she whispered, her hair all mussed and her blazing eyes softened and adoring.

He was looking for the answer, something insulting that would make her know her place, yet something that would keep her coming back to him whilst she pleased him, when the red flashing square of light up in the right-hand field of his vision began to annoy him. He turned to his boys who had been in the room the whole time to tell them to deal with it when he saw them waver and fade. His room turned to smoke and the warm weight of the adoring woman lifted and vanished.

Jace turned in his private VR booth and put his head in his arms and damn near howled with the sense of loss, with the rupture of the two worlds. His body shook and it was some time before he could sort out fact from fiction, so real was the disc that it vied with reality in his memory.

There was no virus. He had not contacted Fee Cambridge. She had not consented to sell her body to him for information.

It was true that he owned a biochemical company that specialised in fluid analysis but that was about the limit of the disc's veracity. His company did mainly hospital work, not public health.

As he recovered from his shock, he began to think

about the disc. Fee Cambridge was on it. The disc had a real person in the VR world. That was illegal, programmers weren't allowed to use real people in the fantasies they wove. It was a very serious crime.

He was in the disc as the user but the disc had real details from his life woven into its VR plot. He wasn't the only owner of a biochem company in the world, just as the disc might have cast the user as a fireman or a statistician, but it was unusual for discs to specify because it could jar with the user. Yet this one not only specified, it specified his particular field. Jace felt very uncomfortable. He was a man who believed in the significance of coincidence, and he was here presented with a coincidence of mammoth proportions.

The disc made it clear that water stock was about to plunge in value because of some mystery virus. That in itself was very very peculiar. Jace could read only one message into it.

The cost of water stock was about to go through the roof. He must mortgage his bubble house as well as his car and buy all he could. He reached for the vidi.

After earnest consultation with his horrified broker, Jace sat back and considered vidi-ing Fee Cambridge. Naturally she would not answer, but he could leave a message on her answertape that she should call him about an illegal VR disc that had fallen into his possession. He toyed with the idea, grinning to himself. He could go straight to the police but that wouldn't be half so much fun. He would rather have an excuse for meeting the legendary Cambridge woman.

He decided that that was what he would do. But he would wait a while first. Since he had the disc, he might as well get the benefit. No one would ever know whether he used it once or twenty times. When he ran over the details in his mind of what had taken place, he found he rather liked the idea of having the VR Fee astride his cock again, pleading for him never to stop, he was so good. Nonsense it might be, but it was thoroughly pleasing nonsense and he couldn't see that it would matter to Fee herself one way or the other however much he enjoyed her simulated charms. He would do the decent thing like the honourable citizen he was and turn the disc in. Eventually. Eventually.

Jace chuckled. Finding a disc with the water baron's wife on it in the water gardens as he watched it start to rain on his way home to bathe just as OWAC were due to announce the new season's price all added up to one thing.

Buy!

Janine knew little of the journey they made to Will's place of safety, though at last there was a bed and she was allowed to lie down and rest on it. She knew that they had followed someone who occasionally whispered to Will but always led them on between broken buildings, through dangerous squares and broken and violated precincts until they were led into the bowels of some dark place and she was allowed to lie down. A girl's voice offered her a place to wash and food to eat but Janine was too tired and so she lay there on the bed as if she had been cast up on a beach, jetsam from a shipwreck.

She slept and dreamed crazy dreams. Sometimes she was in the room where a light always burned and sometimes she heard the rumble of voices, one soft and gentle, one low and rough, and she knew she dreamed of Will. Once she jerked up out of sleep in her dream hearing someone cry out. She looked across the room and saw a man and a woman locked together sexually. The girl's head had dropped back over the edge of her bed so that in her dream Janine saw it upside down, the girl's mouth opened in her ecstasy, her eyes closed, her hair a black curtain hanging below her head. Her arms hung wide in carnal submission and above her slim saffron-coloured proffered body a man pressed heavily, taking his pleasure of her, his wide dark face calm in the release of sexual tension. His eyes opened and for a moment Janine's startled blue gaze met his stone-coloured stare. He smiled a slow cruel smile and lowered his head to kiss the bared throat of the girl sprawled beneath him. He kissed with gentle deep insistence, lingeringly, with a rich sensuality that smothered. Janine knew then that his lovemaking was both luxurious and fierce and something curled tightly inside her and began to hurt.

She woke feeling sick with hunger and dizzy, in daylight. She had very little idea about the events of the preceding night but she was relieved to find herself on a couch though she was fully dressed and felt stinking and dirty. Her clothing was horrible, being what she had taken from the Amazenes. Her throat craved liquid. She overcame her weakness enough to sit up, her hair a vilely tangled mess about her face and shoulders, and she looked about the room where she was.

Across from her Will slept heavily in the arms of a girl with black hair. They had covers over them but the covers had slipped enough for Janine to know that they were both naked. Scenes from her dreams came back to her and she blushed and felt hot with shame. She pulled herself from the couch she was on and trying to be quiet, she went across the room to find something to drink, somewhere to wash.

They had removed her boots and her ankles nagged slightly. Janine found an orange and with trembling fingers she ripped the skin from the flesh and sank her teeth deeply into the fruit, sucking and drinking the juices. After this she stood a moment, shaking, gathering her strength and trying to make her mind work. Then she turned and crept across the room containing the sleeping couple, hearing flies drone in the barred sunlight that filtered through half-shuttered windows. She stole out through the doorway and looked about her. She saw a likely door and mercifully it led to the bathroom.

Janine stripped her awful Amazene clothes from her body and ran water into a cracked basin. She had tried the shower but was unable to make it work. There was no hot water either. She was beyond caring. She would have washed in a puddle if there was nothing else. She began to wash over her body, soaking the Amazene shirt so she could use it as a cloth, and slowly the dreadful hot itch of her dull dirty skin eased.

She heard a noise in the doorway and realised that it had not occurred to her there might be others in the building who used this bathroom. She turned stiffly and saw Will.

He had put his trousers on, she saw with relief. She stood half crouched over the basin, aware of her nakedness and ashamed of it.

'I had to wash,' she said through cracked lips.

His expression was enigmatic. He came towards her and she stiffened disbelievingly but then he turned and tried the shower.

She tried to tell him it didn't work but he kicked it suddenly and the pipes rattled and with a wheezy gush of steam, water began to flow.

Janine turned, trying to resist the temptation to cover her sex. She stumbled across gratefully to the water where it gushed uncertainly, holding a crust of soap in her hand. She stepped carefully into the cubicle and found the water was warm rather than hot. She fell against the wall of the cubicle and began to soap herself in an exhausted way. Her eyes were shut and it was a shock when she felt herself pushed. She opened them and found Will was getting into the shower with her. He had removed his trousers and as he got into the cubicle, his big rough craggy body was pressed close to hers, the water streaming down him in dark runnels of wet hair.

'No,' she whimpered.

'Don't be silly,' he observed dispassionately. 'I don't go in for rape, sister.'

Janine pressed back against the cubicle wall and stared at him. He took the soap from her and began to rub her with it. He was not gentle.

'Listen,' he said patiently. 'We have a long journey ahead. It won't be a picnic. I need you strong and fit. At the moment you are exhausted and you need to rest up and eat. Seeing as you are so well bred you will need to be clean, too, and I don't suppose there is that much water so I am sharing it with you and making sure you get the best of it.' The bored contempt in his voice made Janine's nerves burn. His hands came round her crotch and he scrubbed her thighs, soaping thoroughly and roughly over all of her body. He turned round, handing her the soap. 'Do my back,' he ordered.

She was fascinated. He had a big back by the standards of the men she had known, but what made it unique were the knotted bundles of muscles at his shoulders, and the firm, even harsh resilience of his flesh under the covering of skin. He was scarred also, and she was fascinated by the flaws on him, by the imperfections and calluses that made what should be a smooth surface rough.

His rough handling of her skin had acted on her like a massage and she felt better, more alert and alive. She finished his back and stopped uncertainly. She couldn't get out of the shower because he blocked the entrance to the small cubicle. He turned round and made her turn round and so he did her back.

Janine leant against the wall with her eyes shut, sagging under the heavy pressure of his hands. Water dripped and spouted and trickled over her. He didn't stop with her back but went on down, his hands cupping and soaping her rounded buttocks, momentarily dividing them so that she began to stiffen, but then he had moved on. He must be crouching, Janine thought in a daze, for now his hands circled her thighs again, this time from the back, and he went on down to her calves and ankles. She felt his head brush wetly against her buttocks and when he again made her turn round, she found him kneeling at her feet, his hair slicked back by the water, his dark stony eyes squeezed against it, and his head brushing now against her sexual mound.

He stopped and looked up at her, his eyes so narrowed they were almost closed. She looked down her own body, past her breasts where water gathered and

159

ran out onto the tips and dripped onto him, down to him with his face opposite the dark core of her. Her blood began to sing. He's going to do it, she thought. This is it.

But he did nothing of the kind. Instead he stood up with a grunt and finished rinsing his hair. He pulled Janine against his hard hairy chest and washed and rinsed her hair. She leant against him unashamedly whilst he did this. She had no strength to waste in an exhibition of pride. She had no pride left.

They dried themselves in silence and went back to the main room. The girl still slept. Will went over to one side of the room and found some food for Janine and he made coffee for them both.

'Are we leaving now?' asked Janine.

'Tonight,' said Will with his mouth full.

'Why not now?'

'You can't travel by day in the city.'

'Why not?'

He was silent for a moment and then he grinned sardonically at her. 'Because of the HeliPolice, sweetie,' he said.

'The police? But they will be on our side. You mean they come into the city? Will, that's great news.'

He chewed thoughtfully, allowing her irritation to rise. 'Not really,' he drawled. 'You see, they come in their Helibuzzes for fun. They ride the skies, baby. They don't come down here to ground level. And call me Wolf whilst we are here. Will is a different guy and I don't want to be associated with him.'

'Couldn't we wave to them? Call them down, somehow.'

'Sure. If you want to be shot up.'

'What?'

'They come for target practice, sister. Those cryogen spray guns don't kill, but you can't feel much for a week or so after and the cure isn't the sort of thing a nice innocent little girly like you would appreciate. Most city-folk stay inside daytimes.'

Janine stared at him, shocked at what he said and not really believing him. He was so cynical. 'What if we wrote a message on a roof, in big letters? Painted it or something. Surely that would make them land?'

'I don't think so.' Will remained infuriatingly cheerful. 'They would take it for a trap. City-folk have gotten their own back once or twice with very similar ploys.'

'Won't Fee tell them we are here?' she said weakly.

'I told her to trust me and give me time.'

'You arrogant bastard,' said Janine bitterly.

'And unlike you, Fee understands the city a little and she knows I might need to play it gentle for a while if things don't work smoothly. If we hadn't met the Amazenes we would have been home by now. But we did, and we stirred up a real hornets' nest, and now things are a little difficult. However, we'll make it.' He yawned and stretched, his fine long powerful limbs creaking slightly. Janine was intensely aware of him, of his animal presence. He was aggressively male, bare-chested and wearing the leather trousers that she had ceased to find affected. They suited him. They went with the rawness of his personality. Yet though he was overtly sexual and plainly immensely physically strong, she found that she knew also he was mentally strong, he could control himself and this gave even his roughness a certain sleek grace, an undercurrent of excitement that so much power was under so much control.

She remembered how he had spent part of the night and shuddered within herself. No wonder the black-haired girl still slept.

'I'm going back to bed now,' he announced, 'and I suggest you do the same. We've a hard night ahead of us but I guess we'll be in spitting distance of the Town by the time it's over.'

It was harder than he could have known.

Janine slept more easily now, her belly full and her thirst assuaged, her skin silk clean after the sweaty staleness of the previous three and a half days. She woke towards dusk to realise with a thrill of horror that Will

161

and the black-haired girl were at each other again across the room from her.

She rolled to face the wall and tried to close her ears to the passionate murmurs and half-stifled cries of ecstasy. How could they rut together with her there and probably awake? How much was Will the animal he appeared? Were there no finer feelings in him, no sense of decency or modesty? Janine clawed her ears and bit her lip.

They fell quiet at last. Janine eased her cramped body and found she was trembling. She stared at the wall and tried to imagine herself back into her nice safe life in the Town.

'Hey,' called Will.

She took no notice.

'Hey over there. You deaf? It's time you met our hostess.'

Janine heard the girl giggle and she turned her furious red face to them and sat up, primly drawing the bedclothes up around her.

'Meet Wing,' said Will. He was half-sitting, leaning back against the wall opposite with one arm slung affectionately round the girl's shoulders. He was smoking and his chest glistened with sweat. The room was rank with the smell of sex.

'Hello Janine,' said Wing.

She was Chinese. She had a tiny rosebud mouth with brilliant lips over white even little teeth. Her cheeks were flattened and her eyes were obsidian, black as her hair, narrow and slanting under heavy lids. Her black hair was heavy and brushed the fine thin bones of her little slender shoulders. She was tiny, a delicate pale saffron slip of a girl, black-eyed, black-haired and with coral lips. She was beautiful, and as she sat there laughing, taking daring little peeps up at Will, she let the covers slide to her waist and Janine saw her tiny pointed breasts, coral-tipped to match her lips. She was a jewel, a butterfly.

Will's dark scarred hairy mat of a chest was obscene

against the smooth delicacy of the girl, his body gross beside her slenderness. Janine's mind shot straight to what obsessed her. How could Will's thick clublike thing be allowed near such a girl? She had seen it limp in the shower and knew it would swell to a bludgeon when he was aroused. How could Wing's tender slightness absorb his brutish member? She met Will's eyes and saw they danced with hot lights in them. He knew what she was thinking. Janine blushed.

'Hello, Wing,' she said. 'Thank you for taking us in.'

'It was no problem,' said Wing and glanced up at Will. They grinned at each other and she burst into laughter. 'You fit very well,' she said.

'Wing wants to come with us,' said Will.

'Come with us? To the Town?'

'Yes, please,' said Wing.

'Has W . . .'

'Wolf,' said Will.

'Has Wolf told you about it, then?'

'I knew already. We see things on the Screen, you know. We have it here as well.'

'Why have you not already gone there, then?'

'It is not easy,' said Wing earnestly. 'I know no one there. I do not know how to get a job, how to find somewhere to live, how to get identity papers. I am not sure if I will be arrested by the HeliPolice. But now I have you.' She smiled, triumphantly. 'I will help you here. You will help me there.'

'Quite right,' said Will. His hand caressed her upper arm.

'You can move in with me until we get you a place of your own,' said Janine firmly. She would let the girl know she needn't sell her body to Will in order to get their help.

'You are both very kind,' said Wing. She went up on her knees suddenly to kiss Will. Janine saw her back and the neat small rounded humps of her bottom. She was beautifully shaped, her proportions tiny and perfect. Will's hand slid like a vast blemish across her slender

163

back and descended until he cupped her buttocks. She pressed her little body urgently into his and Janine looked away. She felt fevered and disturbed.

She borrowed a tunic and undertrousers from Wing and they set off with the dark. Wing went ahead via back ways, through silent crumbling alleys, cat-footed over the rubble and safe away from the lights because Will was at her back, knife in hand. Janine followed Will. Wing's feet pattered light and swift but lighter and swifter went the word and slowly about them in the darkness of night the net began to close. The Amazenes were raging at the escape of their prisoner, raging at the violation of the sacred clothing of one of their number, and out for vengeance. They had posted their people. They had laid words and menaces and bribes like light whips upon the scattered people of the city and now their sowing was to bear fruit. As Wing and Will and Janine slipped through the city, eyes saw and mouths told what they saw so that as the three rounded a corner they walked into a trap.

Wing was taken first, lifted clear off the ground, struggling but unable to cry out because her mouth was held. Will hurtled himself forward but sticks were thrust between his legs to trip him and blankets thrown over him to blind him and though he fought with the strength of ten, they had the strength of twenty and ten. Janine fell next to them, but she was easy meat.

The Amazenes had their prisoner again and two more besides. Renegade women. Betrayers of their sex. The city trembled and thrilled knowing there was entertainment in store as the Amazenes exacted their revenge.

Will was chained and taken on ahead whilst the girls were simply tied together and driven on their feet at a run by women guards behind them and to each side.

At this precise moment poor silly Whippet and his gang finally caught up with Janine, whom they had been tracking since she left with Will two nights before. They had met Amazene sentries and been warned off and so had gone around the Amazene territory in ignorance of its nature and the power of the black-clad women with their hanging bare breasts. Whippet's determination to recapture Janine, or to trace her and so keep up some feeble connection with the missing disc, had driven him to browbeat Fruity who wanted to play with the Amazene sentries, not recognising that they were about as fit for sexual toys as scorpions. Dinko and the Zootman both believed that the women were all show and had nothing for them to fear. So the gang had moved in ignorance and stupidity and remained free.

They had become caught up in the thread of excitement generated in the city when the call went out for help to find Will. They didn't understand what was happening, they weren't equipped to understand a culture entirely different from any they had met, but they knew the guilty thrill of wrongdoing and they caught its flavour as they passed among the city-folk. Someone was in trouble. Someone was going to get it. And they all would be invited when it came time for the kill.

The gang was close to its goal when Will broke cover in his attempt to get back to the Town. The spying ones reported the passage of the big man through the night, drawing the vengeful women down upon him. Whippet came pattering in the rear and finally saw Janine, her wheat-fair hair a long pale sheet glimmering in the gloomy shadows of the decaying city. There were women around her but women were of no account in Whippet's version of the world of physical strength, and he brought the gang round in front of the guard detail and challenged them direct.

The guards stopped more from surprise than from any feelings of fear. The four youths ranged themselves in front of them and Whippet went forward.

'The lady with the fair hair belongs to me,' he said as menacingly as he was able.

'Go brother,' said a low female voice. 'Go and you may not be harmed for your insolence.'

'I don't care about the little one but the fair one is ours,' said Whippet obstinately. His knife flickered into his hand.

There were three women guarding the girls. Without further words one stayed with the captives whilst the other two fanned one to each side and took out their machetes. Their actions were poised and fluid. Now they raised their weapons and ran at the four youths.

Wing and Janine turned startled eyes to each other and then Wing kicked the feet from under their guard who was watching the battle. Janine flung herself down on the woman's face and Wing pulled the knife from her belt. She slit Janine's bonds before the woman threw Janine off but now Janine had her hands free and struck blindly.

'Run,' called Wing. The Amazene groped at her feet for her fallen machete and Janine kicked her hard in the face. She grabbed Wing's arm and they fled.

She took the first second she could to slit Wing's bonds so that they both had freedom. Wing led her immediately into a building and they ran as quietly as possible along its corridors, stopping if they saw a light and doubling back till they could stay in the safe dark where no one would see them. They went up and up until suddenly they were under the sky. The tired stars were faint and hazed, the air clearer and cool up here. The city spread in a smudged dim sprawl below them.

'We must hide,' whispered Wing. 'They will think we go home. Or that we keep running. They do not know we go to the Town, do they?'

'I don't know,' muttered Janine. The blood sang in her veins. She felt hoarse with excitement. 'I told them when they first took W – Wolf, that I was from the Town.'

'That is bad. But they are not very concerned about women. They took us because we were with him and with him they are very angry. They might not look too hard for us.'

'We can't leave him.' Janine was horrified.

'Of course not. But I don't think you realise how bad things are.'

'I took him away from them once,' said Janine grimly.

Wing was silent for a short moment. Then she said

166

soberly, her voice little more than a faint susurration in the night, 'The time may come when we have to leave him. But first we shall see if we can help. Yes?'

'Yes,' said Janine. Except that she knew there was only one circumstance in which she would abandon Will in the city whilst she went back herself to the Town with Wing's help.

But he was not dead yet.

They were silent for a while. Then Janine became aware that Wing trembled and shook silently beside her. She looked at the little figure and saw the glistening trails on her face.

'Don't cry,' she said helplessly.

'They will kill him,' snivelled Wing. 'He was brave and strong, like the heroes of old. He had loyalty instead of blood in his veins. He would have saved both of us even at the cost of his life because we slowed him down, it was our fault he was captured, and he must have known it might happen.'

Janine remained quiet for a while, absorbing what Wing had said, seeing it from her point of view. At last she asked quietly: 'What will they do, Wing? Do you understand this?'

'Yes. I understand. When we met he told me he was on the run from the Amazenes. You must know, they do not bother us overmuch being locked in their own strange ways and the rites of their religion. Also they keep men from hurting us because they exact revenge when a man uses his strength against a woman and she does not want it. So many of us are quite happy that they are there. We are not often hurt, you understand, though men are so much stronger. How is this done in the Town? Are there Amazenes there?'

'No. The police protect any of us, man or woman, who might be attacked. It hardly ever happens.'

'The police,' said Wing. 'That will be the strangest thing, to think of them as protectors rather than attackers.'

'What is going to happen to Wolf?' persisted Janine.

Her exultation was leaving her, and a dark tide of grief was washing through her, leaving her weak and with a great sense of loss.

'He will be sacrificed to the god-queen they worship,' said Wing matter-of-factly.

'Sacrificed?'

'Publicly crucified and then thrown into the sacred snake tank. Mambas. Very bad snakes.' Wing shuddered. 'The Amazenes breed them especially and milk their venom. I think they make a drink with it that they use in their sacred rites so that they might make contact direct with the god-queen. But this is rumour. None of us know. They keep their secrets, except when one of their kind has been defiled and then they humiliate and sacrifice the defiler.'

'No,' said Janine.

'It is said,' whispered Wing, 'that they sometimes inject diluted venom into their victims. It makes the man stand ready as if he wanted sex.' Wing giggled. 'You know what I mean. Then the whole pack satisfy their lust on the man and he can do nothing about it. They chain him down and use him as a toy. Maybe twenty, thirty women.'

It was plain to Janine that Wing was fascinated by this idea and for a moment the image came into her mind of Will flat on his back staked out on the ground, naked, his thick pole sticking up from his groin, and woman after woman mounting him and riding him.

'We've got to stop this,' she gasped.

'They won't do that with Wolf,' said Wing. 'I tell you, he will be crucified for all to see, then given to the snakes. It is their way.'

'People will come to watch?' asked Janine in dull horror.

'Of course. Such a thing is a rare occurrence. Not many flout the Amazenes as Wolf has done. And they have been helped. They would never have caught him had we not been spied on. I did not know how angry they were or I would have counselled staying hidden for days yet. But he was anxious to get you home, he said. He was impatient. Now he suffers for that impatience.'

'They never give up a victim? There is no way he can be forgiven? They will take no one in his place?' Janine was speaking almost idly. It was clear to her that Wing had a fatalistic view of the proceedings she so casually described. She might have to attempt this terrible thing of rescuing Will alone.

'The god-queen can order a reprieve, but that never really happens. They always ask.'

'The god-queen speaks?'

'Not in voices you or I hear.'

'How might she speak if we could hear?'

'She would send a challenger.'

'A challenger?'

'One who would fight for him. If the god-queen wishes him reprieved, she will ensure the challenger wins.'

'Does no one ever challenge?'

'Who would fight for a man who has only death ahead of him?'

'I don't understand. Speak plainly to me, Wing. You say we might get someone to challenge them to fight for his life. Is there such a man? Do you know anyone who would help us? What could we offer him in exchange?'

'No, no. The god-queen would use a woman, never a man. The challenger-woman would fight the priestess. The priestess is the pack leader and very strong, their best fighter. It would be hand to hand fighting. It has never been done in my time,' insisted Wing.

'Why did you say the man had only death ahead of him?' Janine could have shaken the girl.

'Because even if the challenger wins, he must drink the cup they offer to prove the god-queen really wishes to let him go, that he is forgiven.'

'What is in the cup?'

'The venom. He must drink the venom. And no one can survive it, whatever they say their god-queen can do. We cannot rescue him, Janine-sister. He is a dead man.'

* * *

They strung Will up in a great empty plaza in which they lit bonfires to signify the phases of the moon. The drums began to beat, bidding the people of the city come and bear witness to the god-queen's vengeance. Great barrels were broached and the thick luscious red wine flowed like a dark river, heating the blood and dazzling the senses so that people reeled and laughed and almost forgot the figure tied above them, his arms outstretched with the bar across his shoulders and manacles at his wrists. Apart from a rag at his loins he was naked. They had oiled his body and it shone in the flame-flicker. He was a captive bull and many found it funny that one so magnificently made should come to such an end at the hands of women.

Beyond the plaza, on its open side where one could see for some distance, there was a distant stripe across the smudged sky. Light hurtled at intervals along this stripe. That the Connets should be so close and so unattainable seemed the final irony to Janine.

'Tonight they will dance,' said Wing. 'Tomorrow night he will die.'

Janine looked across the square at Will. Though he was distant from her and she lurked with Wing in the shadows at one corner of the plaza, she could yet see that on the opposite side to them were the ruins of some pseudo-Classical building of the former age, perhaps once of municipal use. All that remained of its former dignity was the portico, the fluted columns supporting the pediment at the top of a decorous flight of steps, the whole thing like an elegant denture, for nothing of the building remained behind this façade. Will stood chained with his outstretched arms between two of the columns, for all the world like blind Samson, but he could not pull down the building as Samson had pulled down the pillars of the house of Gaza. He could do nothing except watch the revelry build before him, the revelry over the manner of his coming death.

'I will challenge,' said Janine.

'Ah. You feel like that about him. Yet you seemed to hate him when he was with us,' said Wing.

'He came into the city to save me. Now I must help him.'

'Those are very fine words,' said Wing, 'but very stupid. You cannot fight the Amazenes and win, Janine-sister.'

Janine turned her head slowly to Wing as though her neck was a rusty ratchet stiff with disuse. 'I outsmarted them once before,' she said. 'I can do it again. Tell me how the challenger must go about her business.'

'We will need money,' said Wing fearfully. 'Much more money than I have.'

Janine's eyes glittered with red points from the distant fires. 'How does one set about earning money down here? What does a girl do for cash in the city, Wing? We only have tonight and tomorrow. I must be ready by tomorrow night.'

Wing began to explain.

Chapter Six

*I*t was all made easier because Wing was so very beautiful. Janine had her hair cut to shoulder length and dyed black. She painted her lips into a coral rosebud and though she was taller and thicker-set than the little Chinese girl, she was slim and short in stature by European standards. The Chinese girl was saffron but Janine was a clear pale butter-colour with a warmly tinted skin that flushed a faint peach when she was aroused. Her skin had not the smoothness of the Oriental girl's because she was covered in a fine short down of gold-red hairs but this faint fuzz did not show under the spotlights.

Her only shame was that the hair at the base of her belly was dyed to match that of the hair on her head. Strange that this should embarrass her when nothing else did, but so it was. Her mind felt free and loose. She had a superstitious notion that a plan would come to her, help would come to her, and somehow she would win the challenge, save Will from the venomous cup and they would all go free. And live happily ever after.

She knew it was a fairy tale but that did not matter. She could not leave the city and let Will die, even if she had to die alongside him. She could not, of course, ask such a sacrifice from Wing to whom she was a meal ticket, the gateway to a better life. But in exchange for Wing's help at this early stage in her rescue attempt, she gave the girl the knowledge she would need to contact Fee when she entered the Town, telling Wing that if she told Fee she had seen Janine and Wolf, Fee would help her to a new life knowing that she, Wing, had helped Fee's friends down in the city.

'Wolf goes by the name of Will in the Town,' she murmured, 'but do not use that name here.' Janine did not know why Will went under an alias in the city but she had come to respect his knowledge at last and to abide by his decisions. At last, when it was too late. She might not understand the need for an alias, but she accepted that the need was there.

The two girls had hired themselves to a showman who was even now erecting a booth on the edge of the plaza where Will hung for all to see. Many such booths were springing up. For the rest of this night and the next, a great crowd would gather and there was room for sideshows to build up excitement before the main event. Will's death in the snake pit, sacrificed to the Amazene god-queen, was the main event.

The tented structure that was the booth contained some seating and a stage lit from the front and the back with spotlights, and cut transversely by a tissue screen. There would be some titillation in the performance the girls intended to make, a little teasing before the audience saw fully what they were paying for. They would earn fifty per cent of the take between them, to be paid at the end of the night. They had to hope it would be enough for there would be no more time. This was their only chance to get the cash Wing said they needed if Janine was to make an attempt at the challenge. They had to be good.

A strangeness came over Janine that she should be doing this but the strangeness made it easier. It was like virtual reality. It was not real. She did not do these things. She had no responsibility. But though it was strange, it was vivid. All the details had the clarity of details in a nightmare and yet this was no nightmare. She recalled.

The two girls had whispered together.

'I cannot challenge in my own persona,' murmured Janine. 'The Amazenes might take me and Wolf himself might object.'

'I think he will,' said Wing.

Janine looked at her. 'He does not feel for me,' she said gently. 'We have not done the things that you and he have done. He does not want me that way.'

'Then why does he risk his life?'

'Because we have a mutual friend he is very fond of, and he has promised her to bring me home safe.'

'She loves you, this friend?'

'In her way, I think so,' said Janine.

Wing was silent for a few moments, considering what Janine had said, what she had witnessed for herself, what she knew of the relations between men and women.

'Is it that you prefer women?' she asked suddenly, slyly.

Janine was startled. 'I don't prefer women,' she said stiffly.

'You like this thing of bodies with women, though,' persisted Wing. Her face was inscrutable.

'I find men a little frightening sometimes,' said Janine in a low quiet voice. 'I prefer them, but with women it is so easy, so soft, so affectionate. Truly, I have gone very little with them, only with two to be honest, and one of those is my dear friend who sends Wolf to rescue me. And we have not gone together for maybe three years, not as lovers, I mean.'

'Wolf is her good friend, too?'

'Yes.'

'Perhaps life is not so different in the Town from what it is in the city, not as different as I feared.'

'People are the same everywhere,' said Janine.

'If you are not to be recognised when you challenge,' said Wing carefully, 'you will have to be disguised.'

174

'How?'

Wing explained and when Janine understood, she found a pulse throbbed low in her blood somewhere. She might not win, but losing would have a strange black glory. But they would need money. Then Wing explained how they might make money.

'I too like both men and women,' she whispered, 'but I prefer women. It was good with Wolf though he is fierce, very fierce, but that makes me only want a woman's caresses the more. My dearest Janine, men adore to see women at play together. If you are serious about wanting to save this man you say does not like you, then perhaps I can help you. We might play together if the idea does not disgust you, and if we played before an audience we could earn in a short time what you will need to prepare you for the challenge.'

'You and me,' murmured Janine.

'You and me,' murmured Wing, her voice soft as summer darkness and sweet as the rising sap.

So they had hired themselves to a showman and he had made a booth for them in the plaza of Will's death. Janine prepared herself to look as much like Wing as possible, for they would pretend they were sisters and add the bite of incest to their lesbian play. Their show would run for twenty minutes and it would run all evening save for ten minutes' rest between shows when the audience was changed. There were only a few hours of night left to them and they must earn as much as possible. The showman acted as barker, calling the strolling crowds to come into his tent and see rich entertainment.

As the tent filled for the first showing, the girls stripped and dressed for the parts they were to play. Janine found her own body strange, as strange as anything that strange night. Her lips and nipples and fingernails and toenails were all coral red, as they were on Wing. The hair of her head and the hair of her body was black, glossy black like a young tom cat. She and Wing had mapped out what they planned to do but there had been no time to rehearse, no time to refine the details. Yet they must be smooth and slick together. The audience must go away pleased and tell others they were worth watching.

It was to be a little playlet. They were two sisters, one shy, one bold. One would be ignorant, one knowing. One would lead and until a certain point, one would follow.

Wing would lead.

The show opened. Janine's throat constricted. She heard the hungry rustle of the audience, avid for hot entertainment. She was paralysed with shyness. She could not perform in front of a crowd. She could not be naked before them. She could not embrace a woman with others watching. She could not exhibit her vulva in a crude display of sex.

But Will.

The music began. She saw, across the stage, Wing give her an encouraging smile. The back lights were on, the screen in place. The two girls walked onto the stage, shadows only to the watchers, and sat down on chairs ready placed and began to undress themselves.

They were in profile to the audience and they carefully stripped their clothing with large exaggerated gestures. Off came their tops with a pert wiggle. Then they slipped tight skirts down their legs. Each girl sat and removed her stockings in the time-honoured way, one leg held out straight and raised high in turn. Each girl then wriggled her pants down and off.

They were but black body-shapes to the audience, back-lit, but clearly they were naked and everyone knew the screen would be removed. They had paid to see good flesh, not mere shadows, however enticing those shadows were.

The music was sweetly dissonant, the discordancies tinkling until an Oriental effect was achieved. Slowly Wing emerged from round her side of the screen, coming into full view, her slight body oiled and gleaming and beautiful. The audience hissed its appreciation and clapped.

Wing stroked herself, held up a leg, admired it, and turned her back on the audience and made as if to peep through a window or an aperture at her 'sister' within. As her little bottom projected towards the audience, they yelled appreciation.

Janine, still behind the screen, seemed to wake up and hear her sister call. She stood up and stretched and came slowly round the screen. She too was stark naked. Wing ran prettily up to her and gave her a kiss. Then the two girls went to two chairs placed centre stage side by side and sat down, their arms entwined about each other, their knees held primly tight together. Wing laid her head on Janine's shoulder and Janine stroked her hair back. Wing kissed Janine.

Wing kissed Janine. It was supposed to be a stage kiss, a mere pressing together of lips whilst they concentrated on their act. But the girls could not see the audience through the glare of the lights trained on them, and Janine at least had entered a new territory about which she knew nothing.

She could smell the heat of the lights on their bodies. Her eyes were dazzled so she kept them turned to Wing. She could smell the oil on their skin and a faint tang of fresh sweat. She could smell the dye on her hair and she knew that if her nose could be bent to her groin, she would smell it there too, and somehow this disturbed her more than anything, more than her nudity, more than her participation in a sex show, more than her sexual exploration of this almost unknown girl from the city.

Her groin would not smell as it should of warm musk and the rich juices of the natural aroused body. It would smell of chemicals. What man would want her if she smelt of chemicals? A tear gathered in each eye and slowly welled over her cheeks. Janine saw nothing incongruous in this, nothing odd that she should be thinking in these terms. Time itself was misplaced for her. The imminence of her death was a loop in time and she must live that loop first before her lines were nipped off short.

Wing kissed Janine. Janine touched her temples, smoothed her hair, and kissed her back. Their lips opened like petals and they kissed fully and deeply, like lovers, like mourners, knowing that as they gained, so they would lose.

Janine's breast swung round and brushed Wing's. Wing released Janine's mouth and held her head between her two little palms. She mimed speaking, pointing at their breasts and laughing. Janine lifted one of her breasts and held it out to Wing, as if enquiring. Wing laughed naughtily and held up her own little pointed breast and the two girls touched nipples, at first gently, then with more force.

Janine felt her nipple come erect at once. Between her legs a tingling started and she knew she was becoming wet down below. She remembered Will pressing down in sensual abandon on Wing's submissive body. Wing's nipple was slightly sticky with the waxy colour on it, and the slight stickiness was heaven.

Wing lowered her head and kissed Janine's nipple. This was no pretended kiss either. Janine felt her nipple grow and glow in the girl's mouth and as Wing's tongue wrapped about it, something for her alone since the audience could see nothing of it, she felt her breast stretch. She let her head drop back so that her helmet of black hair fell away and the watchers could see her face was intent, ecstatic. Janine slid off her chair and Wing turned sideways on to the audience. Now Janine reached up and kissed her sister's breast, her eyes closed, her cheeks sunken in with the effort she put into it.

She heard a vague roar like distant combers, like breakers on a far shore. Wing bent over her kneeling figure and she lifted her face and they kissed mouth to mouth again, their hands feeling each other's breasts. Then Janine let her head drop. She kissed Wing's breasts again. She kissed her navel. She kissed her belly. Wing let her legs slide apart and Janine reached her head in and kissed her sex.

Now it was her turn to make no pretence. She put her

head right in and poked out her tongue. She licked at Wing's vulva and felt excitement ignite along her veins as she tasted the girl, tasted her musk.

Slowly, taking her time, Wing lifted her legs, bending them at the knees. She then held herself in that position, keeping her legs wide open. She also half turned to face the audience so they could see that Janine really did put her face right in to the Chinese girl's sex. As Janine licked, so Wing's slit began to glisten. Janine sat back on her heels and inspected where she had lapped. The lights shone full between Wing's legs. The audience could see the wet gleam of fruity sexual flesh. Wing had her head back, her eyes closed. Janine reached up an inquisitive finger. Carefully, slowly, she slid it within Wing's body, letting them all see how it sank deeply up into the wet folded flesh, how Wing engulfed the little shaft. Janine moved her finger about enjoying the spongy elastic heat it could feel, then she withdrew it and half turned to the audience. She smiled a slow sly smile and sucked the finger.

She could smell the heat of their bodies now, those who watched, as a great rank animal beyond the lights, pulsating with excitement. They were in her palm, thought Janine calmly. They would respond as she demanded, as she commanded. She smiled wickedly at them again and turned back to Wing's open body. She held her hair back and dipped her face in again. She sucked hard. Wing trembled, balanced on the chair, and Janine caught at her legs, pushed them further apart and sucked as hard and as noisily as she could.

She felt the rush of nectar. It was a honeyed spring, a dewfall, a moist lush outpouring of a woman's gift.

The curtains closed and the showman began to hustle the audience out. The girls had ten minutes to rest and redress and then they must do it again.

'Janine,' whispered Wing. She looked deep into Janine's eyes.

Janine blushed faintly. She could still taste Wing's climax in her mouth.

'You are a very sweet darling,' said Wing and smiled.

Still Janine said nothing. Her own body trembled.

'Should we swap roles for the next show?' suggested Wing.

Janine nodded. She did not want the audience to see her private sexual pleasure. She did not want them to see into her body as they had seen into Wing's. But she wanted to feel Wing's head between her thighs, feel the silken brush of her hair, feel the warmth of her breath, feel her tongue. She wanted Wing's tongue within her body. She wanted to come.

She was lost, far away from her home, among alien people, afraid, hungry, lonely and frightened. She thought she would die the next night. She wanted to come with Wing at her sex. She wanted to come more than anything in the world.

She did.

They performed the show again and again, though each of them had but the one genuine sexual experience. Yet it was the repetition and the exhaustion that forged the real bond between them. They were lovers from the first showing. They loved each other by the end of the night. And as the long night drew to a close and the plaza began to empty, they crept together in an exhausted tangle. At last the showman said that they might as well stop. It wasn't worth keeping going.

'That was quite something, girls,' he said. He sat on the stage with them and counted out the money.

'Yeah,' said Wing tiredly.

'You want another go tomorrow? We could start a couple of hours earlier, make some real dough. You were classy.'

'We'll rest tomorrow,' said Wing. She could feel Janine tremble beside her.

'Of course. You wanna see the show when the Wolf guy gets his. Sure. But we could do this again sometime. Really classy. I reckon you two like it, you know? It felt genuine. Genuine. I shoulda charged more.'

He got up and began to dismantle the screen. 'Is it enough?' whispered Janine.

'I think it will be plenty,' said Wing. 'We are quite rich, sister, for a few hours' work.' She giggled weakly.

'Don't,' groaned Janine. 'I must get some sleep.'

Wing was sober. 'There is much to do, sister,' she said. 'That is, if you wish to go through with what you plan. Might you not change your mind? I do not want to lose you now.'

'Will,' said Janine.

'He is a man,' agreed Wing. 'I would save him if I could for I think he is a tender man and true under his fierce rough ways. But what use is it to him that you die for him, pretty Janine?'

'What use is going home without him?' said Janine.

'So how was your trip?' asked Fee.

'It went fine.' Rollo looked tired. Lines were etched deeply at the corners of his bright blue eyes. As he grew older, Fee thought he grew better looking, if that was possible. Age and the development of his character added a resonance to his features so that you were less dazzled by the man without and more intrigued by the man within. 'We have what we wanted, what we agreed Transflow needed. We can buck those poor quarterly figures now. We always knew it would be difficult at this stage. All the outgoings rising and the incomings still under par.'

'Full carrying capacity is a year off. Then things will take a turn for the better.'

'Maybe a year and a half, Fee. But we can manage now. And it will be a bonanza when it comes.'

After a while he thought to ask how she was, how things were going with her.

'I put in an advert about that missing disc,' she said. 'I took two slots, one morning and one afternoon for the whole week.'

'Any response?'

'About fifty,' said Fee and grinned. 'I'm checking

through them slowly but so far I have identified one genuine and all the rest are false.'

'One genuine? You mean you have tracked the disc?'

'It's the same old story, Rollo. She had it and now it's gone.'

'Anyone we know?'

'A policeman's widow out in Green Vistas, that's the west side of Town. It's funny you know, she kept swearing she sees the girl from the disc round and about.'

'What!'

'She says this girl was on the disc. She sees her from time to time but never to speak to. She sees her on the other side of the park or down a long street or just going out of a shop. The girl sometimes smiles and nods at her but she always vanishes.'

'This clunkhead had a girl on the disc?'

'So it seems.' Fee was thoughtful for a moment. 'Rollo, you know that student who had it?'

'Yes.'

'He had this glove. I mean, the woman on his disc wore gloves and she took one off on the disc and after it was over he had the glove.'

'What are you telling me, Fee?'

'I don't know what I'm telling you, Rollo. Except that it is a very odd disc.'

'I wish I'd had a chance to try it.'

Fee shivered. 'I'm glad you didn't.'

Rollo was quiet, watching her. Then he said: 'So what else is worrying you?'

'I had this crazy vidi-call.'

'Like what?'

'Have you heard of a Jace Harvon? That's the name he left. He says he has some pirate disc with me on it. I took it as a dirty call, Rollo.'

'Tell the police. Let them do some work. I don't like men making those sorts of calls to my wife. Let's burn his fingers.'

'Right.'

'So now tell me what's really worrying you.'

'Will and Janine are still missing.'

'Damn,' said Rollo softly, explosively. 'Damn, damn, damn.'

Fruity had had a very good night. These crazy dames in black had roughed him up a little but that had been kinda sexy in a way. He had been marched with the boys to some place and made to hang around a while but then things had got good. They were all bathed real nice and slow and dirty by some pretty things in flowing frocks with lots of hair, not like the guards who were, after all, kinda frightening. Then he was led to this big room which was warm and full of fancy stuff, silks and brocades and velvets and satins, and left in it without a stitch on. Then the guard-sisters had come in, still with their clothes on but then, what clothes! That big bulgy booby right out on show with tattoos on it. Wow. Then down below – Jeez! These were sisters that didn't believe in overdressing, but somehow you didn't really feel you could take liberties with them. Then they started to take liberties with him and that was the kind of action Fruity loved. He rolled like a puppy squealing with pleasure as the sisters crowded over him and all got their hands in. He stopped feeling frightened, or he learned to ignore their menacing looks, and he opened up and lay with his arms and legs spread real wide and let all those crazy ladies feel him about and play with his dongo. Then one got astride it and they bounced in the same tempo for some time till Fruity let rip and the lady got off. But they weren't done with him, hell no. In a little while he was ready for more and another lady took the heat out of his steam-pipe and if anything, Fruity enjoyed it even more.

They let him be for a little while after that, sitting and talking amongst themselves. There was a Screen in the room and some of them watched it whilst some of them played finger games or cards and one or two smoked. Then they noticed he was in an interesting condition again and one of them with much laughter came forward and Fruity served her good.

After the fourth sister Fruity began to feel a little peculiar. He had imagined his lusts were boundless but he had never had the opportunity to find out before. He was beginning to find the room a little warm and stifling and his knees felt dizzy. He rested a bit limp after the fourth sister but it wasn't long before a couple of them started to play with him. Up came his dongo and one of the sisters climbed aboard but Fruity's heart wasn't in it so much this time. Still, he did his duty, he had a reputation to live up to, and soon the sister was able to climb off him, wet, wet, wet.

Fruity fell asleep after that, at first a shallow nervous sleep but after a while a deep, more relaxed slumber. He put his thumb in his mouth and started to suck it.

He dreamed of vampires, of succubi. He wasn't so far wrong.

Janine slept till midday, huddled with Wing in a corner in one of the thousands of ruined crumbling useless buildings that made up the warren that was the city. After they woke, she and Wing went to a public bathhouse and bought a hot bath and a massage apiece to ease their tired limbs. Then they ate. Then they bought some clothes. At Janine's insistence they bought tunic and trousers for Will, and food that would keep for a while, and a couple of good stout knives, all of which they cached secretly under stones in the direction they had agreed to go if they were able to escape from the plaza. If Wing alone got free – as was to be expected, for her part would end with the falling of dark that night – Janine instructed her again how she could contact Fee, and how Fee would help her once she knew what had happened. Wing would hang around in the shadows, lost among the crowds until she knew Janine had lost the challenge. Then she was free to go.

Janine ate well. It was not a problem, this fuelling of her body. She would need her strength and she owed it to Will not to fall prey to false nerves and so weaken herself. Indeed, she felt light and limber with a kind of nervous strength that one part of her knew to be an illusion though her other parts would not admit it.

The day was a warm sunny one. Few were abroad and Wing and Janine kept to the shadows themselves, mindful of the HeliPolice and their little games. Most of the shops were shut and would not open till dusk fell. Janine needed a pharmacy and it irked her that she must wait because she was not sure if what she wanted was available down here in the squalor. These little plans she laid were the last control she might exert over her life. She wanted them to run smoothly.

At last it was time for her to have her body prepared. It was for this that they needed the money, because what she wanted was expensive. She went to the paint parlour with the faithful Wing in attendance. There Wing bound back her hair (so black, so strange) and Janine removed her clothing. She laid herself down on the couch and closed her eyes. The artist was there. It was time to begin.

He began with her right foot, working slowly up the leg, taking his time, with Wing watching to make sure that he did as they had agreed. Janine did not want to see herself until he was finished. The strangeness that had visited her the previous night was strong upon her now and she felt she floated as he applied his brush. Tomorrow, perhaps, she would wake and all this awful dream would be over. She would be in her large airy apartment with its frescoes and its balconies, its domes and minarets, the long ferny main room sunsplashed and warmly dappled green from her growing plants, the furniture low and firm and good to recline upon. It was all earth colours as she was herself, cream, terracotta, ochre and umber, with trellises to divide it into a work station, an eating area and where she slept, before great windows that overlooked the water gardens.

She was homesick.

She would never go back to her work, she thought. Not because she was preparing to die, but because it seemed empty and irrelevant now. She had learned a great deal about herself and how she felt and all of it meant that she could not go on earning an honest living telling other people how to make love. Not when she hardly knew herself. Not when she was frightened.

The artist was at her thigh; her right leg must be complete. Indeed, he now swapped to her left leg. Complete, that is, from the top. She would have to roll over and be done all over again on her back side. It must be total. The illusion must be total.

The brush was very cool on her skin and pleasant. As the paint dried it shrank very slightly, but it had a certain plasticity and it stretched again and eased. When the second leg was finished on its upper surface, he sprayed her first leg to fix it. Certain areas within the pattern were painted with a resist which he would peel off at the end, so that her skin could breathe. At the finish she would be coated with what appeared to be a continuous layer of paint, but it would be strong and flexible, durable over days rather than hours, and it was because of this latter quality that Janine hoped it would be able to withstand rough treatment.

She was rolled over and he painted the backs of both her legs. He continued on up over the mounds of her buttocks, with Wing holding them apart so that he could work a little within the cleft. Janine didn't mind. She was somewhere else, somewhere far away, probably watching only she did not want to see until the pattern was finished.

After a while her back was finished, and her neck. He would leave her arms till later. Now he made her roll over again after he had fixed her back and allowed it to set. He began to paint her belly.

About this time Janine fell asleep, or into a trance. She became aware again as he decorated her breasts, first one and then the other, which she found very pleasant.

Wing saw her smile. 'Do you want to know how you look?' she asked.

'No, no,' whispered Janine. She could feel the annoyance in the artist as the spell was momentarily broken.

186

She could wait. It was what he wanted, also. The whole was never the mere sum of the parts, nor ever has been. She would wait.

The artist painted her neck, her shoulders, her arms. He applied his patches of resist. He applied his paints in their various colours. He applied the fixative coating and allowed it to set. He peeled the little areas free that would allow her skin to breathe, that would keep her alive.

He painted her face, her ears. Then he stood back.

'It's not complete,' said Janine dreamily. She could hear Wing gasping though Wing thought she made no noise and all her amazement was contained within herself.

'The soles of your feet are clear,' said the artist. He wiped his hands and looked at his work.

'I do not mean the soles of my feet,' said Janine and opened her eyes from her long rest and looked at him.

He was young with wild black eyes and an angry sulky mouth. His talent overpowered him and it hurt him to see what he had created because it drained him and he would be exhausted for days after this work.

'I didn't know that was included,' he said.

'You do now.' Janine's soft blue eyes had become hard somewhere along her travels and his dropped before her blazing look. She opened her legs and he took up his brushes again. He moved the lamp so that he could see the clearer. Once his wet brush tip touched Janine, his trembling ceased and the sureness flowed through his arm like electricity. He painted the country of her sex with short sure strokes so that the little scene grew, the miniature world. Now Janine had the Hanging Gardens of Babylon between her thighs. The pattern was complete.

Very slowly she stood up, easing herself from the table. Wing fell back from her, afraid and captivated at one and the same time. The artist tilted his head to one side and put his chin in his hand. He looked her up and down.

Abruptly he burst into tears. 'I want to be alone,' Janine said sternly and Wing took the tearful man away and took out the money they had promised him for his work. Janine went over to the mirrors and looked at herself slowly, all over, front and back and sideways. She began to smile a fierce quiet smile. She picked up a hand mirror and arranged the light so it was reflected and she looked between her legs at what he had done last.

Yes, she was very pleased. The web closed over her body and she felt charged up, ready for anything. Ready for the challenge. She reached for the bodysuit she had bought that day and slid her magnificence into it. Then she swung a cloak about her shoulders and fastened it with a gilt clasp. She put on the silk mask she had and drew up the hood of her cloak. Nothing showed, nothing of what the artist had done. She was all dark and soft save for the hard glitter of her eyes within the black shadow of the hood. She was faceless, bodyless. So she would be until the challenge.

Will found what had happened to him really quite funny. He had mechanisms available for dealing with excessive pain and they were in full force now because for the better part of eighteen hours he had been on his feet with his arms held up apart, manacled at each wrist with the bar across his shoulders. During the heat of the day he had been allowed to sit down for a while and he had slept then, but now as the evening approached he was prodded back onto his feet. Something fairly nasty was happening to his muscles and the discomfort would be exquisite if he allowed it to bother him, but most of the time he caused himself to be spaced out, high on his own body chemistry and beyond the mortifications of his flesh.

He had rather taken to the Amazenes. Their life had a certain logic to it that he found admirable, even if he was to be the loser by it. Anyone who found a meaning to life in these crazy days was to be congratulated and he didn't see that they were unnecessarily bloodthirsty. They had their code and he had broken it.

He liked their personal courage. He admired their organisation and their discipline and since he had once captained a pirate band, he knew that loyalty had to be earned and could never be taken for granted.

Their rule had an aesthetic appeal also. It was hard but it allowed for plenty of fun. One had to be amazed at women who could take men prisoner and then enjoy them sexually. He had performed willingly enough for them because of what was in it for him and presumably any other male captive, that is the getting together with a fierce and beautiful woman. His lady had been good, very good. She was salty, strong and innovative. It had been very satisfying to sink his hot flesh within her and feel her melt under his embrace. There were some things a woman couldn't do for herself and he, Will, enjoyed helping out. But he couldn't become a pet, no way, not even to save his life. That his future was to be the permanent inmate of a cage, a member of a harem, a plaything of the warrior maidens was simply beyond his capabilities. He would rather die than be so demeaned.

He found time to wish he wasn't so thirsty. He pushed the desire for a drink away and with his lids drooping heavily over his eyes allowed his thoughts to wander in the green places of his life. He wasn't so old but he felt he had outlived his life and times. It wasn't so bad to go in this extraordinary way. By the gathering activity in the plaza as the sun fell low in the sky, he was going with a bang. He would make a lot of people happy that night.

His guards lolled sleepily with their weapons slack on the steps to either side of him. He could hardly escape and they did not fear a rescue attempt. They would wake up fast enough if anyone approached with weapons at the ready, but it was hardly to be expected. The folk of the city were looking forward to their entertainment and would not want it spoiled.

He didn't see when the cloaked figure with the hood

189

up over its head approached carrying a basket over one arm. He didn't see when it knelt and spoke briefly with one of the guards who waved the figure indolently on. The cloaked one came up to Will and stood before his shambling exhausted body. He became aware of her, at least he thought it was a her by the height and the seeming slimness under the cloak, and wondered dully if she had come to taunt him.

She bent over her basket and lifted up a bowl into which she emptied water from a gourd. She took a sponge and reached up and bathed his lips.

It was the best liquid Will had ever tasted. The cool freshness at his mouth told him how parched he was and he began to suck on the sponge. She refilled it with water and gave it to him again. She did this again and again till he felt his thirst diminish and lose its fierceness.

Now she began to sponge his grimy face, washing the dust and the sweat from it. She cleansed his neck and his chest and it felt very very good. He tried to see the face of the charitable one but the cloak made a pool of black that his aching eyes could not penetrate. Once or twice he caught the glitter of eyes and he wondered if she was real, if she was alive.

The sun was a low blood-red disc that flooded his body with a dim crimson radiance and made the figure of the one that served him blacker than ever. His skin absorbed the water and came alive again. His shoulders and arms began to hurt and his leg muscles were a hot agony but he wouldn't have had her stop, not for anything.

She bathed his chest and quite absorbed in her self-appointed task she went on down and washed his belly. He wore only a bit of rag about his hips. Now she washed his legs and they trembled and shook.

His pain, his near future, the bloody sun, the silent witch at his body began to have a curious effect on Will. Absolutely against his will he found his cock hardening and a harsh lusty desire filling him. It brought relief with it because it overrode his aching muscles. My swansong, he thought dizzily, and it was the supreme jest. His body was having the last laugh. He had kidded himself he had the mastery of it but now it was getting its own back.

The grubby rag moved. The hooded figure was bent before him, the guards idle and hardly bothering with the mad-woman. The witch stopped what she was doing and with a swift gentle movement she tweeked the rag away. Her own body was between Will and the rest of the world. She was close up against him and his urgent cock was secret between them.

He could not see into the hood. Its peak touched his belly. He felt his hair stand on end and his eyes came fully open, feeling as though they bulged.

Dear Jesus God, she was sucking him! Will's eyes clamped shut and power surged through his body. Her mouth was wicked and sweet and Will sent up prayers of thankfulness. Life had its ironies, even as death approached.

He felt her hand come up and take the stem of his cock. She worked him rapidly, sucking fiercely and taking the wild honey of his manhood with sure and knowing strokes. He came with merciful ease for he would not have been able to have strength for long, and now she was twisting a fresh cloth about him, hiding him, giving him his modesty again.

She bent low at his feet and washed them, kneeling to kiss them when she had done so. Will felt his heart melt with love for her. That there was this in the world!

She stood up.

'My dear,' he said, his voice a little-cracked with disuse. She laid a finger on his lips, bidding him to silence, and then with a quick soft gesture she drew her finger round his lips. It was a tenderness. Now she lifted a cup and he drank the sweet water, a little running down from the sides of his mouth.

'Thank you,' he said, his eyes and mouth and voice soft.

191

At last she spoke. 'Be prepared,' she whispered. Then she gathered her basket, and was gone.

Shadows filled the square, oozing from under broken walls, from behind gap-toothed buildings, sliding up from the drains and sewers and vacant secret places of the dying city, shadows that by day shrank and lived under stones with the slimy things of the world but by night grew and challenged the dying day till the fading light was all swallowed up and gone. With the shadows came the people of the city, out for a good time. The Amazenes themselves arrived in force and Will's guards stopped their lounging and stood to attention either side of him.

They set up huge trestles and lit fires. Animals were spitted and turned over these fires, and slowly the smell of roasting meat began to hover in the air. Barrels were broached and there was beer and wine for everyone. Booths were set up, minstrels began playing, and the crowds grew thicker and thicker. Will watched it all and thought how in other circumstances he could have enjoyed the proceedings himself.

He didn't know whether to be glad or sorry for his witch-lady. He was more alert, more alive thanks to her, but that was not in itself necessarily a good thing. He would be better being numb as the night wore on. His loins felt good, clean and lively, and he knew that had he met her sooner, felt her sooner, when he still had some say in his own fate, he would not have let her go.

A heavy rumbling filled the square, more deafening than the excited roar of the happy and increasingly drunken crowd. They fell back and quietened. Will looked to see what was going on and saw with a sick lurch of horror that a huge tank was being rolled into the arena before him. Teams of Amazenes strained to tow it into position. At last they were satisfied and they fell back. It was the snake tank. In it the mambas writhed, ready for their little present. For a moment Will's self-defences trembled and he felt the real terror of the situation flow over him. His knees turned watery

192

and he opened his mouth to cry out at the injustice of it, of everything. It was the memory of the witch-lady that restored him, that brought back his courage.

Over the twangings and tinny sounds of the wandering bands of players, an insistent rhythm began to make itself felt. It was the beating of drums. They were quiet at first, but they gained in intensity and volume, and the crowd began to draw back and feel the lick of fear, the lick of sacrifice that was in the air. The foretaste of death. The Amazenes began to look entranced and vivid. They would take on a little of the essence of their god-queen tonight and be raised above the common clay as a result. The drums beat in their blood.

Now the priestess and captain came forward in her ceremonial robes beneath which she was naked but for her holy *caffada*. She sat herself on her prepared seat and was statue still to watch over the proceedings. It was good that the people enjoyed themselves. They might be foolish and heretical, but this time was for them to see the Amazenes at their height and know that queens walked in their midst. And now at last it was time to bring the prisoner forward, tell all the world of his guilt and let him meet his due punishment. She raised her hand and made the sign. On either side of Will the guards stepped smartly forward and each taking one arm they marched him forward into the square.

The crowd surged. It could taste blood. It roared its approval.

Jace stared at his Screen and couldn't believe it. He was frozen immobile. Eventually he was able to halt the transmission and run back and replay the vital part. Yes, it said precisely what he thought it had said, though the words were unbelievable. His Connet was on the line. His bubble house was on the line. His business was on the line. He had raised all the credit he could and bought massively in water stock, and now they were dropping in price. They were dropping the price! They couldn't. They must be mad. No one ever dropped the price of anything except when developing technology sharply dropped production costs and that didn't apply here.

He switched on his personal computer and did some rough calculations. If the stock price held level he would be financially embarrassed for a while but he could ride it out. But if the stock price dropped, as it was bound to do now, he would find that he could not meet his obligations. Unable to repay the money he had raised, plus interest, he would lose his car or his house or his business. Or all three. He would have to move out of the Zoo and become someone's employee.

With trembling fingers Jace worked out the series of price levels that would mark each stage of his personal catastrophe. He would know in an hour or so how far down the share price would go, as the news flew round the world. It would bottom and then bounce up a few points and then settle for the foreseeable future. That would be his foreseeable future and Jace wasn't sure he could stand it.

He flipped the Screen back onto its current transmission mode. There would be financial reports as time wore on. A large knock-on effect would be generated as industries dependent on the water supply became more buoyant. Damn, that was a ghastly pun and quite inappropriate. But though other industries would improve their financial standing, no one, but no one would invest in water stock. Jace gnawed his nails and began to roam up and down his room.

Fee and Rollo Cambridge watched the plummeting of their holdings with more cheer. They were not in hock and could easily ride out the low price. They might even buy a little in a few weeks.

Fee laughed. 'I don't know how you do it,' she said. 'This is perfect for TransFlow but I don't see the advantage to the other members of the cartel.'

'It's the same really only TransFlow needs it more. This will turn eyes off us and over the next couple of years we will get peace from the market. Meanwhile cheap water will make everyone use more of it. Industry will be less efficient. Consumers will waste more, be more generous with it because it is now fixed in their minds as a cheap commodity. By the time we put the price right up in five years' time, they will all have the habit of far greater usage. It will take everyone another ten years to relearn habits of economy and by then, my sweet Fee, we won't be caring very much. We'll have our pile and be wanting to move out of the limelight a little. I intend to move into semiretirement then, you know. I warn you.'

'Nuts,' said Fee amiably. 'You've just halved our fortune.'

'On paper, my darling. I don't think you'll feel the lack of anything.'

Fee turned luminous eyes on him. 'Not as long as you keep up your health and strength,' she murmured. She smiled. 'Let's pass some time, honey. Yes?'

'Yes,' said Rollo, but he kept one eye on the Screen to see just how far down the stock would go.

The door buzzed and Jace's servant went to attend to it. He came through to Jace with the visitor accompanying him. Jace saw a police captain in his room and his mind could hardly focus. What did the man want? Why had his servant brought him in without consulting Jace as to its convenience? Didn't he realise Jace's world had ruptured? How dare he interrupt at this particular time?

'Jace Harvon?'

'Yeah. What is this? Can't it wait? I'm busy right now.' Jace heard his own voice, hoarse and desperate. Yet he couldn't control it.

'I am Captain Pheek MacAvoy, Mr Harvon. I am afraid I am calling over a very serious matter.'

'What are you talking about?'

'We have received a complaint, Mr Harvon, from a lady who says you made her a call that could be described as loose, libidinous and of a sexually offensive nature. Have you anything to say?'

Jace achieved a noise like 'gaa', but really his mouth just hung open, his eyes goggling whilst he stared at the captain like a fish.

'The call was left on her answertape. She does not say you spoke directly to her and she did not call you back. Are you in the habit of doing this, Mr Harvon?'

'I don't know what you are talking about,' exploded Jace, able to command speech at last. Blessedly he forgot his financial ruin for a moment.

'You left your name and your number, Mr Harvon. I don't know what you expected her to do.'

'Who? Who is this crazy dame? Is she some old ugly bitch having hallucinations that men want her all the time?'

'No,' said the Captain and smiled sourly. 'She certainly isn't that. I must tell you that you are forbidden to contact Ms Fiona Cambridge in any shape or form, by letter, by fax, by vidicom or in person or by any electronic means or through a third party and if you do so you will be in breach of order no. 543/81903a given on this day and date. Do you understand?'

'Fee Cambridge?'

'And you are to present yourself at Zoo Central Police Headquarters tomorrow morning at ten a.m. sharp, and your lawyer should accompany you as you may be charged with an offence under the Malicious Communications Act. Do you understand, Mr Harvon?' He touched his breast pocket. 'This communication is being recorded.'

'This is nonsense,' shouted Jace. 'You've got it all wrong. Sure I contacted Fee Cambridge. I found this illegal VR disc with her on it. I've broken no law.'

'I think you had better hand the disc over, in that case. I'm sure the sooner we clear this matter up, the better, Mr Harvon.'

Jace glared at him and stumbled from the room. His servant was standing there all the time, grinning like an idiot. This was monstrous, coming on top of the evening's calamity. He could hardly give it the attention it

196

deserved, though at any other time he would have been crapping his pants because an offence of this nature was a hell of a serious thing and if that bitch pursued him, she could make it real hard for him. She would have the police in her pocket, of course. No doubt she and her high-roller husband gave generously to them. Jace went into his bedroom and over to beside his bed.

The disc wasn't there.

Impatiently he checked round the room. His blood pressure must be soaring because he was getting angrier and angrier and now the damned Captain had followed him and was lounging in the doorway, watching.

'I must've left it in the sitting room,' growled Jace. He went through with the Captain an ominous shadow and searched round the room. It was very large and on all different levels with huge white polyplastic alcoves.

He couldn't find it.

'Perhaps your man knows where it is,' said the Captain suavely.

Jace turned like an embattled turkey cock and glared at his employee. The man shrugged with helpless satisfaction. 'I ain't seen no special VR disc, sir. Your collection is where it belongs.'

Jace had already checked his rows of stored entertainment discs. The rogue was not there. He began to feel very cold.

He made an enormous effort to be calm. 'I can't lay my hands on it right now,' he said in markedly less belligerent tones to the Captain. 'It's here somewhere. I'm all het up and I can't remember where I left it.'

'You have all night to look,' said the Captain. Jace's man grinned. 'But be sure you have it in the morning, Mr Harvon. I guess it's kinda important to your case.' He gave Jace a straight look that was all condemnation and had himself shown out.

Jace sat in his favourite chair. His brain roared and he had to formulate words one at a time very carefully to achieve coherent thought. Well, he wouldn't be charged. He had the disc somewhere and could prove he was reporting a felony, not committing one. He had been a bit naughty going to Fee direct and obviously she hadn't liked that, the bitch, but they could hardly say he was making a loose, libidinous and ... what the hell was it the Captain had said? Jace shook his head. It hurt. His ears roared. If he called an attorney he sure as hell wouldn't be able to pay him. He giggled. He glanced back at the Screen and saw that the stock had dropped another few points. He got up and went to find the disc.

It took him an hour. The damned thing wasn't where he had left it, he was sure. He had searched high and low, it was his evidence of innocence, after all, and he had eventually found it back in the pocket of his jacket, only the pocket had a hole in it and if he had worn it, the disc might have slipped out and been lost. For a while Jace sat holding it. It had a very pleasurable feel in the hand but it had gotten him into trouble and he would be glad to turn it over the following day to the police. He couldn't think how the hell it had gotten into his jacket pocket.

He went back to look at the Screen. After ten minutes or so they went over again to the financial news and he saw the stock had fallen still further.

Three-quarters of an hour ago, he had lost his Connet. Just before the Captain called, he had known his bubble house would go and he would be exiled from the Zoo. Now he saw he would have to sell his business to meet his obligations.

He was nothing. He was nobody. He was poor. On top of everything else the police thought he made dirty vidi calls too. Jace got stiffly to his feet and made himself a big fat drink and poured the whole lot down his throat. It did nothing for him. He poured himself a second. Then it occurred to him that as a sour jest and a way of getting back at that bitch the Cambridge woman he would access the disc again and have her abase herself to him. He would be handing it over in the morning and he would demand a full apology for the smear cast on his good name. He went into his private VR booth and slid his hand up the woman's silky thigh. It was the sensation he adored above all others, cool nylon, warm flesh, the softest brush of a woman's secret hair and the moist warmth of her private place waiting for him to invade it.

She said: 'Mr Harvon?'

'Uh huh.'

'I have this friend who is aching to meet you.'

'That right, honey-chile?' His fingers teased her hair. They were at a benefit lunch and had paid plenty for their seats but all the proceeds were for charity. He should not have been going up her skirt but she was so pretty and so salaciously inviting sitting there beside him that he couldn't resist.

A woman opposite, ugly and virtuous-looking, leaned across to Jace. 'Mr Harvon, you are a respected member of the community, and an important man.'

'How can I help you, ma'am?' said Jace benignly, respectably. He touched his new-found lady-friend's clitoris and she jumped slightly. He wanted to smell his fingers.

'Don't you think it is time some of us older leaders of society drew the line? Stopped all this loose behaviour and overtly sexual clothing? Haven't things gone too far for us to call ourselves members of a decent society, Mr Harvon? What do you think?'

Jace pinched the woman's clitoris and then slid a finger into her. She drooped sideways for a moment and her thighs came wider apart. His other hand lay fat and meaty-red on the white cloth. He used it to take a swig of his champagne. Damned effeminate drink, fit for women and children. He could go for some beer right now.

'I think you are right,' he said earnestly. 'Women expose themselves too much. Why, just a few years ago they went around with their nipples on show. That's not right, fashion or no fashion.'

The old lady gave a crow of delight. 'It is so nice to meet a man with a sense of propriety, of decency,' she said. Jace rolled his finger around in its warm glove and smiled. 'The Zoo has a bad name,' said the woman. 'It needs cleaning up.'

Jace's companion moved her hand onto Jace's lap and began to fiddle with his trouser fastening. He leaned forward even further so that the man in the next seat along to him shouldn't notice what was going on.

'I was thinking of starting a society,' said the old nagbag over the table. 'A moral reform society to bring decent modest manners back into public acceptance.'

'That's a very good idea,' enthused Jace. His friend had his trousers open and he felt her nails scrape along his shaft. It leapt up and he knew that he couldn't get it back inside his clothing now, no matter how hard he tried.

'Would I be able to count on you as one of the founder members, Mr Harvon? It would be quite a feather in my cap.' She smiled winningly. Her diamonds were fabulous.

Jace felt his foreskin being drawn back. He dropped his napkin in his lap for added protection. He got his hand out of his friend's skirt because he was having trouble now keeping his mind on the conversation he was holding.

'Who else has expressed an interest, Mrs Van Mosterly?' he said. He could feel himself starting to perspire. His cock was being squeezed and gently pulled and every so often her nails would brush against his balls.

Mrs V. M. began to list a few prominent names. Jace felt his cock being worked in time to the syllables uttered at him. He groaned slightly and leaned his belly against the table edge.

'A touch of indigestion?' The old dear was needle sharp. 'Let me offer you a jujube.'

'I've dropped my napkin,' announced Jace's friend and she slipped from her chair and ducked under the table.

Jace jumped and felt his face suffuse. She had him in her mouth. The president was standing up ready to make his after-dinner speech. People began politely to clap and Jace felt his cock sucked hard and then released.

Now she was back, a little red-faced herself but grinning wickedly at the same time. Her hand crept over his wet tumescent member and stroked it whilst the president launched himself into a description of the worthiness of their cause and the generosity of its patrons here present upon this occasion. Jace swallowed more champagne and had it refilled by a waiter. He was close to coming now and glad attention was turned away from him.

'I've got a present for a good boy,' murmured his companion in his ear.

'I've got one for you,' whispered Jace. His cock was big and almost there.

'But you'll have to find it, sweetie.'

'It's hidden?'

'Guess where. You have to dig it out.'

'I reckon I can do that. Buried treasure, huh?'

'Buried where only you can find it.' Her mouth was practically against his ear as she pretended to strain to hear what the president said.

Jace came. Quickly she closed her napkin over his spurt of foam so his trousers would not be stained. Jace shut his eyes as he pumped into her hand and felt the blessed release and warm comfort flood through him. He licked his lips and sighed. His friend mopped gently and then withdrew her hand and the napkin. Jace reached down and fixed his trousers. He was having a good time.

The president finished and they all clapped. 'What about your friend?' asked Jace.

'She's very like me. Has the same tastes. I told her about you and she's just dying to meet you.'

Jace slid his hand back up her skirt and worked it so that he penetrated her again. He pushed hard and saw her veil her eyes with pleasure. He hadn't known her when they sat down side by side at the commencement of the meal. She had begun their conversation by brushing across the front of his trousers and then inviting his response.

'How could you tell her about me when you don't know nothing about me?'

'But I do. You see, until my marriage I used to work in a feelie bar. That's something I keep secret now because you know how people are, so damned snobbish. But I knew you, Jace Harvon, and it was delicious. I've always wanted to meet you again. Of course, I am respectable now.' Here she broke off and wriggled on his finger so he felt her pussy all over his hand, wet and eager. He felt something hard and pushed to hook at it.

'I think you have found my treasure,' she whispered. He felt her bear down on him and he felt the little hard object move lower. He finally got a hold of it and worked it free of her lovely sticky clinging intimate flesh.

He looked at it, keeping it below the level of the table, rubbing it with his thumb. 'A pearl?' he said, wonderingly. It was like solidified cream, warm and smooth with a silken lustre.

'My husband is a very rich man but I like you, Mr Harvon. You were good to me when I was a poor feelie waitress. Now I want to be good to you in return. So does my friend. She's very like me, Mr Harvon. Generous, too. She gets bored, you see.'

Jace lifted the jewel and smelled his hand. It was divine. He smiled at his companion and felt his bones relax. He felt genial, rich, sexy, important.

'So I can count on you as a founder member,' insisted the harpy from over the table.

'Sure you can,' said Jace. 'I'm all for moral reform. We need to clean things up in the Zoo, it's all too dirty. No one knows where the limits are any more.'

'I so agree,' said his companion. 'Can you put me down, too, Mrs Van Mosterly? We need to keep things decent.'

The red square was flashing and with the sliding horror of those who see their own death before them, Jace found that he was back in an ugly reality. For a few dreadful moments he coped with the heartstrain of the rupture of the two worlds. Then the details began to sort themselves out in his mind. He was financially ruined. Within a couple of weeks he would have to sell up everything. On the following day he had the sordid business of handing over the disc to prove that Fee Cambridge was on it and he hadn't made a dirty vidicom call. That was a pity. It was a hot disc, like none he'd ever used, though it hurt so damn much when he came out of it he could hardly breathe to begin with.

Like ice, the trickle ran down his spine and for the first time in his life Jace knew real fear.

The disc. Fee Cambridge. It had been different.

He ejected it from the slot in the booth and examined it. He hadn't put the wrong disc in. It was the rogue, all right, smeary markings and all. His hand began to tremble. He hadn't made Fee up. She had been on the disc. So where was she this time?

Tears began to fall down Jace's cheeks. He cursed fluently and terribly. He called maledictions down upon Fee's head, upon the heads of the makers of the disc. Was there more than one program on it? He couldn't see it, he couldn't see how you accessed different programs. What if the police didn't examine it properly? He would need a lawyer after all.

He pulled himself together and his mind hardened and came under control again. He felt very cold. He put the disc in his pocket and poured himself another drink, swallowing it down greedily.

His thoughts became crystal clear. This disc thing would sort itself out but his financial situation would not. Much of what he had taken for granted in his life was about to come to an end. He would not be able to afford the very select and interesting brothels he had patronised so successfully over the years. He would not be able to afford the casual generosity that made him feel such a big man when he went to feelie bars. To get a woman he would be reduced to the laborious but cheap business of courting them, winning their favour, and he didn't like that, not one little bit.

He would have to learn to do without women in his Connet. It was a good place to enjoy what two adults could get up to, bodysynching at three hundred plus miles per hour. Jace made a fresh drink and let his mind grimly catalogue all his expensive pleasures.

Perhaps he should take advantage of some of them whilst he still had them available. He could go to a brothel. He could take his Connet out. It would be nice to scythe the skies one last time. Maybe he would power over to the ocean and go watch the waves for a while. Walk out into them, maybe. Jace poured himself yet another drink and appreciated it thoroughly as it went down his throat.

Hey, that wasn't such a bad idea. Wouldn't a glorious end be better than long years of obscurity?

Jace had another drink. He put the disc on his table and walked to his door. At the door he stopped and feeling irritated he went back and picked up the disc. He hadn't meant to do that. He wanted it with him. He had thought it was in his pocket.

This time he held it firmly as he went to the door and released it. He went straight down into his hangar. The silver gleam of his powertube was friendly and reassuring. Connets were so damn beautiful. Jace let himself in and sighed at the comfort and luxury of the interior. He started up the turbines and programmed the computer. His fingers hesitated. The idea that had been coalescing quietly in his mind all this time came to him in its full naked meaning. Slowly he reprogrammed. The computer flashed up a query as it was supposed to do when it was given an unusual order but Jace confirmed it. He pressed the enter button and the giant car lifted on its airpads and began to float up the ramp until it reached the highway access point. Jace had programmed maximum speed and the shock of take-off knocked him back in his seat. The car shot onto the highway and screamed, a silver streak, out into the night.

Chapter Seven

'*I* challenge,' called a clear voice, clear above the noise and the roar of the rabble and the crackle of the bonfires and the spit of the grease on the roasting meat and the drunken belches and the squeal of eager people scenting death.

The silence rolled slow and shocked over the fuddled crowd.

The priestess stood uncertainly, not sure she had heard right. She held a mamba by its neck and those closest could see its tongue flicker. She was about to apply it to the breast of the man they called Wolf. He stood silent, his arms helplessly outstretched, sweat pouring in greasy streams down his chest and from his brow.

'I challenge,' called the cloaked one. 'In the name of the god-queen I say this man is pardoned and his crime a light thing and he is in no wise to die in this manner.'

The priestess lowered the snake uncertainly. Its body curled in loving embrace about her forearm.

'Come forward,' she called. Her followers hissed and spat in the dust to show their disapproval.

The cloaked and hooded figure came forward, all black, not very tall. Will lifted his aching head and tried to focus his eyes. He was having trouble keeping upright.

The priestess began to smile. 'Those who challenge must fight,' she said.

Janine opened her cloak and let it fall to the ground. The crowd hissed loudly and there were faint screams.

She was quite naked, her hair tightly bound. Her entire skin surface lived in glowing colour, iridescent with turquoise, emerald, sapphire, crimson, gold and brilliant silver. Her skin was all snake, all snakes, living and winding up her limbs in a glorious brilliance of colour that cascaded into the eyes of the beholders and dazzled them. She was a snake, a snake in human form, and as the firelight flickered so the snakes on her body moved and cavorted in their eagerness to fight.

'I challenge,' said Janine softly but all heard her. 'I speak in the name of the god-queen who has sent me to do this task. She is angry with her people and will rain fire from the sky if they continue to disobey her.'

There was an unhappy rustle among the Amazenes. The priestess heard it and the leader in her knew instantly her leadership wavered, was under threat. She dropped the mamba she held back in the snake tank.

'So be it,' she said matter-of-factly. She shrugged her own cloak off and was naked but for her *caffada*. She moved towards Janine.

For the first time since her painting, Janine knew fear. The challenge was absurd. She couldn't beat the women in front of her. She hardly knew what she had been saying. The words came into her mouth as though she were an actress speaking her lines.

Now the time had come to deliver. Janine shrugged mentally. She would fight to extinction and hoped that Will knew why she did it, what she meant by it, if that could help him in his last moments. She hoped Wing was free and clear and would make a successful life for herself in the Town.

The Amazene hit her. Janine fell back gasping. The Amazene followed up on her blow and punched Janine in the breast. Janine rallied a little and tried to hit back but the blow was effortlessly blocked by the warrior maiden before her. The Amazene grinned as she took Janine's measure and closed to grapple. They fell to the ground.

Words blazed uselessly in Janine's mind. She wanted to make a better showing, not be so feeble. Anger helped her and she rolled clear and went into a crouch. She remembered the ballet she had learned and kicked high with one foot, turning on the other and was lucky enough to strike the Amazene in the face. The woman fell back in slight surprise, but she knew her opponent's weakness now and prepared to come in and finish the business.

The disc slid into Janine's mind. This was all for a damned VR disc. They were all going to die for it, she and Will, all who mattered to her. The disc had led them into this. It ought to save her now.

The Amazene lifted a hand and turned it into a blade. She struck for Janine's windpipe and missed, Janine felt her shoulder go numb and staggered back. The Amazene pressed forward to strike again. Janine lifted a feeble arm. This was it. Oblivion crooked a dark finger and beckoned in cold welcome.

The crowd screamed. It was a scream of real fear. The Amazene hesitated, her hand uplifted, but the blow never fell. Her head turned and across the night sky they all saw the huge meteor blazing with fire and showers of sparks. It was incredibly low, incredibly close. The crowd fell to its knees. They felt the backwash of heat and in its train came the thunderous roar of the split air, giant claps of sound that made the ground tremble.

The meteor soared over them, and behind the buildings a couple of hundred yards away it hit the ground. Flame erupted and split the night. The noise was terrific. A huge dust cloud full of bits of masonry flew into the air and crashed around them. Janine hit the Amazene who stumbled, her eyes wide and terrified. Janine hit her again and the woman fell to the ground. A large piece of rotten cornice fell out of the sky and hit her a glancing blow. She lay still. Her breasts moved up and down, the only sign she was still alive.

Helibuzzes, FireCopters and AirAmbulances buzzed overhead. For ten minutes there was pandemonium, then things began to quieten down.

Janine stepped forward and spoke directly to Will's guards. 'I claim the prisoner,' she said. 'He is mine.'

The guards looked at each other uncertainly.

'Unchain him,' said Janine. Now they moved to obey her. Will's wrist manacles were removed. His arms stayed stuck out awkwardly. He could not control them.

'The god-queen is very angry, as you can see,' said Janine coldly. 'I will now take him away.'

Behind Janine the priestess clambered slowly to her feet. She rubbed her head where the stone had struck her. 'The cup,' she croaked. 'First the cup.'

'So be it,' said Janine. 'But I will give it.'

They pushed Will forward, making his arms hang at his sides again, until he was more central in the plaza and all could see him. A religious quiet had fallen on the crowd who were rapidly coming to respect the power of the Amazene god-queen. They had never seen anything like the events of the night. The cup was brought forward, a large silver chalice, and Janine took it. Will was forced to his knees. His eyes were blind and blank. He hardly seemed to understand what was happening.

Janine had one hand between her thighs. She crouched for a moment so that her face was more on a level with Will's. She held the cup carefully. She knew that spilling it would get her nowhere. They would have more.

'It's poison,' she muttered. 'Don't drink.' She got back on her feet standing over the kneeling Will. She put her free hand over his mouth. The touch of him, alive, almost free, was like electricity surging up her arm. He was warm. She was touching him. He had to survive. She must see this through.

Her hand, musk-scented, caressed his mouth. His lips were slightly parted. She held up the cup of venom with the other hand and began to chant. She needed a little time.

'Now may the god-queen make the miracle complete,' she intoned. 'All have seen the sky rain fire. All have seen the challenge completed. Now is the final step. Let the god-queen know peace as her will is done. Let her people tremble and obey. Let her favour shine out once more.'

She bent over Will trying not to sob. Gently she put the cup to his lips. The priestess was close, watching. Janine tilted the cup and its evil contents ran into Will's open mouth. Janine's hand was over his nose, lightly, not preventing him from breathing.

She held up the cup triumphantly. In front of them all she inverted it and they saw it was empty. Her other hand was busy over Will's mouth and then she drew it away. His wide dark exhausted bewildered face was turned blindly up so the firelight flickered across its lean planes.

His throat worked. The priestess sighed.

'Let the drums sound,' whispered Janine but the priestess heard and made a signal and the drumbeat began, ominous, slow, like the tolling of the passing bell, each stroke a year in the life of the one that has died. Only Will was not dead. He went on kneeling, his arms slack at his sides, swaying slightly.

'Stand up, Wolf,' said Janine in a relaxed voice. 'Show you live and are now free. The god-queen forgives your heresy as unintentional and you are punished enough. Stand up and go from this place.'

He did it. Janine felt tears on her cheeks as the effort it took communicated itself to her, but he did it. Through his confusion and his pain he heard the thread of sense that would set him free, and he played his part in the charade perfectly.

Janine turned to the priestess. 'The challenge was fairly won. The cup was fairly given. I claim the prisoner's freedom.'

'So be it,' said the Amazene bitterly. 'May the god-queen continue to protect you.'

Janine did not know whether to construe this as a threat or a blessing, but she took Will by the arm and when this failed to move him she put her hand in his back, and she propelled him from the square. The crowd split like the Red Sea before Moses and Janine walked through the gap, praying Will would not fall down.

They were out of the city. They were free.

The night was old, star-thick, tired. The three of them shambled uncertainly in the open countryside. None of them knew it. None of them had any experience of it. It was forbidden to Town and Zoo-folk. City-folk despised it. They were three babes in the countryside, innocent and ignorant.

It was noisy. Distantly a lion roared. Insects screamed in permanent indignation. A few birds had beaten the coming dawn and trilled and fluted that this particular piece of territory was mine, mine, mine.

They stopped whilst Wing oriented herself, searching for the place she was trying to lead them to. Janine gave Will more wine and some water, and food but he could not take the food. She wished she could see him properly. He needed to be in hospital. She did not want to save him by killing him. He no longer spoke and sat silent, his great chest heaving, whilst the girls anxiously conferred.

Behind them, in the west, the sky was dark and ominously blue, deep velvet blue that sucked light into it and absorbed it and gave nothing back. Above them it was infinitely high, a pure cold arc of blazing colour, a vault that was pierced only by the ringing idiocy of one lone blackbird. Before them it was the gentle colour of a duck's egg, blue, green, softly welcoming. They got to their feet and went on.

'There,' shouted Wing. 'We have arrived.'

The plain was broken by an old fault that made a cliff which ran for several miles. At several places water drained through this cliff onto the lower land, and at one of these places in times past the people had built a pleasure-bath, for not only did the cold clean water drain down through it, but a hot mineral spring bubbled up. Years ago Wing had visited this place and now she led her companions to it.

Will knew nothing any more of what they did. They guided the sick man into the ruined building. Janine sat with him whilst Wing cut grass with her machete. With her harvest they made a thick mattress which they covered with their cloaks. They laid Will down on this rough and ready bed and covered him. They washed themselves a little and they ate. Then they both laid themselves down one either side of Will, and curling their bodies and their bodily warmth against him, they slept. All three of them slept. The sun came up, the daytime insects shrilled, the lion slept and lionesses hunted, the herds moved and grazed and moved on and the sun walked up the sky and began to fall down the other side. Still they slept.

Will opened his eyes and saw he was under water. He wouldn't move his body just yet, he decided. He couldn't for the moment remember why but he was sure deep within himself that it was a very bad idea.

His eyes moved slowly. Even his eyeballs hurt in the green aqueous light. It was all green, humming and green. Ripples of liquid light danced up the walls. Plants hung in riotous confusion dripping from some height above him. He could hear water, its rich moist tinkle.

He was alive. He could see. He could hear. Will moved his body very slightly and pain knifed horrifically through him. He was certainly alive.

Later on someone bent over him. He was lifted slightly, that hurt too, and they gave him drink and spoonfed him liquid food. They washed his face and he slept again.

He came round again and knew he was in a building with a lot of water in it. He could hear the water and there was a funny smell in the air. The building didn't have much of a roof because the weak sunlight flooded gently down through a mass of vines and growing plants. He saw the ripples of light again and knew them for reflections. Shortly he would work out what had happened to him, why he was here, where he was, but at the moment his memory could rest, sealed off. He knew he was safe. He knew he was being looked after. That was enough.

There were two of them and one was horrific, her body a dance of colour that was wholly inhuman. He didn't know if it was tattoo, or liquid crystal, or if she was an alien. But both tended him with gentleness and soon he knew that strength would begin to flow back into his big exhausted body.

They fed him. They washed him. They lay with him in the night and kept him warm.

'Wing,' said Will.

'You are awake. You know me.' Wing clapped her hands. 'You have been so ill but now you are truly better.'

'Where am I?'

'We are nowhere. It is a ruined bathhouse but the water is good. If you feel strong enough you must use the hot springs. It will help.'

'What happened?'

'Ash saved you. She fought the Amazene. She tricked them over the poison. We brought you here. We are safe, Wolf. Quite safe. No one comes here. No one knows we are here.'

'Ash?'

'That is not her name but that is what she calls herself.'

The snake lady.'

'Yes.' Wing looked sad. 'She saved you.'

'Good. I will thank her. Did Janine get away? The Town-sister.'

'Yes, she got away.' Wing looked steadily at Will.

'Good. I hope she's safe. She was real trouble.'

'Are you hungry?'

'Yes, I think I am.'

Wing laughed. 'I will feed you. And I will tell Ash

you are back with us in your own mind. She will be so happy.'

They changed his bedding. They helped him to lie in the hot water and feed on its mineral strength, letting his tortured muscles recover. They fed him and they continued to warm his bed in the night, one each side of him, their naked bodies pressed close to his. For in this warm empty paradise none of them wore any clothes. It had a primeval innocence at first, but as Will's health and strength returned, the innocence began to slip away.

He became bored lying on his back all day in the warm filtered sunlight buzzing with insects. He levered himself from his bed and went out of the ruined building, through its mock-classical columns, to see how the world went on. Out there he squatted painfully and let the heat of the sun penetrate his aching muscles. He must start taking some exercise and loosen up. It was just that he was so tired and there was a voluptuous pleasure in being waited on by the two women, though one of them never spoke and hardly touched him except when it was necessary. He wondered who the snake woman was, whether she wanted to go to the Town. For himself, he felt he could stay here forever.

His tanned body was the colour of stone and it blended with the columns of the building. He sat still and when the two girls came back from wherever they had been, they did not see him. Their heads were close together and they were chattering, laughing, though he could not hear the words or the joke. Will kept still, watching.

They had been gathering plants. They put them down and sat on the grassy ground, stretching and relaxing. Above them the little cliff reared and its vegetation cast speckled shadows. The snake woman rolled suddenly and her body flickered brilliantly, inhuman in its uncertain shape. Wing went over and knelt by her and Will saw Wing bend over the supine girl and lay her lips on hers. Wing's hair fell in a loose black sheet and covered from view the two kissing but Will's heart thundered

213

and he knew what they did. He saw Wing's hand drift down the rounded contours of the painted body, lingering over the mound of the breast, over the inviting softness of the belly. Then her lips followed her hand and slowly in the sunsoaked, shadowsplashed air she kissed the body beneath hers, kissed it with the slow savour of one who does what she does by right, by custom.

The body on the ground moved, lifted itself into the intimacy of the embrace, and the legs came open. Will saw Wing lower her head still further until her hair caressed the thighs and belly of the snake girl, her face bent into the body below her. The palms of his hands were greasy and moist as he saw her buttocks, now facing him, lift as she bent to her self-appointed and so very welcome task.

The snake girl let one hand come up and idly she began to play with the upraised buttocks. She caressed their shape, moulding her palm to each little pointed cheek in turn. Then her fingers slid within the cleft and Will saw Wing push back slightly into the invading hand. Now the fingers ran deep between the cheeks and pushed hard in and Wing's little body jerked. The snake girl had her knees up and Wing was bent right over between her thighs whilst her own more secret place was vulnerable to violation. Will was not close enough to see the moist rosy flesh below where the snake girl penetrated but he knew where her fingers went, what she did.

The snake girl cried out, her body glittering in jagged flames of colour, her hips lifting to the eager sucking mouth. As her passion was fulfilled, so Wing began to cry out, lifting her face and sobbing as her rear clenched the wicked invasive fingers. The snake girl worked them vigorously. Wing sat up, forcing them further in, and plainly came to climax.

She edged forward after a few moments and eased herself off the violating hand. She twisted round and lay on the ground alongside the snake girl. They put their arms round each other and kissed face to face, their bodies pressed together, breasts crushed between them.

Will's skin felt too tight. His chest was constricted and he sweated as if he had a fever. He got quietly to his feet and went into the bathhouse. He slid into the vast cistern where the cold hill water leaked through and swam briefly in its icy embrace. Beyond him in a square-built pool the hot mineral water steamed faintly, sulphurously.

That night Will lay awake in the dark, his mind helplessly running over what he had witnessed. His body, returning to some approximation of its normal strength, burned. At either side of him the two long warm soft forms pressed close.

He lay still, burning, his chest heaving up and down. His breathing was harsh in the silent warm damp air. It was impenetrably dark, so dark it pressed down on him where he lay.

He felt one of them stir. He kept still. She moved slightly and he felt her listening, felt her thinking. Then a hand was laid hesitantly upon his chest. His breathing shuddered slightly and the hand slipped down his body, warm as silk. In his mind's eye he saw Wing, her hand sliding down the snake girl's body. His body leapt in hot response. The hand on him quested lower, crossed his belly, touching his springing hair and found the thick stem of his urgent sex.

Will didn't know whether his eyes were open or shut. He lay on his back and felt the hand grasp his cock and squeeze gently. His whole soul, his whole body, was all focused on the one part of him and its crying need for release.

The hand caressed him with knowledge and experience. He felt lips at his shoulder, on his chest. The figure reared itself beside him in the dark and bent over him. Hair brushed his face. Warm sweet lips touched his cheek, his nose, then found his lips. Will turned to face her and kissed her fully and firmly, his mouth opening hers and tasting hers and his tongue seeking her tongue. He felt her breasts soft against his muscled chest and moved his body slightly so that his skin could distin-

215

guish the feel of her nipples, papery and soft in repose but elastic and firm as they became erect.

His cock was a joy. Her thigh was pressed against his and her hand was busy, squeezing, moving up and down. Then she released him. She felt for his hand, found it, and clasping it lightly she led it over her own smooth body, leading it down till it brushed against warm hair. She curled his fingers and he pressed them gently forward, into her, into her sex, warm and open for him. He caught her head with his other hand and pressed her face into his and then he rolled his big body onto hers, pushing away her hands as he opened her thighs and found the way in. His need was urgent but he controlled himself and was gentle. Her legs were parted and his staff found the damp entrance he needed. He lifted his hips and brought his cock up, pushing in, urging it in, and she drew up her knees and helped him.

He entered glory. She was tight all around him with a lovely firm elastic grip of wet sliding flesh and as he went in and out of her he felt the need to climax rise like a hot flood. He wanted to kiss her breasts but they were below him, under his chest, so he kissed her throat and her ears and her lips.

She was now thrusting up into his body, her own need manifest. He could feel her nether regions tremble and he knew that she too was going to come. He lifted himself up on one arm and thrust savagely into her, using all of his returning strength to pound into her as they came to orgasm together. She cried out and he let go with a sob as his sperm leapt along his shaft and burst forth. He pumped again and again till he was empty. She too came to quietness beneath him and her body drooped back and he bore down softly now, letting her relax with his slack member still firmly held in her hot wet embrace.

He got his arm under her shoulders and held her to him in the dark. He had forgotten the other girl but now he felt her move as they rearranged themselves. Tiredness washed over him. His body was peaceful. In the watery murmur of the hiding place he fell profoundly asleep. He did not know which of the girls he had made love to.

Will assumed he had been with Wing. Ash, the snake girl, kept away from him apart from in the darkness of the night, and he found himself unsurprised by the knowledge that Wing enjoyed sexual relations with a woman. Some dark part of him liked it. He found the sight of two women in erotic combination inflaming, and that he might use one of their bodies himself was also immensely satisfying to him. Since his sexual rebirth, neither girl had put any clothing on so he followed suit, staying naked himself in their bizarre Eden remote from the rest of mankind. His physical prowess, his muscular strength, returned in a slow wave through the passing hours and days and he experienced a deep mental contentment.

It was to get better.

The next night he slept at first but woke in the murmurous dark to the quiet splendid joy of the two women pressed against him. He moved slightly, savouring the feel of them, the knowledge that they were there and that they waited on him by day and one of them served him by night. It was all the finer because he was strong again. He was a muscled package of energy, of fierce strength, of endurance, of great stamina, with intelligence as well as power, and it pleased him to lie idle in the sun and be fed and washed and be their purpose in life.

A hand was on his body and he sighed deeply and happily. His penis was springy and erect. His balls glowed in anticipation. Hair brushed his shoulder. Lips found his. Her sweet individual woman-smell touched his nostrils. He kissed her, nosing against her face in the dark, tasting the shape of her features. He turned to face her so that he might feel the points of her breasts brush his chest, so that she might rub her body like a cat against his and press her little belly forward into his loins catching his rigid shaft between the two of them, squeezing. Her breathing deepened and he could feel the rise and fall of her breast as she pressed against him. He pushed a leg between her silky thighs and she began to fall back, wanting him on her, wanting him in her. He kissed her throat, her nipples, feeling her arch her back, feeling the heat from between her legs beat up against him.

She drew her legs right up, so far up that for moment he was confused in the dark. Then he understood. She hooked her legs over his shoulders so that her femininity reared beneath him, open, begging for penetration, offering the maximum exposure, the maximum entrance. For a moment he held her legs and dropped his head, feeling his hair brush her inner legs. He took her into his mouth and sucked. She rolled under him and he heard her gasp and moan with delight. Her taste was nectar, sweet, musky, rich and powerful. He sucked and then let his tongue invade her, tasting the inside of her, running his tongue round and feeling its pulpy excitation. He found her clitoris and sucked it till she cried out.

He pulled himself up and lowered his flaming shaft into the place he had sucked. He was holding her by her calves, her body doubled right over to receive him, and as his cock slid thick and hard into her vibrating inner body, he felt her twist and push to draw him in, further in, till he was buried deep inside her.

He was racked by his lust. He began to thunder into her. His body hit hers with a loud slamming motion and his balls slapped against her. She must have squeezed her muscles because he felt them grip his shaft as he rammed it home again and again, beside him, caught in his fierce dark joy, wanting her hard and wanting her to want him hard.

He gave a sob and his prick felt as if it burst as he shot inside her. She was throwing her body up to take him, to make his fierce thrusts fiercer, and suddenly her sex was all different and she was coming around his climaxing tool. Still he thrust into her but now he was letting her down, letting her relax. He let her legs slip down onto the bed and as his belly touched hers, he felt it throb and flex with the potency of her orgasm.

She clung to him, utterly his in the moment of supreme capitulation. He lowered his great head to rub it against her in his wordless joy, and he felt the salt tears on her cheeks. He licked her tears and kissed her face, cuddling her to him. After a moment or two she moved so that she was leaning up over him and now he lay on his back. She stroked his hair back from his brow, kissed his face, and then his mouth. He found her very sweet, very affectionate, and he kissed her back slowly, gently, lovingly.

His body jumped. He felt her kiss his belly, his hips and then slide on down till her face was buried in his hot hairy groin with his still-wet tool. Only – she still was kissing his mouth. Another mouth kissed his cock. He lay warm between the two poles of desire. One girl kissed his mouth, his eyes, his face, his throat. The other kissed his slick manhood. He lay feeling her kiss and gently suck what she found there, rubbing her face in him, and he began pleasurably almost to doze, allowing them both the freedom to play with his body and do as they wished.

All about him warm soft flesh pressed. He stirred slightly and moved his hands finding breasts and buttocks. He stroked what he found, fondling a nipple, letting his hands slide within the cleft of buttocks, feeling moist flesh in secret places quiver as his fingers ran lightly over it. The girl at his groin was stroking him, sucking him and caressing his balls. He felt power return to his shaft and it lifted and firmed a little.

They moved and he became aware in the thick darkness that both had their heads bent together over his sex and that two tongues wove about his lifting cock. His exploring hands found a double set of buttocks lifted before him, one to each side, and he stroked them, running his fingers down between them and then seeking lower, further in.

There were two pouting sexes. He had known it, known there were the two girls, but that they should simultaneously give him their bodies, excite and arouse him, argued a generosity of spirit he had no right to expect. For days they had both looked after him. At first they had even half carried him out to perform his necessary body functions, he had been so weak. They had tended him, almost worshipped him here in this templelike building with its eternal spring of pure water and the endless sunlight pouring through the tracery of vines that was the roof. They had dealt with his every physical need and they still did. Here in the liberating privacy of the night they caressed his skin with theirs, their skin a soft push on him. They took his intimate body and pleasured it with skill and willingness and emotional abandon. Will slid his fingers into the two uptilted vulvas and felt the one soupy wet and the other slightly moist, unused, needing to have its springs released to flood it with the sweetness of its sister.

He pulled himself up and put his face to it. He kissed it, felt it shudder deliciously, and suddenly she rolled and fell across him on her back. He kissed her there again and began to suck her in earnest. The other girl was up kissing his shoulders, his neck, his hair. He pushed the girl down and came forward onto his knees to plant his rod where he had sucked. Behind him he felt hands flutter over his buttocks. He went into the opening that beckoned in the dark and began softly, gently, to bring himself and it to climax, lifting her with him, fondling her inner places with his veiny member, rubbing on her clitoris with each inward thrust.

Behind him a wicked wet finger found his rear and began to press on it. Will gritted his teeth and contained his growing excitement.

Around his cock he felt the silky smoothness begin to grow hot and coarse in its demands. Its heat enveloped him. It seemed to suck his goodness from himself. It throbbed and he felt it vibrate. At his rear a finger slid inside him and he exploded.

'Damn!' he shouted. He reached his climax with violent shudders. He jerked helplessly but though he had come before he meant to, teased by the delicious invader in his rear, he felt the urgent throb around his slackening cock, so he pushed in as hard as he could though his erection waned even as he did so. She came, hot and thick, a rumbling juicy flow that was lava-hot. He pushed in a few more times feeling her contract about him. He stopped, his head hanging so that his hair brushed her breasts. His arse was being penetrated rhythmically by the finger. He got his arms under the girl he had just filled and held her, pushing his face into her soft pillowy breasts. He grunted as his violation continued. His rod slid from its warm bath as his rear pushed backwards towards its invader. Suddenly her other hand came under him, felt his dangling slack damp member and his loose swinging balls. The finger came out of him. Warm lips pressed sweetly to him, kissed his anus, kissed his cock, sucked it a little and then he was allowed to lie down.

They rearranged themselves silently, Will between them, each girl again pressed warmly to his sides. Will held each of them, an arm about her. His cock and balls felt fine and glittery. His backside tingled faintly, deliciously. His belly was soft and empty. Four breasts pressed against his sides. The two girls were his, his to play with, and he was theirs. He knew now they were both skilled at lovemaking. They could turn him inside out with their sweet demands if they chose and he would die to keep them satisfied and coming back for more. That was all right. That was good. This would be a sweet death, night after night in the watery murmur of darkness. Will felt sleep wash in a velvet flood over his body and he gave way to it, relaxed, a fine animal full-fed.

They were running out of food. Will became aware that the girls fed him as much as he required but ate little themselves. Their bodies were lissom and delightful, barring the extraordinary, brilliant and terrifying

221

snakeskin. He had not been close enough to her in the daytime to find out whether it was decoration or in some ghastly way a natural phenomenon.

He was sitting in the sun when the snake girl suddenly appeared out of the undergrowth quite near him. He gasped in shock. She carried her machete and across the weird mural of her body blood was splashed in big red gouts. He sprang to his feet, terrified suddenly for Wing. What if this monster had killed the little Chinese girl? She was a freak and he had all but forgotten it in the hot strong pleasures of the night. Now he could smell the blood on her body rank in the sun and because she was close to him, he saw the streaky little cloud of hair in her groin.

'Where is Wing?' he said roughly. He would kill this thing if she had harmed his little lover.

The snake girl turned and stood to one side. Wing came out of the brush behind her carrying some flayed rabbits. They had been hunting, that was all.

He looked at Wing and the snake girl went by him into the bathhouse.

'What is it?' asked Wing, puzzled. 'We needed meat, Wolf. I think we will have to go soon for we do not have much to eat now.'

'Nothing,' said Will. He was ashamed of himself. Wing went by him and vanished into the bathhouse in her turn.

After a while Will followed them. The snake girl had saved his life and he had not yet thanked her. He felt bad about his suspicions. She had shown no sign of jealousy that he coupled with Wing in the night. Indeed, she had joined in. He had accused her in his mind of murder.

They were in the cold cistern together, gasping and laughing as they washed their bloody dusty bodies. They were fooling like puppies together, pushing each other under, coming up underneath each other, kissing, touching, rolling in the water. He squatted in plain view and they ignored him. Instead they wove their bodies together using the freedom of the water. Now they kissed more often and finally they climbed out of the water, shaking themselves, rapt, it appeared, for each other.

Wing kissed the snake girl. It was the closest Will had been to her in the daylight since his recovery. He could see how her hair was oddly streaked and pale at her skull as if it wanted to lift itself away from her. Her patterned skin shone through the water droplets. She was passive as Wing kissed her and when Wing opened the girl's legs, Will's eyes narrowed in shock. Wing held her legs apart and the snake girl lay with her eyes shut, ignoring them both. Will looked where his eyes were led, invited, and he saw that even here the flesh was decorated with patterns woven into the sexual flesh itself. Wing peeped slyly at him, held her hair back with her two hands, and buried her face in the snake girl's body.

Will felt faint shock. The two girls were so close, so deliberate in their actions. Wing had lifted her rear provocatively just in front of him and was wiggling her behind as she sucked down on the other girl. Slowly Will reached forward.

He touched the warm pale saffron buttocks and then he opened them and looked down into the cleft. Wing's little fawn strawberry-shaped bottom puckered and he knew she was deliberately working her muscles. Below he saw the moist webbing of her sex, the skin of her outer labia a darker colour than the rest of her body. He came forward on his knees and began to slide his erect cock into her body, into her, even as she sucked at the snake girl.

His heart pounded as he thrust into the wicked invitation. He began to pump hard so she juddered against the open sex of the snake girl. Somehow he was angry and he knew his body was dancing to their tune, to Wing's tune. He wanted to come quickly, rudely, but it was too good, a feast too good to gobble. He slowed down and with long firm movements sank deeply into

223

her body and then withdrew till only his hot swollen tip remained within her. Watery light rippled along his shaft when it was withdrawn. Wing's bent back before him was pale green in the filtered sunlight, the incestuous plants writhing together above them forming a natural trellis with their tendrilled embrace.

Wing trembled and he felt her change and knew she had orgasmed. She held herself for a moment as he still rode into her, and then she lifted her head and broke free from his cock so that it hung before him, erect, a viscous film of her come draped over it. She rolled from between the thighs of the snake girl leaving them open to Will's eyes, his unsatisfied cock pointing at the magic painted secret flesh of her body. He stared. The snake girl opened her eyes wide in shock. They were vast and blue and brilliant as the sky. Will's hot stone-coloured eyes absorbed her open body, split in welcome to his needy cock. He lurched to his feet and stumbled out of the bathhouse.

He went over through the grove of trees to the cliff. He dealt swiftly and unsatisfyingly with his need and cursed the worm in paradise that must needs spoil what they had here. He began to run out onto the prairie, forcing his body into a rhythm it could maintain. He needed to find out if his strength had fully returned. Their time was over here.

They ate the rabbits that night and agreed to leave for the Town the following morning. Wing did not know how far away they were. They had to go north and make a westing also, but they did not want to come back to the city and must be careful.

Still the snake girl did not speak. Will and Wing went to bed together that night but the snake girl did not join them and Will found he missed her warmth at his side.

He woke very early in the morning hearing the slight shrieks of the creatures of the dawn though it was still dark. He could see very faintly the dark vines above him twisting across a slightly fainter sky. He slipped from the bed and went over to the hot pool where he slid eel-like into the water and allowed its goodness to penetrate his sleepsoaked skin. Then he went over to the cold cistern and washed the faint sour-egg smell from his body. He was cold as he went outside. The air was aching in its purity and the dew was falling. The sky glowed, light over the horizon but still dark above his head. The stars were invisible except far to the west, the shout of the coming dawn washing them from the icy loft of the sky.

The east began to flood softly with light and in its low rays he saw the snake girl sitting on the wet grass, shivering. He stayed still, watching her.

As the sky lightened a mist began to rise from the vast grassland about them so that the light became pearly and dull for a while. Will saw the snake girl move and then take a long iridescent shard of multihued colour and lay it on the ground. After a few minutes, the sky perceptibly brightening, she took another great strip and laid it beside the first.

She was shedding her skin.

When she had peeled her shoulders he went over to her. She jumped slightly when she saw him and he saw how strange she was.

In the night she had cut her hair. Its curious ugly streaky blackness was gone and she had a short pale-wheat fuzz like thick deep-piled velvet over her head. Beads of dew lay on it. As he looked at her she peeled another great strip of snakeskin as he saw cold naked pink raw flesh revealed underneath. She was shivering uncontrollably.

He sat beside her, watching. After a few minutes he began to help her, picking off the frozen shards of colour. All around them mist spiralled silently upwards into the opalescent sky. It was flushed a deep peach in the east.

Will peeled her back and saw ordinary cold human skin revealed more and more. He felt her jump slightly each time his fingers brushed her back. He moved round to her face, his gold-flecked stony eyes softened and greenish-brown. He peeled what remained on her front. She was passive, quite passive, submitting to his hands over her body. He touched her breasts, her inner thighs, her cheeks, her brow, under her arms, and at last she was all naked, freshly skinned and vulnerable.

The mist was nearly gone and the sky was red-streaked. Will ran his hand over the soft warm thatch on her head and his penis leapt. It was the sweetest thing his palm had ever felt, the warm soft velvet of her head. Like moleskin it had no lie of its own. It lay the way he stroked it.

She lay back and opened her legs. Will looked at her, considering what she wanted. Then his fingers went in and he found the last of her false skin and gently he peeled the tiny landscape of her sex.

Her body was shivering hard now. He came up over her and slid into her. He rested there for a moment. She was dry inside and not ready for him. Holding his cock in her, he began to kiss her face, her breasts, her trembling throat where a pulse beat.

Her eyes were open and they changed first, their blue brilliance becoming hazed. Her skin warmed and flushed partly from the rising sun and partly from the inner heat building in her, the fires he lit with his patient cock waiting for her to respond. Her breasts rose and her nipples hardened. Her arms came round him and she made whimpering noises in her throat and pressed up into his warm strong body. Her passage softened as it gloved his prick and he felt moisture spring from her inner flesh to bathe and lubricate him. She brought her legs right up and folded them around his body, clinging to him, and at last he began to work his cock in her, shafting her new-made body, letting the sun make a warmth on his back as his hardness made a blaze in her body.

He began to buck more strongly and he felt her rise to take him. Her teeth were at his shoulder and her fingers dug into his back. She was hot, very hot about him and he got an arm under her arching body and pulled

226

her tight to his chest. Her head dropped back, her lips slightly parted, her eyes closed. Her face was drowned, ecstatic.

His belly was on fire and he burned to climax now. Her body was shuddering against his. Her inner walls gripped him with tight spasmodic contractions. He plunged in and let his climax come. He felt his shaft ripple and he did not know whether it was from her or himself. Her submission was gone. Her teeth were bared and she fought greedily to drain him, ripping her pleasure from his body and not hiding the extent of it from him.

When he lay beside her she came up and was astride him. Her face was tender and fierce and she kissed his chest and bit his nipples gently. She held his slack cock within her still, her inner cushioning softly holding him.

'Janine,' he said. 'You saved my life. Thank you.'

'I've changed my name.'

'But not your nature.'

'You think not?'

'I think this is how you always were, only you hid it.'

'I hated you going with Wing.'

'I kinda liked it, but I guess I'll stop. I think she prefers you.'

'I like it. I like her,' admitted Janine. Her voice sank to a low note. 'But women are breast-milk and I guess I'm weaned.' She bent her head and nuzzled him, licking his skin, smiling at him. 'I must look terrible,' she said suddenly. 'I couldn't bear my head black any longer.'

'You are beautiful,' said Will with sincerity. 'Darling, so beautiful.'

She lifted herself slightly and squeezed her muscles. His cock jumped slightly and began to firm again. It was very slidy, bathed in the combined juices of their two bodies. Janine held herself slightly up from him and began to caress the reawakening creature using only her inner muscles. She squeezed and stroked and rode very slightly up and down and all the time he filled and firmed within her.

'I wanted you,' she whispered as her core cradled his sex, rocked it. 'I've wanted you so much.'

After a while he caught her under her buttocks with his two hands and held her just over his belly. He pushed up, jutting into her with little gentle slithery movements, his arm muscles trembling with the effort but whole and strong again.

'I thought you hated me,' he said.

She pushed his hands away and now that he was a rigid pole joining their two bodies, she began to work just the very tip of his cock in rapid fluttering movements, concentrating on his most sensitive part, squeezing it with the tighter neck of her entrance. His breathing changed and his shaft swelled tighter, filling her until she could no longer bear to deny its full presence. She rode down hard on him, feeling the glory of his strong manhood pulsing within her, and suddenly she felt herself flame inside and she lost control so that Will took over and with a rapid series of powerful plunges up into her orgasm, he brought himself to climax once again.

'I was frightened of you.'

'Not any longer,' he murmured. 'Christ, you're so sweet.' Janine climbed stiffly off Will and kissed his body now warm and flooded with sunlight. She knelt over him and he felt her lips roam up and down him as he half slept, his every part comfortable and at ease. She began to lick his groin, lick his curling springing hair, lick his soft wet cock, lick his balls.

After a while she made him roll over and she kissed his back, under his hair, down his spine and on to his buttocks. He felt her hold his buttocks open, he felt the sunlight on his arse, he felt her lips silky as they kissed and sucked him there.

She made him roll over again so that he was on his back, and she laid her body on top of his. She lay on her back with her head in his groin and her legs one either side of his shoulders. When he lifted his head he looked straight up into her body laced with his own juice. Her

228

labia, dark-tipped and pansy-soft, wove about the curious little wrinkled lumps and strange bumps and cushionings on her inner sex. He found he felt odd in his throat and there was a tightening in his chest, pleasurable, sore. He brought his arms round under her thighs and felt for her breasts. He caressed them, squeezing the soft flesh up into its points, using his thumbs to nuzzle the sensitive tips. After a while he sat up and holding her legs open he bent his head and kissed at her sex, tasting her, mapping her intricate flesh till it was known territory. His territory. His tongue staked a claim on her and when he finally drew her tired body alongside his so that she could sleep, he was smiling.

Last of all she took his hand and turned it palm up. She touched the sapphire stain under the skin where the Amazene had marked him.

'I'm sorry for this,' she said seriously.

'It could have been worse,' he murmured. He grinned at his small joke but Janine shuddered. He had so nearly died.

'That meteor saved you,' she said, 'whatever it really was. I was a little beside myself at the time but the HeliPolice were out in force, you know. I don't think it was a natural phenomenon.'

Will leant on an elbow and looked down into her quiet face. 'You saved me, hero. The special effects were extra.'

'Is this gratitude?'

He kissed her. 'No. Self-indulgence. And long overdue.'

Wing woke them an hour later. It was time to eat what food they had left and to go. Wing saw the peace they had in each other, how their limbs glowed and were relaxed, how their eyes were soft and hazed with carnal release, and knew her time with their bodies was over. She didn't mind. She had not yet found what she wanted, though now after this time in paradise she knew more clearly what it was. She wanted the strength and vigour of man coupled with the softness and intimacy of a woman. She did not really want a man's sex, but she wanted to be mastered and to submit as well as being free to steal and invade. No matter. She would make a life for herself in the Town and perhaps there find what she wanted.

Whippet had found paradise in the city. He had forgotten the disc. It had been meaningless, a fantasy, and now he had reality. His friends were there, all safe and well. Each day was a delight. Whippet could not have believed this was possible.

The vast series of rooms where Whippet and his friends and some other men were kept were all warm and well-furnished and exquisitely comfortable. There were vidi-books, the Screen, VR discs, a swimming pool and a roof garden under a woven trellis to keep them happy and occupied. There were all kinds of games, card games, jacks, everything man had devised down the long inevitable ages that the Amazenes could get their hands on to keep their pets happy.

Every day the bathhouse girls with the long hair came in and brought them all breakfast, whatever they wanted, with beer and coffee and fruit-juice and anything they asked for that the Amazenes could supply. Then the bath girls washed them, a couple of girls to each youth, and Whippet found this time of lying in warm scented soapy water whilst girls' hands roved his body one of the nicest times of the day. He generally got a hard-on and the girls would squeal and play with his erect soldier, foaming it, soaping it and slithering their hands up and down his shaft till it was big and happy and ready to oblige some needy female.

By mid-morning a couple of the Amazenes often came by to see if they could get the benefit of the pets' morning wash. The boys lay about with little black leather pouches on and waited to be selected, or they even approached the guards themselves and aroused their slim muscled bodies. Whippet grew so used to synching through the weaving of the *caffada* that he found total nakedness slightly indecent in a woman. It had taken him a little while to realise how brave they could be with the threatening-looking women, but now he would kneel and suck at the exposed breast if he felt like it, and the Amazenes really loved it.

Every day brought new delights. Sometimes he would pass the day in a VR thriller, or using up his muscle power in a little workout in the gym. In the evening he would service one or two of the girls so that his cock felt good all the time. After servicing an Amazene warrior, a bath-girl would wash his equipment and this was the nicest finish to sex that Whippet could imagine, gentle hands cleansing him, stroking him, worshipping his male member and giving it its due. When he had the resources available, he liked to come under water and watch the pearly streams float from his body like strung jewels. The bath-girls always squealed extra loud if this happened.

There were hectic times too, when a group of warriors came into the harem wanting a party. There would be drink and music. The bath-girls would wait on them all and Whippet would find he had the powerful thighs of a warrior clamped about his ears as he sucked fervently at her musk whilst another was sprawled across his body sucking him to climax. Whippet liked these times when his blood ran thick and hot and they were all a little crazy. A huge net hung over one wall in the general room and Fruity would hang upside-down on it, his knees hooked through the net and bent to support him where he hung, his hands gripping the webbing. An Amazene would run up the net agile as a monkey and squat with her open sex over his mouth, taking Fruity's pride into her mouth, and Fruity would come in this curious fashion at least twice in a night to the Amazenes' amusement and pleasure.

The Zootman had a lower libido than his erstwhile gang members but he had the most curious tastes. His pretty face would shine with happiness while his pole invaded the arse of a warrior till she screamed with the fatness of his climax in her. He would tongue a warrior too, whilst she was busy with her other end, tongue her sex and her arse with delicate probing titillating darts till her sex-flesh was flushed dark with desire.

Dinko was like Whippet. He enjoyed it all. When he had had enough, he slept. It was a lifestyle Whippet could not have imagined being offered to him. No work. As much tool-work as he required. Comfort. Luxury. No responsibility. Entertainment.

Whippet grew stronger and healthier than he had ever been. He never saw the locked doors that led to the outside world. They might never have existed as far as he was concerned. There is only one freedom that matters, and that is the freedom to do as you please. Whippet had that. He wanted for nothing. The pain of his former life, the pain of the disc (it was a silly fantasy, all those girls dripping round him because he was the star – it made him embarrassed to remember it) all drifted away as day succeeded day in safety and peace. His past was grey in his mind, grey as the smoke that had filled its corners ever since he had used the strange disc so much. His memory blurred. Why remember, when the present was always so good? His thoughts were thin and ephemeral but his life was rich and full. It was enough.

Janine, Will and Wing returned to the Town. There was something odd in their threesome that made the people they passed look askance at them. There was an aura, a power about them, a felt emanation that disturbed. Janine knew that not only could she not return to her insipid and pointless job, she now felt ill at ease in the environment that had bred and reared her. Vile as the city undoubtedly was, it had changed her for the better in that she felt her character and experience was now three-dimensional instead of flat. She wondered about Will. She knew nothing of his former history. But at last she could see why he stood out like a sore thumb among her former acquaintances. He was a misfit. Now she was. The Town was a neat passionless blur topped by the white aloof glitter of the Institute of Science. It was all very pretty but it was so very dull.

She wondered what had happened to the disc. It seemed to have passed from their lives absolutely long ago, when even Whippet had lost it. She wondered about Whippet himself and had ventured a remark to this effect to Will. He had bared his teeth wolfishly and said that as far as he was concerned, Whippet had made his own bed and could lie in it.

Neither of them appreciated the rich irony of this comment but Janine stopped bothering about the foolish youth. Will's broad exotic face filled her mind. The rugged power of his body flooded her blood. His dark flinty eyes softened now for her yet she felt the psychic strength of the man, his control over his own vast appetite, his ability to manipulate his desires and channel the force of his own personality.

She knew nothing of his history, of the range of his mind, of the power of his intellect, of the depths of his experience. She wanted to know it all. She was only twenty-one. He was forty-five. She felt herself a baby with him, yet she felt old when she saw the bland smug faces of the people of the Town.

Chapter Eight

The news ran through the Zoo like a bush fire. Jace Harvon had committed suicide using his Connet. The Zoo felt proud of its unpopular member. If a Zoo-denizen had to go, then he or she should go in as expensive a blaze of glory as could be managed and Jace might have been pork rind in his life but he was a true native son in his death. Apparently he had gone bust over some crazy water deal. That he should prefer death to expulsion from the Zoo was very right and proper. Jace had never been so well liked.

Diva Jackson, that bitter jewelled turtle of a woman, first told Fee, glittering with excitement. Then Fee had it over from her good friend Diana, the big blonde sexy Scandinavian with whom she went to the gym a couple of times every week.

She told Rollo and he laughed. He had no compassion for a man who made a fool of himself over money. Money was a cold joy to work and construct and manipulate and cause to bloom. Only the ignorant threw it away before they had extracted the infinite pleasure of its juice. He made arrangements to buy Jace's stock cheap. That controlled the downward push on the share price, levelling it off, and it was all money in the bank for when TransFlow manipulated the market a second time and caused the share price to escalate, as it would eventually do. Rollo was always a man of infinite resource.

Fee aged a little at the loss of her friends. She filled the void in her life with the youth Caz. His power over her grew as if he had second sight. He could read her. He could foretell her feelings and use what would happen in the future to control the present. He thrilled her with his slender mysterious half-fulfilment of manhood and she felt intuitively that when his body fully ripened, he would lose this otherworldly quality and become ordinary. He might still be captivating. He would probably be better at sex. But he would go from four dimensions down to the normal three, though this might even be a relief. She was tangled in him like a webbed fly but she wasn't struggling to get free, not yet. If ever. He made her happy.

The vidi call from Janine left her thunderstruck. She was amazed, incredulous, bewildered and delighted. Janine was back, safe and whole. Will was back, as hungry and as wolfish as ever. And they had someone with them, a delectable little thing that looked Chinese and as original as sin.

Quite privately, Janine made an appointment with Rollo. Will had gone over to his own place to settle Wing in there. He spent a great deal of his time with Janine but they had made no formal arrangement and he was often busy. He was picking up the threads of his business life and sorting out the mess that had developed after he had disappeared.

Rollo came to Janine's apartment. She admitted him, unable to prevent her heart from thumping. He was so good looking, so beautiful, a panther of a man. He had that off-hand contained manner that is the hallmark of the truly self-confident. A man who is so sure of himself that he has no need to prove it by bragging is supremely attractive. He had been her first male penetration, her first experience of the full act of sex, and she had believed herself to be in love with him for five years, though she had never told him so and never would.

She made him a drink. Like all illicit lovers, they knew each other's tastes in these small intimate matters. They sat on her balcony, private in the tall shrubs and potted trees she grew there.

'What happened to your hair?' asked Rollo.

'I had to dye it black. I grew to hate it. I cut it all off with a knife. It's been tidied up since but they didn't have much to work with.'

'It's extraordinary. Beautiful.'

'I feel like a freak.'

'No.' There was arrogance in his denial. He expected her to accept his word on the matter.

They were silent, Janine examining her own feelings. Then Rollo put down his glass and came and stood over her. His very blue eyes glittered. 'Make love to me,' he said. He smiled, his head slightly on one side, pretending it was enough of a query to undermine any offence. Janine stood up, mesmerised, and led the way through to where she slept.

Rollo eased himself out of his clothes and lay down on the bed, half propped on the pillows. His body was smooth and golden, the slight sheen on it making it look like satin. Her skin trembled knowing she was going to touch him again.

Janine undressed. Her warm skin tones caught the sunlight. The faint red-gold fuzz of her body hair softened her contours.

'You are slimmer,' said Rollo. 'Did you have a hard time?'

'Yes.'

'Maffick brought you back OK.'

'Yes.'

'He took his time. Why was that?'

His voice was lazy yet his eyes pierced her. Janine smiled slyly in her turn and knelt by the bed. 'He was sick,' she said lightly. 'Wing and I looked after him.'

'I thought you were dead.' Rollo's voice was suddenly harsh.

'You know, I think that crazy business saved us, the one that did himself in with his Connet.'

236

Rollo laughed and grabbed her, pulling her naked body down onto his, catching and crushing her mouth. His hands ran round and over the soft curious thickness of hair springing from her head.

'Rub me with it,' he said roughly. Janine slid down the bed between his legs. She pushed her head into his groin and rolled her head there so her hair frotted his member and aroused it with its soft dense texture. Rollo lay with his eyes shut feeling the blunt furry nuzzling in his groin. When he was hard he sat up and moved round till he was astride the girl. He pushed his cock between her young firm breasts and squeezed them together over his shaft. He began to rock backwards and forwards. Janine saw the naked tip of his cock, the foreskin withdrawn, every time he came forward. He moved down her and entered her in a liquid movement. He began to move in her and stopped.

'What is it?' he said.

'Nothing.'

He looked down at her thoughtfully. Her hollow was moist and cool around him. He was used to her body almost weeping when he entered it, so wet and hot he sometimes thought she had already orgasmed before ever he got into her. Now he pulled out of her and walked through to her kitchen where he rummaged in the cupboards.

He came back and saw her lying pale and sweet on the bed. His cock roused harder at the sight of her apparent innocence. Vulnerability always excited him, brought out the bastard in him. He sat on the bed and pushed his arm under her knees and lifted them up. He pushed the spray can in under and stuck the nozzle into her cool hole. He squeezed and rocked with laughter as she yelped and wriggled.

When he released her Janine gasped with shock and let her legs open whilst she craned to see what he had done. Whipped cream foamed from her body and all her vulva oozed with it. She could feel its cool slidiness within her. Her clitoris tingled within its frothy slipperiness. Rollo tossed the can away and, still laughing, pinned her to the bed and again slid into her. He pumped into the slithering mess and withdrew from her again. He came up over her and presented his bristling length to her face. His smile was sly invitation. Janine began to suck.

She sucked him to climax, taking him in her mouth, tasting him through the creamy mess. She held the long smooth creamy member with one of her hands, stroking his balls and inner thighs with the other, and she savoured him in her mouth, remembering the size of him, the length, the texture, the way he shuddered slightly as she increased the power of her mouth, the individual taste and feel of him, how good it was. How perfect, to take this thing into her mouth and suck it till it juiced hot and hard, till all the power of the man was reduced to a pelvis-thrust which she controlled. How perfect, his pleasure in submitting his vulnerability to her in this way. How perfect, the act of sex between consenting partners.

When he lay slack across her on the bed, his eyes heavy-lidded in his bodily content, she moved herself free of him and went through and cleansed herself. She came back to the bed and sat by him, stroking his hair, thinking.

More than ever he was like a cat. Currently he was satisfied but the predator in his nature would soon wake. She kissed his golden body but she could feel he was puzzled by her behaviour.

Her door buzzer sounded and over her nakedness she slipped a shirt that came decently down to her thighs. She released the door and Will was there. He was inside before she had time to think and he bent and kissed her with a fierce fiery sweetness that made her loins bubble in the way that Rollo had missed. She made a small sobbing noise and looked like a terrified rabbit.

'What's the matter?' said Will without heat. His free hand slid up her thigh and he felt her naked parts below the shirt. He ran a finger straight within her slidy damp body and felt her soft arousal, her readiness for sex.

'Baby, you feel good,' he whispered and bent his head down over hers, making her head go back as he took her mouth more strongly, his body beginning to press urgently against hers as her sexuality brought his to leaping life. His mouth was sweet fire, spiced fire, beautiful.

Janine tried to think. Her body, aroused but not satisfied by Rollo, rubbed itself into Will, wanting him fiercely. When he released her mouth she stammered: 'No,' but he only laughed and swept her up into his arms and carried her through to the bedroom area.

He slid her round till he carried her in front of him, her legs wrapped around his waist, her arms about his neck, his mouth locked on hers. His effortless strength made the coming crisis even more threatening. He carried her into the sunny room and went straight up to a wall. He lifted her even more, working her shirt up, manipulating his stiffened organ free and penetrating her pinned against the wall. He bent his knees slightly and drove his cock deep up into her body. It slid in with succulent ease and for a moment his belly hurt because it was so good to be in her.

'No!' howled Janine. She lifted her head so sharply she hit the back of it against the wall, hard enough to make herself dizzy with the blow. His cock was hot fire in her and she wanted to be taken by him.

Will laughed, his face dark and alive with mischief. 'Why not?'

'Please,' said Janine, wanting him to stay inside her forever. She burst into tears.

At that he did stop, puzzled. He slid out of her and gently let her down to the floor.

'Hi,' said Rollo from the bed.

Will turned round slowly and carefully. He backed away from Janine and stood by the floor to ceiling windows so that he was black, with light flooding in all around him. The ugliness came from him like a living force.

'You want me to go?' Rollo's tone was light and insulting, full of the private joke.

239

'No,' said Will. It cost him an effort to speak and his voice was harsh, a crow's croak. He turned his head and looked at Janine cowering by the wall. 'My mistake,' he added bitterly.

Janine flew across the room and drew back her hand. She hit Will across the face with all the force she could muster. He blinked and shook his head slightly. His arms hung by his side. Janine hit him again, so hard her palm stung. She hit him with her left hand then, and a ring she wore tore his cheek slightly so that a trickle of blood began to ooze down his face. She hit him again, again and again, as he stood there faintly rocking on his feet.

'You fool,' she sobbed. 'You bloody fool. You fool.'

She kept hitting him all the time. Rollo gave a great crack of laughter and began to roll helplessly on the bed as he gave way to mirth. He made no effort to cover his glorious naked body. Will reached up a trembling hand and caught Janine's wrist. He looked over at the laughing man.

'Your wife is far too good a lay for a bastard like you,' he said with concentrated venom. 'She's wasted on you.'

Rollo stopped laughing abruptly. The two men looked at each other. In the silence Janine made a small terrified whimpering noise.

'No,' she whispered.

Rollo stretched himself on the bed. It was a long sinuous movement in which his lean muscled body rippled with contained power. He put his hands behind his head and smiled.

'Not that you're ever going to have her again, Maffick. You'll have to make do with memories.'

Will made a small movement. Janine wrapped her arms tightly around his chest and pressed her face into him. 'No,' she begged in a muffled voice. She didn't know whether she shook with her own fear or with Will's rage communicating itself from his body to hers.

'And little Janine there isn't bad,' continued Rollo. 'I've broken her in for you and I'm quite pleased with my handiwork. She likes to come back to the master, of course, from time to time. You have to accept that. Still, you're used to your women preferring me.'

The door buzzer sounded. Janine felt Will relax. He looked down at her and picked her off his body effortlessly. He smiled at Rollo and pushed his sleeves up his arms. The door buzzer sounded again and Rollo got off the bed warily and stood to face Will.

'I'm going to enjoy this,' said Will. He licked his lips, letting the bloodlust rise strong and hot in him.

Janine said in a loud voice: 'If you two fight I'm going into the kitchen to cut my wrists.'

'Haven't you done enough damage already?' asked Will unpleasantly.

'I think I'm going to enjoy it, too,' said Rollo. He swayed in anticipation.

A voicethrough sounded in the apartment. 'This is the police. Let us in or we will break the door down.'

'Rollo, stop it,' pleaded Janine. 'Think of Fee.'

'You think of Fee,' said Rollo, not taking his eyes off Will. 'Your lover would walk over you any day of the week to get up my wife. He's an insect, buzzing round the honey.'

'This is the police,' boomed the voicethrough again. 'Open the door immediately.'

'I'm going to kill you,' said Will. His eyes were brilliant, mad. He took a step forward and Janine punched him in the belly. Rollo put on a robe and went to answer the door.

Will looked down at Janine when they were alone together. 'Go away,' he said in a voice that was suddenly tired. 'Leave us to see this thing through.' The blood was smeared on his cheek. Janine moved back from him and fetched a chair. She was almost a foot shorter than him. She stood on the chair and sank her hands into his mane of hair. She pulled his great lion head against her breast and rubbed her cheek on him, curled over his protectively. Then she forced his head back and began to kiss his face. His arms hung at his side all the time, as they had when she had hit him.

241

Rollo led the two policemen into the kitchen. Only a trellis densely woven with greenery separated them from Will and Janine.

'What is it?' he asked. He looked very relaxed. He was clearly naked under the robe.

'Ms Janine Conroy. Doesn't she live here?'

'She does. She's, ahem, in the bedroom.' Rollo grinned conspiratorially.

'And you are?'

'Rollo Cambridge. I live in the Zoo. I'm just, ah, visiting. Ms Conroy is an old friend of mine.'

He watched the two troopers working out who he was. He watched their manner change by subtle degrees from belligerence to deference. It was a process he had witnessed many times in his life and it never failed to amuse him.

'Ah, Mr Cambridge,' said one of the men. 'Tell us, if you don't mind, do you know a Will Maffick?'

'Sure. My wife knows him better than I do. They work together sometimes.'

'You know anything about his past history, sir?'

'Can't say as I do. He's a good biochemist, so my wife says. He must have attended an Institute of Science somewhere, I guess.'

'Do you know how well Ms Conroy knows him?'

Rollo shook his head thoughtfully. 'You'd have to ask her that.'

'Could we, er, see her?' asked the older of the two policemen. Damn Zoo bastards synching shamelessly wherever they went, he thought sourly. This man was so cool, here with his lover whilst he talked about his wife.

Rollo grinned again. 'Perhaps I'd better fetch her,' he said. He walked easily out of the room.

Janine was standing on the floor tight up against Will, her arms round him and his head bent over hers.

'Janine,' said Rollo.

'Go away,' pleaded Janine. 'Just go, Rollo.'

Will lifted his head and looked hungrily at Rollo.

'The police are here,' said Rollo clearly. 'They want to know if you know someone called Will Maffick. Apparently they are looking for the guy.'

Janine felt Will jerk in shock.

'You'd better put something on and come through, honey. It seems to be serious.' Rollo kept his eyes on Will and comprehension passed between the two men.

Janine broke away from Will and looked bewildered.

'Here,' said Rollo gently. He guided her out of the room. 'No city,' he breathed. 'Otherwise as near the truth as possible.'

Janine looked at the two troopers. She had no idea how fear had tightened her skin. She looked marvellous, other-worldly. The troopers thought her manner was because they had interrupted her sex with Rollo. He stood over her now, guiding her to sit down at the table, his hand resting lightly, possessively, on her shoulder. Gently he caressed the nape of her neck where her skin was pale from being long covered up by her hair.

The troopers were embarrassed as Rollo meant them to be. But they remained dogged, doing their job.

'We understand you know a Mr Will Maffick,' one of them asked Janine.

She looked puzzled. 'Yes, that's right.' Her voice was cool, a little husky. Both troopers felt a thrill of envy for the big golden man who had just had his body pleasured by this lovely young creature. She had the quality of ethereal innocence with her pale peachy downy skin and her big candid blue eyes, serious, absorbed, but her innocence lay like a translucent skin over something else, something that glowed from within her, warming her superficial purity and contradicting it. Underneath she was corrupt, knowing, wise to the needs of men, the slut within the nun.

'How long have you known him?'

'Less than a month, I should say. Why do you ask?'

'Do you know him well?'

In the silence Rollo said: 'My wife knows him pretty well, I guess. Do you want to talk to her? I could vidi

243

her and see if she is at home or in her office. She's always glad to help the police.'

'Do you know where Mr Maffick is now?' the older of the troopers asked Janine.

She felt Rollo's pressure on her collarbone. 'No,' she said. 'Should I?' She leant her head sideways and rubbed her cheek against Rollo's arm. She looked up at him and smiled lovingly. She seemed to forget the troopers' presence.

Rollo was amused and casually possessive. He touched her cheek with the back of his hand and then ran a gentle finger over her slightly parted lips. It was an intensely sexual gesture, intimate, familiar. Janine gazed adoringly up at him.

'I'll vidi Fee,' said Rolo.

'There's no need,' began one of the men.

'It's no bother.' Rollo was charming. He put in the code for Fee's office. Janine sat quiet. The troopers watched.

Fee's secretary put Rollo straight through.

'Honey,' he said easily. 'I'm at Janine's.' Both troopers went red. This would be a story to relate. Bastards, Zoofolk, there was no doubt about it. Rollo was clearly wearing a bathrobe and as clearly wearing nothing else.

'Yes,' said Fee. Her image was alert, neutral.

'Some troopers are here. They are asking about Will Maffick. I told them you knew him best of any of us and they ought to see you.'

'What do they want to know for?' asked Fee.

'Why do you want to know?' asked Rollo, looking across the room.

'We'd rather not say just now.' Both troopers felt that obscurely they weren't in control of this interview. As indeed they weren't. They knew they should not have let Rollo forewarn Fee yet they did not see how they could have stopped him, nor exactly why it was important.

'You catch that?' Rollo asked his wife.

'Yes. Do they want to interview me now? I'll be here

for an hour yet but I have an important international call coming through.'

'Is that all right with you?' asked Rollo politely.

'Yes, sir. Thank you. We'll get right on over.'

Both men stood up. Rollo and Janine saw them out. Rollo went back to the bedroom, Janine following. She was bewildered.

'You put them onto Fee,' said Will accusingly.

'She can dance rings round them,' answered Rollo absently. He looked speculatively at Will. 'This changes things,' he said.

'Yes.'

'What is all this about?' asked Janine.

'Bad or very bad?' asked Rollo. 'I have no details, you understand.'

'She's a hell of a woman,' said Will. 'I'm sorry.'

'Isn't she just.'

'Very bad, at a guess, to answer your question.'

'You'd better give me power of attorney,' said Rollo. 'I'll handle things this end for you. Here, I'll give you my scrambled business line so you can contact me.'

He scribbled the number down and handed it over. Many businesses paid for a coded line that could not be tapped to protect their industrial secrets. If Will used it, he would have private untraceable communication with Rollo that could not be overheard.

'Learn it and destroy it, huh? I don't want it getting out.'

Will scanned it a few times and gave it back to Rollo. 'OK.'

Janine couldn't understand the transition that had taken place. These men had been going to kill each other a short time ago. Now they were calmly discussing Rollo handling Will's business affairs.

'What's going on?' she asked again.

Rollo began to dress. 'Have you anywhere to go?' he asked. 'You'd better not go home. I don't know how safe this place will be.'

'I don't know.' Will looked doubtfully at Janine. 'Wing's at my place,' he said with an effort.

245

'Wing? Oh yes, the girl you brought out of the city. Look, hadn't I better go over and warn her? They'll have your vidi tapped. I could get some things for you, too.'

'I'd be grateful.' Will still looked doubtfully at Janine who was completely at sea.

Rollo laughed. He was ready to go. 'You are a fool, Maffick, like she said. She was just checking out the dream against reality. The dream was failing to come up to standard, too.'

'Hmm,' said Will. He followed Rollo and told him a few of the things he wanted. Then Rollo was gone.

Will came back to Janine. She was sitting on the bed and he came and sat by her. He ruffled her hair.

'I'm a criminal, baby. You know I used to be in the city. I escaped from jail way back. With Fee's help I made a new identity for myself. It looks as though the police have just cracked the code. I think I'm on the run again.' He watched her quite carefully as he said all this.

'Why were you in prison?'

'I was a pirate. Fee met me down the city. She came looking for a little rough. Then the police busted us and I went to her for help. She hid me out in her apartment. That was five years ago.' Will did not add that he had seen Janine in bed with Fee, locked in her arms all those years ago, and been haunted ever since by the carnal images of the two women.

Janine made a giant effort to absorb what she had been told and act. Will's character came fully into focus for the first time for her. She understood so much of his behaviour and personality that had been mysterious.

'You need a place to hide?'

'Just for a short while. I'll have to go away, of course.'

'I still hold the lease on my offices. It doesn't expire for another ten days.'

'Why did you shut your business down?'

She managed a ghost of a smile. 'You know that. We'd better get you over there, and get some food in and stuff.'

* * *

They made the journey safely, unobserved. The offices were dismal and empty. Janine took Will through the waiting room, the outer office and the inner office. Then she showed him what had been her pride and joy.

'I rented this,' she said. 'It was repaying the investment, though.'

It was a microgravity chamber. In it, when it was switched on and in working order, the effects of gravity were nullified and you were in free fall.

Will switched it on. 'What's it like?' he queried.

She reddened. 'I don't know,' she said breathlessly.

He turned to her an incredulous face. 'You don't know? You haven't tried it?'

'No,' she mumbled.

He looked at her thoughtfully. 'How many men have you synched with apart from Rollo?' he asked.

'Some,' she said defensively. She shrugged. 'You know.'

'No, I don't know. How many?'

'Two.'

'Is one of those two me?'

'No. Two plus you.'

'Full-blooded affairs or one-offs?'

'Will!'

'Answer me.'

'One-offs, I guess,' she mumbled.

'At least that little scene I came in on back at your place is easier to understand now.'

'I'm sorry,' said Janine miserably. She hung her head.

'So few men because you prefer women?'

'No!'

Will put his arms round her and began to kiss the moss-soft springing thickness of her hair. 'Show me how sorry you are,' he said. 'In there.'

They stripped and went in through the door. Once they were inside the warm padded room, Janine operated the gravity-null control. Gradually their bodies became light and began to float. Will bounced himself round the chamber for a little while getting used to it.

Then he swam across to Janine. 'You owe me,' he said. 'I'm waiting to be paid.'

'I don't want you to go away,' Janine blurted out.

'Come with me.'

She laughed, cut herself short to check that he meant it, then came across to him and ran her body against his in an upward spiral that took her into a stately backflip. As she circled round she angled off to the control panel and played with the buttons there. One by one the walls began to glow. A deep rich blue, almost blue-black, filled them and in the dark pinpricks of unwavering brilliant light appeared.

'Starlight,' said Will.

'Exactly. We're in space, Will. It's just you and me and a million miles to Pluto. How are we going to fill our time?' She got herself upright in front of the space-vision so that the galaxy lay behind her dazzling in faint light. Will drifted down beside her and stood there. Slowly she knelt at his feet and bent over them. She kissed them both as she had done when he was chained in the plaza of death. Now she kissed his thighs and outlined by the universe she brought up her head, still kneeling, and took his sex in her mouth.

To begin with he was slack. She ran her hands up the backs of his thighs, feeling their iron-hard muscles and sinews with the thick goatish covering of hair. She ran her open palms hard up onto his buttocks and slid her fingers into the warm cleft his body made there. His cock lifted in her mouth and she sighed, nuzzling his balls with her chin. She worked her fingers deep between his buttocks and prised them apart. Her fingers came probing down, feeling his seam, feeling his hair, feeling his warm and intimate places.

She sucked very slowly, very gently, tantalising him, taking the time she needed to know him. His thick strong cock came hard erect and stood out high and proud before him, unbowed even by gravity. She released it and gently pushed herself off from the floor. Or wall. Whatever. She floated up past his body and arched

248

her back hard so she drifted over again. But this time she caught him with her legs, holding him about his waist, letting her upper body arch right back till her head almost touched the wall/floor. She opened her legs wide before him so that he could look straight down into her.

He flipped himself gently and let his legs come up behind him. He caught Janine by her waist and laid his face into her groin. He kissed her vulva. She pushed hard down and they both floated in midair. Will pressed his face into her, her legs held wide, and they rotated slowly. Jupiter began to heave monstrously into view behind them. The chamber was washed with pink and cinnamon light, full of deeper blood-red hues, orange, terracotta and pale pale rose. Silently the great storm whirled in its violent oval. Will and Janine whirled, locked together as silently, Will's mouth busy at Janine's sex, running over the bumps and dips of her woven elastic arousable flesh, sinking into the warm musk-filled pits and crevasses of her.

He released her. She swam between his legs and came behind him. She caught hold of him and began to kiss and bite his back, his buttocks, letting her hands come round him to feel his chest and belly and cock. Still they spun.

She came round him above his head and let herself slowly fall with her knees tucked tight until she was sitting astride his head, her shins on his shoulders. His mane of silky hot tangled hair was warm against her vulva. She rubbed herself and felt its luscious abrasion on her sensitive parts. Then she curled her head down and round till it was level, though upside down with his.

'I remember,' she whispered. 'Will Kid.'

'That's why I didn't want to be called Will in the city. They might have remembered, too.'

'Thief,' she said and kissed his eyes.

'Plunderer,' she said and kissed his mouth.

'Violator,' she said and kissed his cock. She came back up his chest and kissed it as she came, kissed the scars she understood at last. She angled herself so that had he been lying flat, she would have been astride him. She moved herself so that she drifted against him, her crotch homing in on his hardness. She touched it and bounced gently. Will caught her and pulled her back. She bounced softly, wetly, slightly stickily on the end of his cock. Her body was crying out to be penetrated, to feel this man within her, to feel his power in her, but her mind wanted to extend the pleasure infinitely, to draw it out till it became almost a pain.

She bent her legs round him to hold herself at his body now. The rings of Jupiter glittered behind her. The moon Io was in the frame and with a tiny silent sulphurous puff, a volcano erupted on it. Janine locked onto Will's body and felt the greediness of her desire. She was all vacuum, all emptiness, an aching void that needed the life of Will's sex within her, to warm and fill her and make her complete.

The chamber was dark within itself, dark as the inside of her body, but all four walls padded with translucent material had quite disappeared. All around the spinning lovers was the blue-black matrix of space lit by the faint dazzling stars, stars in their billions, the fires of the universe, burning, burning. She felt Will's maleness at her, pushing, and though she could see nothing but spangled darkness and the bloody vast gas giant of Jupiter, she opened and she pushed with her feet into Will's back, pulling him in.

There was yet that delicious hesitation to overcome. Always her passage was tighter at its neck. His cock was biggest at its end. The swell of his glans forced itself through the gates of her body, squeezing them open till he was firm inside, just his head, and she was closing valve-tight on his stem. Her insides vibrated deliciously, her walls trembling with pleasure, wanting to suck him further and further in till her body was speared to its depths and could take no more. She felt him sink into her, felt herself open to draw him in, felt herself give way and melt around him till she was him, was of him, was his absolutely, possessed by and of his body. He came on into her swelling as he came till she began to cry with the delight of being filled by him. He drew back, pushing himself against her body, then pulled in again, hard this time. Janine cried out and helplessly they spun, a wheel of sex, coupled against the starlight, against the slow majesty of the frozen voids of space.

She was almost in pain. He was so big in her. It was as though each nerve in her sex cried out at the pressure it was subjected to. He came in and out of her again, in again, and she was hot inside, blazing and bulging with him. Inside she was like the tentacles of an octopus. She gripped and sucked at his cock as it went in and out, as though it was being massaged by a thousand pairs of lips, kissing and sucking in harmony the length and breadth of his shaft.

Each powerful deep hammer blow in her body tolled like a great bell. The music built up in her body as a vibration that intensified as it was continually reinforced. She had forgotten herself, forgotten him. She was a container and she was full, burstingly elastically full. Soon she would overflow.

She felt a wet drop on her breast. As she spun, she had met her own tears caught in drops in the air of the chamber, tiny jewels unseen in the dim brilliance of the solar system.

Will's fingers hurt her hips where he held her. He slammed into her and she felt his shaft pulse as his climax overtook him with surprising intensity. Her own body shook into orgasm and ripples from her beating sex made her skin tremble. She bore down on Will in her, squeezing him, crying out as she shivered out of control, sucking at him and taking his desire, his goodness, his benison.

They floated slack, Janine numb from the shockwaves in her body. Warmth flowed in a slow tide up her, there was a gentleness in her belly and very slowly she began to feel within her body again. Will was soft within her and there was a ripe wetness about his sweet gland.

Will drew her off him and brought her to lie against his chest. He stroked her hair and she felt the slow thud of his heart. He kissed her face, then her throat, then her breasts, sucking her bright tips and making of them little pinnacles that glistened wetly when he released them. Janine saw a pearlised string beading the air. She was puzzled. Then Will saw it and he laughed. He drew slightly back from her and opened her legs. From between them their juices oozed out to float in free fall like themselves. Janine caught some on her tongue and then doubled over and fastened herself to Will, tasting his body wet and salty from their lovemaking. He was delicious. She licked him, savouring the taste of him. Will shivered. It was a sexual trick he adored, to be tongued after penetration by the woman he had had, yet he knew that Janine had learned it from Fee, from Rollo, and that she did it to him because she had learned doing it for Rollo that men liked it.

She floated up to his face.

'You'll take me with you?'

'If you want to come. It won't be a life like this.'

'No. Good.'

'The whole planet isn't like this. There are parts of the world that haven't changed in fifty, a hundred years, where cities are still alive and functioning economically. I don't mean the desperate open sewer down there beyond Townsend. I mean old-fashioned places.'

'Yes. I'm not totally ignorant.'

'And there is the wild, where they say we are forbidden to go. In the city there used to be rumours that people are living there again, like cavemen, you know. I'd like to see if that was true.'

'Yes.'

'It might be dangerous.'

'There are other dangers more insidious.' Janine shivered suddenly in the warm chamber. 'The Town is too comfortable, too easy. There's no need to strive. Comfort is like a radiation. You can't see it or really feel it when it is always there. But it is death by slow numbing degrees. The death of fear, of hope, of excitement.'

252

'I was glad at first when I lived here,' said Will quietly. 'But it never was enough. I'm not sorry to be forced away.'

'Will.'

'Yes.'

'The disc that caused all this recent trouble. Tell me about it.'

'It was symbiosis, honey. The disc biochemically bonded directly to the brain. We must have been mad. It wasn't virtual reality. It was hallucinatory, closer to a shamanistic trance state. It was a complete other world, by this world's standards, but real unto itself with its own images drawn from the depths of the psyche. It could produce artefacts that existed in this reality, too. Damn it still being loose. It's really dangerous.'

'What happened to you when you used it?'

Will was silent. One side of his face was lit with reflected light from the disappearing Jovian monster. The other side was dark. Janine felt his cock stir softly against her thigh. It occurred to her she would like to feel his strength, feel a little savagery in his lovemaking to go alongside the tenderness he had just shown her. She had a feeling he had a lot to give.

'I saw you,' said Will.

'Me? On the disc?'

'You,' said Will and he felt lust rise sharp and hard in him. He spun Janine over and entered her from behind.

He rather liked this microgravity chamber.

'Ms Cambridge,' said the older of the troopers. Hell, what a woman, what a beauty! How that husband of hers could go elsewhere, even with that little juicy thing he was with, was beyond Trooper Allison Jones.

Fee was at her desk. Her computer-links crowded the space on top of it. She was dressed in slick formal clothes, businesswear, and was formidable by any standards even if you did not know her background or reputation.

'It's about Will Maffick, I understand,' said Fee. She

253

wished she knew what had already been said. Rollo had done well to warn her.

'How well do you know him?'

'He is a close business associate. We have worked on several experimental projects together.'

'How did you meet him?'

'That's a difficult one. It was about four years ago, I think. At a biotech conference, as far as I can remember.'

'Can you be more specific?'

'Was it the Neural Web International? Or the Biosynthesis Symposium in LA? Damn. I go to so many of these things,' she added vaguely. 'I suppose they all keep records? If it is important, you can check.'

'Perhaps you can list the most likely ones for us.'

'Sure,' said Fee easily. She had first met Will by the bonfires in the city. He had held a knife to her throat until she persuaded him to lift her leather skirt and make use of what he found there. They had coupled on the bare earth in public like dogs. She still got a buzz out of the memory.

'Can I ask you gentlemen why you want to know? I have worked closely with this man and perhaps if you have information to his disadvantage, I ought to be told for my own self-protection.'

'He isn't who he says he is,' said Trooper Jones. 'We'd like to know who he really is.'

'You mean, he is using a false persona? Good God.'

'No, not exactly. He is not on any records further back than five years ago. He appears on the Central Social Statistic from nowhere.'

'I thought that was impossible.'

'Not to a computer expert.'

Fee was silent. 'I see,' she said. 'He is certainly very knowledgeable about computers, I can testify to that.'

'What sort of projects did you work on, Ms Cambridge?'

'Biosynthesis, mostly. I'm being indiscreet, now, you understand. The first person to patent a neural computer that can link directly into the brain so that a human can access the computational logic processes and data banks just by manipulating his thought patterns will go down in history. No screen. No console. Just the hardware that nature provides all of us with, the brain, and the software no more difficult to access than our sensory perception of the world around us, which is software, if you think about it. You just think yourself into what you want to know. After all, we have known for generations there is a lot of spare capacity in the brain, up there in the cerebral cortex.' Fee smiled. 'It's a glittering prize. Will and I worked on it. I know more about computers. He knows more about the molecular structure of the brain.'

This much was true. But Fee knew that the essence of a good lie is to embed it deeply in a sea of incontrovertible truth.

The troopers were fascinated as she intended them to be. The more they were distracted, the better.

'Are you close to this?' Jones demanded.

'We made something like a VR disc but it was a disaster,' said Fee lightly. 'You couldn't control it and you didn't know you were in it and when you were jerked back to this reality you felt like death. But we'll improve it. I hope you don't arrest this man. He has a good brain.'

'We need to have the anomaly explained.'

'Yes, I understand that. The Central Social Statistic is more important than my neural link.' Fee grinned. Will had used the equipment in this office to put himself into the Central Computer. She couldn't have the troopers knowing that.

'Has he ever told you anything of his history? Where he grew up? Where he was educated? If his family are still alive?'

Fee slitted her eyes. She thought about Rollo's penis, about sucking it, how it stretched in the membrane of her mouth. She expanded her chest and exuded sex as a palpable force across her desk to the troopers.

'You will think me dumb,' she said sweetly. The

troopers were not thinking of her dumbness at all. Both were a little red. 'I just don't talk about the past. I'm not interested in history.' She glowed forcefully. 'I use a man,' she said, leaning forward and allowing her heavy breasts to swing slightly under her clothes, 'for what he has, what he knows. Will knows a hell of a lot about molecular locks, about biosynthetic systems. I sucked him dry, gentlemen, on that issue. But as far as what school he went to, I never thought to ask. I didn't give a damn. I couldn't tell you what school my husband attended. It isn't relevant to our relationship and I am not a woman who has ever been interested in irrelevancies. There isn't time enough in the world for what I want to know, for what I want out of a man. An associate, I should say.'

She sat back and crossed her legs with a silken rustle. She eased her shoulders and pressed a button under her desk, out of sight of the troopers. They were still struggling for words when her desk buzzer went.

Fee flipped open the line to her secretary. 'Yes.'

'Professor Lapetev is on the satellite from Brasilia, Ms Cambridge.'

'Put him on, please.' She looked apologetically at the troopers. 'This is a booked call. I have to take it. Have you anything else you want to ask me?'

One of her screens glowed and a good-looking Russian came on. 'Fee,' he cried jovially. 'I kiss your cheeks. All of them. Are you ready for the data-stream?'

Fee did some keying. Her eyes flicked up. 'I expect to be kept informed,' she said crisply. 'Sergei, you dog, how were the harmonic equations? Have you the result yet?'

Her fingers were busy. The troopers stood up awkwardly. 'Keep in touch,' said Fee. 'I have the right to protect myself.' Her screens were filling with mathematical equations. 'Did you double-check the chaos integrations, Sergei?' she asked.

As the troopers went out, Sergei Lapetev was asking Fee to take a note of results of the quantum-space transformations. As soon as she was sure they were gone, Fee closed down her systems. She had taken the call the previous week. She had been playing a recording to get rid of the troopers. She had a standing arrangement with her secretary to use some recent call to help her get rid of unwanted visitors. Her secretary would assume she was getting rid of timewasters, as usual, rather than fighting for her own freedom from criminal indictment.

'Oh Will,' she said sadly. She had been so pleased to have him back, back from the dead. Now he would go out of her life again, and she would lose the wickedness he put into it, the unpredictable savagery of his lovemaking that thrilled her, the honey of his loins. She had walked in the primaeval forests of the north with him and he had preyed upon her, coming down on her with the rapacity of the wolf. She had loved it. His wildness was sweet like the briar, a beautiful and scented pain that her harsh nature had doted on. The boy Caz was the well at the world's end. She drank from his youth and grew younger herself on it. But Will had given her experience. Will could quiet the beast in her, the incessant beast in her nature that wanted release, satiation, glut. Will could fill her, run her to exhaustion, surprise her, bend her to his will, abase her and lift her up again. Will was the only man who had ever run Rollo close in her life and she was faintly surprised that Rollo had accepted him, her ferocious lover, albeit a tacit acceptance. Maybe he had never realised that there was a danger in Will, that his lovemaking was so rich. That was a good thing. She did not want to lose Rollo. He wasn't just a man, a man who meant so much to her, a man she loved in her furious way. Rollo was a package, a lifestyle, a social standing as well as a brilliant and sometimes terrifying lover. But it was a pity she was losing Will.

The police were not entirely gullible. They felt watched, all three of them, Rollo, Fee and Janine. Will must go and soon or they would all stand condemned.

There was the problem of what to do with Wing. She could not stay in Will's apartment which by now was under surveillance. Janine was selling hers ready to go away with Will. They needed Wing away from the contaminating criminality of association with Will. If the police got to her and found she was a non-person from the city, she would be in no trouble herself and they would register her on the Central Computer, but they would find out from her how she had come into the Town. When they had leisure, Rollo and Fee could concoct a story to explain her arrival that did not include Will or any of the truth of her coming. Meanwhile they searched advertisements for a place for her to stay.

Rollo took her out. Janine had taken her shopping using Will's money and Wing had been delighted with what was available in the Town. She had a somewhat dramatic taste, much to Janine's amusement. She noticed that Wing had an effect on the men who saw her. Yet Wing preferred women.

Now Rollo took Wing out in his Connet. This fulfilled a powerful ambition in her. All those who had lived as rats in the city had seen the powerful cars soar above them, splitting the sky, carrying the very rich unharmed, since the passing of the pirates, through the very poor. When Wing discovered that these powerful and beautiful friends of Janine and Will owned one of the turbo-monsters, she wasted no time in asking for a ride.

Rollo was a man of powerful sexual appetite, but he managed it with an iron hand as he managed all his resources. His attitude to Wing was avuncular, paternal. He was providing the child-woman with a treat. She certainly piqued him. She was twenty, as far as she knew, which was young in the Town and the Zoo. But the city-bred Wing had a cunning and a sophistication that ran deeper than her ignorance of technology, her lack of formal education. She was a born manipulator, a survivor, one wary eye always open to the main chance.

Rollo and Fee's Connet was tobacco coloured, opaque glass smoky over the titanium rocket body. The interior

258

to Wing was a miniature palace of luxury, the couches, the computer console, the ambience of sensual indulgence coupled with speed. Rollo took the great car out of its hangar and up onto the nearest access ramp. He programmed a distant destination and set it to maximum speed. The machine hummed with restrained power. One had the feeling it was limitless if unleashed. It rose high on its airpads and suddenly they were thrown back into the padded sides as it shot onto the highway, the engine note rising from a whine to a shrill scream before it was out of auditory range.

Rollo watched Wing with indulgence. She was gaping at the screen that showed what they passed over. Since they went too fast to see anything directly, what she saw was more and more out of synch with what was passing outside but Rollo didn't trouble to explain. He felt Wing wasn't a girl to look for intellectual rationalisations of the world around her. She was too busy experiencing it.

Eventually she turned to him, her face thrilled and alive.

'Would you like a drink?' he asked. She nodded and he made her a martini, very dry, and watched her screw her face slightly as she tasted it. Synthetic alcohol had a sweetish tang that he found deeply unpleasant. What he gave to Wing was the real thing.

She looked wide-eyed around the car's interior as she sipped her drink. Then she finished it. Rollo said nothing, watching her. At last she looked at him and he saw the speculation in her almond eyes. He did not like gaucherie. He had no objection to Wing weighing up in her mind what she wanted to do. He had no objection at all to being the focus of attention of this little slip of a Chinese girl, full of weasel cunning and slick with human experience.

She stood up and took off her dress.

She wore nothing underneath it but body jewellery. Three silver chains lay in parallel, one about her neck upon her fine straight little shoulders, one below her little pointed breasts, and one low on her waist. They were connected by a single vertical chain passing from her throat, between her breasts and over her navel. Below she wore across her hips a broad belt inset with a mosaic of coloured glass that winked and twinkled as she moved. It was tight about her hips and below it her sex pouted with its fine delicate silky trail of black hair. At the top of each leg she wore a very tight metal belt, buckled at the front, so that the tops of her thighs were squeezed, opening between them a wider gap that was the entrance to her sex.

Her lips were vermilion in her pale jasmine face, the colour caught and echoed by her painted nipples. The nipples were flattened still from her clothing, bent over and soft. Before Rollo's eyes they lifted and firmed, like a flower opening under the sun. But it was Rollo's hot blue eyes that brought them to erection.

She began to dance, slow movements designed to exhibit the beauty of her slim tiny body. Rollo lay on the couch and watched as she performed for him. He saw the subtle curve of her back, the rounded swell of her bottom, the boyish slimness of her hips, the tiny cones of her painted, pointed breasts, the blued cup at the base of her throat as delicate as porcelain, her very straight, bird-brittle shoulders. Her black hair hung heavy as steel, swinging slowly with each slow movement, her face closed and secret and clever. She brought up a foot and laid it on the couch by Rollo.

He picked it up and kissed it, allowing his hand to slide slowly up her ankle, her calf, her moulded thigh to the abrupt constriction at the top. His fingers sampled the metal as his lips touched her foot. His fingers slid over the belted skin until he just touched what lay beyond. It was a moth's touch, his fingertips on the extremity of her labia, barely grazing her intimate hair.

She liked him for his self-control. He was like the car, all contained power, exquisite promise waiting to be released.

Rollo looked up at her, his eyes bird-bright, his fingers just touching her private parts. She squatted slightly to increase his pressure on her. She clenched the muscles of her vagina and he felt the movement as a faint flutter at her sex. She did it again, so that he was kissed on his fingertips by her vulva. Then, with her foot still upraised and resting on the couch, she leaned forward and down, bending her knee. Rollo kept his hand steady and so she impaled herself on his fingers. They sank up into her and she smiled down into his face. Still she worked her muscles so he could feel the little convulsions in her cushioned sex-flesh about his fingers.

Very slowly, keeping him within her, she moved over to the couch and got onto it, squatting open-legged above him. She undid his shirt and exposed his chest as he fondled deep within her body. She bent between her own knees without lowering her body any more and kissed his chest, nuzzling it, allowing the cloak of her hair to sweep heavily across it. She began to rock slightly so that now she masturbated using him, using his fingers. She brought her head up and put a hand behind her, on him, on his groin. She began to rub him gently across the bulge of his awakened manhood, lightly scratching the material that covered him, frotting him and teasing him whilst all the time she rocked gently on his fingers, working herself and her sexual juices on his fingers.

Rollo took it for so long. His cock ached. She was sensual bliss to his fingers. He could smell her running juices. Her painted nipples danced slowly above him. Her jewellery winked. Her sly face was the invitation to sin that he loved. He closed his eyes for a moment, trying to control his breathing. She pressed hard on his shaft and he groaned.

'Christ, oh Christ, do it,' he said between his teeth. Sweat broke out on his forehead. 'Do it,' he whispered.

She stripped him at lightning speed. But when he reached to penetrate her, she leapt away across the car.

'What?' he said. His eyes were dark and she would not stop him now.

She crouched on the opposite couch and grasped the

261

handrail that ran along the side of the roof of the car. Her back was to Rollo and her feet were apart. Slowly she straightened her legs so that her bottom lifted and projected back into the body of the car, back towards Rollo. She gripped the handrail, her knuckles white. Her feet were planted firmly. Her bottom thrust back at him. Rollo stood up and put a hand on her thigh.

'No,' she said. She wiggled her rear and gripped the rail afresh, bracing herself.

Rollo looked up to where a central rail ran the length of the car. He took a hold of it with both hands and placed his feet firmly on the floor. He brought his naked groin forward and brushed his heavy cock against Wing's rear. She pushed back, inviting him.

Her sexual flesh was very dark, very wet. Rollo's cock pushed, seeking the way in through her pulpy aroused vulva. Without using his hands he managed to catch the swollen end of his member up in her and then he used the force of his hips to push himself right within her.

She cried out and squeezed down on him. 'Hard,' she begged. 'Make it hard.'

Rollo was a strong man in perfect condition. His hands had a good grip. His feet were stable. Using his haunches with all the power of his sleek muscled body to drive them, he began to plunge into Wing's braced body as hard as he was able, great slamming blows.

The car hummed and sang the sweet music of its power. The naked man with upraised arms in its central aisle was silent except for soft grunts as he drove with full force, bucking his hips into the rear of the straining girl. Under the violence of the pounding Wing cried out her savage joy, begging him for more. Her mind, her body, were all splintered light. The beauty of the insanely expensive car, the beauty of the rich, powerful Zooman, the thunder of her depths as he tore her orgasm from her were all designed to break her apart, destroy the impoverished city-bred crawling slimy thing that she had been, to screw out of her her past life and in the catharsis of his exploding sex, create her anew.

She came first and felt him follow her, felt him spasm inside her, felt the diminution of his lust. His cock eased and slackened. He kept up his penetrations though he slowed and softened them until he was sure her own sexual need was satisfied. At last he was still, pressed into her, her bottom pressing sweetly into his belly.

He brought down his hands and caught her about her hips, feeling the strange band that held her there. He pulled her stiffly from her position and turned her to face him, holding her to his chest.

For a moment she stood in his arms, swaying very slightly with the momentum of the car. Then she lifted her wicked little face and looked up at him.

'You lie down now,' she said.

Rollo did as he was told. She bent over his body and kissed his damp part. She licked the sticky juices gently from it.

Rollo reached down a long lazy arm and hooked a finger in her belt, pulling her up the couch.

'Come here,' he said softly.

'Why?'

'I want to kiss you where you are wet.'

'I wish we had a woman here. After I have been used by a man, I like a woman to touch me, to kiss me, especially between my legs.'

For a moment Rollo's brain rejected what his ears had heard. Then he began to shake with laughter.

'You lascivious little bitch,' he said. 'Next time I'll provide one. Meanwhile, give me what I want. You'll have to make do with my mouth.'

'Then you must be very gentle with me,' said Wing. She arranged herself quickly and with supple ease so that she lay on her back on top of Rollo, her hair hanging in his groin, her legs open either side of his face, and her mound exposed below his face on his chest. Rollo lifted her at her hips and brought her sex to his face as though it was an oyster on its shell, the prepared muscle ready to slip into his mouth. He put in his tongue with great gentleness, as she had commanded, tasting the flow of his spunk mixed with her musk. Her chains hung below her body and brushed his chest and belly. He licked with tenderness and skill and Wing lay supported by him with her eyes closed, feeling the soft pressure at her bruised vulva, feeling the release of good sex, of a lover's lips and tongue easing her need, balm to her frightened and insecure youth and a sign that there were better things to come.

Fee and Will met in secret in the Town to say goodbye. They chose a cheap bar and sat down in a grubby shadowy booth.

'We've had hot times, lover,' said Fee with an awkward grin.

'Maybe I'll get back someday and we'll run over a few again,' said Will. He touched his forefinger where he had implanted the tiny polarising device that had enabled him to use his genetic code to work doors, financial transactions and all the paraphernalia of life in the Town and Zoo in the twenty-first century. His unpolarised genetic code was on his police record. This simple device had kept him safe for five years. Now it had apparently outlived its usefulness. 'I just need something cleverer than this,' he said.

'You hacked the Central Computer once, pirate. Maybe you should do it again, making a more thorough job of it.'

'You do it, Fee. It's the sort of thing that should appeal to you. It breaks the law. It's one in the eye for the society that nurtured you and gives you a damned good life.'

'Not good enough for you, Henson Carne. Will Kid. Will Maffick. Wolf. How many names, Will? How often will you go on?'

'Till I drop. I'm restless. You know that.'

'Janine goes with you?'

'Sure. Green?'

'In your place, tiger. You are getting above yourself.'

Will laughed. Fee would never admit to jealousy. 'I'll be in touch,' he said presently. 'Rollo will make more money out of my business for me than ever I did. He'll send me what I need when I ask for it, wherever I am.'

He saw Fee's eyes glitter ice-green in the gloom. 'He's glad to do it,' she said abruptly.

'Glad I'm going, you mean.'

'Yes, I mean that.' Fee knew he understood the compliment she paid him, that he threatened her stability with Rollo, that no other man could do that.

'I guess I owe it to him to stay away for a long time. I don't mind so much. There's a big world out there. We live small in the Zoo, Fee, smaller and smaller.'

'I'll let you know when you can come back, when I've fixed things. But you won't have to come then. It's just that you'll be free to. Janine might need that one day, you know. She was bred in the cage. She's used to it. Her wings aren't so strong.'

'I was bred here too. Henson Carne is a graduate of that damned wedding cake up there on the hill.'

'I know. I asked a few careful questions. There's a student there I'm friendly with. You broke the bars a long time ago, Will. It's different for you.'

He reached out and ran a fingertip down the cicatrice on her cheek. 'My brother did that,' he marvelled.

'He's dead,' said Fee. 'I reckon even if you hadn't left all this and gone to the city for his sake, you would have turned pirate. It was too strong in you.'

'And in you, sweetheart. You made one hell of a pirate, Fee.'

She laughed delightedly.

'If you get the disc back, destroy it,' said Will. 'That was a bad thing we did. That cleaner lady from the Institute, she brought back a whip from her discworld. Bitch,' he added, reflectively. He eased his shoulders. 'I don't go for that.'

Fee crowed with laughter. 'My student brought back a glove,' she said. 'He saw my light-bed in it when I didn't have one. I wasn't on his disc, but he had an older woman. I was on someone's disc, though.'

Will had seen Janine on the disc in all but name and

the experience still haunted him. 'What do you mean?' he asked.

'That crazy guy who topped himself in his Connet. He made me a dirty vidi call saying I was on a pirate disc, yeah. He synched with me in VR. I told Rollo and we sicced the police on him. Then he blows his entire fortune on water stock which falls, thanks to Rollo's twisty behaviour, and goes loopy on the starways and makes a rocket out of his Connet. Isn't that weird?'

Will's hand trembled. 'What if it was our disc?' He had never known Fee so stupid.

'What?'

'His death saved my life,' said Will roughly. 'Janine was fighting for my life and losing. That Connet went over like a meteor and Janine used it to win.'

Fee stared at him, her mind working freely at last. 'What happened to the messenger boy who stole it, who kidnapped Janine?'

'I think the Amazenes got him. If they did, he'll be in a harem.'

'I never got back to that widow lady I told you about, the one who kept seeing the black-haired girl all over.'

'Get back to her. Take Wing with you. Prime her over what to say. The widow is a policeman's widow, remember.'

'What did we make, Will? What was it? A gate? Or just telekinesis?'

'Perhaps it went in the Connet, Jace Harvon's Connet. Perhaps that's where it is now, all burnt.'

'What if it didn't?'

'Walk on the quiet side, Fee, for a while. Keep your eyes open. Promise me you'll destroy it if you find it again.'

'Yes.' Fee was submissive.

'What was on the disc for you?' whispered Will. 'Tell me.'

'Will, I . . .'

'Tell me.'

'I can't.'

266

'Were you a whore, Zoo-lady? Is that it? You like it rough, don't you? I hope you miss me. Jesus, the way your breasts tremble when I take you.'

'Let me be, you bastard. In every sense.'

Will leaned closer. 'You took Janine and put her in your husband's bed when she was a virgin.'

'She wanted him. He was better than some callow youth.'

'Better than your student?'

'Leave him out of this.'

'Then you got in the bed, too, didn't you?'

Fee looked at him wildly. She didn't understand him. Why was he angry? It was all old history and nothing to do with him.

'It was a long time ago.'

'Rollo doesn't let go. Don't you understand that yet? That's why he's so damned good with money.'

'He's let Janine go.'

'No. I took Janine away from him. You be warned, Fee Cambridge. What you put in his bed will stay till he tires of it, and he is slow to tire. He is not a greedy man in that sense. But what he has, he holds. If I wasn't going away there would need to be a judgment of Solomon between us because we'd rip that girl in half.'

Fee shook herself irritably. 'I don't like you in this mood. We are saying goodbye, goddamn you, and you are being horrible.'

'I give you good advice as a parting gift. You are the most woman I have ever had, you beautiful witch. Stay in there, baby. Make sure you keep winning.'

Fee looked sulky. Will stood up and leaned over the table between them. 'I want to feel your breasts,' he said. He put out his hand and slid it down the neck of her garment. She sat looking up into his wide face, his eyes of stone. His hand roamed in the full ripe flesh, found her nipples, stroked them, palmed them when they were erect.

'Remember me,' he said. He lowered his head slowly and took her mouth, softly at first, then with increasing force. Her lips parted and he tasted her wine. His own mouth was spiced and subtle with promise, hot promise of fierce joining. He released her and drew back.

'I'll remember,' she promised.

They were ready to go. They had packs prepared with survival rations, Sludge, medical kits and spare clothing, basic cooking equipment. These were deposited in Fee's name at a depot on the outskirts of the Town. Their goodbyes were said, their arrangements all made. Still they evaded the police. Now, on this last night, Will had come by secret ways to Janine's apartment that they might sleep in comfort till the pre-dawn when they planned to go, to slip like ghosts from all that they knew into the unknown.

All that Janine feared was her dependence on Will, but she didn't tell him that. She was not herself a criminal, not a known one. Fee had told her she could come back any time, and to let her, Fee, know. She would always help wherever Janine was in the world.

Will woke all of an instant, the hairs on him prickling in atavistic warning. There was danger. He could feel it.

The girl slept in the crook of his arm, her breathing gentle, relaxed and deep.

Will lay very still, listening. His nerves screamed for him to move. Then he heard it again, the faint scrape at the door.

He leapt from the bed and slid into his trousers and shirt. Janine was startled, sitting up, bewildered.

'Dress,' he whispered. 'Fast.'

Blessedly she obeyed without question. Will took the rope that lay in the room. He should never have come here.

The noise came from the door again, louder. Janine heard it and in the dark Will felt her turn to him, questioning.

'Window,' he breathed.

They went over to it. Will touched it and it slid silently open. He had attached the rope whilst Janine dressed.

Now he pressed their masks on, one over her face and one over his own. They were unpleasant and difficult to breathe through, but they filtered the oxygen from water and enabled a human to breathe submerged.

'Don't wait,' he whispered. He threw the rope out and slid straight down it into the damp greenery of the water garden shrouded in darkness below. On the ground he jumped lightly free of the rope, and held it, feeling Janine's pressure, knowing she was following his descent.

Lights blazed everywhere. The police were there. Will stepped back into a bush and vanished. Janine was stark, brilliantly lit on the rope. As she slid down it the police fired at her, cryogen spray guns. She screamed and fell off the rope.

Chapter Nine

Fee and Rollo were entertaining Wing and Lexie. The policeman's widow was incurious and happy. Her black-haired girl was found and was moving in with her, into her apartment in Green Vistas. She had had explained to her how Wing had come to the Town and how Rollo had found her. Lexie would now inform the police and act as Wing's sponsor whilst the girl was registered on the Central Computer. Once Wing was accredited, she could begin to take some part in the life of the Town. She could get education and training. She told them she wanted to become a dancer.

Wing liked Lexie. The plump motherly woman was generous with her body, with her life. She absorbed Wing's wicked talents easily and was undisturbed by any serious question about Wing, or what they did together. This was a moral climate Wing appreciated. Yet Lexie's life was so straightforward that Wing could adjust to her new society, learn its rules by mimicking her sponsor. Lexie was gentle in sex, very happy, yet her nature was to give rather than to take and she did not make demands on Wing as to how she filled all her time. She was content to share. She did not wish to own.

Fee had been curious to meet Lexie. The woman was so unharmed by the disc. She didn't even know how she had come by it, couldn't remember and didn't seem to care. Perhaps their fears had been absurd. They had made of it a monster, between them. It was just a disc.

Rollo's work station indicated a call had come in. He apologised and went off to answer it.

It was his private coded line. Will Maffick was calling him urgently from his telecommunicator.

'What is it?' asked Rollo. He hadn't even known they were still about.

'I'm by the west hydroponics houses. The police busted Janine's apartment. She's been hit. I need your help.'

Rollo suppressed his instinctive urge to break the connection, deny responsibility.

'Is she hurt?'

'No. Cryogen spray guns. I've nothing with me. I haven't been able to pick up our packs. I can't even give her a stimulant.'

'These things don't kill?' That was the police line.

'No. They blast the nerves. They deaden all feeling in the affected area.'

'What do I do? I could get an AirAmbulance.'

'She'll go to jail if you do. She can ride it out. It takes a week or ten days to clear the system. Or there's a cure.'

'A cure?'

Will explained the nature of the cure.

'We can't,' said Rollo.

'We must,' said Will.

'OK,' Rollo capitulated.

'Can you bring Fee and Wing? Wing understands. She knows all about this. We'll need their help.'

Rollo thought rapidly. 'Get under the highway,' he said. 'I'll bring self-climbing rope. We'll have to use the Connet.'

'Yes. That's a good idea. Bring the packs. When we've done, we'll just go off. Right?'

'How did you get away?'

'We went down the water pipe, the main feed for the water garden under Janine's apartment. I had oxy-permeable masks.'

'You weren't completely unprepared, then.'

'No. But we were lucky. I'll see you soon.'

Rollo got rid of Lexie as fast as he could and told Fee and Wing. Wing looked horrified. She had seen city-folk suffering from the effects of the cryogen guns. The police did not let on to the Town and the Zoo exactly what the guns did.

Will waited anxiously under the highway. The occasional Connet howled by far above him. He felt Janine begin to come round again. He clamped his hand over her mouth as she opened it to moan. She writhed in his arms, fighting to feel something. She didn't know who he was or what was happening to her. She was going mad with the numbness which filled her body, blotting out all sensation upwards from where she had been struck. Even Will's great strength was tested as he gripped her and tried to comfort her.

A Connet came slow and stopped above him. Will sobbed in his throat and used a pressure point to put Janine out. He slung her limp body over his shoulder and ran along in the dark, stumbling on the rough ground, till he was under the stationary Connet. The self-climbing rope came snaking down. Will tied it rapidly round him, picked up Janine and held her tight. The rope pulled them quickly upwards.

Hands helped him over the fence that angled out from the side of the highway. Another Connet swept by. Most Connet owners did not look at the world outside their cars. They had to rely on that for the time being. In seconds Will and Janine were in Rollo's Connet. Once everyone was inside, Rollo programmed the computer and the car shivered into action.

There were five of them, two women, two men and the insensible girl. She was moaning, beginning to come round. Will laid her on the floor in the central aisle of the Connet. Wing pulled Janine's clothes open and bared her lower body.

'Are you sure this is right?' asked Rollo. His eyes glittered and his breathing was hard.

'It's the only way,' said Will. 'There are no drugs that cure. Only this.'

Fee was trembling with excitement. This was frightening, but strangely exciting. She knew Janine was in no long-term danger. But to do this to her seemed distasteful. Yet Wing and Will had no doubts.

'Who's first?' asked Wing. She looked at the two men. 'You aren't enough,' she whispered.

'We've damn well got to be,' said Will.

'You,' said Rollo. 'You first.' He sat down, his face blazing queerly, watching.

Janine looked up at them plaintively. 'Please,' she beseeched them. 'It's the only way.'

'That's it,' said Will. 'We have to go through with this.'

'Do it,' said Rollo.

Will took off his trousers and knelt before Janine.

'We must help him,' Wing said to Fee. 'That's why we are here.'

'Yes,' she whispered. 'I understand.'

They made Will erect. They stroked him, teased him, caressed him and aroused him till he was able to penetrate Janine and work his cock in her limp body. Long ago the city-folk had discovered that the best antidote to the cryogen guns was prolonged physical stimulation – the most efficacious of all being sexual intercourse. It all depended on the men having the stomach, the balls for it. Rollo felt very queer indeed, knowing that he and Will had to fuck Janine till she they neutralised the cryogen spray.

There was no question that Janine's life was in danger, however numb she was. Yet it was bizarre enough to turn a weak stomach. Some part of Rollo knew that he was on trial, he would be proving to Will he was the man he made himself out to be. That he could do what Will could do. Another dark part of himself thrilled at what was happening. For though Maffick was jealous of him, longed to kill him probably, though he had stung the man beyond endurance and then put salt in the wound by helping him, by tending his affairs, Will now

273

had to beg Rollo to synch with Janine as much as he could in front of him. So part of Rollo gloated. Life played into his hands. Will was dependent upon Rollo handling his affairs, which he naturally would do to the best of his ability just to make Maffick grind his teeth the harder. Will needed him to get his woman right. And Rollo would oblige.

First Will. Then Rollo. Then Will again. Fee and Wing worked the two men and as they did it they made a silent promise, one to the other. They recognised a like desire. They wove what sexual webs they could, together at each man in turn, but increasingly their attention slid to each other.

There was a strange aura in the Connet, sweat and pheromones overlaid with tension. But when Rollo came into Janine for the second time, she had revived noticeably.

Wing stroked Janine's brow after this. The girl's eyes were open, focused, her body tingling.

'Once more, maybe,' she said. Her dark eyes were sly. 'Such big men,' she murmured. 'You do the work of five city men.'

Rollo looked across the Connet. Will was stretched on the opposite couch, his eyes shut, his face calmer now that Janine was so much better. Fee bent over him, eager for his body, stirring him, pleasing him, doing things to him to bring him up triumphantly once again.

Will opened his eyes and met Rollo's blue flame. He looked down at Fee. He smiled across at Rollo and leaned back again, content.

When they reached the ocean, Janine was curled asleep, peaceful at last. Will carried her out into the early day and laid her, wrapped in her cloak, on the short rabbit-nibbled turf of the machair. He took their packs.

'She'll be all right now,' he said. His eyes danced. 'Thank you.'

Fee kissed him on the lips, holding him tightly, then she broke away and climbed back up to where the Connet sat reflecting the brilliance of the low sun.

Wing stood on tiptoe and kissed his chin till he bent down and kissed her on the mouth. 'Good luck,' he said.

Then Rollo faced him. Slowly he raised a hand and offered it reluctantly to Will. For a moment Will did not respond. The girls were back in the Connet. Then Will took the offered hand, held it with his own and clasped both with his other hand.

'I respect you,' he said grudgingly. 'But we need space between us.'

Rollo laughed. 'And different women.'

Suddenly the two men hugged briefly, then Rollo was gone. The Connet quivered in its net of dawn-radiance. Will heard it hiss as it rose on its airpads and then its engine whined and it was gone.

He arranged the packs about the sleeping girl, covered by a cloak. He lit up a smoke and sat peacefully there, watching the great roll of the opalescent sea. He was very tired. After a while he had a drink and a bar of Sludge. Then he curled himself by Janine, protecting her body within the curve of his own. He fell asleep to larksong.

A week later, Wing, Fee and Rollo took another ride in the Connet. This time they were concerned with no one but themselves. Wing took off her dress, an extraordinary affair of bronze plaques that tinkled as she moved, and Fee saw her body jewellery. She wore the chains as before about her shoulders, ribs and waist. About her hips this time she wore a string on which were more of the bronze plaques in a minute skirt, inches deep, that hid nothing of her charms. She reached up and grasped the central handrail that ran along the roof of the Connet. Lithely she swung herself up so that she hung from her arms but her feet were hooked in it too, her body doubled. Her legs were apart. Her little skirt fell back with a faint ringing noise.

Fee came forward to where Wing bat-hung, exposing herself. The girl had unearthly beauty in her sexual parts. Her outer labia darkened like petals to their outer edge. They held together, flesh nestling to flesh, until Fee reached up and very gently separated them a little.

275

Between them the strange lumpy wrinkled soft cushionings that lay within Wing were exposed, pink and gleaming, inviting, interesting, intricate. They were tiny animals in her private body nest, eager to feed, to caress what came within their soft grasp. The flesh was sugar-sweet, clean and musky. Fee adored it with her eyes, adored it the more because it echoed what she had herself, what lay within her, her woman's part.

Below Wing's sex lay another mystery to tease the eyes. Like a tiny strawberry, her anus with its puckered flesh nestled similarly within triangular dark-petalled skin, pansy-soft, strokable.

Wing swung, doubled up, to the faint motion of the rushing car. 'My bag,' she whispered to Fee. Fee fetched it and opened it. She withdrew from it a small wooden ball to which were attached two strings of tiny silver bells, some eight inches long.

'In me,' whispered Wing. Her head hung back now, her hair a black heavy curtain.

Hesitantly Fee touched the vulva before her.

'No,' said Wing.

Fee touched the strawberry. The puckered flesh leapt. 'Yes,' sighed Wing.

Behind them, Rollo watched, his blue eyes dull flickering flame.

Fee put the ball into her mouth and briefly sucked it. She took it wet from between her lips and then pressed the warm thing to where she had been commanded.

Wing groaned. Her flesh quivered. Fee pressed and it gave under the pressure. The ball popped within Wing's body and the bells hung from her, ringing, tintinnabulating softly, silver-sweet.

Fee lowered her face into the naked invitation and bit on Wing's succulence. The bells in her tail rang. Rollo stood up and lifted his wife's skirt. He crouched slightly, bending his knees, and as Fee sucked Wing, Rollo penetrated her from behind.

They dropped Wing off, very late, at Lexie's. Together,

tired, satiated, always wicked, Fee and Rollo went home to the Zoo.

Fee went through to shower whilst Rollo went into his work station to see if any urgent messages had come in. He came back out and locked the door, standing for a moment near to the door of the bubble house, yawning, rubbing his neck, his mind running agreeably over what he had been doing, what he had witnessed that evening.

The door buzzer sounded.

Rollo checked his watch, irritated. Then he released the door to see who had come so late.

It was a messenger delivering a package. 'Cambridge?' he asked.

'Yes.' It was a hell of a time to get mail.

'Sign here, sir.'

Rollo signed the proffered clipboard. He meant to speak to the youth but he faded rapidly back along the corridor that led to the walkway. Rollo could hardly see him. His uniform was grey, smoky, his edges ill defined.

Rollo shut the door and rubbed his eyes. He examined the package. It was slim and flat, addressed to himself.

He began to open it. He could hear Fee, hear water run. She must have left all the doors open. He took out a sheet of paper wrapped around something.

It was a disc, a VR disc. Rollo examined it. The wrapping was smudged, he couldn't read it, but he could see the small green triangle on one corner.

A sex disc?

He turned to the letter.

Dear mr Cambridge,
This is what my Master, the late Mr Jace Harvon, got into trouble over. He was in a mess over money too, but now I got to clear his things, the police tell me too. I was his houseman. There aint no family and anyway it was a Pirate disc and your lady was on it and I reckon the police shouldnt have that oh no. So I give it back to you

I never used it I aint that kind of bum. I got respect
for Zoo and your lady is Zoo all thru.I got respect.

All the best, mr Cambridge, dont worry none.
No one got this disc, I looked after it good when I
found it. Now you have it and alls right.

Sam Mason

Rollo turned it over in his hand. It was warm, friendly. This was the disc, then. The disc Fee and Will had
made.

He knew he should drop it and grind it under his heel.
Fee had used it. Will had used it. Only he, Rollo, had not.

It was quiet from the bedroom now. Fee would be
wondering why he had not come.

Fee was OK. Maffick was OK. Why should they be
stronger than him? The disc had harmed no one that
they knew of, except possibly Jace Harvon, and he had
been a gambler, a screwball.

Jace had tried to harm Fee. He had synched on disc
with her and the disc had bitten back. But Fee, who
made it, was all right. Fee was fine, glowing, happy, the
beast in her momentarily tamed.

Maffick was fine. The sonofabitch had his, Rollo's,
woman all to himself, adoring him. Maffick had the potential for sexual fidelity in him, too, if he had the right
woman. Rollo knew because he had it himself. It was the
women who were wild. He had been faithful to Fee till
she put Janine in his bed. He still didn't sleep around,
not like Fee. Not like Wing.

The disc had saved Will. That was what they thought.
Jace's death had saved Will when Janine fought for Will
in the city.

Would she have fought for me? thought Rollo and his
face twisted wryly. Maffick was a lucky bastard.

He put the disc in his pocket. It was easy. He would
use it, then he would destroy it. It wasn't cocaine, for
Christ's sake. It was just a biosynthetic disc. The biosynthetic disc. The only one. He would learn his heart's
desire on it, after all. That was what it did.

Rollo grinned and walked firmly into the bedroom.

He stopped dead.

The light-bed was on, glowing weirdly, shining up with cold silent brilliance.

A man sat on the bed. A young man. No, something ageless, divine, demonic.

He sat cross-legged. His slim chest was bare and silk-skinned, sweet with flat nipples in pale chestnut brown. The column of his neck sprang clean, his throat soft and strong, to his eternally young face. He was smiling, his eyes merry. In his curling hair two pretty little spiral horns curved up. His ears were pointed. His pupils were black bars set in amber, goat's eyes.

His hips, his loins, were honey-wild with the promise of coupling. His thighs were covered in thick coarse hair that came all the way down to his hooves, where they were crossed on the bed. The light shone up through his springing hair, made a sheen on his human chest, lit his chin from the underneath and caught the tips of his horns in a twinkle.

Fee knelt on the bed watching him. She was naked, white with the bed's own lustre. Her great breasts were swung slightly forward so that they hung clear of her body. The tips pointed towards the goat-man, pointed in invitation. Her body was static, enthralled.

The upwelling light made sockets of her eyes and her cheeks so that her face was like a skull, an eager skull facing the goat-man, facing Pan. Rollo followed the direction of her eyes.

From the lap of Pan sprang his penis. It was long, very long, an upward curving arc of manhood, of godhood, the club-end clear in the light from the bed. It was a slender delicious naughty curve, maybe fourteen inches long. Pan was all wicked boy, inviting, suppressing laughter, wanting to play. Fee swayed forward, mute, adoring.

Rollo tried to speak, to stop her. He couldn't. He looked down his body and it was not there. He had no voice. He could not see himself. Before him his wife leaned forward till she knelt before Pan and his monstrous naughty toy. Rollo heard the pipes, heard the music of the gods at play.

His hip burned. He felt the disc glow through the fabric of his clothes. High to one side of the room, up in what would be the right-hand field of Fee's vision, he saw the dull red square, not lit. The time was not yet.

Pan tempted and Fee fell forward into the temptation and Rollo could not do a damn thing about it.

It was Fee's disc. Fee's fantasy. Fee's creation. Fee's other world. Here, Rollo was the cyberghost.

Fee touched Pan and he laughed.

NO LADY
Saskia Hope

30 year-old Kate dumps her boyfriend, walks out of her job and sets off in search of sexual adventure. Set against the rugged terrain of the Pyrenees, the love-making is as rough as the landscape. Only a sense of danger can satisfy her longing for erotic encounters beyond the boundaries of ordinary experience.

ISBN 0 352 32857 6

WEB OF DESIRE
Sophie Danson

High-flying executive Marcie is gradually drawn away from the normality of her married life. Strange messages begin to appear on her computer, summoning her to sinister and fetishistic sexual liaisons with strangers whose identity remains secret. She's given glimpses of the world of The Omega Network, where her every desire is known and fulfilled.

ISBN 0 352 32856 8

BLUE HOTEL
Cherri Pickford

Hotelier Ramon can't understand why best-selling author Floy Pennington has come to stay at his quiet hotel in the rural idyll of the English countryside. Her exhibitionist tendencies are driving him crazy, as are her increasingly wanton encounters with the hotel's other guests.

ISBN 0 352 32858 4

CASSANDRA'S CONFLICT
Fredrica Alleyn

Behind the respectable facade of a house in present-day Hampstead lies a world of decadent indulgence and darkly bizarre eroticism. The sternly attractive Baron and his beautiful but cruel wife are playing games with the young Cassandra, employed as a nanny in their sumptuous household. Games where only the Baron knows the rules, and where there can only be one winner.

ISBN 0 352 32859 2

THE CAPTIVE FLESH
Cleo Cordell
Marietta and Claudine, French aristocrats saved from pirates, learn their invitation to stay at the opulent Algerian mansion of their rescuer, Kasim, requires something in return; their complete surrender to the ecstasy of pleasure in pain. Kasim's decadent orgies also require the services of the handsome blonde slave, Gabriel – perfect in his male beauty. Together in their slavery, they savour delights at the depths of shame.

ISBN 0 352 32872 X

PLEASURE HUNT
Sophie Danson
Sexual adventurer Olympia Deschamps is determined to become a member of the Legion D'Amour – the most exclusive society of French libertines who pride themselves on their capacity for limitless erotic pleasure. Set in Paris – Europe's most romantic city – Olympia's sense of unbridled hedonism finds release in an extraordinary variety of libidinous challenges.

ISBN 0 352 32880 0

ODALISQUE
Fleur Reynolds
A tale of family intrigue and depravity set against the glittering backdrop of the designer set. Auralie and Jeanine are cousins, both young, glamorous and wealthy. Catering to the business classes with their design consultancy and exclusive hotel, this facade of respectability conceals a reality of bitter rivalry and unnatural love.

ISBN 0 352 32887 8

OUTLAW LOVER
Saskia Hope
Fee Cambridge lives in an upper level deluxe pleasuredome of technologically advanced comfort. The pirates live in the harsh outer reaches of the decaying 21st century city where lawlessness abounds in a sexual underworld. Bored with her predictable husband and pampered lifestyle, Fee ventures into the wild side of town, finding an urban outlaw who becomes her lover. Leading a double life of piracy and privilege, will her taste for adventure get her too deep into danger?

ISBN 0 352 32909 2

AVALON NIGHTS
Sophie Danson

On a stormy night in Camelot, a shape-shifting sorceress weaves a potent spell. Enthralled by her magical powers, each knight of the Round Table – King Arthur included – must tell the tale of his most lustful conquest. Virtuous knights, brave and true, recount before the gathering ribald deeds more befitting licentious knaves. Before the evening is done, the sorceress must complete a mystic quest for the grail of ultimate pleasure.

ISBN 0 352 32910 6

THE SENSES BEJEWELLED
Cleo Cordell

Willing captives Marietta and Claudine are settling into an opulent life at Kasim's harem. But 18th century Alergia can be a hostile place. When the women are kidnapped by Kasim's sworn enemy, they face indignities that will test the boundaries of erotic experience. Marietta is reunited with her slave lover Gabriel, whose heart she previously broke. Will Kasim win back his cherished concubines? This is the sequel to *The Captive Flesh*.

ISBN 0 352 32904 1

GEMINI HEAT
Portia Da Costa

As the metropolis sizzles in freak early summer temperatures, twin sisters Deana and Delia find themselves cooking up a heatwave of their own. Jackson de Guile, master of power dynamics and wealthy connoisseur of fine things, draws them both into a web of luxuriously decadent debauchery. Sooner or later, one of them has to make a life-changing decision.

ISBN 0 352 32912 2

VIRTUOSO
Katrina Vincenzi

Mika and Serena, darlings of classical music's jet-set, inhabit a world of secluded passion. The reason? Since Mika's tragic accident which put a stop to his meteoric rise to fame as a solo violinist, he cannot face the world, and together they lead a decadent, reclusive existence. But Serena is determined to change things. The potent force of her ravenous sensuality cannot be ignored, as she rekindles Mika's zest for love and life through unexpected means. But together they share a dark secret.

ISBN 0 352 32912 2

MOON OF DESIRE
Sophie Danson
When Soraya Chilton is posted to the ancient and mysterious city of Ragzburg on a mission for the Foreign Office, strange things begin to happen to her. Wild, sexual urges overwhelm her at the coming of each full moon. Will her boyfriend, Anton, be her saviour – or her victim? What price will she have to pay to lift the curse of unquenchable lust that courses through her veins?

ISBN 0 352 32911 4   *April '94*

FIONA'S FATE
Fredrica Alleyn
When Fiona Sheldon is kidnapped by the infamous Trimarchi brothers, along with her friend Bethany, she finds herself acting in ways her husband Duncan would be shocked by. For it is he who owes the brothers money and is more concerned to free his voluptuous mistress than his shy and quiet wife. Alesandro Trimarchi makes full use of this opportunity to discover the true extent of Fiona's suppressed, but powerful, sexuality.

ISBN 0 352 32913 0   *April '94*

HANDMAIDEN OF PALMYRA
Fleur Reynolds
3rd century Palmyra: a lush oasis in the Syrian desert. The beautiful and fiercely independent Samoya takes her place in the temple of Antioch as an apprentice priestess. Decadent bachelor Prince Alif has other plans for her and sends his scheming sister to bring her to his Bacchanalian wedding feast. Embarking on a journey across the desert, Samoya encounters Marcus, the battle-hardened centurion who will unearth the core of her desires and change the course of her destiny.

ISBN 0 352 32919 X   *May '94*

OUTLAW FANTASY
Saskia Hope
For Fee Cambridge, playing with fire had become a full time job. Helping her pirate lover to escape his lawless lifestyle had its rewards as well as its drawbacks. On the outer reaches of the 21st century metropolis the Amazenes are on the prowl; fierce warrior women who have some unfinished business with Fee's lover. Will she be able to stop him straying back to the wrong side of the tracks? This is the sequel to *Outlaw Lover*.

ISBN 0 352 32920 3   *May '94*

Three special, longer length Black Lace summer sizzlers to be published in June 1994.

THE SILKEN CAGE
Sophie Danson

When University lecturer, Maria Treharne, inherits her aunt's mansion in Cornwall, she finds herself the subject of strange and unexpected attention. Her new dwelling resides on much-prized land; sacred, some would say. Anthony Pendorran has waited a long time for the mistress to arrive at Brackwater Tor. Now she's here, his lust can be quenched as their longing for each other has a hunger beyond the realm of the physical. Using the craft of goddess worship and sexual magnetism, Maria finds allies and foes in this savage and beautiful landscape.

ISBN 0 352 32928 9

RIVER OF SECRETS
Saskia Hope & Georgia Angelis

When intrepid female reporter Sydney Johnson takes over someone else's assignment up the Amazon river, the planned exploration seems straightforward enough. But the crew's photographer seems to be keeping some very shady company and the handsome botanist is proving to be a distraction with a difference. Sydney soon realises this mission to find a lost Inca city has a hidden agenda. Everyone is behaving so strangely, so sexually, and the tropical humidity is reaching fever pitch as if a mysterious force is working its magic over the expedition. Echoing with primeval sounds, the jungle holds both dangers and delights for Sydney in this Indiana Jones-esque story of lust and adventure.

ISBN 0 352 32925 4

VELVET CLAWS
Cleo Cordell

It's the 19th century; a time of exploration and discovery and young, spirited Gwendoline Farnshawe is determined not to be left behind in the parlour when the handsome and celebrated anthropologist, Jonathan Kimberton, is planning his latest expedition to Africa. Rebelling against Victorian society's expectation of a young woman and lured by the mystery and exotic climate of this exciting continent, Gwendoline sets sail with her entourage bound for a land of unknown pleasures.

ISBN 0 352 32926 2

BLACK
lace

WE NEED YOUR HELP . . .
to plan the future of women's erotic fiction –

– and no stamp required!

Yours are the only opinions that matter.
Black Lace is a new and exciting venture: the first series of books devoted to erotic fiction by women for women.

We're going to do our best to provide the brightest, best-written, bonk-filled books you can buy. And we'd like your help in these early stages. Tell us what you want to read.

THE BLACK LACE QUESTIONNAIRE

SECTION ONE: ABOUT YOU

1.1 Sex (*we presume you are female, but so as not to discriminate*) are you?

      Male   □   Female   □

1.2 Age

      under 21   □   21–30   □
      31–40   □   41–50   □
      51–60   □   over 60   □

1.3 At what age did you leave full-time education?

      still in education   □   16 or younger   □
      17–19   □   20 or older   □

1.4 Occupation _____

1.5 Annual household income

      under £10,000 ☐   £10–£20,000 ☐

      £20–£30,000 ☐   £30–£40,000 ☐

      over £40,000 ☐

1.6 We are perfectly happy for you to remain anonymous; but if you would like us to send you a free booklist of Nexus books for men and Black Lace books for Women, please insert your name and address

_____

_____

_____

_____

SECTION TWO: ABOUT BUYING BLACK LACE BOOKS

2.1 How did you acquire this copy of *Outlaw Fantasy*

    I bought it myself ☐   My partner bought it ☐

    I borrowed/found it ☐

2.2 How did you find out about Black Lace books?

    I saw them in a shop ☐

    I saw them advertised in a magazine ☐

    I saw the London Underground posters ☐

    I read about them in _____

    Other _____

2.3 Please tick the following statements you agree with:

    I would be less embarrassed about buying Black Lace books if the cover pictures were less explicit ☐

    I think that in general the pictures on Black Lace books are about right ☐

    I think Black Lace cover pictures should be as explicit as possible ☐

2.4 Would you read a Black Lace book in a public place – on a train for instance?

    Yes ☐   No ☐

SECTION THREE: ABOUT THIS BLACK LACE BOOK

3.1 Do you think the sex content in this book is:
    Too much ☐   About right ☐
    Not enough ☐

3.2 Do you think the writing style in this book is:
    Too unreal/escapist ☐   About right ☐
    Too down to earth ☐

3.3 Do you think the story in this book is:
    Too complicated ☐   About right ☐
    Too boring/simple ☐

3.4 Do you think the cover of this book is:
    Too explicit ☐   About right ☐
    Not explicit enough ☐

Here's a space for any other comments:

SECTION FOUR: ABOUT OTHER BLACK LACE BOOKS

4.1 How many Black Lace books have you read? ☐

4.2 If more than one, which one did you prefer?

4.3 Why?

SECTION FIVE: ABOUT YOUR IDEAL EROTIC NOVEL

We want to publish the books you want to read – so this is your chance to tell us exactly what your ideal erotic novel would be like.

5.1 Using a scale of 1 to 5 (1 = no interest at all, 5 = your ideal), please rate the following possible settings for an erotic novel:

Medieval/barbarian/sword 'n' sorcery ☐
Renaissance/Elizabethan/Restoration ☐
Victorian/Edwardian ☐
1920s & 1930s – the Jazz Age ☐
Present day ☐
Future/Science Fiction ☐

5.2 Using the same scale of 1 to 5, please rate the following themes you may find in an erotic novel:

Submissive male/dominant female ☐
Submissive female/dominant male ☐
Lesbianism ☐
Bondage/fetishism ☐
Romantic love ☐
Experimental sex e.g. anal/watersports/sex toys ☐
Gay male sex ☐
Group sex ☐

Using the same scale of 1 to 5, please rate the following styles in which an erotic novel could be written:

Realistic, down to earth, set in real life ☐
Escapist fantasy, but just about believable ☐
Completely unreal, impressionistic, dreamlike ☐

5.3 Would you prefer your ideal erotic novel to be written from the viewpoint of the main male characters or the main female characters?

Male ☐   Female ☐
Both ☐

5.4 What would your ideal Black Lace heroine be like? Tick as many as you like:

Dominant	☐	Glamorous	☐
Extroverted	☐	Contemporary	☐
Independent	☐	Bisexual	☐
Adventurous	☐	Naive	☐
Intellectual	☐	Introverted	☐
Professional	☐	Kinky	☐
Submissive	☐	Anything else?	☐
Ordinary	☐	_____	

5.5 What would your ideal male lead character be like? Again, tick as many as you like:

Rugged	☐		
Athletic	☐	Caring	☐
Sophisticated	☐	Cruel	☐
Retiring	☐	Debonair	☐
Outdoor-type	☐	Naive	☐
Executive-type	☐	Intellectual	☐
Ordinary	☐	Professional	☐
Kinky	☐	Romantic	☐
Hunky	☐		
Sexually dominant	☐	Anything else?	☐
Sexually submissive	☐	_____	

5.6 Is there one particular setting or subject matter that your ideal erotic novel would contain?

_____

SECTION SIX: LAST WORDS

6.1 What do you like best about Black Lace books?

_____

6.2 What do you most dislike about Black Lace books?

_____

6.3 In what way, if any, would you like to change Black Lace covers?

_____

6.4 Here's a space for any other comments!

_____

_____

_____

_____

_____

Thank you for completing this questionnaire. Now tear it out of the book – carefully! – put it in an envelope and send it to:

Black Lace
FREEPOST
London
W10 5BR

No stamp is required!